MW01118226

SEERS OF VERDE

THE LEGEND FULFILLED

BOOK ONE

M.L. WILLIAMS

See More:
Great meeting you
at Cracked Walnut!
Myron Williams

Seers of Verde — The Legend Fulfilled: Book One

Copyright © 2015 Myron Williams

This is a work of fiction. All characters, organizations and events portrayed in this novel are products of the author's imagination or are used fictitiously. Any resemblance to actual people living or dead is coincidental.

All rights reserved, including the right to reproduce this book, or portions thereof, may not be reproduced without the written consent of the author, except for the use of quotations in book reviews or literary publications.

Covers by: SelfPubBookCovers.com/rgporter

Back cover photo by Robert Davis

Published by All Writes Reserved Publishing, LLC

ISBN-10: 1530053692
ISBN-13: 978-1530053698

DEDICATION

To all my loved ones who have passed on but would have enjoyed seeing this book come to fruition: my parents and two brothers. Also for my gentle cousin who inspired the Tevan character.

TABLE OF CONTENTS

ACKNOWLEDGMENTS

Many people have helped me get this story published. Thanks to Tony Brimeyer, Linda Fritts and Bob Davis for their expertise and invaluable assistance.

Special thanks to my family — Connie, Laura, Phillip and Amy — for their love and support over the years. It actually was their "gentle" nudging that got me back to working on the novel. After the first draft was written, I let it gather dust for far too long before the characters started to appear in my dreams, demanding a resolution to their story.

I also appreciate the support from authors Dennis Green, Cheryl Corbin and Lennox Randon who took the time to answer questions and offer encouragement.

ARRIVAL

1

Commander Yermak Halpan paced in his cabin aboard Brak's Revenge, the pride of the Tanlian space fleet. It had been eight lunar cycles since his ship had taken trophy. The last two raids on Earth colonies had been disastrous. The colonies had launched early warning satellites and installed ground defensive weapons with enough firepower to ward off his lightly armed ship.

The colonists were not only aware the raiders were coming, but also had their weapons powered and ready. Yermak had to call off the attacks before they could even start.

The Tanlians were renegades, descended from prisoners who had mutinied against their overseers and taken control of the planet, Tantalum 2, a Colonization Alliance of Independent Nations (CAIN) incarceration and mining camp. Yermak's grandfather, Brak Halpan, had helped lead the revolt.

After capturing a fleet of deep-space Earth ships, it had not taken long for Tanlian raiders to discover how easy it was to attack and plunder Earth colonies. These new bio-formed worlds had no defensive systems and the colonists were lightly armed at best.

A buzz at Yermak's door comm brought an agitated response. "Who disturbs me?"

"This might brighten your mood," said Rolid, the commander's brother and second in command, his scarred face breaking into a predatory smile.

Yermak knew what the smile meant — a raiding opportunity. "What have you found?"

"It looks like colonists have arrived at XR-309. We just received the signal from the beacon we set up on the planet's large moon," Rolid said.

"I thought CAIN had abandoned that planet because it was so far from their other worlds. We restocked supplies and hunted there two lunars ago. There was no sign of colonists," Yermak said. He recalled the great sport his crew had hunting the wildlife, especially the four-legged and winged predators.

Many trophies were taken and bragging rights declared for the biggest creatures killed and most kills. The bloodletting had been a welcome respite after months of frustration for the Tanlians.

The grazers were plentiful and easy targets. The killing spree meant the ship would have fresh meat for weeks. His crew had filled up with raw supplies and water, leaving after a week.

"It appears, brother, the colonists arrived just days ago," Rolid said, his bright blue eyes shining.

"Recently arrived?" Yermak repeated, not believing their good fortune.

"They may not have had time to set up their defenses. Their cargo may still be waking," Rolid said.

"How far away are we?" Yermak asked as he pulled up star charts on his monitor.

"Ten days at trans-light nine, but we will be stretching our fuel reserves at that speed," Rolid answered. "We will need enough fuel to reach the nearest GEMS (Galaxy Exploration and Minerals Syndicate) buyer."

Yermak stared out his portal. "It might be too late if we take that long to get there. It may give them time to put up their defenses. I might lose this ship and crew if we return to Tantalum with nothing to show for it. If we are successful, I'm sure one of our Tanlian brothers would be more than happy to send us supplies—for a cut, of course."

Rolid nodded. Taking longer to arrive would be a dangerous gamble.

"See if you can get us there in less than ten days," Yermak said, walking toward his brother and looking him in the eye. "We need this raid. It's the best chance we've had in months."

Rolid turned to leave, prepared to give the orders to speed to XR-309, but Yermak stopped him.

"One more thing," Yermak said. "Locate the nearest Tanlian ship and inform the crew we're going hunting. Tell them we will do the work if they bring us fuel. We will be happy to work a trade. But, delay that message until we are halfway there. I don't want any over-eager *friend* taking our prizes from us."

"Yes, Commander. That's a good plan." Rolid bowed to his brother and left.

That colony better be soft, Yermak thought. *We don't have any extra reserves for a long fight or to chase them around that planet.*

The commander could not wait to get on with the hunt. He would have no trouble convincing his crew to be thorough when harvest time came. It also had been months since they had had women to enjoy for themselves.

First plunder is always so delicious, he thought as a vicious smile spread across his face.

2

Captain Hector Nandez couldn't help himself. His dark eyes moistened as he looked out the window of the *Colonia Nueve*. No long-distance imager was needed. The planet Verde Grande shone like a great shining emerald in front of him.

At last, after eleven years of traveling at trans-light seven, the Earth colonists had arrived at the planet his grandfather, Emilio Nandez, had discovered almost a century ago. Suspecting conditions on the planet were favorable for life, Emilio had convinced the Colonization Alliance of Independent Nations to send an auto-ship on a scouting mission. What the ship found exceeded even Emilio's wildest dreams.

Even though the planet had one small continent above sea level, it offered an interesting geological formation: a huge fissure that split the continent in half. Millions of years ago, the planet's tectonic plates had formed a mountain range, leaving two valleys on either side. Dark green moss covered the thousands of canyons of the planet's large valley, which was thousands of kilometers in length and stretched for hundreds of kilometers in width.

Rivers, some a kilometer or more wide, and others narrow enough for a man to jump across, ran through the canyons, which split off from the large valley like branches on a tree. Spectacular waterfalls fell thousands of feet to the valley below.

On the other side of the huge mountain range, far taller than anything found on Earth, was a much narrower valley that had been created over millennia by a river that coursed through it. The narrow valley looked to be rich in mineral deposits, though it would be a challenge to navigate. Seeing an excellent opportunity to set up an agrist and mining colony on one world, the colonization council dispatched a bioforming party to study the terrain and release Earth flora and fauna.

Hector could see the bioformers had outdone themselves. Almost every Earth species they had planted or released had flourished. Giant pines spread up the mountains. In the valleys, grasses, ferns and wild flowers were everywhere. Dozens of tree species had grown into thick forests, exploding in different shades of green. The planet was named Verde Grande, meaning grand green one in old Earth Espanol.

Hector's concentration was broken by a slap on the shoulder from Lar Vonn, the ship's chief security officer.

"I bet you can't wait to get down there," Lar said, studying Hector's face.

"I didn't think I would feel this way," Hector said shaking his head, feeling a bit embarrassed at being caught in an emotional moment. "My grandfather and father dreamed of visiting this place. They were denied the chance because the bioforming wasn't complete."

"Bureaucrats," Lar snarled. "Verde Grande was ready for colonization fifty years ago. They should have gotten the chance to see this."

"Well, at least we made it. No problems after the longest colonization flight in history," Hector smiled, looking at his friend, a smallish but muscular man with sandy blond hair and bright blue-green eyes "How are the sleepers doing?"

"They are all a bit groggy," Lar said of the two thousand colonists, many of whom had been in deep sleep for more than eighteen months.

"All those bodies, colonists and crew members, awake at once will create chaos. I'm accustomed to the two hundred who were awake at one time," said Lar.

Hector nodded, remembering the three times he had awakened from transport sleep — the headaches, blurred vision and uncooperative muscles. All crew members and colonists were required to undergo this deep sleep for the majority of the trip. The ship was equipped to sustain only about two hundred awake humans at one time. Hector had used his captain's prerogative of staying awake through at least half the trip.

"Permission to take a scout flyer on a test run," Lar asked, his square face breaking into a smile.

Surprised, Hector looked at Lar. "And who would you suggest as crew for the scout?" Hector grinned, already knowing the answer.

"I think only a couple of senior crew members could be trusted for this mission," Lar said with fake military propriety. "We would need a capable pilot, Captain. Got any suggestions, sir?"

"Do you think we should?" Hector said, while rising from his seat and heading for the door.

"You're the captain. Who's going to tell you no?"

"Well, you could object, Security Chief Vonn," Hector said.

"We've scoped the planet and nearby star systems. It's all clear as far as we can tell," Lar replied.

"Any biologists and geologists awake?" Hector asked. "If so, find a few and let's take that scout out. Maybe test its landing and takeoff capabilities from the planet. Just a test mind you," he said with a wide grin.

"They are already standing by. We can be off as soon as you are ready Captain," Lar said, turning to head out the door. He did not wait to see the surprised look on his captain's face.

¶ ¶ ¶

Hector steered the flyer into narrow canyons, avoiding outcroppings and peaks by mere meters. Years of waiting for the opportunity to visit Verde Grande and all that time cooped up in the transport ship were released as he swooped down on the planet like a bird of prey chasing its next meal.

"Nice flying, Captain," Lar said, not bothering to disguise his amusement when they had landed. "Scouts handle a bit differently than deep-space transports, don't they?"

Hector couldn't help but laugh. "I missed that mountain peak by at least fifty meters. Got to remember not to judge by sight."

Lar shook his head and glanced at the other twelve crew members, who looked a bit green after the wild ride to the surface.

"I'm not sure, Captain. Geologist Bergmann fainted and Biologist Ensgstrom just vomited behind those bushes."

"They'll be fine," Hector said, hoping to convince himself more than Lar.

"Permission to fly the scout back to the *Colonia Nueve*, Captain. I — um — could use the practice," Lar said, saluting.

Hector started to deny the request, but glanced at the crew. Instead of scurrying around the planet, most were hunched over or sitting on the ground and eyeing him a bit warily.

"Permission granted," he said with a sigh. "I'm glad you want to brush up on your pilot skills, Security Chief.

"Thank you, sir," Lar smiled. That confirmation was the remedy the rest of the crew needed. They were soon on their feet and exploring the countryside.

¶ ¶ ¶

After her stomach stopped churning and the throbbing in her head eased, Nira Engstrom attempted to slip away on a quick fact-finding mission.

"May I join you?" asked Wald Bergmann, the geologist. "I didn't enjoy the captain's ride any more than you did. Besides, my interest lies over this mountain. I would be happy to act as a lookout."

Nira started to make an excuse then remembered the captain's orders to travel in pairs and report in every fifteen minutes. She didn't mind the company. "Of course. You can keep me from getting lost."

"Please call me Wald. My talents at finding our way back will rely on GPS and communicators, I'm afraid," he said with a grin.

The plants and trees fascinated Nira. Barely a century old, the deciduous tree were huge — some were dozens of meters tall. Their thick limbs stretched out like giant umbrellas, and large leaves created canopies. In the shaded areas, huge ferns blanketed the forest floors.

Birds chirped and flitted by. Some of the species were almost unrecognizable. They sported unique color variations to blend in with the new environment. Even their songs and calls were different than what she had studied.

"What a dream to see this," she said. "Thousands of years of evolution accomplished in so short a time."

"I'm no biologist, but I don't recognize any of these birds," Wald said.

"The adaptor gene has helped the species here thrive," Nira explained. "What a wonderful tool to speed up bio-forming." She stopped to take notes and vids on her micro recorder.

"Ah yes, the biologists' holy grail," he said. "Since it doesn't affect the geology of a world, I haven't concerned myself over it." Wald noticed Nira's shocked look after hearing his admission. "I do find it interesting," he added quickly. "Please educate me, Nira."

"This is only the second colony planet to have adaptor species seeded on it," she explained. "It looks like it has been a marvelous success. The gene is implanted in first-generation plants and animals to help them evolve and thrive in new worlds. You called it our holy grail. Yes, Earth scientists believe they have unlocked the key to evolution. This gene is triggered by stressors to its host. It expresses itself by producing changes to react to those stressors in following generations."

"It works this quickly?" Wald said, jumping out of the way when something that resembled a rabbit bolted out of the underbrush.

The dark brown spotted creature was smaller than most wild rabbits on Earth. Its round ears lay flat as it scampered away in a blur.

"Apparently so," Nira said laughing. "In animals, the gene helps produce longer legs for chasing prey or escaping predators. Plants develop wider and different colorations to allow them to make use of the different amounts of sunlight and moisture."

"Larger predators?" Wald asked, fingering his energy-pulse weapon.

"Don't worry, there shouldn't be any monsters lurking about," Nira said. "To control wild evolutionary swings, scientists encrypted a terminator marker, which dilutes the adaptor gene after ten generations. It was designed as a survival tool."

Nira's smile changed to a look of concern as she and Wald topped a hill. Below them, the valley widened as two rivers flowed together. What captured her attention were the hundreds of birds and other carrion feeders gathered in one area. Using her power-binos, she gasped, sunk to her knees and let out a heart-breaking sob.

"We have to go down there and investigate," Wald said frowning after looking through her binos. "Even I know that many dead animals can't be natural."

¶ ¶ ¶

"Tell me what you found, biologist," Hector commanded Nira after she and Wald rejoined the landing party.

"Yes, Captain," Nira said. "After we were feeling better..." She stopped with an embarrassed silence. Wald shifted on his feet, not wanting to make eye contact with Hector.

"Go on, Nira. Nothing to worry about. Security Chief Vonn already scolded me."

Nira smiled then continued with her report. "After we felt better, we walked over a rise to get a better look at the valley. I saw an unusual number of carrion eaters, especially birds, gathered in one spot — hundreds," she said, shaking her head.

"That meant there was a big kill down there. We went to investigate."

"A big kill?" Hector asked.

"Yes, Captain. Hundreds of skins and bones were scattered around a large bend in the river. It's such a waste," she said, her green eyes filling with tears. "Many of the carcasses only had heads, claws, or fangs removed. Some were skinned. And …" she paused, fright taking over where there had been anger.

"What else?" Hector asked, getting impatient.

"Scorch marks in the earth, Captain," Wald said frowning.

Hector glanced at the geologist, the little man with short, scruffy brown hair and a pinched face was employed by Universal Mineral.

"The scorch marks were made by a lander," Nira said. "Humans have been here, probably killing everything they could find. They left such a mess." She frowned.

This time it was Hector's turn to look worried as a shiver ran through his body. He turned to Lar.

The security chief scowled. "Tanlians, Captain. I don't know who else would land, plunder like this, and leave."

"No permanent structures were built, just some temporary huts, skinning racks and smoke pits. They weren't here long," Wald said.

"But they know about the planet. They've been here and they may well come back," Hector said, combing his fingers through his thick black hair. "How long has it been since they've been here?"

"From the looks of the decaying carcasses, three to four lunar cycles," Nira said. Wald nodded in agreement.

"We need our defenses set up quickly, and we need to find shelter sites for our people. Get those colonists awake and ready to work," Hector commanded as they rushed back to the scout flyer.

3

"Nine days. Nice work," Yermak Halpan said as the Tanlian ship slowed its approach to XR-309's largest moon. The commander gripped his viewer's console as the moon came into view.

"Hug the surface," he barked. "I don't want the colonists to see us."

Rolid nodded as he piloted the raider toward the surface, getting as close as he dared.

"Locate that ship. I'm sure they've launched landing parties by now. Find out where those colonists are hiding on the planet. We may have to attack quickly, not take the time for a two prong," he said, referring to the Tanlians' favorite maneuver of assaulting from two directions.

The wait seemed interminable, but four hours later the Earth ship came into view as it orbited the planet.

"Look at the size of her!" Rolid shouted. "How many of our favorite cargo do you think she's carrying?"

Yermak stared at the *Colonia Nueve*. It was the largest colony ship he had seen. "The ship obviously was built for transporting a great number of people and equipment," he said. "It looks like a cargo ship, but it's sleeker. It might be armed."

The commander frowned. "Any movement on the surface? Any communication going on?"

"Not that I can find, Commander," Ossor Vallon, the comm operator said. His fingers flew over his console and then tapped at his earplugs.

"I don't like it. That's not a good sign — silence," Yermak said, looking at Rolid.

"Commander, I have something," Ossor reported. "Magnify sector C3 on your viewer. A lander is coming from the planet heading toward the mother ship."

"Excellent, we're in time," Yermak said, smiling. "We may just have a good hunt, yet. Can you open a channel? I want to hear what they are saying. We need to find out how far they are in to their little adventure."

"Yes, commander." Ossor's fingers flew over his board, there was a loud crackle, and then voices came over the speaker system.

"Lander One requesting permission to dock. We need fuel," the voice said.

"Fuel already?" a second agitated voice asked. "That's only been two trips pilot. We need to move faster than that."

"I'm sorry, Captain," the first voice said. "The equipment is taking longer to load and unload than we expected."

Yermak and Rolid looked at each other, smiling.

"They are still transporting to the surface, equipment, and perhaps people," Yermak said.

"Do we go now?" Rolid asked, looking forward to an easy hunt.

"No, we need to find out where the people are," Yermak said. "Are they on the ship or on the surface and where? We don't want to strike the wrong target and have them warn the others."

Rolid raised his eyebrows, but didn't challenge his brother.

"Patience," Yermak ordered his crew, but directed the remark toward Rolid. "If we listen and watch we will find out where the supplies are going and what kind of cargo they are hauling. That captain is impatient. They will lead us to the women. In the meantime, tell the crew to prepare for attack. I want all four scavenger flyers powered up and their crews armed and ready."

"As you wish Commander," Rolid said, now smiling. This would occupy the men until they were ready to attack. And from experience, he knew Yermak would not wait long now to strike.

4

The colonists were not moving fast enough for Hector. It was taking too many hours to move all the equipment into the landers and get it to the surface.

He signaled Lar Vonn. "How are the shelters coming?"

"The colonists are working hard, although a few are still a bit groggy, Captain," Lar said.

Lar's status had now changed. He was in charge of the activities on the planet. Hector was not to be questioned concerning ship's business, but now they were contemporaries.

The colonists were cooperating well. Search parties had located caves that could serve as temporary shelters. The mountains would serve as formidable fortresses once they had time to shape them with their laser cutters.

Lar even had to credit Wald Bergmann. The Universal Mineral geologist had taken a party over the mountain range and found a labyrinth of caves while searching for mineral deposits. Perhaps those caves could function as mining headquarters or even human habitation.

The valley where Wald had searched did not look promising for colonizing. Its narrow, sheer mountains emptied into the river at the bottom of the meandering valley.

The security chief marveled at the success of the bio-formers. Many of Earth's plants and animals thrived here, as well as genetic successes from some of the other colonized planets.

Even Wald's valley teemed with deer, rodents, predators, birds, and fish. The bio-formers had not missed any opportunities to establish ecozones everywhere. Most of the zones expanded across the planet, except at the highest altitudes where the native moss still grew.

Thank the heavens most of the colonists are on the planet, Lar thought. One more lander trip should be able to bring down the remaining colonists. But there was always more equipment.

"We're right on my schedule, but behind on the captain's. Typical," he said to no one in particular. As he walked toward a group of colonists moving equipment, he noticed Taryl Bryann standing a few meters away, waiting to get his attention.

The Seer had made him nervous when they first met. He couldn't help it. The diminutive woman was beautiful, with bright red hair and eyes so dark they reflected his image when he looked into them.

Lar was not shy around most women. He liked nothing better than to laugh and talk with them. He was quite charming and no stranger to sharing his bed.

However, Taryl was different. The quiet woman kept to herself and would interact with the rest of the crew only when necessary.

Lar did not understand her abilities. In the past few decades, many Earth colonies included Seers. They were always women, and their ability to sense emotions in others had proven valuable for colonists when dealing with humans from different cultures.

Could she read my mind? he had wondered, but then tried to shed that thought, embarrassed.

The two had been on the same sleep/wake cycle during the voyage to Verde Grande. Lar often woke up to find Taryl glancing his way while fighting off effects of transport sleep. At other times, Taryl would be fighting the deep-sleep grogginess and find Lar gazing at her.

The security chief intrigued Taryl. When she connected with him, she saw her eyes staring back at herself. However, she felt warmth from him, not the usual fright or lust she'd felt from the others.

Lar couldn't help but stare at those beautiful dark brown eyes. Something in them stirred his soul. He wanted to reach out and stroke her hair. The security chief enjoyed being with women, but this one had softened his heart. While on his rounds in the ship, he found himself thinking about her and made excuses to be near her when he could.

It wasn't long before the two were often seen walking together down the halls of the ship. They often shared meals and met in the observatory late at night, looking at the stars while the ship sped toward Verde Grande.

Innocent touches led to hand holding and more intimate gestures. Lar ran his fingers through her hair and she smiled at his attention. She liked to touch his well-muscled arm while they talked.

Their good-night kisses and hugs lasted longer and longer. Parting left them both anxious to see the other as soon as they were awake. After one long good-night kiss, Taryl took Lar by the hand and led him into her quarters. The next morning was the only time the security chief was ever late for his shift.

No one had objected when Lar asked Taryl to fly with the first group to Verde Grande's surface.

"I do not mean to bother you, Lar, but I believe we might be in danger," Taryl said, putting her hand on his shoulder.

"What is the problem?" Lar asked, appreciating she was not mincing words.

"I believe we are being watched and listened to by others," Taryl said, fear shining in her eyes.

Lar stared at her. The hair on the back of his neck was standing. "Go on, what you have found might be very important," he told her.

"I was meditating alone, trying to get away from all the activity. I was having a hard time concentrating," she said, looking at Lar.

Taryl knew "normals" did not understand that the hustle and bustle of human activity and frantic thoughts that went with those activities could upset Seers. To escape this explosion of images in their minds, they had to refocus their thoughts.

She saw Lar frowning and tried to explain. "I felt others. I believe they are watching us," Taryl said, gesturing skyward.

"Do you mean the *Colonia Nueve*?" he asked, but feared it was something else.

"No, not from our ship," she struggled to explain. "I can see through their eyes. I see images. The watchers can see Verde Grande and our mother ship."

"Our scans have not picked up anything, heard no communications," Lar said.

"They are there, Lar. They are listening to our communications. They are very interested where our people are going. And one other thing," she said looking at Lar's deepening frown. "They are anxious and excited."

Lar did not argue with the Seer. What she told him was too serious. In all likelihood Tanlians were observing them, waiting for an opportunity to attack.

"Yes, they must be Tanlians. I saw a star chart with routes all leading to the planet Tantalum 2," she blurted, startling Lar with her confirmation of his thoughts.

"Thank you, Taryl. You may have saved us, if we can act fast enough. Can you tell me more about them?"

"No," the Seer said. "But I will concentrate on them. I will inform you of any changes."

"Please stay close," he said bending down to give her a hug. "We will need your assistance and besides I feel better when you stay close to me." Lar allowed himself one more long look into her face and then went to work.

"Requesting to speak to *Colonia Nueve* Captain Hector Nandez," he spoke into his communicator.

Hector frowned as he received the message, recognizing the danger code formality. "Yes, *Colonia Nueve* security chief?" he answered in like formality to let Lar know he recognized the code.

"The weapons are in place and everyone accounted for. Defenses are approved," Lar said in his best formal tone.

Hector feared the worst, but continued the charade-like conversation. "Perhaps you should join me on ship and we can pick out test targets, security chief. I want to see these sonic cannons in action. I'm glad the colonists, except for a few stragglers, are all on surface and accounted for."

Lar understood the last message — there was a large group of colonists remaining to be transported to the planet.

Sonic cannons? he thought. *That should give the Tanlians something to ponder.*

5

Second in command Rolid Halpan shouted in surprise after hearing the last transmission from the planet to the colony seeder.

"Defenses are up? One hour ago, they were fretting about their timetable. A colony has sonic cannons? I thought only new military ships carried those. They're supposed to be experimental."

Rolid stared at his brother who was deep in thought.

"Something has changed down there," Yermak Halpan said, drumming his fingers on his command console and glaring at his personal screen, which was filled with the image of the green planet.

"They were in an uproar only a short time ago. What happened? Have we been scanned? If someone has broken communication silence, I will have his tongue as a trophy."

The comm operator, Ossor Vallon, shook his head. "There have been no transmissions, Commander. I have detected no echo pings. They have not scanned us."

"Maybe they are trying to scare us off?" Rolid said in frustration.

"They don't know we're here. They may suspect something or be playing a trick in case they think someone is listening,"

Yermak mused. “The Earth ship should have sent an auto scout to look for us. They have not launched a defensive satellite. No, the Earthers are up to something.”

“Are the collector flyers powered? Crews armed and ready?” Yermak asked Rolid.

“Three of the four are in fly-out position, Commander,” Rolid answered. “The fourth flyer will be at full power shortly. The crew is waiting for its pilot.”

“What are you waiting for?” Yermak said, smiling at his brother. “Get to Collector One and be ready to lead the squadron to that planet.”

This time it was Rolid’s turn to smile. “A real hunt this time. We will return with our cargo bays full of their women,” he boasted.

Yermak nodded, enjoying his brother’s enthusiasm. “Do we have an accurate fix on the colonists’ location?” he asked Ossor.

“They seem to be working in two locations, commander,” the comm operator answered. “There is a great amount of activity in the smaller valley. Large equipment is moving around there.”

“Two locations, hmm,” Yermak again tapped his fingers. “The Earthers have been busy. What did the ship’s captain say in the last communication?”

“He asked the security chief to return to the ship,” Ossor said.

“Tell the collector pilots, including my brother, to be patient for a bit longer,” Yermak said, his face revealing an inspiration. “They have one more transport group left. Probably the officers, and maybe that captain. Wherever that lander goes will be the prime colony site. That’s where the women will be.”

Ossor requested permission to speak. Yermak waved for him to continue.

“Commander, why would the colonists locate to that narrow valley? It looks to have few resources.”

Yermak was silent in thought. “That narrow valley makes defending it easy. Easy to get their people to safety. We will have to strike quickly, maybe decoy their defenses to get in there.”

He turned to Ossor. “Tell the collectors to follow that lander when it leaves the mother ship. I want what’s on board and I want all the prizes we can find on the ground. It's going to be a good hunt." He slammed his fist into the console.

6

"How many people are left on ship, Captain?" Lar asked as soon as he was back on the *Colonia Nueve*.

"Almost six hundred counting the ship's permanent crew," Hector answered. "Both landers are docked. Between them they will get our remaining people to the planet."

"Barely, Captain. They will be full with all our people on board. What if we have to outrun the Tanlians to the planet? We still have equipment to move to the surface, too," Lar said, shaking his head.

"We have the scouts, too," Hector reminded him. "We can carry any overflow in them."

"Taryl Bryann tells me she feels the Tanlians are growing impatient. Those scavengers may not wait much longer if they want to catch us by surprise."

Hector shook his head. He was uncomfortable in putting his trust in a Seer — someone who could feel others' emotions and see through their eyes.

"She told me what she … saw," Lar struggled to explain something he did not quite understand. "The Seer described the console and the viewer the Tanlian was using. She claims to see through their communicator. He is monitoring all messages between our ship and the planet. Taryl was telling me what was going on with our people before they reported to me. Everything was accurate."

"I believe you Lar, but it is just such a strange talent. If she was a machine, I could understand how she worked."

"She was born in a machine, as was I," Lar reminded the captain.

"It makes no difference to me whether you are a clone or natural born," Hector said. "You have nothing to be ashamed of being a clone, Lar. I wish all the so-called 'naturals' were as trustworthy and honorable as you."

"You would be surprised how many clones are on this ship and who they are," Lar said.

"I don't understand her talents. I am wary of trusting her, but we have no choice as I see it," Hector shrugged.

"You always have treated the clones equally as you have the naturals among the crew," Lar said. "I trust Taryl. I have looked into her eyes. My instincts tell me she believes what she sees. There is no other way to explain why she can see what she does."

¶ ¶ ¶

Taryl Bryann felt very alone after reporting her experience to the security officer. She sat on a hill watching the other colonists rush to build temporary shelters from the ship's supplies.

She was only twenty-three when she left the Siriusian shipyards on the *Colonia Nueve*. Today her natural age was thirty-four. Yet physically she had only aged three years, thanks to the slow aging of transport sleep.

The first connection with the Tanlians had startled Taryl into breaking the mental contact. Her heart had raced so hard her chest hurt. She blinked, trying to refocus from her waking dream.

Realizing what she was seeing, Taryl calmed herself and allowed her mind to open back up, searching for the connection she had just made. For several minutes her mind wandered, then she could "see" inside the Tanlian ship again. This time she was able to slip into the "sight" with greater ease.

She had connected to someone named Ossor; he appeared to be a communications specialist. He was monitoring all their transmissions from the planet and the mother ship.

Fear gripped her again, but she forced herself to relax, take deep breaths, and not break the connection. Taryl found herself fascinated by the experience. It was almost a sensual voyeuristic sensation.

After several minutes, though, the dangerous situation crept into her consciousness. Taryl forced herself to leave the Tanlian. Trembling again with the realization of what she had seen she went to find Lar Vonn.

Taryl felt relieved the security chief trusted her. She did not need her talent to read him. It was obvious from his expression and tone of voice that he believed her. However, his parting words frightened her even more.

"Stay with these Tanlians. What you find out may warn us about their intentions and save all our lives. The safety of the colony may depend on what you learn from them. You are better than a weapon," he said taking her by the shoulders and looking straight into her eyes. "Through you, we can react to them as soon as they make a move."

Lar then took out a communicator and tuned it to a secure scrambled frequency. "This is a direct comm to me. Our link can't be broken," he said, then paused as if unsure of himself.

"I understand," Taryl assured him. "The comm will be my link to you. Do not worry about my 'sight.' I will be concentrating on the Tanlians."

7

Hector did not like the conclusion he had arrived at. After speaking to Lar Vonn, he knew the remaining people on the Colonia Nueve were in great danger. He was sure the landers could not outrun or outmaneuver the Tanlian raiders for long. Their only hope was to land quickly and get the people to safety.

The captain also did not like the idea of leading the Tanlians to the Fourteen-hundred colonists on the planet who were scrambling to safety and making security preparations. Lar had left two hundred men and women of his well-armed security force on the surface.

Hector doubted the Tanlians would want to engage in a bitter fight with colonists equipped with laser rockets and energy-pulse weapons. From what he knew about the raiders, they liked surprise attacks, grabbing what people they could before the fighting got too fierce.

However, the problem remained how to get the last six hundred colonists and ship's crew to the surface. Every option Hector considered always led to the same answer, which made him sick.

Hector called Lar to his cabin to tell the security chief of his decision. Upon entering, Lar could tell Hector was troubled. The captain offered no greeting. The usual smile was replaced by stone-faced formality.

"Captain, you have orders for the crew?" Lar asked.

"Yes," Hector said, unable to keep from frowning. "Gather everyone not on ship's duty to loading dock one. I want to talk to them."

The security chief, who was normally unflappable, felt his throat tighten in nervous anticipation. "Yes, Captain. Most are gathered at the landers, getting ready to go."

As the door slid shut behind the security chief, Hector signaled Geologist Wald Bergmann.

"Yes, Captain?" Wald responded, surprised at being hailed. He knew Hector was doing his duty by cooperating with him. His company, Universal Mineral, was helping to fund the colonization mission.

The two had a mutual understanding: The captain would drop Wald's equipment and workers where he requested, and the geologist would ask no further assistance from the ship's crew.

"Geologist Bergmann, I want to commend you on your fine work of securing safety for the colonists," Hector said with false cheeriness, hoping Wald would recognize the formality code.

Wald paused, not sure how to respond. Not having military experience, the geologist only concerned himself with ship business or security worries when they affected his interests. The captain's formal tone told him something was wrong.

"Thank you, Captain, just doing my duty. The, umm, colonists are settling in fine," he responded, growing more nervous with every passing second.

"I hope you made enough accommodations," Hector said enunciating each word. "We seem to have a few stragglers up here who seem to think they need safe, secure living quarters."

The reality of what the captain was telling him sent a shiver down Wald's spine. For some reason the ship was sending him the last batch of colonists and they needed protection.

How many colonists? Protection from what or whom? he thought. *Tanlians?* The word exploded in his brain. What else would cause the captain to ask for his help?

"Of course, Captain. We have plenty of room here for the last of the colonists. Nice safe accommodations, just like home."

Hector nodded after hearing Wald's response. The geologist understood. "Very good. The colonists are looking forward to getting down to the planet and seeing your handiwork. Oh, and don't worry about the scientists on the other side of the mountain. They plan to camp there to study the wildlife. A scout will bring them to the colony when they are ready."

Hector hoped Wald had enough time to scout those caves. They may be the only hope for the remaining colonists.

After signing off with the captain, Wald wasted no time. He signaled the heads of his working crews on a scrambled frequency.

"We need to make secure preparations for possibly …" Wald paused. *How many?* He took a wild guess. ". . . several hundred colonists. Mark those caves in code and prepare yourselves for an attack. Lives depend on you. Get to work!" he shouted.

¶ ¶ ¶

The gathered colonists waited quietly in the loading dock of the *Colonia Nueve*. There was none of the usual good-natured chatter as they stowed gear and readied themselves to be ferried to the planet.

It was unusual for the captain to address outgoing flights. While friendly when speaking one-to-one, the captain tended to shy away from large groups. He was content to let one of his junior officers make speeches.

Hector looked out over the faces of the colonists. They represented all the races of Earth. However, there was something else familiar about many of them. He shouldn't have recognized many of them by name, but he did.

The realization shocked him — clones! Almost half of those looking up at him were the gene-alt clones. Their telltale blue-green eyes gave them away.

Damn the official colonization protocol, he thought. Disembarking to a colony was regulated by strict rules. Those with "important" duties were first — the engineers, biologists, geologists, chem experts, med teams, surveyors, and a security detail to protect them.

Hector looked at Lar and now understood why the security chief had not objected to bringing his elite security team back to the ship. They felt a loyalty to their fellow clones.

The people before him had signed on knowing full well the dangers of being colonists. They were adventurers, willing to risk their lives for a dream. By pure chance, the fate of this group may suffer a different fate from their counterparts on the planet. Drawing strength from his anger, Hector addressed the crew.

"Thank you for your attention. You soon will be heading to the planet, but we have had to change our landing site."

Standing next to the captain, Lar could see Hector was struggling with his emotions. The captain held his arms behind his back. His clenched hands were turning white.

Seeing their worried and anxious looks made Hector pause. *No need to cover up the reason with political double talk. These people deserve the truth*, he told himself. "Crewmates of the *Colonia Nueve*, we believe Tanlians are observing us. We need to get you to the surface as quickly and safely as possible," he said.

Some of the gathered colonists gasped. A few sobbed. All gazed up at him.

"All the other colonists are on the surface, getting ready to defend themselves. They may not be able to hold off an attack. We need to draw the Tanlians away from our people on the planet. The landing site has been changed to Universal Mineral's valley on the other side of the mountains. We hope to get you down safely before the Tanlians attack."

To his amazement, none in the group shouted objections. This last group consisted of hunters and agrists. Making sacrifices and living with plans that changed at a moment's notice were nothing new to them.

"Captain, an observation if I may?" Riss Nels, one of Lar's security force, broke the silence.

"By all means," Hector said, looking at the young lieutenant. Lar started to reprimand the young officer, but stopped when the captain held up his hand.

"I grew up in a hunter/agrist family, sir," Riss said. "There was an Earth bird called a kildeer that acted wounded to protect its nest. It would draw danger away. Is that what you are asking of us?"

Hector smiled at Riss. "Yes, Lieutenant, that is what I am asking this brave group to do — draw the danger away from your fellow colonists, and then fly to safety when you get the chance."

The gathered colonists were silent, thinking about their predicament. After about a minute, a man with curly red hair stepped out of the crowd. Hector recognized him as Neb Klinfer, another clone.

"Captain, I am a hunter. Will we get a chance to defend ourselves?"

Hector nodded. "You have my word. I will do everything I can to get all of you safely to the planet. It may be up to you after that."

"Thank you, Captain. That's all we can ask," the hunter said. He bent down, picked up his equipment and strode toward the waiting lander. Without another word, the colonists all turned and headed toward their assigned ships.

8

Lar Vonn did not mask his vigorous objection to his captain's plan.

"Be careful, security chief, or I will . . ." Hector stopped when he saw the grave concern on his friend's face, knowing whatever threat he issued would be worthless.

"Throw me in holding?" Lar finished Hector's sentence, flashing a smile that quickly disappeared. "You can't do this Captain. There's got to be another way. We can outrun them to the surface and then make a stand there. Everyone gets an equal chance that way."

Lar's face flushed with anger when he'd heard Hector's plan to stay on board the *Colonia Nueve* to divert the Tanlians from the escaping colonists. A half-dozen loyal crew members volunteered to stay with the captain to help with defenses, communication and navigation. This plan was contrary to all of Lar's instincts to protect the crew — *everyone* in the crew, especially the captain.

"If all goes well, my friend, we will scatter their raiding landers and chase the mother ship from the planet," Hector said, feigning bravado.

"And if it does not go well?" Lar snapped. "You will be a big target for the Tanlians. Another prize."

"Under no circumstances will the Tanlians capture the *Colonia Nueve*," Hector vowed. "I promise you that."

Only then did Lar grasp Hector's plan — divert the Tanlians at any cost, even if it meant losing the *Colonia Nueve* and those manning it. He stared at Hector, but could manage no words.

"Let me finish the job I swore an oath on, Lar," Hector whispered, grasping his friend's shoulders.

"I swore to do everything in my power to safely deliver the colonists to the planet," the captain said with conviction. "That is what I intend to do. I need you to do what you swore to do, too, Lar. Protect the colonists from all harm. I want to give you the best opportunity to do that."

The security chief nodded and offered Hector his hand.

"May we both do our jobs well and live to tell stories about our victory," Lar said. He started for the door, but turned in the entry, snapped to attention and saluted Hector.

"Captain, it's been an honor."

Hector returned the salute. "You are the guardian of my grandfather's dream, now. May all of Earth's gods be with you."

Lar nodded, turned and walked away. The door swished shut behind him.

¶ ¶ ¶

Ossor Vallon tapped his ear plugs, shook his head, and then pounded on his console. Listening intently, he looked at Yermak Halpan.

"Well, what is it? What are the Earthers chattering about now?" the Tanlian commander growled at his comm operator.

"Nothing commander. They are silent. No contact between the ship and the planet. Very strange."

Yermak's eyes slit in thought for a moment and then he shouted at Ossor. "Launch the collectors! The Earthers are leaving!"

Before Ossor could relay the order, Yermak opened his comm link to his brother who had been waiting with eagerness to lead the four collector ships to the planet.

"Rolid," Yermak barked, "it's hunting time. Follow those Earthers to the surface. Launch."

¶ ¶ ¶

Lar's voice crackled over the comm system. "Captain, Taryl Bryann says the Tanlians have launched."

Hector looked at his comm operator. Startled that a human had detected the ships before his scanners, Yoshi Watanabe confirmed Taryl's warning. "Yes, captain. It's four small ships and a larger vessel. It must be the mother ship."

Surprised that the Tanlians hadn't waited for the *Colonia Nueve* to make the first move, Hector ordered the landers to launch. "Give me an open frequency," he ordered.

When Yoshi nodded he had one, Hector began, "To the commander of the Tanlian ships. I urge you to call off your ships. We are prepared to defend ourselves."

Hearing the message, Rolid signaled his brother. "What are your orders, Commander?"

"Keep pursuing those ships. I will deal with that mother ship," Yermak barked. "Let's see what this Earth captain is made of. Direct link me to that ship."

Once the link was established, Yermak spoke again. "Earth ship captain, this is Commander Yermak Halpan of Independent Tantalum 2. I order your lander ships to set down at the first available site and surrender. If there is no trouble, we may leave a few of your pathetic colonists alive. You will stand down from that seeder ship, captain, and be prepared to be boarded. It will make a fine addition to the Tanlian fleet. Offer no resistance, and we will return you and your officers to an Earth colony after the proper reward has been paid."

Hector looked at Yoshi Watanabe. "Did we expect anything else from these bastards? Let's see how bad they want us."

Yermak watched in disbelief as the *Colonia Nueve* turned away from the planet.

"Commander? Our fuel supplies are low. If we chase that ship . . . " Ossor didn't get a chance to finish.

"Intercept her," Yermak yelled. "They are trying to trick us. Tell the collectors to find the colonists on the planet. There may be no one on board those landers."

Hector watched with grim satisfaction as the Tanlian mother ship turned to follow his departing vessel. "Whoever said divide and conquer better be right," he told his crew as they waited for the inevitable.

¶¶¶

Sitting apart from the other colonists as they scrambled to safety in the large valley, a frightened Taryl Bryann broke from her trance and spoke into her communicator. "Lar, two of the Tanlians have broken away and are headed toward us."

The security chief winced as he flew the first lander full of colonists toward the planet. He had hoped to get his cargo safely on the ground before the Tanlians followed them in.

"Taryl, is someone with you? One of my officers?"

"Yes. Lieutenant Navrakov is here," she said.

"Lieutenant, you may get a good shot at one of the Tanlian ships. Make it count," Lar said. Uri Navrakov was an efficient and competent military man who would do his duty to the death.

"That second ship will be the problem, we don't know what kind of weapons they have. If they spot you … " Lar stopped, knowing he did not need to say more.

Lar had one last order for Uri. "Lieutenant, you must trust Taryl completely. I have full faith in her. She may be your best hope for survival."

"I will, Security Chief," Uri said, looking at the frightened young woman. A twenty-year veteran of deep-space missions, the lieutenant had been skeptical about heeding the advice of this strange Seer. However, he did not question Lar, whom he respected without question.

"We will defend the colonists," Uri answered. "Good luck to you, sir. You have your own Tanlians to worry about."

"We're entering the atmosphere. I pray we all survive this. Good luck," Lar signed off and concentrated on getting the ship to the ground.

"I wish I knew when we could expect the Tanlians," Uri said, as he turned toward the colonist encampment.

"The Tanlians estimate arrival in eight minutes," Taryl murmured, her eyes closed.

Uri spun around, his mouth open in shock and then remembered Lar's words. "Are you sure, Seer?"

"Yes," she answered as if in a dream. "One of the pilots just signaled his crew."

Uri clicked on his comm and spoke to his waiting troops. "Two raiders arriving in less than eight minutes. Let's prepare to welcome them. Battery one, we may only get one shot."

¶ ¶ ¶

As expected, the first Tanlian collector crested the mountain top and headed toward the valley. It streaked by the false encampment the colonists had built, hoping to decoy their enemy.

"Wait for him," Uri whispered into his comm. "He should scout it two more times before he lands." True to Uri's prediction, the Tanlian collector screamed over the encampment two more times.

"Send the runners now," the lieutenant ordered. Over a dozen troops dressed as colonists bolted from enclosures and ran for "safety." The Tanlian collector hovered near the encampment and started to land.

"Fire!" Uri shouted. Two laser-guided missiles shot out from their hidden launch pads on the mountainside. The Tanlian collector exploded in a bright flash. Nothing was left except for small bits of metal.

Uri turned toward Taryl. "And the other?"

"They are watching from above," she opened her eyes gazing at a tiny silver dot in the sky.

Uri followed her gaze with his power scope and spotted the other ship. "That one won't make the same mistake. Get everyone to safety."

As he spoke, two energy-burst rockets slammed into the mountain, destroying the two launchers that had shot down the first Tanlian collector. A series of energy rockets splattered over the mountain, causing small avalanches.

"We can't take too many of those hits," Uri warned. "We're not equipped to handle bombardment."

"I can see the pilot's controls," Taryl said, relaying the numbers she saw on the Tanlian control panel.

"You can see the panel readout?" Uri asked in amazement.

"Yes," she answered. "I have been trying to … divert him."

"What? Explain," Uri said.

Taryl hesitated. "I, ah, can change what he sees. He has had to recheck his console many times. I have tried to confuse him."

Uri stared at the small innocent-looking woman gazing at him. "Can you tell me what he sees as he is flying? Can you hear me when you are, are …" he fumbled for the right words.

She nodded. "I can see what he sees and hear you, yes."

"Listen very carefully, Taryl and tell me what you see. Will you do what I tell you to do?"

This stunned Taryl. She broke her trance and stared at Uri,who returned the gaze. Seers were not accustomed to taking orders. They often were left alone and offered advice when asked. A shudder ran through her body. What did he want her to do? "Yes, lieutenant," she whispered.

He nodded, clicked his comm on. "Tanlian ship, we surrender. Don't fire, we have suffered too many losses."

Taryl gasped, but stopped when Uri held up his hand.

"Bring your people out into the open, so we can see them," snarled a voice over the comm in broken Universal Anglo.

"So you can slaughter us? No," Uri said not masking his anger. "Those bursts nearly wiped us out," he said, hoping his lie was believable. "My people are afraid."

The Tanlian laughed. “You should not have fired on us. We can defend ourselves, too, Earther. We do not want to kill you — at least your women.”

Uri and Taryl watched as the Tanlian collector descended on their position. Knowing the ship would be ready for another missile launch, Uri waited for the right moment.

“Eight thousand meters,” he counted as his mag-scope gave him the information. “Seven thousand. Six thousand. Come on,” he whispered as Taryl gazed at him.

“Five thousand. Fire,” he yelled to the remaining batteries. Two more laser missiles launched out of a higher point in the mountain and raced toward the Tanlian ship. Reacting quickly, the invader shot higher into the sky, heading toward the mountain peak in an effort to lose the missiles.

“Now Taryl, tell me what the pilot is seeing,” Uri said.

The Seer, already watching through the pilot’s eyes, repeated what she saw on his chronometer. “Nine thousand meters, ninety-five hundred meters, ten thousand meters..." She kept counting.

Uri interrupted her. “Make him see Nine thousand five hundred meters.”

Taryl twitched but kept her focus. “Nine thousand, five hundred.”

Seconds later, the colonists watched as the remaining Tanlian ship slammed into the mountain, hundreds of meters from its peak. Only Uri heard Taryl shriek in terror then faint as she watched the Tanlians die through their eyes.

9

"How far behind us are they?" Lar shouted as he guided the lander through Wald's obstacle course of a valley. The two ships could barely navigate through the rock outcroppings that were everywhere.

"Two to three hours," Riss Nels answered the security chief. "At least the Tanlians have to slow down through this rock maze, too."

"True enough, lieutenant. Their ships aren't much bigger than our landers. How is the other lander faring?"

Riss checked the comm and smirked. "Lieutenant Dhar doesn't appreciate this obstacle course, either."

Geologist Wald Bergmann signaled the ships. "Landers, you're only five Kms away. Prepare to set down."

"I would if I could see where," Lar snapped.

"You will see a gorge shortly. Land there. We are in the caves right above there," Wald answered.

"I see it now," Lar said. "Signal Dhar to follow me. We need to get these ships down, and the people need to get out quickly." The colonists poured out of the ships in a rapid but orderly fashion, helping each other when needed.

Wald hurried over to Lar. "The caves are ready, security chief. Once your people are inside, the Tanlians will have trouble finding them."

"Thank you, Wald, excellent," Lar said, slapping the geologist on the shoulder. "But we have some able bodies who want to face them out here. Those who don't have weapons can follow you."

"Very good. My people will guide them to safety. We have arranged a welcome for the Tanlians." Just as he spoke, the roar of flyers echoed in the valley, sending the landing parties scrambling to safety.

Tanlian pilot Rolid Halpan guided his collector through the jagged valley. "I've flown through worse," he bragged, while his crew grew more nervous with every near miss of hitting a rock outcropping. "Tell number two to keep up. We need to get down there before they have a chance to hole up."

Wald cursed as Rolid's ship streaked through the canyon. "We missed that one, but here comes the other," he said to Lar as they hunched behind two boulders that had been maneuvered into defensive positions.

As the roar of the second Tanlian ship grew, Wald flicked a switch on a handheld remote. Explosions rocked the narrow canyon. The walls disintegrated, sending boulders flying like missiles.

The second Tanlian ship was knocked out of the air. It somersaulted to the ground and lay buried by debris.

Lar smiled. "Good work. Now we only have to worry about one Tanlian flyer."

Seeing the explosion destroy the second collector, an angry Rolid guided his transport out of the canyon and returned from the other direction. The two grounded Earther landers were perfect targets. They exploded under a barrage of energy bursts from the Tanlian ship.

Rolid then swung his collector around and released sonic and gas bombs, hoping to knock out his opponents long enough for him to land and release his trained killers upon the colonists. Lar and Wald were prepared for this tactic. All their people on the ground had been given ear plugs and safety breathers.

"No one move," the security chief spoke into his comm. "Let them think the bombs worked. Wait for my signal."

Rolid made one more swing over the area. Seeing no movement, he set down his collector ship. "Kill all those damn men and take every woman or girl you find," he ordered. Fifty armed Tanlians came storming out of the ship, found defensive positions and crept toward the caves.

At Lar's signal, a woman in one of the caves screamed. The Tanlians rushed forward like a pack of Earth wolves advancing on helpless prey. A second signal launched a barrage of weapon fire on the Tanlians. Energy bursts, pulse grenades and bullets filled the air and brought down half of the Tanlians.

The surviving attackers didn't stop. They rushed the cave only to be confronted by Lar and his men. Too close to use weapons, the Tanlians and *Colonia Nueve* defenders fought hand to hand. Trained to fight as a unit, the security force formed a defensive circle to fend off the Tanlians. Although fierce and having the advantage of greater numbers, the attackers fell one by one.

Lar took quick stock of the situation. Seven of his men were badly wounded, but none were killed. Dozens of Tanlians lay dead. The defenders had no time to rejoice. The roar of an engine filled the air as the Tanlian collector lifted off and shot out of the canyon.

"That damn pilot didn't have the courage to join his men," Lar shouted to Wald, who emerged from his hiding place. "Can't we shoot him down?"

"We have no rockets, security chief," Wald yelled back. "We've used all our explosives."

¶ ¶ ¶

Stunned by the outcome of the short-lived battle, Rolid fired his engines, concerned now only with escaping this planet and returning to the Tanlian mother ship, even though it would be in disgrace. Shaking with fear, he flew out of the valley. Several times he swore his altimeter gave him the wrong reading. With sweat dripping down his face, he wiped his eyes to make sure he could see.

"The instruments are never wrong," he thought to himself, as his ship exploded into thousands of pieces of debris.

¶ ¶ ¶

"What just happened?" Wald asked, his mouth agape at seeing the collector crash into the mountain.

"I think our Seer has become a weapon," Lar said, smiling. "Let us hope she uses her talents wisely."

On the other side of the mountain range, a pale and shaking Taryl Ryann looked up at Uri Rabakov. "All four Tanlian ships are destroyed, Lieutenant. As well as our landers." She paused. "I've killed today. I've broken the ancient code not to do harm."

Uri knelt beside Taryl. "You've helped save almost two thousand people who would have been killed or captured. What you have done here will never be forgotten by our people," he said, holding the trembling Seer as tears streamed down her face.

10

Yermak Halpan could not believe his good luck. The escaping ship offered no resistance. The Earth craft had been built for deep-space transport and sported no weapons to defend itself. However, the Tanlian commander was angry the Earth captain had refused to stop the colony ship. Both vessels had barely broken out of orbit.

Yermak wanted to take the ship back to Tantalum 2 as a trophy, but the other captain was forcing his hand. "Very well, we have no choice. Target her engines — fire."

Two energy-pulse missiles shot out of the Tanlian ship, hitting the *Colonia Nueve's* engine compartment. The Earth vessel was finally forced to halt.

"Prepare to dock. Fasten all clamps," Yermak ordered his navigator. "Tell the crew to be careful. We don't know how many armed men there are on board. Kill any who resist."

¶ ¶ ¶

Hector stared at his command console. He heard the screech of the alarm on the docking port. It was just one of many warning signals sounding through the ship, but it was the one they had been waiting for.

"Are they attaching their docking clamps?" he asked his comm operator.

Yes, Captain. Their clamps are descendng," Yoshi Watanabe answered.

Hector nodded. Yoshi had determined that the Tanlian ship was built as an old Earth-class transport. It had forty attachable clamps, as well as another forty clamp ports aligned with the *Colonia Nueve's* design.

"Give me a countdown on those clamps"

Yoshi took a deep breath. "Ten seconds, nine, eight, seven, six…"

"Attach clamps," Hector ordered. At his signal, forty of the colony ship's docking clamps ascended and locked into the Tanlian ports. The Tanlian ship shuddered after the docking was complete.

"That was a rough one. Is there a problem with the dock?" Yermak asked Ossor Vallon.

"Docking was successful, Commander, but …" Ossor studied his console, puzzled.

"Well, what is it?" Yermak demanded. "We have the Earth ship."

Ossor looked up. "The readouts are unusual Commander. There are twice as many docking clamp confirmations than there should be. Our forty clamps are secure, but I have eighty confirmation lights. Very strange."

"Sounds like a problem for engineering," Yermak snapped. "Turn these ships back to the planet. We may get some decent salvage out of the Earth ship, as well as that hulk it left behind. Why haven't I heard from the boarding party? Stetter, are you on board yet?"

Tanlian lieutenant Jor Stetter winced when he heard Yermak's voice. "The main dock entry has been sealed shut commander. It looks like they have tripled-shielded hatches."

Yermak was livid. "Well blow them open, Lieutenant. Get into that ship."

"Yes, Commander, but it will take a few minutes for us to burn through each dock."

Hector studied his console. Alarms started screeching as small explosions echoed through the ship. His console flashed: “Docking port one open. Unauthorized entry. Docking port two open. Unauthorized entry. Docking port three …"

He turned toward his crew. Their eyes fastened on him. “I’m proud of you all. We have given the colonists their best chance to survive. Now it’s up to them. Let’s give the Tanlians a warm welcome.”

Hector whispered a quick prayer. “Grandfather, I pray your dream comes true. May Verde Grande flourish.” Hector then entered in his last command code, signaling the self-destruct program. The explosion from the *Colonia Nueve* swept through the open ports the Tanlians had just opened and enveloped their ship as well, giving the intruders no time to react. Yermak Halpan only had time to hurl one last curse at Hector before the firestorm enveloped both ships.

11

Colonists on both sides of the mountain range were regrouping in the early evening hours on Verde Grande. The wounded needed to be attended to and meals were being served from rations left over from the *Colonia Nueve*.

The first of Verde Grande's two moons, the giant Luz Primo, was climbing on the horizon. It would be several hours before the smaller moon, Luz Nino, joined it in the sky.

"It's no use. Our communicators aren't powerful enough to reach the other group," Uri Navrakov said as he approached Taryl. "We need the *Colonia Nueve* to relay our signal to them."

"I am very tired. Today has been terrible," Taryl said, still looking withdrawn and pale. "I know what you want. I will try to see the others." With a heavy sigh, the small woman sat upright and closed her eyes. Her breathing slowed to a steady, rhythmical pace.

Uri looked at the Seer, hoping the exhausted woman could use her talents once more. As if in answer to his unspoken question, Taryl lifted her face, her eyes still closed.

"The others have survived the Tanlian attack. They have many wounded, and some have died, but they have shelter and are being cared for," she whispered. "They are talking about the colonists on the other side of the mountain — us. Their landers have been destroyed. They cannot get to us or we to them."

Mixed emotions flooded Uri. He was thankful the others had survived. But how would they reach each other without the flyers? How would they reach the *Colonia Nueve*, if it had survived?

If the mountains were as treacherous as he had seen, it would be a dangerous task to attempt a climb, but they may have no choice.

As Uri gazed up the mountain, pondering the situation, a thunderous clap broke the silence. The sky was illuminated by what appeared to be a giant meteor falling to the planet. Fire trailed it for hundreds of kilometers.

Wald Bergmann jumped when he heard the explosion and searched the sky. "Are the Tanlians returning?" he asked, desperation giving away his emotion.

Not getting an answer, he turned toward Lar Vonn only to see tears streaming down the security chief's face. The geologist paused and gulped. "The *Colonia Nueve*?"

Lar cleared his throat. "In all probability. If I know the captain, the Tanlian mother ship is part of that, too."

The colonists in both valleys stood as one gazing into the sky, watching the blazing ships fall to the planet. Prayers to all of Earth's gods, saints, and holy people were murmured in thanks as well as in final tribute to the ship that had safely brought them to the planet.

12

"Damn Tanlians, they must have gotten to the colonists before they could get to the planet. Two thousand people lost," said a red-faced Jamison Gresser, Director of Colonization Alliance of Independent Nations, as he slammed a fist on his desk.

"Are you sure? What was the last communication from Verde Grande colony?" asked Per Vosberg, chief of Universal Mineral.

"Captain Nandez reported Tanlians were attacking the colonists on the planet and he was trying to draw the mother Tanlian ship away," Gresser said. "That was three weeks ago. There's been no communication since."

"No communication satellite was launched?" Vosberg asked. "All those people," he shook his head. *All that equipment and investment*, he thought. *Wald Bergmann finally chose the wrong project. Too bad I can not tell him personally.*

Jamison was now pacing around his office on Sirius 7, the launching point for all CAIN's colonization efforts. "Verde Grande is too far away to send military flyers," he said. "It would take them years even at trans-light nine to reach the planet."

Per shifted in his chair, frowning. "I apologize for putting this loss into financial terms, director. However, Universal Mineral cannot afford another loss like this. We are facing too much competition from the Galaxy Exploration and Minerals

Syndicate. Combine that with the danger from the Tanlians, and it is too much of a drain."

Jamison nodded. He knew dramatic changes to their colonization efforts needed to be made. The Tanlians were forcing new colonies to shore up defenses. The Syndicate was seeing success with their colonies. Jamison and the other CAIN officials were unaware of how their competitors were avoiding these troublesome raids.

After four years of unsuccessful attempts at fending off the Tanlians, Galaxy Exploration and Minerals Syndicate sued for peace during secret negotiations. Each GEMS planet agreed to pay an annual "tribute" to the raiders. In exchange, the Tanlians agreed to leave those worlds in peace.

The Colonization Alliance of Independent Nations had refused to deal with renegades, thus starting decades of attacks and kidnappings. The Tanlians had successfully defended their home world against two invasions by CAIN forces.

The Earth people had underestimated their opponents' skill, determination, and size of their force. CAIN could not muster the number of ships and men needed to take back the ship-building planet.

The Tanlians soon learned women were the most valuable commodity among the expanding Earth colonies. Due to the shortage of females, especially on GEMS mining camps and security posts, officials often looked the other way when Tanlians delivered the precious cargo. After all, women were in great demand by their inhabitants, no matter that it came at the cost of human suffering.

The women were stolen from CAIN colonies. So it was no concern to the Syndicate, which often had trouble competing with its rival for scarce new planets that could be bioformed.

The Tanlians were paid with fuel, food and raw materials they could trade for the latest tech gear or light weapons. Now those raiders apparently had taken their biggest prize — an entire settlement of colonists.

Per studied Jamison, who was gazing out his window, deep in thought. "How much longer do we wait until we count Verde Grande as lost?" he asked the director.

Jamison looked at the mining chief. "If we don't hear from them in one more lunar cycle, we will withdraw all interest from the planet. Excuse me, Per, I have two thousand souls I want to pray for."

¶ ¶ ¶

"It is not like Yermak Halpan to be late," Tanlian transport commander Masat Ebber complained. "Are you sure these are the coordinates we were given to meet his ship?"

"Yes, Commander. Tantalum 2 moon base Octavius 7 were the coordinates they gave us," comm operator Kor Vens said. "I have sent messages every thirty minutes. They have have not answered."

Masat stared out of his command cabin's window. "Eighteen hours is too long to wait. We need to get our perishables to Tantalum 2."

The ship was carrying food, oils, live animals, and vegetation from New Arabia 3. Officials on the GEMS colony were generous in paying their tribute to the Tanlians.

"How many colonies are within minimum traveling range?" Masat asked Kor. "Yermak said he was low on fuel or he wouldn't have asked for our assistance."

Kor frowned as he scrolled through the star charts on his console. "The only established colony is eight lunar's travel, and that is Nouveau France 4."

"Too far away, plus even Yermak wouldn't dare attack a Syndicate world. Not with them being so generous to us," he smiled. "How many seeder worlds are being bio-formed?"

Kor shrugged. "My guess is more than twenty, commander, and those are the worlds we know about. We may not be aware of all the bioforming activities, especially with the CAIN Earthers."

Masat nodded. "Yermak is out there somewhere. Perhaps he stumbled upon a fat trophy and is taking his time. Launch a signal beacon along the route he was taking. If he needs assistance, he can send another message.

"Chart the bioformed worlds we are aware of. We will return and try to find our wayward brother after we make our delivery to Tantalum 2. If Yermak has found his favorite trophies, I'm sure he won't mind sharing with his fellow Tanlians," Masat smiled. "Lay a course for home. We are late as it is."

SEPARATION

1

"How long have they been gone?" Wald Bergmann asked, as he gazed up at the treacherous mountain, hoping to see the small party of men returning safely from the hazardous climb.

"Just a day longer than you asked last time. It's been two weeks now," Riss Nels answered, trying not to let Wald know he was just as worried. "Chief Vonn and that hunter, Neb Klinfer, can take care of themselves." This didn't help calm Wald's fears.

Lar Vonn, former security chief of the *Colonia Nueve*, had grown anxious in trying to organize a climbing team in an attempt to find the other stranded colonists. Only Neb and a handful of other hunters had volunteered to join him on the dangerous trek.

Few of the colonists in their valley were experienced mountain climbers. Neb and the other hunters were the only ones who knew how to scramble over boulders. The others were accustomed to flyers that transported them over mountains or to specific locales in the mountains. Climbing was becoming a lost art.

"I'm afraid we may not know if they ever find the others. We just may never see them again," Riss said, hoping he was wrong.

"I should have gone with them. I've been climbing over rocks on five worlds. It's just that ..." Wald's voice choked.

"That's nothing to be ashamed of, geologist," Riss said, seeing how upset Wald was with himself. "Many of us don't like heights except when we are flying, including myself."

"You? Afraid of heights? Come now, Lieutenant, I appreciate you trying to make me feel better. But a CAIN pilot and security officer afraid of heights?"

"Flying is different than climbing mountains or trees," Riss said. "You are in charge of a machine that gets into the sky quickly, unlike the danger of falling and injuring yourself."

Wald felt a bit better after hearing the lieutenant's confession. He did not doubt Riss's bravery after watching him, Lar, and eight others fight off and kill the Tanlian attackers in a bloody hand-to-hand struggle.

However, his gaze returned to the mountain. "I don't care what Lar Vonn ordered. I say we give them another two days and then send a search party," Wald said, glaring at the other man.

Riss shook his head. "So we can lose more men? No. Even if we followed their tracks and signs, others could become just as lost. I have to agree with the captain's orders, no search parties. The best we can hope for is to see them return with colonists from the other side."

Riss saw Wald frowning and shaking his head. "I know how you feel, but we can't spare more men, especially you. We are responsible for the safety of the colonists in this valley and you are too valuable. Who would help us maneuver in these caverns and carve out living quarters? You have done an admirable job."

Wald shrugged, but smiled at the compliment. "Any of my men are capable of digging through rock. They can help as well as I have."

After the Tanlian attack, Wald and his miners had undertaken a task they had not expected: carving out living quarters from the network of caves for themselves and the six hundred stranded colonists.

Fearing another Tanlian attack, the miners fashioned dead-end shafts that would lead attackers astray. They also created dozens of escape routes and exits. These doorways to safety emptied into small canyons inaccessible from the air or behind waterfalls where people could hide indefinitely.

Food and other supplies were hidden along the escape routes, marked by scratches or cracks in the rock. Nesia Weeber, a young geologist, designed this peculiar code, which all the colonists soon learned.

Certain scratches identified a supply cache or a safe route. Other markings, which looked almost identical, were added as decoys. The miners worked with efficient speed. The colonists had to be protected if the Tanlians returned.

However, the shortage of fuel for their digging and excavating machines was the most important factor and concern. Six months had passed since they had been stranded, and fuel already was running low. Wald feared their supply would run out in another few months at the pace they were working.

Riss and the others who knew how to hunt had been successful in finding plentiful game. They were lucky to have a few biologists and agrists among the group who harvested edible vegetation, and even started planting for the next season. Even in this valley, the bioformers had established groves of pecans, apples, pears, and plum trees. Dozens of berries and even grapevines grew wild.

Another thought edged into Wald's mind. "When can we expect rescuers from Sirius 7? I know the captain sent a distress call. The colonization council will wonder about its people. And Universal Mineral will be curious about my findings, as well as its equipment."

Riss was silent for a moment. "We had better learn to be comfortable here. My guess is the fastest ship could reach us in seven years, unless one can be dispatched from Brasilia Dos. That still would take two and a half years."

Wald's mood darkened even more. "My Lord, two and a half years at the fastest? The whole Tanlian fleet could visit us over and over again. We could be decimated."

Riss leaned over and put his hand on the smaller man's shoulder. "Well, we will just have to make their visits very unpleasant. The Tanlians like quick attacks, easy plunder. The more difficult we prove to be, the less likely they will want to come back and suffer losses."

Wald shook his head. He felt pessimism growing in him — a cold shiver coursed through his body. The geologist had been so busy planning the living quarters and escape routes, urging on his workers and rationing the fuel supplies, he hadn't considered the magnitude of the situation.

Riss knew the eccentric little man could get lost in his own fears. Wald had not planned to be a colonist. His stay on Verde Grande was supposed to be short term according to space travel standards, maybe ten years.

The geologist was an expert at finding valuable mineral deposits in mountain ranges, caves, and valleys on the new worlds being colonized. He and his men would mark the deposits, start a dig or excavation site and move on to the next promising site.

Wald was happiest when he was in the middle of a project. Riss hoped the geologist would be interested in a plan he had been working on for several weeks. "I need your opinion of a project I have been thinking of," Riss said.

Taken by surprise, Wald's eyes narrowed with suspicion as he looked at the young lieutenant. "Need me to dig more holes for you?" He didn't mask his sarcasm. However, he changed his demeanor when he saw the look on Ris's face. "What is it Lieutenant?"

"Yes, as a matter of fact, I was thinking about digging more holes," Riss answered. "We can't deceive ourselves that the Tanlians won't come back. Even with your ingenuous cave system, attackers could still capture or kill many of our people."

Wald stared in disbelief, mulling over Ris's words. "So what we are doing here may not be good enough, lieutenant? Do you have another plan?"

"What we have done on this site has been excellent, geologist. However, if our people were scattered through various canyons, out of harm's way, it would make it difficult for the Tanlians to find all of us. They don't like to work too hard."

Wald stared past Ris, deep in thought. “We don’t have the time or fuel to build another complex like this,” the geologist said more to himself than to Ris. “But we could fashion smaller habitats for perhaps a few dozen people. There are many canyons scattered through the valley.”

Riss smiled. He could see the other man warming to the idea.

“We just might be able to dig those holes for you, lieutenant.”

For the first time in weeks, Wald smiled. He had another project and another deadline.

2

A somber Jamison Gresser shuffled out of the chambers of the Colonization Alliance of Independent Nations Council during a recess. As he feared, the council was leaning toward abandoning Verde Grande.

The council members had been horrified at the apparent loss of life at the hands of the Tanlians. A century of work and billions worth of currency and credit shares were going to be counted as a loss.

Jamison, the colonization director, had argued in favor of sending a rescue ship. Even the fastest deep-space flyer would take almost eight years to reach the planet and eight more to return. However, they would receive the ship's signals in weeks. At least they would have an answer.

"We owe it to those two thousand colonists to find out what happened," he argued before the council. "There may be survivors waiting for supplies and reinforcements. We cannot leave them to the whims of these predators."

Per Vosberg testified what the loss of just the mining equipment alone would be worth. His estimate did not account for the *Colonia Nueve* or any of the other supplies and tech gear the ship was carrying. However, he supported his friend of thirty-something years before the council. The two men had formed a close relationship during the colonization of many worlds.

Universal Mineral had earned huge profits from its association with the Alliance. Vast supplies of iron ore and other precious minerals flowed back to the other CAIN worlds and even to Sirius 7, Earth's first colony and now the center of colonization efforts.

Jamison leaned against a dappled blue marble wall, which had been mined from New Canada, the first world he and Per had worked on together. "Old friend, we will convince them," Per said. "There have been too many losses to the Tanlians and Verde Grande seems so far away, even to us."

"Most of the council seems to be very determined not send a ship," Jamison said, sounding defeated. "They are letting the Tanlians dictate what worlds we can settle. I would not be surprised if the rights are sold to the Syndicate. What a sad day. I'm glad Emilio Nandez is not here to see this."

Jamison and Emilio Nandez, Hector's grandfather, had worked side by side for many years. Almost sixty years ago, he and Emilio had taken part in the last bioforming mission to Verde Grande.

Both men had fallen in love with the lush green world and its rough but beautiful terrain. Jamison and Emilio were in charge of wildlife population control. They visited hundreds of the smaller valleys, checking on the success of the ecosystems. If it looked like grazer, rodent, bird, or predator numbers were down, they released more or different animals to create a healthy eco-balance.

A loud gong rippled through the halls of the council building. Not long afterward, a polite but insistent aide told the two men the council was reconvening.

"Cheer up, Jamison. It's my turn to address the august body, and I can be quite persuasive," Per said.

Jamison smiled at his taller friend. Most passersby would not give Per more than a cursory glance. His stringy blond hair looked windblown most of the time. He appeared to have picked his clothes for comfort rather than for fashion. One would never know this man presided over one of the biggest CAIN conglomerates.

The two men walked into the council chambers. It was a small auditorium. Seats on twelve levels encircled a speaker's podium on the first level. Jamison stood at the podium, waiting to be recognized.

Council Chairman Beppe Lazano looked up. "The chair recognizes the honorable Director Jamison Gresser. You have the floor, Director."

"I wish to yield to my colleague from Universal Mineral," Jamison said gesturing toward his friend seated beside him.

The chairman nodded. "So be it. The chair now recognizes Per Vosberg of Universal Mineral."

Per smiled, thanking Beppe and the one hundred council members for hearing him. "Honorable council members, we have indeed suffered a great loss at the hands of the Tanlians. We have lost people, we have lost equipment, and we may have lost a promising world this group has overseen for more than a hundred years. I understand your trepidation of sending a manned ship to Verde Grande. How much more time and funds should be spent on this planet?"

At this comment, Jamison turned with a shocked expression and stared at Per, who shot him a quick glance and a smile. "Universal Mineral has invested millions in the Verde Grande mission. We also have more than fifty men as well as equipment stranded there."

Per paused for a moment and then began again. "I don't need to remind the council of how lucrative our association has been."

Many of the council members nodded and smiled. Most of the members were leaders from Earth, Sirius, and the other new worlds. Universal Mineral had helped build their cities and fuel their economies.

Per waited a bit again for effect and continued. "I have been trying to factor this next cost, but I seem to be having somewhat of a problem, honorable council members. CAIN dispatched two thousand colonists to Verde Grande. I cannot estimate what it cost to send those people — thousands of currency each, a million possibly."

This time there was an uncomfortable shifting of seats, clearing of throats, and a few nervous coughs among the audience. Jamison was now smiling, seeing how Per was setting up his argument.

"My colleague and good acquaintance, Jamison Gresser, has eloquently argued about rescuing the survivors, if there are any, on Verde Grande. Those colonists were the sons and daughters of the CAIN worlds," Per said, his voice gathering in strength. "Sons and daughters from Sirius 7, New Canada, Orion 2, Brasilia Dos, Latino Hermano, Hawking 4 and New Iowa. I understand that even our brethren from Earth had representatives among the colonists."

The discomfort among the council members grew. Each councilperson had hosted gatherings for the colonists from their worlds. They had shaken the colonists' hands, posed for vid photos and given them good luck hugs.

"And don't forget what the Nandez family has meant to the colonization program. How many worlds they discovered and helped make livable. Why a Nandez — Hector I believe — captained the *Colonia Nueve*, christened by his father. It appears Captain Nandez gave his life to get the colonists to the planet."

Per now shifted to a hushed tone, making his listeners sit up, straining to hear him. "Council members, I have a compromise for you to consider. We do not have to endanger more people on an unknown rescue mission. We could, however, send a robot ship to investigate."

Per and Jamison could sense excitement growing in the audience. "The robot ship could reach Verde Grande much faster than a manned vehicle. If there are any survivors, its scans would detect them or pick up any signals they were sending. I propose having a rescue ship on standby on Brasilia Dos, ready to launch if we find our people still alive."

Per paused, taking his time to look around the room as if to make eye contact with everyone and then shouted, "Honorable council members, what do you say?"

Rising as a wave, the one hundred council members shouted aye and applauded. Waiting for the commotion to quiet down,

Chairman Lazano called for a vote, which was approved by an even louder roar.

3

Lar Vonn woke up with a start, sitting up straight from his bedroll. For a few seconds he wasn't sure where he was. Only a dim light glowed from the heat lantern. Breathing heavily, he looked around the cave. A shadowy figure was sitting only a few meters away, looking at him.

"Was it the same dream again, chief?" Neb Klinfer asked. Recognizing the hunter, Lar shook his head. "Is she showing you the others again?"

Lar took a deep breath. "It was different this time," he said focusing on Neb. "There were other climbers — maybe twenty of them. The sun was at their back as they were climbing, not in the eyes as it is in ours in the morning. She is showing me these things. It has to be."

Every night for the past nineteen days since Lar, Neb, and four other trusted hunters had started their climb, the security chief had awakened from dreams about the colonists on the other side of the mountain.

At first he had shrugged off his night visions as his concern for his fellow *Colonia Nueve* shipmates. The dreams seemed so real. He could see the other colonists at work building shelters, preparing food — everything. They appeared to be well and working hard.

However, the warm feeling he experienced after awakening convinced him it was more than just a dream. Taryl Bryann was directing his dreams.

"Other climbers? Do you recognize them?" Neb leaned forward.

Lar had been in awe of Taryl's talents since in a vivid dream he had seen the fleeing Tanlian ship smash into the mountain, destroying it after the colonists had thwarted the attack on their encampment. The ache of being separated from her was almost too much at times. He was thankful the climb required his full attention.

Lar smiled while stretching his aching back and shoulders. "Yes, I know all of them. They are all security forcers from the other side. It looks like they are trying to scale the mountain to reach us."

Neb raised his eyebrows with surprise. He had gotten accustomed to hearing Lar's accounts of the other colonists, but this was different. "Can you tell where they are, chief? Did you recognize the landscape?"

Lar shook his head. "No, but I got a full panoramic view as if ..." He stopped, realizing what he was seeing. "I am not seeing through Taryl, but through someone else's eyes. She is acting as a mental portal."

"Twenty men, a much larger party than ours," Neb said. "They must be outfitted well and have plenty of supplies. I wish we knew where they were. We could leave markers for them."

At the mention of supplies, the hunter shook his ration bag. It was low. The first week of their trip the hunters had successfully bagged several mountain goats, giving them meat for a short while. But the six men could only carry so much besides the gear they needed to survive the elements.

In the past week, the party had bagged only a few small rodents. Supplies were growing thin, temperatures were dropping the higher they climbed, and still thousands of meters of rock still loomed ahead of them.

During their trek, Lar and Neb had grown to respect each other. Both were no-nonsense men when it came to climbing or hunting, but they loved to share stories after settling down for the night. Lar did not need a translator to understand Neb's actions. He knew they were low on supplies and it appeared the climb was only getting more treacherous. The temperatures and high altitude slowed them down, even with their insulated suits and breathers, which someone had the foresight to grab from the lander.

The security chief frowned, looking up at nothing but rocks. The rocks seemed to rise unmercifully into the sky. "How many more days of climbing will the supplies sustain us?"

Neb shook his head. "My guess, less than a week. We haven't seen game for a while. We may have to consider how we will get back to the others," he said gesturing down the mountain.

This was the answer Lar had feared. The security chief was desperate to continue, but he was a realist. It appeared the climb would take longer than he imagined. A much larger party would be needed to scale the mountain, about the size of the other group coming from the other side.

"You make a good argument, hunter. I might be stubborn, but I want to live to try again."

Neb smiled at the compliment and looked at the other four hunters who already were starting to pack for their descent. "Our laser cutters have plenty of energy left. Let's burn signs in the rocks within two hundred meters of this place. Maybe the climbers from the other side will see them."

"I hope we can find your marks on the way down or Wald Bergmann may find us sleeping permanently among these boulders," Lar said with a smirk.

"A blind man could find our marks and the cut rocks," Neb answered, then laughed at the good-natured insult. "Even a security officer may be able to find his way."

¶ ¶ ¶

Lt. Uri Navrakov volunteered to lead the climbing expedition in hopes of reaching Lar Vonn's stranded group. He and the chief were not close, but the two men respected each other. Taryl

Bryann was the key factor in his decision. He saw how important this mission was to her — how much she must care for the others.

The Seer had been sick for three days after the Tanlian attack on their valley. Uri felt responsible for her. It was at his direction she had steered one of the fleeing attack ships into the mountain. He did not realize she had repeated the feat hours later to destroy another fleeing Tanlian flyer to help the others.

It had been six days and Uri's party was already feeling the toll. The going was slow, their supplies were heavy, and none were experienced climbers. This party did not possess survival hunting skills, so they ate from the stores they carried.

Every trail they followed ended in a dead end. This forced them to backtrack as much as going forward. Uri looked up. The boulders seemed to get bigger. They were scattered everywhere. The top of the mountain still loomed in the far distance.

Never one to shirk his duty or complain, Uri urged his men on, but he could see their spirits were running low. Many of the climbers had volunteered, hoping a saunter up the mountain would be a welcome break from the constant building, moving supplies, and foraging for fresh food. Now their bodies were sore from sliding over rocks and jumping crevices. Their hands were bloody from being torn on jagged edges.

Three days later and only two thousand meters higher, Uri halted his exhausted group for the night. The mountain still rose before them as if daring the climbers to continue. Their supplies were running low. They had maybe ten days' worth left if they were frugal.

In the morning, the lieutenant made the difficult decision to turn back. His group also had marked their way with laser cutters. Perhaps another party would try again, guided by their signs. The descent went much faster. They reached the colonist encampment in five days.

Taryl was the only one not happy to see them return. She was waiting for the climbers at the foot of the mountain. At first surprised to see her waiting exactly where they emerged, Uri caught himself. Of course she had been watching their movements.

Uri could not bear to look the petite Seer in the eyes. She stood before him, hands on her hips, her face almost as red as her flaming hair. Her expression softened as she saw his men shuffle past. They too were embarrassed at being forced to abandon the expedition early, but exhaustion was evident in their movements and faces.

Every other man sported bandages. Four others were carrying a stretcher. The injured man had broken his ankle in a fall two days earlier.

"I'm sorry, Taryl. We were unable to complete our mission," Uri said, bowing his head. "It was rough going up there. I was afraid we were going to run out of food and healthy bodies to continue."

Tears ran down Taryl's cheeks. "I know you tried your best, lieutenant. Your men look exhausted. I watched when your man broke his ankle. How awful."

"We can try again in a few lunars when the weather clears," Uri said, trying to cheer up the despondent woman. "A second group won't make the same mistakes we did. We marked our path very well."

Taryl nodded and allowed herself to smile. "CAIN security forces must be well trained, lieutenant."

Uri looked at her, puzzled. Was she mocking them?

"Lar and some of his men met the same fate you did," Taryl said. "They were out almost three weeks, but could not continue. They are returning to their camp now."

Three weeks? Uri was shocked. He knew Lar's group did not have the benefit of half the supplies and gear his climbers carried, but they had lasted longer on the mountain. Of course, Lar was as determined a man as Uri had met. He should not be surprised.

"It may take many attempts to climb, but we will keep trying. Our people will get better with experience, and we will keep forging a trail."

Uri could do nothing to comfort the Seer. He knew she was struggling with her emotions. It was no secret Lar and Taryl were lovers. However, not many knew the Seer was pregnant with the security chief's child.

Uri was privy to the fact because Taryl had seen his wife, Franca. A med tech, Franca had examined the Seer and found her and the baby to be in good health. However, Taryl was anxious about the others, especially Lar.

"Thank you Lieutenant for your worthy efforts and your words," Taryl said, trying to mask her feelings. She knew another group of climbers was still struggling to make it off the mountain. She felt utterly helpless. She could watch her beloved Lar and the others, but she could not send aid.

Taryl turned and started walking toward camp, rubbing her stomach in an effort to soothe herself.

4

Masat Ebber had expected to be called before the High Council. The transport captain had abandoned another Tanlian captain who had requested his assistance. It didn't help that the other captain was Yermak Halpan, grandson of the hero of the great revolt.

To make matters worse, he was facing another Halpan — Drace, Yermak's and Rolid's father — and even more importantly, the leader of the High Council.

Drace was an imposing figure. A long gray braid hung over his shoulder. Each knot signified completion of a successful mission. His bushy eyebrows stuck out almost four centimeters.

"How long did you wait for my favorite sons?" Drace boomed, glaring at Masat.

"Eighteen hours, High Councilman," Masat answered. "Transport law required me only to wait twelve. Yermak did not leave the coordinates of his mission, only where to meet him when he returned, which he did not."

"Do not quote transport law to me, Captain," Drace said, glowering at the man standing before him. "I wrote that law. I waited four days once for a fellow Tanlian to return."

Masat relaxed a bit. He had heard that story before. Last time, Drace had claimed to wait two and a half days, and this was the first time he had publicly claimed Yermak and Rolid were his favorites. The old man had fourteen sons, and all had been pronounced as his favorite at one time or another.

"I am prepared to take a faster ship to search for him," Masat offered. "If I know Yermak, he has found a fat colony and is enjoying himself."

Drace smiled in spite of himself. Yermak was famous for disappearing — sometimes for lunars on end — and then showing up with the most succulent cargo. Yermak always saved the best trophies to bring back to Tantalum 2.

"Take your pick of the best trophy ship in our fleet then, Captain."

Masat looked at Drace and folded his arms. "Trophy ship, High Councilman? Is that necessary?" Masat asked. He had stopped collecting female trophies more than ten years ago. Masat's last trophy hunt had gone poorly. After raiding a CAIN colony encampment, his men killed many of the male colonists who tried to defend their families.

The sonics and gas were ineffective that day, which left many inhabitants alert and ready to fight. The women and children screamed and fought as they were taken from their shelters and separated from the bodies of their dead husbands and fathers.

Children of all ages were taken this time. The Tanlians were collecting women, girls and even young boys. Tastes varied among their buyers.

Masat had trained himself to be oblivious during the collection of trophies. However, that day he found himself watching a mother and two young girls being forcibly carried out of their home. The girls were small, about the ages of his daughters, and their mother had long dark hair, much like his mate.

After that trip, Masat swore never to carry human cargo again. Drace was aware of the captain's vow, but he needed a trophy ship to search for Yermak and Rolid in case his missing sons needed the help.

"I know of your dislike for trophies, Captain, but the High Council requests this of you one more time," Drace said, his ancient face cracking into a rare smile. "Don't bother yourself with the collection, Captain. And besides, I will guarantee you double the earnings from this trip. Do you have any idea where this wayward Halpan might have gone?"

Masat frowned but agreed to Drace's offer with reluctance. "We will have several worlds to investigate, High Councilman. Yermak said he was low on fuel. We will visit each bioformed planet within low-fuel range."

Drace nodded in agreement. Only Yermak would take such a foolhardy chance with low fuel reserves. It was like him to call for help, but not give away a good find.

"Permission to leave and prepare for the journey," Masat bowed to Drace, and waited to be dismissed.

"One more thing before you go, Captain," the high councilman said. "Perhaps you would appreciate some, ah, assistance." Masat looked up and folded his arms, waiting to hear what was requested of him.

"The Galaxy Exploration and Minerals Syndicate is interested in CAIN bioforming activities. They are very knowledgeable concerning the locations of those worlds. Perhaps a guide from our Syndicate — let's say allies — would be a valuable passenger."

Masat did not hide his look of shock. A non-Tanlian had never traveled with a native crew. *Allies?* he thought. *Since when has Tantalum 2 considered the Syndicate as an ally?*

Masat had visited many GEMS colonies and gathered their tributes to take back to Tantalum 2. He had never considered them willing partners. He all but ignored the Syndicate officers when he loaded his cargo. They were lucky he wasn't interested in their women.

Drace was not surprised to see the captain's reaction. Masat, a powerful man of more than six feet tall, was known for his ability to glean more out of the tribute payers than the agreed-to amount. He would glower over the records handed to him by a GEMS representative and then complain in his booming baritone voice that the cargo had been shortened by at least ten percent. Almost always he was successful in bullying the extra ten percent out of the colony paying the tribute.

"Captain, I know we have never allowed non-Tanlians to fly with us, but I believe this GEMS representative could save you time," the high councilman said. "I would prefer you find Yermak quickly instead of taking lunars guessing which world he might have landed on."

Masat knew he was in no position to argue. "Yes, High Councilman. Will this Earther have run of the ship?" he asked not masking his disgust.

"You are the captain," Drace assured him. "You can be as generous or as restrictive as you wish. Although I recommend you giving him access to a computer and star charts."

Masat bowed again, waiting for Drace to wave him away. "As you wish, High Councilman."

5

The trip down the mountain was much easier for Lar Vonn and his companions. They seemed to breathe easier with each step. The trail they had marked on their ascent helped them on their return.

Lar led the way. The security chief wanted to prove to the five hunters that he could manage just fine. His heart grew even heavier the farther he walked from the summit.

This path was taking him away from his beloved Taryl, but the party had been forced to turn back. They were running out of supplies and the climb got more treacherous with every meter.

After a week of the descent, the six men had run out of food. However, the hunters did not despair. On this sunny day, they had seen raptors and signs of four-footed predators. Where there were predators, game could be found. They didn't care what form they'd be in — grazer, rodent, bird or reptile. Almost anything would be edible.

"We will be more effective if we split into two groups," Neb Klinfer said as the group hunched down for a midmorning rest. The six men had already been traveling for four hours.

"That's a good idea, I agree," Lar said, forgetting he was not in command.

"Well, then, I guess it's unanimous," Neb said, as he and the other four hunters broke into hearty laughs.

The security chief shook his head. “Sorry, sometimes I forgot I don’t have to lead. As far as hunting goes, I will try not to get in your way.” The other five hunters chuckled while they unpacked their gear. Neb took out his bow, an anachronistic but effective weapon from Earth.

Each of the others carried a favorite weapon. Drever favored a handheld energy burst tube with laser-guided site. Zek and Hart pulled out old Earth rifles, also favorite Earth weapons.

“A real hunter uses his own eyes to bring down game,” Zek said, smirking at Hart ’s scope, and demonstrating how he peered down the sight of his rifle’s long barrel.

“I want to bring down a meal, not a trophy,” Hart said, not bothered by his friend’s taunt. “Besides, I’m too clumsy to sneak up on anything close enough to use a sight.”

All eyes turned to watch Marco unfold what looked like a small rocket launcher. Looking up, he smiled. “I am not ashamed to use a little tech to bring down game. This is a sonic launcher. I auto-sight an animal and fire the projectile.”

Lar was dubious as he examined the weapon. “A sonic, but that only stuns things.”

Marco smiled. “I just need enough time to get to them and then I go to work.” At that, he pulled out a huge knife, almost a half-meter long. The steel glinted in the sunshine as its owner demonstrated his throat slitting technique.

The other hunters looked away from Marco’s demonstration and finished readying their equipment. Lar stared for a bit and shook his head. He felt for his weapons, a much smaller knife than what Marco carried and a short-range energy pistol. The game would have to be small and nearby if he was going to contribute to the meal.

“Why don’t you three with the noisemakers team up?” Lar said, looking at Zek, Hart and Marco. “Drever, Neb and I will try to stay upwind of you. Between the two groups we should at least have rodents to roast.”

Before setting out, Lar reminded the hunters to keep their comms turned on in case the groups lost sight of each other.

One hour later, Neb, Drever, and Lar had sighted a white grazer standing on a boulder about two hundred meters away. The white animal had two short horns and a beard.

"It looks like an Earth mountain goat, only smaller," Neb whispered. "I won't get close enough to get a shot." He nodded to Drever. "In range for you?"

Drever nodded and readied his energy-burst tube. All he needed was to lock his laser on the animal and it would be a smoldering carcass a second later.

At that moment, two loud cracks and a muffled explosion cut through the air. The three men flinched from the sound. Their prey was no longer perched on the rock, having scrambled away to safety.

"Sounds like they're fighting Tanlians," Drever scowled, disappointed at not getting a shot off. "They had better have bagged something with all that noise. We won't see another animal for a kilometer or two now."

Neb smiled. "If they didn't bring down anything, they should have to eat a rock lizard."

Drever laughed. "I would like to see Marco eat one of those. Perhaps he could slit its little neck to make him feel better." Lar and Neb chuckled. All three turned and walked in the direction of the other group, hoping there would be meat to roast this night.

It did not take long for Lar's group to find the other three hunters. Marco and Zek were cleaning the animal, another mountain goat, but smaller than the one Drever had wanted to bring down. Hart watched as the two worked on the animal, a big smile on his face.

Neb surveyed the scene. "Let me guess who was successful." Not willing to answer, Marco and Zek shrugged and kept working. They had it gutted and were dragging it to a nearby pine to hang it and let it bleed out.

"We had a bet. The other two would clean the first kill. Early Earth tech proved to be the better weapon," Hart said brandishing his scoped rifle.

"Zek shot the tail off a big one, and Marco scared the rest of the herd away. Good thing I was here. We will eat well tonight."

Marco glared at Hart. "You could have killed the big one. Why this one?" he growled.

"I wanted something tender to eat, not tough jerk that would take all night to cook," Hart said. "Sometimes you have to take your best shot, not wait for a trophy. Besides we would not be able to eat one of those big rams. It would be a waste."

"You are a strange hunter," Marco said. "My trophy rooms on Sirius 7 are full of the biggest specimens one can hope to find on the colony worlds."

Hart shook his head at Marco. "But how did they taste? When you are hungry it does not matter if it is the biggest in the herd."

Lar, Neb, and Drever smiled as they began to dig a fire pit and build a spit. They were just glad to have fresh meat.

The six felt like kings that night. Each one tore into huge slabs of roasted meat. Neb had found some kind of fruit growing on a nearby tree. None of the men could identify the dimpled yellow fruit, about the size of an apple, but the taste was sweet and intoxicating.

Hart peeled skins off the fruit, collected a small pile of seeds, and boiled some of the pulp down to a syrup, which he poured over the roasting goat. Fresh, cold water from one of the rushing mountain streams was carried to camp. The six men circled the roaring fire. No one said a word. They had not eaten this well in weeks.

After telling a few lies and poking fun at each other, the six men were more than ready to curl up in their bedrolls.

"We had better keep the fire going all night," Neb said. "Some of the predators may smell the meat and want to join us."

Lar looked around. "Is there anything big enough to worry about? I thought the bioformers didn't release anything that could harm humans."

The other hunters smiled. All of them had seen tracks of various size beasts such as grazers, rodents, and predators. One set of tracks looked like it was made by a big cat big enough to bring down one of those mountain goats.

"I looked at the bioformer release reports," Drever said. "They unleashed many kinds of animals and were thorough with their eco-planning, especially in the wild areas they did not expect people to settle."

Lar looked puzzled.

Neb laughed. "What he means is there could be all sizes of beasts out here. We have seen some impressive tracks. Some of them might think we would make a good meal."

The security chief required no further explanation. Now awake and imagining eyes watching them from the darkness, he volunteered for the first fire shift. The others did not argue as they settled down to sleep.

¶ ¶ ¶

First light had not broken over the mountains, but Neb stirred. He had slept soundly, his belly full from the night's feast. Something tugged at his consciousness — that feeling that something was not right. He shivered from the cool night air, causing him to sit up and look around with a start. The fire had burned down to embers.

Cursing, Neb slowly arose looking to see who was on watch. It was almost pitch black. He could hear the others sleeping. Some were snoring with gusto.

After fumbling for several seconds, he found a heat lantern and turned it on. He identified the sleepers as he crept by them. Marco was not among them — he had to be the one who was on watch.

Gathering more sticks, Neb soon got a nice blaze going and then went to search for his missing companion. The lantern was weak, illuminating just a few meters in front him. It made it difficult to search.

"Marco!" Neb shouted, slowly walking in larger circles around the camp. Waiting a few seconds after each call, Neb called louder. Hearing his voice, the other men woke and joined the search, each bringing a lantern.

Marco's name soon was being called in all directions, but the pitch-black night made the search difficult. The five remaining men met back at camp and waited for dawn and for light to continue their search. The grim-faced climbers ate a quick meal and readied their weapons. As Verde Grande's sun peeked over the mountaintops, they continued their search.

This time, Lar took charge of the mission. No one argued. They divided into two groups and started to search in ever expanding circles around the camp, stopping to report their whereabouts every ten minutes.

The security chief and Drever were together when they came upon the carcass of the mountain goat. The entrails and hide had been dragged about fifty meters from camp so predators wouldn't be tempted to visit the camp. After examining the carcass, Lar noticed one of the goat's horns lying about twenty meters away near some bushes. The sun glinted off an object near the horn. It was Marco's knife.

Lar quickly called the other three men to their position. It did not take Neb long to find the blood trail. Something heavy had been dragged through the bushes and over rocks. A large cat's tracks sunk into the ground, with an occasional bloodstain filling a print.

After two hundred meters or so, the tracks ended among some trees at the edge of a cliff. The search party circled the area, looking through the brush, finding nothing.

"Have you ever hunted cats before?" Lar asked his companions. They all shook their heads. Big cats had been protected for centuries on Earth and even the other colony worlds. The eco-experts wanted to maintain a viable population. Killing such an animal was punishable by a hefty prison sentence.

The security officer kept circling the area. "It's a cat, correct?" He asked, but did not expect an answer. "What do cats do when they want to hide?"

Neb looked startled and shouted, "They climb!" All five men looked up and started searching the trees. Not long into their search, Lar spotted something hanging in the fork of a large oak.

"Over here," he called to the others. "I think I found Marco." Lar started to scramble up the large oak whose wide branches protruded into the sky.

A concerned Neb stopped him, nodding toward the canopy. "The cat may be up there. We can't see much beyond his body. Go slow, my friend, and make sure we can see you at all times."

Lar tossed his climbing rope into the branches. It caught on the first try. As he started up the tree, his four companions took positions around the tree, each poised with his favorite weapon. It did not take long for the security chief to scale the twelve meters to the body.

Frowning, Lar could see the cat must have broken Marco's neck when it attacked him near the camp. He was amazed an animal could drag the 250-pound man that far and then carry the body up the tree. Lar shivered at the thought of what the scene must have looked like.

Lar fought off a gagging reflex after examining the scene. Parts of the body were missing, most likely eaten. It looked like the cat had tucked away the remainder of its kill in this crook for safekeeping. Grimacing, Lar tied another rope around the body and prepared to lower it to the ground when he heard an almost imperceptible noise, almost like thunder in the distance.

Instinctively, he flattened himself against the branch just as the cat leaped past. One of its claws ripped into his back. The big animal bounded onto another branch and stopped to poise for another leap at Lar when two loud cracks and two softer thuds made the cat twirl on its perch. It screamed in pain and fell writhing to the ground.

The men could see why the cat had no trouble dragging a human. The animal must have weighed almost as much as Marco. Its tawny, dark splotched body was still smoldering from the energy burst. Two bullet holes and an arrow also had found their mark.

¶ ¶ ¶

Riss Nels and Wald Bergmann heard the other colonists yell before they saw the climbers returning. It had been almost five weeks since the six men had left, but now they were returning. The shouting ceased after the men came into view. Only five had returned. They walked with a slow shuffle, their heads down.

A large group of colonists rushed to the five men, carrying food, water, and aid supplies. It was evident the survivors were exhausted and in need of rest. Not starving, they still welcomed the food, and especially appreciated the water offered to them.

The people gathered around the five men and waited to hear their story. Lar told those gathered that the climbing party had buried Marco. They had placed a large pile of rocks over the grave, etched his name in the largest boulder they could roll to the site, and said prayers and incantations the best they could remember. Wald looked startled after hearing about the size of the animal and the ease in which it had killed Marco.

"It appears Tanlians are not the only enemy we have to be wary of in this valley," Riss said. "It is apparent this valley is not the paradise we were promised. I wonder how many more times we will have to fight for our lives here?"

6

"I'm worried about her," Franca said, looking at her mate, Uri Navrakov. "Taryl has eaten very little for a week. She and the baby she is carrying need more sustenance."

Uri shrugged and continued eating his evening meal. "All you can do is check her and bring food. She is worried about Lar and the other climbers. They have been on the mountain for weeks now." Uri had just finished speaking when he and Franca were startled by a soft rap at the door. It was past dusk and the stars were beginning to glow in the sky, an unusual time for a visitor.

Franca peeked out of the door to their shelter and stepped back in surprise. "Taryl! Do you need help? Are you ill?" the med tech hurried forward to help the Seer into their shelter. Uri stood as the two women crossed the room.

"I just wanted to thank you for the delicious food you have been bringing," Taryl said, her face glowing. "I'm afraid I haven't properly thanked you for taking care of me."

Uri studied Taryl and smiled. "I assume Lar and the other climbers are safe?" His expression changed at a sudden thought. "Did they make it over the mountain?"

"Lar and four of the others are safe," Taryl said. "One of the hunters was killed by a big predator, a cat I think. No, they had to turn back and return to their camp." Relief showed in Taryl's face. She had slept well the night Lar and the other four climbers had returned to the colonists on the other side of the mountain.

Taryl told the couple about the search for Marco after he disappeared, and how the hunters had killed the cat after it tried to attack Lar in the tree. Uri and Franca were spellbound at the Seer's vivid description of the events as if she had been there.

All three were surprised by a murmur from outside. Franca had forgotten to latch the door when she helped Taryl inside. They had not realized a small crowd had gathered, listening from the doorway. Many of the other colonists were in awe of Taryl. They knew the Seer had helped save them from the Tanlian attack.

Uri walked to the door and started to close it, angry at the intrusion. "Go away, busybodies," he snapped. "Taryl is visiting us and deserves privacy." One of the women in the crowd apologized, but the others stood frozen. Uri was surprised at the expressions on many of the others' faces. It was a combination of fright mixed with reverence.

Taryl turned to face the crowd. "Please, my friends. I will gladly retell the story tomorrow, but I am a guest here." At her urging, the crowd, which had swelled to almost fifty people, began to disperse. Some of the listeners bowed slightly and whispered farewells to Taryl, Franca, and Uri.

"That was the other reason I wanted to talk to you," Taryl said, nodding in the direction of the door after the three had returned inside the shelter. "The others are treating me differently. They bring me gifts and food, too. I am followed and watched wherever I go."

Uri looked surprised. He had noticed the extra attention being showered upon the Seer. The lieutenant did not think twice about speaking to or being near Taryl. The two had worked together to thwart the Tanlians. He had seen how vulnerable she was, but respected the Seer for her unique gift. "How long has this been going on?" he asked. "Do you feel threatened?"

Taryl shook her head. "No, not threatened. But I feel strange about being watched. It's been going on since the Tanlian attack.

I much preferred how I was treated before the attack. People were polite, but left me alone."

Franca smiled and put her arm around Taryl's shoulder. She had seen the Seer as a patient, someone who needed urging to eat to keep up her strength. But the two women had also shared confidences as sisters would have and had grown close.

Uri sat deep in thought, gazing at the door. "Your isolation may have added to your mystique," he said. "If you feel well enough, perhaps you should visit with more of the others, help with the day-to-day activities as best you can."

Franca glared at her mate. "Uri, how could you suggest such as thing after what she has been through? She needs to rest and recover her strength."

Taryl smiled at her friend. "I think Uri may be correct I have not done my fair share of the work in camp. I am capable of helping out, even if I do move a bit slower. Maybe when the others see me sweating alongside them, they will treat me as any other colonist."

Franca laughed, "If they let you lift a hand, that is. You may find it difficult to pick out your own food. And when the others discover you are with child, you may be treated as old Earth royalty."

Taryl lifted her eyebrows in surprise at Franca's last statement. "I want to be treated the same as any other colonist," she said in her soft voice. "My gift should not set me apart from the others."

7

The GEMS representative was not on board yet and already controversy had been stirred up. The official had requested space for six persons. Masat Ebber denied the request, refusing to even meet with the Syndicate people. The captain had been ordered to take one of the foreigners on his mission to find the missing Tanlian ship, Brak's Revenge.

An hour later came a new request — permission for three GEMS representatives to board the ship. Masat refused again, his patience growing thin. He had received no new orders from the Tanlian High Council; the decision was his.

"Tell the Earther that this ship is leaving in one hour," he said to his comm operator. "If he is not on board, we fly without him, and relay my orders to Tanlian command." Barely ten minutes later, Tanlian command signaled Masat. None other than High Councilman Drace Halpan requested to speak to the captain.

"High Councilman, you honor us on our departure," Masat said, not bothering to mask his concern. A smiling, almost grandfatherly Drace appeared on Masat's private viewer. "Ah, Captain, it appears we have a situation with our Syndicate ally. The representative wishes to be escorted by traveling companions. They had not communicated this request before now."

Masat folded his arms across his chest. "The original request was for one GEMS passenger to travel with us, High Councilman. We travel fast and efficiently. More than one stranger may complicate the ship's operation." Masat was disturbed by the benevolent-looking high councilman. The captain was accustomed to a scowling, irritable Drace, not the one who appeared to be sympathetic. "Captain, apparently it is a clan custom for them to travel with an escort, especially in special cases such as this. Would you kindly consent to two passengers?"

Masat was puzzled. The high councilman had said this was a special case. What did that mean? Seeing the look on the captain's face prompted Drace to answer the unspoken question. "I might as well tell you now, Captain, to avoid more angry communiqués between us. Your primary passenger is a woman. She requires at least one male escort. Perhaps an aide, guard or someone else," the high councilman said, this time breaking into a familiar sneer.

Masat was speechless. A woman with access to crew quarters and flight command? The only women "allowed" on Tanlian ships were trophies, and they were limited to the cargo holds or private quarters of officers.

"You would make a bad diplomat, Captain," Drace said, his laughter booming through the speaker. "This passenger is important to the high council. She apparently is an expert on bio-form worlds and has knowledge of Colonization Alliance of Independent Nations activities. I want to know what happened to Yermak, Rolid, and the Brak's Revenge, and I want to know quickly."

Now the high councilman resembled the image Masat had expected — a scowling old man with little patience. Knowing he would lose this argument and perhaps have the ship taken away from him, Masat gave a perfunctory bow. "Tell the two Earthers we fly now . . ."

Drace interrupted him. "You will leave in two hours, Captain. It appears your passengers need the time to load their personal items." The high council leader broke into a booming laugh at the look on Masat's face.

¶ ¶ ¶

Masat's ship had been on its mission for a week before he consented at last to meet the Syndicate passengers. He had politely refused their entreaties to a meeting before then. The Earthers had delayed his launch by almost three hours. They were subject to his rules now that they were on his ship. He had limited their access to the ship's galley and navigation room. He was told the two were never separated. Four Tanlian "escorts" kept a respectful distance, but accompanied the visitors wherever they went.

Now his curiosity needed to be assuaged. The passengers had invited him to dine with them. They promised specialties from their home world of Kenyata. The opportunity to try new food was tempting — they had found his weakness.

Masat was warned the female was beautiful. His crew members were not bashful about casting admiring glances at the woman during her short trips through the ship's corridors.The captain had not believed the descriptions of the Syndicate woman. Many of his Tanlian crew ogled any female they met on colony worlds. But Masat was struck almost speechless when he met Ismala N'pofu.

The tall woman was just shy of six feet. She could almost look him in the eye. Her dark complexion and coal black eyes were striking. Two large, black ringlets of hair rested on her shoulders. Something else about this woman was familiar. She reminded him of someone, but who? A second later, the thought shocked him. This woman looked like a combination of his two sisters. She could pass as a relative.

"Greetings, Captain Ebber, Shadra and I wish to thank you for your hospitality," Ismala gestured toward her somber companion, who bowed to Masat. The captain stared at Shadra, who also could pass as a member of the Ebber clan. "We appreciate you taking time from your busy schedule to meet with us," Ismala said with a wide smile, her eyes sparkling.

Masat nodded, wincing a bit. His crew had tolerated the Earthers, but had shown the pair little hospitality. The captain studied the woman. Her smile seemed sincere. He sensed no mockery in her words.

"I trust you are comfortable and have everything you need?" Masat asked, allowing himself a moment to glance around the pair's cabin. To his surprise, the cabin had been transformed with soft cane furniture and a wide-leafed plant that looked like a fan filled a corner. A large vid screen covered one wall. It displayed the ship's present course in the center. Plot marks spread out in five directions, ending at five CAIN worlds.

"Yes, Captain. We are quite comfortable and have everything we require," Ismala said. "We are ready to dine at your convenience." This was all very strange to Masat — a woman inviting a stranger to a meal. Tanlian women were always subordinate. Many females on his world had arrived as trophies plucked from other worlds or were descended from trophies.

Masat's eyes drifted to Ismala's companion, who had not said a word but stood nearby attentively. "My apologies, Captain. May I present my brother?" Ismala said, noticing Masat's interest in Shadra. "It is Kenyata tradition for our women to travel with escorts, preferably male relatives. He is my protector."

Masat cast a wary look at Shadra. The well-muscled Kenyatan was taller than the captain by several centimeters. He would make an imposing foe. "You will not have to defend your sister on this ship, you have my word." Masat smiled at Shadra.

Shadra's eyes were wide with surprise at being addressed. He looked at Ismala, who nodded slightly to him. This exchange was not lost on Masat.

"Thank you, Captain. That is most reassuring. I have sworn to defend my sister to the death," Shadra said slowly in a baritone voice. Masat nodded, understanding the other man's serious tone.

Tanlians had built their reputation on plunder, especially of women. This Kenyatan would not relax on this ship of trophy hunters. "Permission?" Shadra said, again looking at his sister.

"Speak freely here, Shadra. Their customs are different than ours," Ismala said.

"Captain, if I may be so bold, you appear to share common blood. You could pass for a Kenyatan," Shadra said, studying Masat. The smile faded from Ismala's face as she glared at her brother. Masat threw back his head and roared with laughter. It was the first time on this voyage the captain had enjoyed himself. Ismala and Shadra were startled.

"You echoed my thoughts, Shadra. Both of you could pass for Ebber clan, even siblings of mine. We obviously share common heritage. Tanlians are descended from Earthers of all origins. We are not ashamed of that."

Shadra and Ismala smiled. First contact had gone much better than both hoped. "Thank you, Captain. It is an honor to be hosted by a distant cousin," Ismala said, smiling and breaking into a soft laugh. "I assure you, Captain, we intend to be perfect guests. Our only interest is to help find your missing ship. If by chance we get an opportunity to visit several CAIN worlds, so much the better."

Masat smiled. Ismala had laid out her plans. The Earthers were not interested in the goings on of the Tanlian ship, but had their eyes on bigger prizes.

Walking to a comm next to his guests' door, he typed in the code for an all-ship broadcast. "This is Captain Ebber. All Tanlians under my command are ordered to show our Kenyatan guests every courtesy. I believe they feel comfortable enough coming and going. No escorts are necessary. I will personally deal with any incidences of misconduct."

Ismala bowed to Masat and thanked him. This meeting had gone better than she had hoped. Seeing the captain's renewed interest in the table full of food and native Kenyatan wine, she gestured for him to sit.

8

Lar Vonn tried to keep himself busy helping the other colonists. Several weeks had passed since he and his four companions had returned from their unsuccessful climb. The trip had been a disaster. Not only had they not come close to scaling the mountain and reaching the colonists on the other side, but also one of their party had been killed by a large cat.

After hearing the story of the ill-fated attempt, Lar could get no one to agree to even talk about trying to climb the mountain again. His friend and fellow climber, Neb Klinfer, was sympathetic, but not eager to try that adventure again any time soon. The colonists stranded in this wild and treacherous valley were concerned about protecting themselves from future Tanlian attacks.

Geologist Wald Bergmann and security officer Riss Nels had supervised the building of nine additional shelters, sites cut out of rock or expanded cave systems. Some of the new sites were several kilometers away from each other. Even in his dark mood, Lar had marveled at Wald's workmanship. Tunnels and rooms for dozens of people had been carved out with care.

Using survival training, the colonists agreed to multiple living sites. The Tanlians perhaps could attack one group, but the others would have an excellent chance of escaping. The six hundred colonists already were divided among the sites. Leaders had been chosen for most of the groups.

Lar had been given first choice to lead any group, but he chose to stay at the original landing site. If the Tanlians returned, it was likely they would be attracted to this spot again. The security chief was not afraid to be part of the first line of resistance against any attacker.

Neb and Riss had been chosen to lead different groups and were busy settling in and establishing defenses. Wald declined the offer to be a group leader. He opted to stay with Lar in the first cavern maze he had designed.

Now the situation arrived that Wald had been fearing for weeks. His excavating machines were almost out of fuel. Even the laser cutter power packs were running low. At Lar's request, all ten group leaders met at the security chief's site to discuss what to do.

"Once these machines are out of fuel, what can be done with them?" Wald asked. "Should we shelter them somewhere in hopes we someday may be able to use them again?"

Lar smiled. The idea of doing anything but preserving the geologist's beloved machines broke Wald's heart. The others kept their silence as they sat around the fire. Neb drew circles in the dirt with a stick, something obviously on his mind. After spending weeks with the hunter, Lar had gotten to know him well. "What do you think, Neb?"

The hunter stopped drawing and looked at each leader. "How will we defend ourselves once the power packs are drained and all the bullets have been used from the Earth rifles?" he asked. "It could be years before any rescuers could reach us. We may have enough weapons to ward off one more Tanlian attack, but what if they return more times?" The other nine shook their heads, but kept their eyes on Neb. It was clear he had an idea. The hunter pulled out his archaic bow, unslung the arrow quiver from his back, and also pulled out a knife. He held up his weapons of choice.

"These do not need energy packs or powder projectiles. We can make hundreds, perhaps thousands of arrows that can be used for many years. And knives are very effective from close range, especially in the caves."

The other leaders all started arguing at once, contradicting Neb and pointing out the benefits of their favorite weapons. However, no one had a solution to the problem of what to do when the rifles ran out of bullets and powder and the energy weapons ran out of power. This stranded group of colonists did not have the equipment that could manufacture ammunition for the tech weapons.

Neb said nothing as he drew his designs in the sand. It did not take long for the others to come to realize their modern weapons would be useless shortly. All eyes stared at the patient hunter.

"How do you propose we make your weapons?" Wald asked, fearing he knew the answer.

"We have plenty of metal available to us and enough power packs to run the laser cutters for weeks," Neb said looking at the geologist. "If your machines are out of fuel for years, what good are they to us? Their metal may save our lives and be useful for many years."

Wald started to object, but he realized he could not refute Neb's logic. The flickering firelight made his frown look ominous. He would be lost without his machines. Useless. The diggers and the rock carvers were Wald's poetry. He could use them in dozens of ways to be beneficial, whether it was unearthing valuable minerals or boring shelters and tunnels for habitation. But, now they sat quiet. The dribble of fuel left would barely start the machines.

No one said a word to Wald. All realized they owed their lives to his efforts and ingenuity in carving protection for them out of the rocks. Lar took out a flask of his favorite Siriusian whiskey and took a sip.

"Got any left to share?" Wald asked. "It's been months since I've had anything stronger than citrus tea." The security chief placed the cap on the sliver flask and tossed it to the miner. Wald took a long draw and smacked his lips, much to everyone's surprise. Most had figured the little man for a no-nonsense type

— someone who was only happy when he was working, and who never relaxed.

After a long pause, Wald looked around the fire. He had never been the generous type, but he had rushed to save these people and now he faced another decision. "I suppose we can't throw the damn diggers at the Tanlians, can we?" he said with a half-sneer. The other nine roared with laughter. The uncomfortable silence was broken.

"We can drain all the energy packs to power the cutters. I can even build a smelter that will speed things up," Wald said. Then he turned to Neb. "Hunter, I will make you knives that will cut through bone like soft cheese."

¶ ¶ ¶

Lt. Uri Navrakov was not happy with the colony's defenses in the large valley. Only two laser-guided missiles were left. Twelve launchers had been built and placed in strategic locations throughout the mountains overlooking their shelters, but only four missiles had been transported from the *Colonia Nueve* before the first Tanlian attack. The only two activated missiles had been fired.

His security force had energy-pulse rifles, and their power packs were charged, but they would empty quickly if used in a battle. Almost all the colonists had been issued hand-held energy pulsers. If the Tanlians avoided the pair of missiles, there would be bloody hand-to-hand combat.

He wondered how much the invaders would want to fight. Tanlians were opportunistic raiders. They usually liked to pounce on a defenseless village and escape without suffering losses.

The colony's most potent weapon, however, might be a small red-haired woman — Taryl Bryann. The Seer had confused two Tanlian pilots, making them crash into the mountain. Uri smiled, despite himself. No one would have guessed the person who was almost left off the colony ship may be its most valuable member.

Taryl's pregnancy had slowed her down. Most of her energy was devoted to the unborn baby. Sometimes it was days between her meditations. She could see through Lar's eyes and was able to tell the colonists how their counterparts were faring on the other side of the mountain.

Uri was surprised Security Chief Lar had allowed the second group of colonists to be split up into so many small units. The lieutenant preferred to have the colonists under his protection in one spot, rather than be separated and picked off.

Each colonist also carried a personal comm. This made it easier for groups searching for food or exploring the countryside to keep from getting lost. However, those comms would make it easy for an enemy to key in on the colony's coordinates.

To prevent this from happening, Uri had established a warning system. A high-pitched blast lasting five seconds was the signal for complete comm silence, no exceptions. The security lieutenant made it clear that anyone breaking the silence during an attack would be treated as an enemy.

This is all we can do for now, Uri thought. *We will keep building permanent structures hidden in the rocks and trees and be prepared. If the Tanlians come, we won't be easy targets. I hope Lar and the others fare as well.*

The lieutenant's musings were interrupted by Ilysa Grohweg, one of his mate's med aides. The young woman was breathless and could hardly speak she was so excited. "Franca says it's time," the aide blurted. "It's early, but everything seems fine so far. She wanted me to find you."

"Is something wrong with Franca?" Uri asked, looking puzzled. His mate had been well when he left her this morning. They had shared first meal, and she had scolded him for all the things he had left undone, as usual.

The aide, a tall blonde who reminded Uri of a river willow, stared for a moment and squealed, "No, not Franca. It's Taryl. The baby is coming." Now Uri understood what all the excitement was about.

Taryl was in labor, about three weeks earlier than expected. This would create an uproar throughout the colony. The first baby born on Verde Grande and of course it would have to be the venerated Seer's baby. Taryl had been unsuccessful at convincing the other colonists she should be treated the same as anyone else. It seemed the harder she tried, the more the other colonists grew in awe of her.

"Does anyone else know about Taryl?" Uri said, gripping Ilysa's shoulders. "Did you go screaming through the encampment about the baby?"

"No, no, sir," the girl blinked almost in tears, surprised by the painful grip. "Franca told me to tell you and no one else." Uri relaxed and apologized for scaring her.

"Thank you, Ilysa. The last thing Taryl needs is for a crowd to gather during this time. She is uncomfortable with the attention from the others. The most important thing for her now is to concentrate on the baby." The lieutenant smiled. "What an honor for you, Ilysa. You will help deliver this world's first human baby. We had better return to camp and see if we can help. Let's try to act like we're late for second meal. We'll be less likely to draw a crowd."

¶ ¶ ¶

Ismala N'pofu studied the scans of planet WN-588. The Tanlian ship had orbited the world for four days. They had found nothing. The Syndicate woman was dubious this was the world they had been searching for. The planet was only reaching its second stage of bioforming. It was barely habitable for humans.

The Tanlians found no signs of colonists or even a scientific study team. The planet was quiet. They monitored no communications. Scout ships searched any reasonable hiding place — nothing.

Captain Masat Ebber stood nearby, also studying the readings. "I had my doubts about this place," Ismala said, looking at Masat. "But it was the closest CAIN world. It was interesting to see an early bioform planet. I have to admit the Alliance is adept. Their worlds are ready to settle almost fifty years faster than ours."

Masat smiled. "I'm glad you are able to garner scientific information, but we can't afford to linger much longer. I am ready to depart this world. We have two more planets to scour for our missing ship."

Ismala nodded in agreement and studied the star chart on the large vid screen in her quarters. "The next planet is XR-309, a fully bioformed world. However, it appears the Alliance may have abandoned it. The planet has been ready for at least fifty years. It is eleven years away from the nearest CAIN colony. Perhaps you Tanlians have frightened the Alliance away. It would make a perfect addition to the Syndicate."

Masat laughed. "It's about time CAIN realizes we Tanlians rule space travel. But perhaps they think we have forgotten about this planet, too."

Ismala's fingers flew across her keypad. A line appeared on the screen and inched its way to XR-309. "I estimate about twelve days' travel to the planet," she said.

Masat agreed after studying the giant chart. "If nothing else, this planet may make for interesting study. It also appears to be a likely place where my men can recreate and hunt. My crew likes good sport when they get the chance."

9

Lar Vonn awoke from the most realistic and disturbing dream he had ever experienced. He had been fitful all night, tossing and turning on his cot, getting up to pace around his living quarters. Something was making him ill at ease.

The security chief checked with the guards around his encampment's perimeter so many times even they were growing irritable with him. He even signaled the other nine camps. Nothing. All was well.

Lar usually welcomed sleep. For the past few months, his beloved Taryl Bryann had communicated with him through his dreams. He would wake in the mornings and relive the vivid images she had etched in his subconscious. He could describe in great detail what the colonists on the other side were doing.

The others were faring well under Uri Navrakov's guidance. Shelters were erected to blend in with the landscape. Uri had established an excellent defensive scheme.

This night, Lar was getting flashes of pain. He would wake up in a cold sweat, the dark room spun, not unlike the feeling he got after swigging too many Siriusian ales. Finally unable to stand it any longer, Lar rose, slipped on his clothes and headed outside for fresh air.

Signaling the guards that all was well, he took his time navigating through the rock-strewn path. Verde Grande's two moons both shone brightly, illuminating the countryside. Making his way past the various camp enclosures, he heard machinery grinding and hissing. Only one other person would be awake at this hour — Wald Bergmann.

The geologist was busy reforming the metal sheets that had been cut off his digging and carving machines. He had built a form in which twenty knives could be poured and formed at once.

"I see I'm not the only one who can't sleep this evening," Lar said as he walked into Wald's work area. The other man almost dropped the form containing the hot liquid metal.

"Lar, what in the gods' names are you doing up at this hour?" the geologist snapped while catching the form. Wald had recognized his voice and had not bothered looking up. When he did look at Lar, he almost dropped the form again. "What happened? Are you ill?" concern showing in his voice.

Lar looked puzzled, then shrugged. "I did not clean up before going out. I've had a restless night. I can't seem to get to sleep." He frowned.

"You look like you have been in a fight," Wald said, looking at the other man's disheveled hair and bloodshot eyes. Seeing Lar in this state alarmed Wald. It was usually Lar who had calming words for the excitable geologist.

Now the security chief was bothered by something. He stared in front of him with a vacant expression. Wald studied his companion for a bit and decided not to press him for information. "Well if you're going to stand there, why not lend a hand or is that below the dignity of an elite security forcer? I could use a break. Might be enjoyable to watch someone else work for once."

Lar seemed to snap out of his stupor a bit and walked over to where Wald was working. The geologist explained the procedure while pouring and cooling off a mold. After several clumsy attempts while handling the mold, Lar soon settled into a rhythm, much slower than Wald's pace, but the workmanship improved with every attempt.

"Do you stay up this late every night, Wald? It seems you are always working on some sort of project or another."

The geologist nodded. "I only require maybe four hours a night. But I also slip away for two hours during midday. Too much work to do. Too much on my mind."

The two men had not started out as friends, but each one had grown to respect the other. "Ah, I understand having too much on your mind." Lar paused, and then continued slowly, "My dreams have been strange tonight, almost painful. Not the usual at all. I'm worried."

Wald was surprised at Lar's candor. "Usually your dreams are very, ah, precise. Not so tonight? Perhaps Taryl is preoccupied or dreaming herself."

Lar nodded. He had considered many scenarios and none had pleasant outcomes. "It is difficult not being able to be there, to see for myself what is happening with her," he said. "I may not be able to stand another night of this."

Wald was silent for a moment, rose, and started to shuffle through his tools, looking for something. "Here it is," he said holding up a large flask. "There might be enough of this elixir to take the chill off the night for both of us."

Lar accepted the offer, took a drink and handed the flask back to Wald. The two men sat in silence, passing the drink back and forth and watched the sun rise over the mountain.

¶ ¶ ¶

A large crowd gathered outside the bioshelter. The people were quiet. Only the occasional murmured prayer could be heard. As much as Uri and Franca tried to keep news of Taryl's delivery quiet, word somehow had gotten out that the beloved Seer was in labor. The scene inside the shelter was noisy and hectic. Taryl had been in labor for eight hours now, and there seemed to be little progress.

The petite woman's red hair was soaked with sweat and her cheeks were flushed from the contractions. Franca hovered nearby, monitoring Taryl with handheld med scanners. She was worried. The baby and mother both seemed to be doing well at the moment, but that could change in a blink.

The med tech was frightened at the possibility of delivering the baby via C-section. Franca had assisted at several such procedures, but had only done one herself. She had the necessary equipment, but her confidence was shaky. During a pause in the contractions, Franca looked toward the door.

"Is Uri still there?" Ilysa scuttled over and nodded, seeing the broad back of Franca's mate. "Tell him I need him." Uri entered, looking worried. This situation was out of his control. He felt helpless.

"We may need blood for a transfusion," Franca said, glancing at him. "Can you find volunteers?" Uri straightened up and nodded. "We have a whole camp of volunteers outside the door — hundreds," he said.

"Good," Franca said. "Gather all the other med techs and aides and start collecting blood. Ilysa, you can help, too. Most should be compatible, but do the quick test anyway. She is not progressing well. I may have to operate."

Taryl rose halfway out of the birthing bed and groaned with another contraction, gritting her teeth and then collapsed back down. Uri's face drained of its color. Ilysa took him by the arm and led him outside to begin their blood drawing. The contractions kept coming, and Taryl weakened with every body-racking spasm. Franca monitored her for another hour, and then made her decision.

"Do we have enough blood drawn?" she asked, when Ilysa re-entered the shelter.

"Yes, Franca. We have fifty bags drawn already, and hundreds more people are in line to give."

"Tell the other aides to keep drawing and tell my med tech team I need their help. We can't wait any longer."

¶ ¶ ¶

Uri paced outside the bioshelter for what seemed to be countless hours. He had heard prayers from all the known Earth and Siriusian religions and some that were unfamiliar to him. Almost all the colonists from the camp were gathered, waiting.

The door to the shelter opened and a tired and haggard-looking Franca stepped outside. “Mother and daughter are well,” she announced, breaking into a smile. “Both are resting.”

The gathered colonists slowly stood. Many beamed from ear to ear as if they were proud uncles and aunts. Others wept with joy. Singing broke out in many languages.

Verde Grande’s first baby had been born — a red-haired girl.

10

Kasan Inabritt's loneliness gripped his soul. The young man had to accept the fact he may be stuck on Verde Grande for the rest of his life. He could not believe his bad luck. The Tanlians had forced the colonists to split up and then brazenly attacked both groups.

To his surprise, the colonists not only had repelled the attackers but apparently had exterminated them. Kasan wondered if this had happened before. What would the other Tanlians do? Did they know what had happened here?

He feared he would die a failure, the first Syndicate spy to successfully infiltrate a CAIN colony world but unable to reveal his location. Kasan had signed on as agro tech, an expert in agronomy and horticulture. He had attended the best universities and claimed to be the only living descendant of a prominent Earth agrist family.

The Syndicate had patiently waited for years to get one of their own on a CAIN colony seeder expedition. However, the ship's destination had been a closely guarded secret. Alliance colonists volunteered to go wherever the governing council decided to send them.

Kasan remembered he had been warned it could be years before he would be contacted or had the opportunity to communicate with someone from the Syndicate. He expected to be rescued by a stealth deep spacer.

For now, the agro tech busied himself with the duties he was expected to perform. He completed soil tests to determine what crop would grow best in which location. Kasan helped construct the greenhouse and was in charge of rows and rows of young plants that would be the parent lines of generations of food crops for the planet.

Kasan enjoyed this work, spending hours tending to the plants. During these busy times he even put his prime mission in the back of his mind. Almost against his will, the young agro tech found himself enamored with biologist Nira Engstrom. The two had worked together to identify and categorize Verdian plants.

Nira had been with the first group from the *Colonia Nueve* to land on the planet. Her reports of the wildlife and native plants had been fascinating. Kasan had attracted Nira's attention by his avid curiosity concerning the wild grasses and fruit trees.

The biologist also had made the awful discovery of the hundreds of carcasses left by a Tanlian hunting party. Even Kasan was disgusted by the waste and offered a sympathetic ear when Nira broke down while retelling the story.

Kasan and Nira spent more and more time together: midday and evening meals, walks at night through the wild fruit orchards, sitting on grassy hillsides, gazing at Verde Grande's two moons and talking about the future of this fertile planet. They had not slept together, but their evening farewell hugs grew longer and good-night kisses also grew more passionate. If he had to be stranded, spending the time with Nira would make it tolerable.

¶ ¶ ¶

Ismala N'pofu and Masat Ebber studied XR-309 from the ship's imager. The planet appeared to be a viable candidate for a colony settlement. Fully Earth bioformed, it looked lush and green. Water was plentiful.

"The planet seems to be deserted," Masat said, looking at Ismala. "There are no defensive satellites. We are detecting no communications on any wavelength, Tanlian or Earther. The Brak's Revenge is not answering our hails."

"We are too far away to pick up person-to-person chatter," Ismala answered. "It looks like we can safely orbit the planet and examine it from close range. "I'm sure your men are anxious to hunt."

Masat nodded and gave the order to orbit the planet. Even if they found no humans, he was looking forward to relaxing under a shade tree, maybe even doing some hunting himself. Less than an hour later, the Tanlian trophy ship was orbiting the planet. As Masat was preparing to take a scout flyer to the surface, he saw Ismala waving to get his attention.

"Captain, I have a favor," she said flashing one of those beautiful smiles that captivated him.

Masat gestured for her to continue. He gave her a puzzled look.

"I have a specific-wave signal I would like broadcast to the planet. You have my word it is of no danger. In fact, it may make our job of finding the colonists easier, if they are there." Ismala said, answering his unspoken question.

Masat looked at the Earther woman for a moment, and some of his old doubts about non-Tanlians flashed through his mind. "Have you been hiding something from me?" he asked, not bothering to mask his suspicion. "Do you have information about the colonists?"

"I have not intentionally misled you, Captain," she said, her expression serious. "If the colonists are there, one of them may be sympathetic to the Syndicate. We need to be orbiting to receive the signal."

"A Syndicate spy among CAIN colonists," Masat said flashing an approving grin. "So that is why the Tanlian Council insisted I take on passengers."

Ismala answered with a smile. "We shall know shortly, Captain, if our sympathizer is down there."

¶ ¶ ¶

"Oh, Kasan, she's such a beautiful girl," Nira gushed. This was the first time the biologist had seen Taryl's two-week-old baby. "You should see her red hair, just like her mother's."

Kasan smiled at Nira's enthusiasm. He was about the only colonist who didn't seem interested in the infant. The agro tech would just shrug and say he was nervous around babies and try to change the subject.

"Tomorrow you are going with me to see her. Maybe you can even hold the baby," she teased, knowing he was uncomfortable around children.

A second in Kasan's implanted earpiece startled him. A moment later, he heard three short clicks, one click, followed by five long clicks. It was the signal he had been waiting for. The signal he had almost forgotten about.

Nira laughed at Kasan, misinterpreting his expression. "Don't worry. We probably won't even get close to the baby."

Kasan took a deep breath to get himself under control. He had to get his transmitter to send a reply. It was his duty. A pang of guilt swept over him as he looked at the trusting woman beside him. What would happen to her?

Sweeping all thoughts aside, Kasan cut their walk short. "I have to get back to the greenhouse. I forgot to enter some important data. It may take me a few hours. I'm sorry, Nira."

Nira pretended to pout. "Data? Can't you do that tomorrow? Is data more important than this?" She kissed him.

"The agrists need it first thing in the morning," he said. "It must have slipped my mind while I was thinking of you." The lie oozed out so sincerely it even surprised him.

"Oh, you just know the right things to say," Nira cooed, blinking innocently. Surprised by his intense expression, she let him go. Kasan gave her a good-night peck on the cheek and hurried away. Curious, she stared after him, wondering what data could be so important.

11

Taryl Bryann had no trouble finding volunteers to help her with the baby. All the women in the colony had offered to help. She appreciated the aid after her Caesarean section. Franca Navrakov had skillfully delivered the infant.

Taryl felt better every day, and the baby was in good health. The little girl was a miniature version of Taryl, with thick red hair and charcoal eyes. However, the Seer was growing irritated at being peppered with the same question from everyone: "What are you going to name her?"

Taryl would politely explain she would name the baby when the time was right, according to her people's ways. This puzzled many of the questioners, and if they persisted with more inquiries, she would dismiss them, barring access to her and the infant. It did not take long for word to spread among the colonists that asking this question was taboo. This just fed the growing mystique that surrounded the mother and child.

Taryl's family were descended from Gaians, followers of Mother Earth. They were sensitive to the environment and its affect on the human spirit. On Earth, some called them witches. Many had made their living as mind readers and spiritual healers for centuries. Now they had earned respect among the new colony worlds as Seers — a talent often passed from mother to daughter.

It was a Seer tradition to wait to name a newborn until the mother had a vision. Sometimes it was weeks or even months before the baby made it clear in a dream what its name was. Taryl had meditated before sleeping, hoping she would wake up in the morning and know her baby's name.

A familiar knock at her door told Taryl that Franca was there for a visit. The med tech had been Taryl's steadfast friend throughout her pregnancy and delivery. Uri's wife did not bother the new mother about the baby's name. She was even known to scold anyone who asked. Taryl smiled as Franca entered her shelter with a large basket of food.

"I don't understand it," the med tech said with a chuckle. "I can't seem to walk anywhere near your shelter without collecting treats for you. Everyone seems concerned with fattening you up."

Taryl laughed. It always seemed Franca knew what to say to cheer her. The other woman wanted nothing from her. Their friendship grew with every visit.

"So how is the little mysterious one?" Franca said while picking up the baby and cooing at her.

Taryl would have been upset if anyone else had said this but smiled at the reference. "Still nothing this morning, Franca," the Seer said with disappointment. "I have to be patient. I was dreaming of Lar." She was a bit embarrassed to admit it.

"Perfectly understandable," Franca said. "I'm sure the father of your baby is concerned. Is there any way he knows what happened?"

Taryl shook her head. "I have been too tired to ..." she paused, searching for the right words. "To touch his dreams. Before the baby was born I was able to communicate with him almost every night."

The usually unflappable med tech stopped and stared despite herself. She struggled to regain her composure. "Forgive my meddling, Taryl, but perhaps this is unfinished business. He needs to know, somehow. Maybe that is why your dreams are of him and not the baby."

Taryl looked at her friend for a moment and nodded. She had missed the comfort of female family members. There was no elder Seer to offer guidance on this planet. What Franca said seemed to open a window in Taryl's mind. It was so obvious to her now. Tonight she would try to reach Lar's dreams and tell him about their daughter.

¶ ¶ ¶

"It is unlike him to miss first meal with us," said a worried-looking Dorin Luja, one of Lar Vonn's security guards from the *Colonia Nueve*. "None of us has seen him this morning."

Wald Bergmann was surprised that one of Lar's men was confiding in him. The guard looked worried, but protocol forbade him from disturbing his superior. "You are asking me to check on the security chief?" the geologist asked.

The guard looked down for a moment and nodded. "Yes sir, if you could find the time." It was not unusual for Wald to be brusque with Lar's guards. They often stopped him on his nightly walks and checked on him while he worked all hours of the day. The security chief's people must be concerned if they came to him for help.

"Give me a moment. Let me finish this mold and I will find out why the old chief has overslept."

Dorin paused and smiled. No one but Wald could get away with such a description of the respected officer. "Thank you sir," he said, nodding to the geologist.

Wald knew Lar had been sleeping better since the night when the two had toasted the rising sun, but the security chief was still bothered by the lack of communication from Taryl. The geologist did not understand the connection between the couple, but he did not question it.

Even Wald found himself getting nervous as he approached Lar's quarters among the maize of tunnels in the mountains. Trying not to make much noise, the geologist walked up to the heavy curtains that covered Lar's doorway.

Wald paused, not quite knowing what to say. "The cooks want to know when you are going to honor them with your presence, security chief. First meal is getting cold."

"Enter," a muffled voice answered.

Wald walked in slowly. Lar's voice sounded very different, not like the deep baritone that easily issued commands. The security chief was sitting at a small crude desk he had crafted out of native wood. His back was to the door, which was an uncharacteristic position. Lar was hunched over, frantically working on something.

"You have the whole camp worried, chief. You don't miss many meals," Wald said haltingly.

"One moment, I almost have it," Lar said softly, almost choking on his words.

The geologist kept a respectful distance and patiently waited. He lost track of how many minutes he stood there before the other man turned around and held up a drawing.

"This is my daughter, I don't know her name, but I do know she and Taryl are well," Lar said as tears ran down his face.

¶ ¶ ¶

That same morning, Taryl awakened feeling more refreshed than she had in weeks. Hearing the baby cry, wanting to be changed and fed, she peered over her daughter's crib and smiled. "Good morning, Larinia. It's going to be a wonderful day."

12

One click snapped over the Tanlian ship's comm system. It was followed by three short clicks, then one click followed by five long clicks.

"They are down there," Ismala N'pfou said, smiling. "We will need our sympathizer to signal for several minutes before we can get a lock on his position."

Masat Ebber clapped his hands, impressed with the Earther woman's success. His men had been searching the planet with a scout flyer with no success. The Tanlian captain was puzzled. His ship could detect no power readings or communication signals — very strange for a colony world. If this was the planet Yermak Halpan had raced to, then where was he?

As an afterthought, Masat ordered a beacon activation signal to be broadcast. They had been trying to signal the other Tanlian ship. Just seconds after his order, a second signal beeped back to the ship. "Where is that signal coming from?" the captain shouted, recognizing it as an answering beacon.

"It's coming from the largest moon," answered the ship's comm operator.

"Send a flyer there immediately," Masat said. "Maybe it has some information that will help us." The captain looked at Ismala. "Let's hope that spy of yours keeps broadcasting. We need to determine his coordinates."

For the first time since they left Tantalum 2, the Earther woman frowned at Masat. The captain laughed. "I see the word *spy* does not sit well with you. But if your sympathizer, as you call him, is an uninvited guest among the colonists, I'm certain they would consider him a spy."

Ismala shrugged, turned and continued to broadcast the signal to her contact on the planet.

¶ ¶ ¶

The celebration stunned Taryl. After announcing her daughter's name, an instantaneous festival broke out. In less than an hour, most of the colony was standing in front of her shelter. Music was playing, and people were dancing, laughing and cheering.

"Why are they doing this? Larinia is just a baby," Taryl asked Franca, who also was amazed at the colonists' reaction. Franca and Uri had arrived just before the other celebrants.

"You and the baby are the first thing we have had to celebrate," the med tech answered. "Whether you approve or not, it appears you and the child are special to these people. Let them have their celebration. Life has been hard lately, and they are doing no harm."

Taryl cast a sad glance at Uri. "Can't you make them stop?" she asked. The despondent tone in her voice was evident. "We just want to be part of the colony. Not treated as special. What will Larinia think when she is growing up?"

Uri shook his head. "I couldn't stop them if I tried. I agree with Franca. Let them have their fun. Perhaps life will settle down after this is all over."

Seeing Taryl watching them, many in the crowd started chanting her name. Shaking her head, the shy young mother ran back to the shelter with Larinia in her arms. Franca waited a moment and followed the Seer inside, expecting to see her angry. She was trying to think of a way she could console the new mother.

Instead of fuming about her quarters, Taryl froze where she stood, almost transfixed, her eyes staring straight ahead, focusing on nothing. Never having seen Taryl like this, Franca summoned Uri. Her husband stood beside the Seer and waited, taking care not to disrupt her.

He looked at Franca. "She is seeing something with her *sight*. This is how she acts." He turned to Taryl. "What do you see?"

"They are looking for someone," the Seer said dreamily. "They think they have found him."

Uri leaned close to Taryl. "Who is looking for someone?" he asked, fearing the answer.

"Tanlians. They are looking for someone among us," Taryl said, still staring ahead. "I don't know who it is."

Uri needed to hear no more. Grabbing his communicator, he transmitted a five-click signal to all the colonists. Waiting another five clicks, he delivered a second even louder signal. Grim faced, he marched outside to the stunned colonists and ordered them all to their shelters.

¶ ¶ ¶

Kasan Inabritt hunched over his micro transmitter, which he had hidden in the greenhouse. He had answered the signal and was taking great care to relay coded information to the ship orbiting Verde Grande. The spy was surprised a GEMS deep-space vessel had ventured this far out of its territory. However, he did not question his duty. His people were up there. Signaling had to be slow. He did not want the colonists to trace him. Kasan was not privy to the colony's communication capabilities, or even worse, what kind of defensive capabilities were left.

He knew, of course, the colony's defenders had fired two laser-guided missiles, hitting one of the Tanlian collectors. Uri Navrakov had let it be known that many missile launchers were in place, but he did not divulge the number of missiles left. The launchers were all guarded. There was no way of knowing if they were armed.

Kasan did not know what to think about the Seer. He had seen her coming and going through the colony. She looked quite harmless. Possibly the story of some mysterious ability was a hoax. D-a-n-g-er he clicked into the transmitter.

"Damn this code," he thought. "Each letter takes too long." Waiting for the confirmation felt like it took at least an hour. Finally, receiving the confirmation, he clicked again: M-i-s-s-i-l-e-s. Again an agonizing wait, and at long last, confirmation, followed by a message relayed by a combination of clicks: *Keep transmitting. Need to lock on your position. Attack will follow when lock confirmed.*

"What? Attack?" a surprised Kasan said out loud, almost dropping the transmitter. Why would the Syndicate attack a CAIN colony? The two groups had honored the Earth nonaggression treaty for centuries. Such an attack could have bloody consequences on the home world.

He sat there puzzled for almost a minute before a click from the ship demanded his attention: *Confirm last message.* Kasan shook his head and transmitted the confirmation code.

¶ ¶ ¶

Ismala N'pofu was growing frustrated at how slowly her spy was transmitting. Every time he paused, the Tanlian ship lost its lock on his signal. "He must keep transmitting," she snapped. "It will take too many hours this way."

Masat Ebber smiled at her. "You are sounding more like a Tanlian now. Impatient to get to action. Remember, he is among an enemy. He may be putting himself in danger by transmitting. The colonists will probably kill him if they discover him. Have patience."

Ismala nodded thoughtfully. "I assumed he was hidden in the mountains and could transmit at will. Apparently he is among the colonists. I will try to be more patient."

"If your man is a trained spy, he has been among them this entire time, learning as much as he can, gaining their confidence," the captain said. "What is he telling you?"

Ismala quickly translated the code. “He says the colony has missiles, but he does not know how many. They fired two during a Tanlian attack,” she looked at Masat, who was now frowning.

“The colony must have fired on Halpan’s collectors, but what happened to Brak’s Revenge?” Masat asked, not expecting an answer. "No land-launched missile can bring down a deep-space ship. Get more information out of him.”

Ismala broke into a wide smile. “Ah, as a wise man once told me to have patience. It appears we have many questions that need to be answered.” She broke into a laugh at Masat’s glare.

¶ ¶ ¶

The transmissions from the ship were strange. “How were the Tanlian attackers killed? What happened to the transport ship? Did the Tanlians capture any colonists?”

Kasan confirmed the destruction of the two collectors that had attacked the colony. He doubted any colonists had been taken and relayed the mother ship’s fate. Growing frustrated at the questions, Kasan found the nerve to transmit his own question: “Why the interest in Tanlians?’ As an afterthought, he clicked in code: “They attacked and paid the price.”

Kasan was shocked at the answer. “Our Tanlian hosts want to find their sister ship.” Tanlian hosts? His people had traveled here with Tanlians? Even though the consortium had sued the Tanlians for peace and paid tribute to them, most GEMS people still looked down on them as thieves and slavers.

He was transmitting the colony’s coordinates to Tanlians. If they were successful with their attack, it would be a bloody and terrible scene. The colony’s men most likely would be killed and the women captured for sale. Frantic thoughts raced through his mind. What would happen to his beloved Nira? Could he protect her from that terrible fate? Maybe they could escape to the mountains.

In the interim, Kasan stopped transmitting, ignoring the ship’s incessant requests for more information. “Tanlians,” he said out loud in disgust, putting his hands to his face and shaking his head in disbelief.

"Yes, Tanlians," said a voice behind him. The startled Kasan spun around to see Uri Navrakov and a dozen other security guards watching him. All of them had energy pulsers pointed at him.

Nira stood behind Uri. He could tell she had been crying. She mouthed the word, "Why?" No one spoke. The tension was thicker than the heavy humidity that hung in the greenhouse. Kasan's transmitter started clicking, sounding like a cricket on a hot summer night.

"Don't answer that," Uri ordered. "You have endangered this colony enough as it is."

Kasan shook his head. "I was placed here by the Galaxy Exploration and Minerals Syndicate, not the Tanlians. I had no idea . . . " his voice trailed off. He looked at Nira. She was sobbing. Her body shook.

"You have plenty of time to plan your defenses, Navrakov," Kasan said dropping the transmitter but raising his energy pulser. "The ship only has its lock down to five hundred kilometers. I did not mean to bring you harm."

Uri shook his head at the threatening gesture, but Kasan stepped forward and took aim. The sizzle of energy pulses echoed through the greenhouse. Kasan was dead before his body slumped to the ground. Beside him, the micro transmitter clicked again and again. Uri crushed it under his boot.

¶ ¶ ¶

Masat Ebber listened to the message, which confirmed what they had expected. The signal beacon on the planet's large moon had detected an orbiting colony ship and Yermak Halpan had responded.

"At least we know Halpan found them, but I don't understand what happened to his ship. The Earthers don't appear to have sufficient defenses."

Ismala N'pofu was silent, but kept trying her transmitter with no success. "No confirmation click for twenty minutes now. I am not reading a signal. I do not understand his last message. Then he asked about Tanlians. Very strange."

The captain shrugged. "Maybe your spy has discriminatory tastes. Did he know it would be a Tanlian vessel that would contact him?"

Ismala shook her head. "It should make no difference what ship we arrive in. He answered the signal as he was ordered. I will keep trying to reach him every half hour, but I have a bad feeling."

"Your spy may have been discovered by some unsympathetic colonists," Masat said. "If so, there may be no more signals. At least we have the location narrowed down to a searchable area. Our scout flyers will find them. The colonists can't hide like rodents forever."

13

Wald Bergmann had just fallen asleep in his quarters when something kept intruding on his slumber. A strange noise — irritating clicks, like some bothersome insect. He rolled over in his cot, wondering what was making that sound.

With his head foggy from slumber, he stumbled to his doorway and pulled back the curtain. Nothing. No one could be seen and he could detect no voices. Another click made him turn around. The noise was coming from inside his quarters.

The geologist walked into the middle of his room and waited; he heard it again. Walking over to his desk he had hand-carved from a felled oak, he stood in front of his communication receiver not daring to believe what he suspected.

Reaching down, he increased the volume and was rewarded by a loud series of clicks. Stunned, he listened for a moment, but did not recognize the code. It was nothing he knew was being used by the colonists. The clicks were coming in a series, pausing, then one click would begin a new series.

He grabbed his personal comm and called Lar. "Wald here. Can you come to my quarters? I'm getting something very unusual from my receiver. Some kind of code I don't recognize."

Lar wasted no time answering. "Code on your receiver? I will be there immediately." Hardly fifteen minutes had passed when

Lar charged into Wald's quarters. The security chief, out of breath from running, struggled to choke out his words.

Wald held up a finger to his ear. The chattering continued: long and short clicks, followed by pauses.

"Can you tell where they are coming from?" Lar whispered, listening intently. "Are you recording them?"

"Yes, I'm recording, but I can't tell where they are coming from. Neither signal is close to us. One of the clicks has a slight echo," Wald said. "Whoever is sending them must have a powerful transmitter."

Lar frowned and pointed up. "Like something on a deep spacer?"

"That would be my guess," Wald said. "It sounds like two parties having a conversation. My automatic modulator located the signals and locked onto the wavelength."

The security chief started pacing back and forth, his brow furrowed in deep thought. "If it's Tanlians, why are they bothering talking in code? They could communicate ship to ship or on personal comms."

Lar stopped as a thought stabbed through his consciousness. "Did you say one of the signals had an echo, like a land comm we are hearing through the receiver?"

Wald paused and turned the receiver to almost full volume and waited. One set of clicks chattered away. The second set answered. A distinct echo could be heard. Both men looked at each other. It was obvious: one party was probably in orbit and the other was on the surface. But where?

"Are the Tanlians in the valley?" Lar asked.

Wald shook his head. "No, I could pinpoint them to within five thousand kilometers. Both signals are too far away to trace."

"Too far away, but one is on the surface," Lar repeated, walking faster. "They are trying hard to stay secretive, very unlike Tanlians."

A strange look formed on his face. "The colonists on the other side of the mountain! The land signal must be coming from them." As suddenly as the clicks started, they stopped. After a long pause, the ship kept repeating its signal, but the surface signaler did not answer.

The geologist thought for a moment and nodded. Then a smile slowly crept in at the corners of his mouth. "If the other signaler is on a ship, we can send our code in a short burst on their wavelength. We just might have enough time to warn the others."

"Do it," Lar said. "Maybe it will take the Tanlians a few minutes before they understand what we are doing."

Wald grabbed an earpiece and his hands flew over a few keys. Three minutes later, he looked at Lar, "Ready to send it. Let's hope someone is listening on the other side of the mountain" Both men held their breath as Wald sent their coded burst: "Danger. Tanlians. Ship. Surface. Lar."

Several minutes later, a familiar code answered: "Tanlians confirmed. Spy killed. Luck to you. Uri." Lar and Wald let out heavy sighs and looked at each other, sharing the same somber expression. Once again the Tanlians were threatening them.

Rushing out of Wald's quarters, Lar paused, "I need to contact the other camps. Prepare your tunnel traps geologist, it looks like we may have uninvited guests."

¶ ¶ ¶

"Very strange," Ismala N'pofu mumbled. "Those were odd static bursts."

Masat walked over to her station. "Did you say bursts? Close together? Let me hear them." Ismala replayed the bursts again. At Masat's urging she slowed the signal to half speed. Each burst changed to beeps of different tones, but seemed to have a coordinated rhythm.

"Have you kept your transmitter on the entire time you have been trying to contact your spy?" he asked, growing more impatient by the second.

"Yes," she answered. "I have been trying to re-establish contact."

The captain hurried over to the ship's comm control and shouted, "Launch all scout ships to the last confirmed coordinates. The colonists are down there and they know we are here. Stay out of missile range. Look for thermal signs. Listen for communications." Turning back to the surprised Ismala, he growled, "The colonists have used your transmission to communicate. We no longer have surprise on our side."

Ismala called to him as he was striding out of the room, "Why would they need to communicate through us if they are together? Is there more than one group?"

Startled, Masat walked back, thinking. "Can you trace those signals? One or both groups must be in trouble if they had to use us. Perhaps Yermak did more damage to them than we thought." Ismala replayed the colonists' coded bursts again and again, running the signals through the computer's tracking program and matching that to the 3-D map vid.

"It appears the colonists are separated by a mountain. My spy said nothing about a second group. Perhaps their defenses are not so fierce." This time, Masat smiled. He much preferred easier prey if it was available.

14

"Here comes another flyer," Taryl Bryann said in her dream state. "He is very high and moving very fast." Uri, who was sitting next to the Seer, glanced toward the spotter who was using the magni-glasses to scan the horizon. Not long after Taryl had spoken, the spotter waved, indicating a flyer. A tiny almost imperceptible silver dot streaked across the sky.

"They are growing restless," Taryl said in a monotone. "They want to fly lower, but are afraid."

Uri smiled. "Afraid of our missiles, I'll wager. Their spy must have warned them about our defenses. Good thing he didn't know how few are left or we would be fighting Tanlians right now."

The colonists had been cowering from the overhead threat for three days. Flyers cut across the sky at any time, keeping no particular schedule. Sometimes it would be two or three hours before one was sighted by either the spotter or Taryl. Other times two, three or four flyers would follow each other by only a few minutes. They often crisscrossed one another's paths. Taryl could feel them flying closer at night, always looking for the colonists to give themselves away.

"They are doing exactly what I expected," Uri said to Franca. "Flying lots of missions at irregular times, looking for thermal readings or lights at night. These Tanlians are much more patient than I expected. It could only mean they are serious about finding us."

The security officer had expected an attack before this. The waiting made him edgy. The colonists had been prepared for an attack from either the ground or the air. The Tanlians could have landed a few hundred kilometers away and may be working their way up the valley, hoping to flush the colonists out. But none of the sensors they had set up for kilometers in all directions could detect anything.

¶ ¶ ¶

A frustrated Giovan Choi stood before Masat Ebber. "Nothing," the Tanlian scout pilot reported. "We are detecting no communications, no thermals, no movements, and no lights. The missile launchers, if they have any, are not locking on us."

The captain looked at the other pilot, who was standing next to Giovan. "I assume you have nothing to report either?"

Jibril Bala shook his head. "No, Captain. The second valley is so narrow, we cannot fly very close. The colonists could be dancing down there, and we would not know it."

Ismala N'pofu raised her eyebrows at the tone in which both pilots had spoken to Masat. But, the captain did not react. "You both have done well. We know one group of colonists has undetermined defenses. We don't want them shooting you out of the sky. A whole Tanlian ship has disappeared at the hands of these CAIN vermin. Don't worry, we will pluck them out."

"Yes, Captain," Giova said. Jibril nodded, smiling.

"Go tell your squads to return to the ship," Masat said. "We are going to change our tactics. We will need you to be fresh."

"New tactics?" Ismala asked.

"Tomorrow night I am ordering all the men to the surface. We will have eighty groups of four men each scouring that terrain. I want every kilometer searched until we find those colonists." Masat knew he ran the risk of sacrificing a group of men or two if the colonists discovered them on the ground or fired their missiles at the landing ships. If that happened, so much the better. Then they would know where to find their prey.

"We can't use the same tactic for the second group of colonists, but I will hold back the remaining one hundred men in case they are needed," Masat told Ismala. "The terrain in the small valley is too treacherous to land a ship safely. There are too many ways we could be attacked there."

"Perhaps I can draw out the other colonists," Ismala smiled. "I am quite experienced at negotiations. If they are isolated, these people may be open to a creative proposal."

Masat stared at her, shaking his head. "What could you offer them that would entice them out into the open?"

"Why, dear Captain, their safety. I'm sure they would be very interested in that."

¶ ¶ ¶

The message stunned the colonists led by Lar Vonn. A woman with the Galaxy Exploration and Minerals Syndicate had proposed the colonist groups meet peacefully in a meeting to discuss a solution to this stalemate. She gave her word as a representative of the consortium that no harm would come to those who agreed to the meeting.

"So, GEMS has become more closely aligned with Tanlians. That is not a good sign," Wald Bergmann said to the ten colony leaders who had gathered to discuss the surprising situation.

"We should not give the Tanlians coordinates to any of our sites," Riss Nels said. "It still could be a trap to find our locations. Why should we believe them? Tanlians have never been negotiators." The other leaders echoed his sentiments, wary of this new alliance between two enemies.

Lar spoke. "We have their assurance no harm will come to us. Also, she said they will land a small party wherever we tell them and the ship will leave. The Syndicate people will be at our mercy. We cannot live like this forever, hiding during the day and moving at night. If they attack, either we defeat them or they kill or capture us. This waiting is becoming unbearable."

No one argued. The leaders sat contemplating their options. Neb Klinfer broke the silence. "The meeting location should be as far from our camps as possible, and it should be well defended. If we are attacked and captured they should not be able to find the other colonists."

Lar looked at Neb. "Your group is the farthest from the other sites. Is your surface rover operational? How far could it travel in a day?"

Neb nodded, "Yes, we still use the rover. If we start at dawn and end at dusk, perhaps fifty kilometers or so. We could snake through so many canyons, the Tanlians or Syndicate, whoever they are, would never find our people."

¶ ¶ ¶

The colonists messaged the Tanlian ship with their terms to meet. Masat Ebber was not happy. "Why will it take them two days to tell us the coordinates? And why do they insist on meeting with only five people? We cannot adequately defend that few."

"I am not surprised, Captain," Ismala N'pofu said. "They do not want to give away their location. They may want the time to set up their defenses."

"Or a trap," Masat interrupted with a snarl.

"Remember, we are hunting them," she said. "They will feel less threatened if we land with a small group."

The captain had to agree her reasoning was sound. "Who will be our negotiators?" he asked. "I assume you. And who else?"

Ismala stared for several seconds, then smiled. "Shadra, my brother, would never let me go to the surface without his protection. We would need at least one other who could pass as if he were with our party. The others can be any security you choose."

She paused, not saying another word. Masat looked at her puzzled, waiting for her to tell him who would play the part. "Well are you going to privilege me with an answer?" he demanded. "Which of my crewmen do you require?"

"None of your crew, Captain," she answered, looking at him with a sly smile.

He stared back. It took a moment for him to understand who she was talking about. "Me?" Masat asked. "I am no negotiator."

"Why, Captain, that is not what I have heard about you," Ismala purred. "All the GEMS colonies hate it when a certain Captain Ebber visits to collect the treaty tax. He always seems to negotiate more than what the agreement has called for."

Masat was amused at her story. He had never considered himself a negotiator, but he had never been turned down. "You call your tributes treaty taxes, eh?" he said, laughing. "I never considered myself a tax collector."

15

Martje Ryyt tried one more time to capture Lar Vonn's attention. She had memorized his early day schedule: exercise at 05:30, bath at 06:30, and first meal at 07:00.

As one of his security force, Martje had worked closely with him even before the *Colonia Nueve* had left for Verde Grande. She had told herself long ago she would not turn him down if invited to his bed. However, she had found herself thinking about him ever since that early morning when she had helped him back to his quarters after he spent the night drinking with Wald Bergmann.

Martje had just finished washing in the women's bathing area and was walking back to her quarters when Lar stumbled down the hall. It was obvious the captain was having trouble finding his way, so she put his arm around her shoulders and half-dragged him home.

As she was putting him in his cot for some well-deserved sleep, his hand clutched her robe and pulled it off. She stood there, her hair and body still wet from the bath.

Half-opening his eyes, he smiled when he saw her and mumbled, "Ah, you are a magnificent woman." Reaching for her hand, he pulled her toward him, asking for just a kiss. Martje did not resist. His other hand caressed her body.

It did not take her long to strip Lar of his clothing. However, the lovemaking was over almost as soon as it began. The security chief wrapped his arms around her in a tight embrace for a few delicious seconds then collapsed in a deep slumber.

Martje lay close to him for almost an hour before leaving for her quarters. Later that day, after Lar had slept off the strong drink, she saw him at second meal. He was polite to her as usual. She was crushed he didn't remember their encounter. Now, the tall well-muscled woman was doing everything in her power to be noticed.

At early exercise, she would wear thin tight-fitting garments and position herself to either be in front of him or next to him. After bathing, she made sure they would "accidentally" meet after leaving their respective areas.

Martje knew Lar missed Taryl Bryann, his lover who had been stranded on the other side of the mountain with the other colonists. But it had been months since Lar had been with another woman, and Martje worked to make herself available.

Lar had not been immune to all this attention. It was easy to notice Martje. The statuesque woman was ruggedly attractive. She had let her light brown hair grow since landing on Verde Grande. The long ringlets softened her squarish face. Her green eyes were captivating. Her breasts were not large, but the clothing she wore accentuated them.

The security chief found himself taking cooler baths in the deep cave pools. But this did not seem to help because she always seemed to be there when he left the water. She would smile coyly, a threadbare robe barely covering her body.

Lar had heard the whispers that Martje was a voracious and aggressive lover. It was said men would leave her bed exhausted and sore, and none would retell their adventures. The stories and this woman intrigued Lar, but each time he was stopped by a pang of guilt and longing for Taryl. He had given his heart to the gentle Seer, but she was so far away.

The new Tanlian threat also occupied his mind and most of his time now. After the council meeting with the other colony leaders, Lar wanted to clear his head. He wanted to think. He visited each guard position, stopping to talk with whomever was on patrol.

Not knowing who was scheduled where, he called out the password and walked close to the nearest guard. "All goes well?" he asked.

The guard was barely a silhouette. Luz Primo was rising, but was only a half moon tonight, and Luz Nino had to appeared yet. Lar was greeted by a muffled, "Yes, Captain." Curious, he stepped closer and saw Martje standing there, crying.

"What is it, Martje?" he asked, surprised to see her weeping.

"The Tanlians, sir," she said trying to compose herself. "I do not object to fighting and dying, but I don't want to be taken alive by them to be sold." Instinctively, he put his hands on her shoulders to comfort her. "The way you can fight Martje, the Tanlians will be lucky if you don't kill all that get close to you."

She stepped forward and put her head on his shoulder and sobbed, hugging him. He embraced her tightly as well. Not long after that, they shared a long passionate kiss. Hands quickly unfastened each other's clothing. The half moon of Luz Primo and full moon of its smaller sibling made a perfect setting for making love.

¶ ¶ ¶

Tears streamed down Taryl Bryann's face. Concerned about Lar, she had meditated to be with him, to see through his eyes. The Seer wanted to be comforted that he and the other colonists were well. She had watched with trepidation all those "chance" meetings between Lar and Martje, knowing full well the intentions of the other woman.

Her heart swelled with joy each time Lar turned away from Martje, but a part of her could tell he was weakening. Feeling like a voyeur, Taryl watched as Lar comforted the other woman. Her stomach churned into knots, and she became ill as he and Martje started to make love.

Her crying turned into uncontrolled sobbing. She could do nothing but watch and forced herself to break the mental connection. Frightened by the sound, Larinia woke up, crying. The only comfort Taryl got that night was rocking her daughter back to sleep.

She and Lar had not been bonded in a traditional ceremony. They had hinted at their life together once they were both settled on the new world, but those plans had been torn apart after the Tanlian threat had separated them.

The next morning, Taryl woke feeling detached. Her world only seemed to come into focus when she snuggled and fed Larinia. Franca was concerned when she visited Taryl later that morning. Taryl's good friend could only elicit short, polite answers from her. There was no laughter and small talk.

After an uncomfortable silence, the Seer thanked the med tech for her intentions and then dismissed her as a superior would give leave to a minion. Surprised and hurt, Franca left the shelter. Uri Navrakov looked up in surprise when his mate slammed the door to their shelter and slumped into a chair.

"That is unusual for Taryl," he said after hearing Franca's description of her encounter with the Seer. "We both know Seers are subject to mood swings because of their gifts. We have not seen that in Taryl so far. Perhaps something she has seen has upset her."

Franca nodded. "But, she was so cold, so distant. It was like she was another person. She treated me like a servant."

Uri agreed to check on Taryl later in the day. He hoped the Seer may just have needed some time to herself. The chance to visit Taryl came much sooner than Uri expected. Barely an hour after second meal, one of the other colonists sought him out, telling him the Seer had summoned him.

Now it was Uri's turn to feel concerned. He took his time making his way to Taryl's shelter and was surprised to see one of his security guards posted outside her door. Recognizing Ells Castanda, Uri stopped before the young man who stood blocking Taryl's doorway, his arms crossed.

"I gave no orders for special protection. Move aside."

"The Seer requested assistance," Ells said, not bothering to salute or acknowledge Uri's rank. "I shall tell her you are here."

Ells knocked at the door and entered, letting the security captain wait outside. A moment later, the guard stepped out and held the door open for Uri to enter.

"We shall discuss your behavior later," Uri snapped as he entered the shelter.

"I don't think so, sir," Ells paused and shrugged. "The Seer has requested our assistance. We are bound to her."

Taken aback by the private's behavior, Uri walked into Taryl's quarters, his face turning red with anger. "Taryl, I demand to know what is going …" but what he saw inside left him speechless. Four of his female security force stood protectively near the Seer and had taken defensive postures when he walked in. Two other women fussed over Larinia.

Taryl had not bothered to look up but was busy working on a large sheet. "Ah Captain, thank you for coming," the Seer said, coldly formal. "These kind people have accepted my invitation for personal assistance. I trust the colony can function without them for a while."

Not waiting for an answer, Taryl gestured for Uri to examine her work. It was a grid of about 500 square kilometers surrounding the colony. The precision of the map was startling, as if an enlargement had been made from an overhead vid record.

"The Tanlians are preparing to search every kilometer until they find us. I have seen their plans," Taryl said. After watching the Seer use her special sight firsthand, Uri did not doubt her.

Pointing to the map, she showed him where the Tanlians planned to land and start searching the valley. One of the search parties was going to be less than one hundred kilometers away. Uri studied the map, forgetting his surprise and anger for the moment.

The Seer had marked all the Tanlians' proposed landing sites and charted their expected daily forays. After a few moments, he glanced at Taryl. She was smiling at him as a teacher waiting for a student to understand a lesson. "I have done my job, Captain. Now we need your military expertise. How should we address this situation?"

16

Choosing the right five people to negotiate with the GEMS representatives was a difficult decision for the ten council leaders. Especially infuriating was the request that one of the five colonists should be a woman. In the end, the leaders chose Lar Vonn, Neb Klinfer, Wald Bergmann, Riss Nels and Martje Ryyt.

Martje was chosen for her heroism and the superior fighting skills she had exhibited during the first Tanlian attack. No one questioned why Lar excused himself when the council voted for her. None of the colonists knew what to expect from the Tanlians and their GEMS allies. They all suspected a trap.

"For a man who does not like to be involved in the mundane activities of the colony, you seem to have become very prominent," Lar teased Wald after the other council members left to finalize defenses for their camps.

The geologist cocked an eye at the security chief and flashed a sly smile. "And you, my friend, will have your own, ah, body guard, I see," Wald said, referring to Martje. Lar faked an angry frown, then nodded, conceding the verbal jab.

A few people knew of Lar's tryst with Martje the night before, but it was not a topic of main concern with the colonists. The Tanlian threat was much more important. The private affairs between a man and woman usually stayed private.

"You have chosen the meeting site well," Lar said. Wald had picked a small canyon with natural rock walls that ran straight up for hundreds of meters and almost closed at the top. The canyon split off the colonists' valley, but it snaked around, dividing into two more side canyons that would serve as a more than adequate escape route if needed.

Seeing Neb, Ris, and Martje walking toward them, Lar turned to Wald. "Let's invite our guests to our lovely valley."

Ismala N'pofu accepted the colonists' invitation to the planet and relayed the coordinates to Masat Ebber. The captain shook his head. "Damn colonists. It will take us an hour to reach them once we land, and they could attack us from anywhere."

Ismala shrugged. "Would you have expected any less? They will watch our every step. Would not you do the same thing if you were them?"

Masat grumbled, but agreed he likely would be just as wary.

"Before we go, I ask permission to send a message. It may seem strange, but trust me," she said.

Masat nodded and gestured for her to make her transmission. The captain watched with interest as Ismala typed a complicated code into the ship's communications board. After double checking her readings, she recorded her message.

"This is Ismala N'pofu, colony director of the Galaxy Exploration and Minerals Syndicate, calling the Colonization Alliance of Independent Nations. My transport ship attempted to answer a distress call from planet XR-309. We were unable to locate the source of the call. However, we regret to inform you that your new colony has been attacked by Tanlians."

She paused for dramatic effect. "We have found no living colonists after many days of searching this lovely world. I fear the worst for your brave people. The attackers have vanished and so have your colonists. I am transmitting images of the burnt-out settlement. This world is very close to Tanlian transport flights. As you know we have a treaty with the Tanlians. The Syndicate would gladly trade XR-309 for one of our planets in the bioforming stage, closer to your territory. Again, my sympathies on the loss of your people."

Ismala looked up to see an impressed Masat smiling at her. "This message will transmit on a continuous loop for two hours. The Alliance should receive it in a week. This planet will make a wonderful addition to the Syndicate."

¶ ¶ ¶

Taryl stopped giving orders to her new attendants and stared straight ahead. She felt the presence of intruders, but the time was all wrong. The Tanlians were preparing to land in their valley at night to begin their forays. One of her aides brought her a chair and guided the Seer down into it. None of her new followers had witnessed her experiencing "second sight." The room was hushed except for Larinia's happy gurgling. Taryl breathed deeply, letting her sight find the strangers.

Startling images slowly came into focus. Something was wrong with this experience. Taryl found herself looking across a rough-hewn table at Lar Vonn and four other colonists, including the woman he had slept with the night before. The shock of seeing the colonists almost made her lose concentration, but Taryl held on to the sight. The trembling woman tried to see who she was seeing through, but could not.

Her "host" did not look away from the colonists. Lar and the others were solemn, listening to whoever was speaking. Finally, her host glanced around the table. Two Tanlians and two people from GEMS sat opposite the colonists, sitting together — like allies. A chill radiated down her spine.

Now her host watched Wald Bergmann speak. The geologist was smiling and gesturing, occasionally he waved in the direction of the mountain that separated the two groups of colonists. It appeared the other colonists were surrendering or even worse, revealing her group's position.

Finally breaking the connection, Taryl sat wide-eyed, not believing what she had seen. After having her heart broken the night before, she suspected the worst of Lar and his group. He had betrayed her once, and it seemed his group were endangering her people.

Her people? What an interesting thought. It just felt right. Taryl considered herself as the colonists' protector.

¶ ¶ ¶

Masat Ebber and the red-haired colonist across from him stared at each other. He sized up this thin colonist as prey, mentally going through the motions it would take to kill this man if necessary. However, the Tanlian captain got the uneasy feeling his counterpart was doing the same thing.

Neb Klinfer was wary about this meeting. But the large man in front of him commanded his attention. The hunter could tell there was something different about him, the way he scanned the horizon and took in every detail of the others.

At times, the Syndicate man seemed to have a far-away look as if he were distracted by something. Perhaps listening? That thought disturbed Neb. The other man may have a listening device. Who knew what was being planned?

Neb readied himself for a possible attack. A throwing knife was tucked just inside his sleeve. One quick motion was all he needed to bring down the big man. Breaking the stare with a bored look, the hunter glanced at his companions. Everyone but Wald was intense.

Martje was stone-faced as she and the large Syndicate males exchanged cold stares. The lead negotiator acted too pleasant for the situation. She took turns talking with and smiling at Wald and Lar. The geologist seemed captivated by her presence, but Lar stayed serious. The security chief occasionally looked up and down the table, studying everyone. Neb could tell Lar was sizing up the potential combatants.

Wald and the Syndicate woman babbled on, discussing trivialities. Neb grew more uneasy with every second. The air seemed charged with energy. Words now ceased making sense to the hunter, and time slowed. He could almost count the breaths from everyone.

When Neb returned his gaze to the man across from him, the other bore a far-away intent expression. Slowly raising his hand to his lips, the man coughed and announced the need for a break. His female companion glared at him, but nodded her agreement.

"What is it Masat?" Ismala demanded, struggling to keep her voice low. "We must put these people at ease, show them we can be trusted."

The Tanlian captain scoffed. "These colonists will never trust us. I have information from my ship comm operator. Apparently the colonists on the other side of the mountain are willing to trade these people for their safety. We have been given the location of all their nests in this valley. This group has no missiles. They can only offer hand-to-hand resistance."

Ismala stared at Masat in disbelief. "The others have betrayed these people with no provocation? How can we believe them?" she asked. "Perhaps the others are the ones with no missiles and are trying to save themselves. Have you studied these five colonists?"

"I sense some nervousness, but no fear, except for Wald. The only unusual thing I noticed was the feeling I was being watched, but that has passed. Let us return to the table and see what information we can find."

¶ ¶ ¶

The five colonists gathered to discuss the visitors. "These Syndicate people are acting strange, especially the large one across from me," Neb said. "I suspect he has a listening device. Something happened that made him want to leave momentarily."

Lar nodded and looked at the others to get an indication of their feelings on the subject.

"I agree," Martje said. "It felt like the man across from me was measuring me for a fight."

Wald shrugged. "I cannot tell the woman's intentions other than she is a skilled negotiator, smooth and unafraid. We may find out soon. They have returned to the table."

Ismala flashed a warm smile at Wald. "What can you tell us about the others? The ones across the mountain. Why are there two groups?" Wald raised his eyebrows at such a direct question. Her tone had changed after the break.

"Oh, those are several dozen researchers who got separated when the Tanlians attacked the first time," he said with a shrug, matching her smile. "They have blamed us for being stranded, but we warned them."

"Researchers?" Ismala said, not bothering to mask her surprise. "But the other valley looks like a much more suitable place for a colony." Wald smiled, but did not answer.

"Let us part peacefully," Ismala said with a graceful wave. "As I said, you have my word your people will have safe passage back to the nearest GEMS outpost if you willingly give up this world. The Syndicate has offered your Alliance a trade for a more suitable planet, one out of harm's way. Until we meet again."

As Ismala and her party rose to leave, Neb and Masat glared at each other one last time.

"I look forward to our next meeting, colonist," Masat said, his lips curling into a snarl.

"The pleasure will be mine," Neb said, grinning at the other man's reaction.

¶ ¶ ¶

Back on the ship, Masat laughed at the audacity of the colonists in the large valley. Without remorse, they had revealed the positions of the group he had just met with. But, whoever sent the message from the surface had threatened the Tanlians with death if they kept searching the valley.

"The CAIN traitors may be scared of being discovered," he said to Ismala. "Perhaps we are getting close. It won't hurt to sweep one more sector. We may be able to capture both groups.

17

Uri and one hundred men of his most trusted security forces lay in wait for the Tanlian ship to land and unload searchers. The lieutenant and his men had camouflaged themselves well among the trees or dug into positions in the ground.

Uri left half of his troops to guard the colonists. Those he left behind were exhibiting an annoying loyalty to Taryl Bryann. Uri planned to deal with that situation when he returned to the settlement. The Seer had undergone a troublesome change and now apparently was growing accustomed to issuing orders.

After about one-half hour, a small ship appeared overhead, exactly where Taryl had indicated it would land. It silently lowered itself to the surface, powerful search lights flashed back and forth, examining the area. It hovered overhead for several seconds, then landed. A hatch swooshed open and a swarm of humanity burst out, running to take protective positions.

After all the Tanlians were safely out, a commander must have given an all-clear signal. The intruders rose as one and started separating into small groups. It looked like they outnumbered the colony defenders two to one.

Uri buzzed his troops on a secure channel. "On my signal, fire the sonics and energy bursts. Then pick a target and drop as many as you can. Ready men." He waited for a few seconds, and then gave the order. The first barrage from the colony defenders caught the Tanlians by surprise. Many were knocked to the ground by the onslaught of the sonics and energy bursts.

Confused and dragging their wounded, the invaders tried to make it back to their ship as Uri's soldiers kept firing, killing many more. An energy cannon swiveled around from the collector ship and fired in the direction of the colonists. Not having a clear target, the bursts fell where the colonists had been, but Uri's group had vacated their positions to chase the Tanlians.

As if on cue, another Tanlian collector appeared out of nowhere and fired into the colony defenders. Shocked, Uri looked up thinking, *That ship is supposed to be ten kilometers away*, but he didn't have time to dwell on the thought. Grabbing his handheld rocket launcher, Uri sprinted toward the Tanlian ship on the ground. The ship's door was starting to close as the last of its crew tumbled in.

Uri crouched, took a deep breath, and fired. His missile shot through the door. The Tanlian ship exploded into a fireball. The overhead Tanlian flyer opened up on the colonists, covering the area with large energy bursts. In less than two minutes, Uri and his men lay dead.

¶ ¶ ¶

Hearing the report of the battle, Masat shook his head in disbelief. The first group of his landers had been taken by surprise and wiped out. But the second collector received a message telling them the coordinates of the colony fighters and rushed to the site.

"I think the colonists in the large valley have proven their point," Ismala said. "Your men all could easily have been killed by that ambush. But then they were saved by the colonists' message to our second collector."

Masat rested his chin on clenched fists. "Enough with this side of the mountain," he said raising his hands in frustration. "Let's go after easier prey. I have unfinished business with that red-haired colonist."

¶ ¶ ¶

Taryl opened her eyes and let out a heavy sigh. Feigning sorrow, she told her attendants Uri and his men had been killed defending the colony. "The Tanlians are leaving. It appears we have convinced them we can defend ourselves." Some of Taryl's attendants hugged each other, knowing their Seer had saved them once again. A few others wept with joy.

Taryl smiled at her group. She had strengthened her influence on them even more. It would not take much convincing to win over the remaining colonists. "Someone please inform Franca and the other women that their brave mates have died as heroes," the Seer said in a somber tone. "After they have mourned, invite them to join us."

¶ ¶ ¶

Lar Vonn was yawning and stretching in his cot, trying to wake up, when the alarm sounded. Jumping up, he rushed to his doorway to confirm what he heard. Up and down the rock hallway, the other colonists poked their heads out and looked at the security chief.

Martje Ryyt came running toward Lar. She was dressed and armed, carrying an energy-pulse rifle, and knives of all sizes almost dripped off her. The look on her face was all Lar needed to know. He grabbed his weapon belt and a protective tunic.

"We are under attack!" he yelled as he ran through the cave warrens. "Those able to fight, take your positions. You others get to the escape routes and stay in the safe areas until we come for you." With no more urging, the colonists poured out of their rooms without a word.

Lar and Martje ran for the entrance and were joined by other colony fighters filing out from other tunnels. The sound of sonics and hisses of energy blasts greeted the colonists as they poured out of the cave to join the guards outside.

Seeing Wald among the rocks, Lar sprinted over, keeping low. The geologist glanced to see who had joined him and then returned to gazing through his magni-view.

"How many?" Lar asked, watching the Tanlians sprint from rock to rock, trying to hide from the colonists' protective fire.

"More than we can defend with our present numbers, although there are a few less Tanlians now. They stumbled on our warning mines," Wald looked up and grinned, but changed expression quickly. "We won't be able to hold them off for long."

Lar nodded. "We won't need to. The others have had time to get to safety by now. We can retreat to the caves and fight them there." Wald shuddered. The security chief put his hand on the geologist's shoulder. "All your traps and plans have worked well. They have kept us alive and given us a chance. Now it comes to man against man. We will inflict great losses among them if they keep attacking. It's time for you to escape now, my friend."

Wald shot Lar a somber look. The two men had disliked each other after the escaping colonists had landed and sought refuge in Wald's beloved caverns. Now the geologist was having trouble saying good-bye in this moment of danger. Clasping the security chief's hand in the old Earth custom, Wald managed to choke out, "Good luck." He turned and scurried back into the caverns.

¶ ¶ ¶

Neb Klinfer watched the Tanlians swarm toward his encampment. Lar's group had warned them they were under attack, and soon afterwards, Neb's scouts sounded a similar alarm. It appeared the Tanlians and their Syndicate allies were approaching the colonists at both ends in an attempt to trap them in the middle.

The hunter watched the attackers, trying to determine what they were up against. "It looks like over one hundred," he said to Drever Zanden, who was standing nearby.

"How did they find us?" Drever said shaking his head. "Our encampment is the best hidden. A stranger would have to know where to look."

Neb shrugged. "Maybe spies. It's too late to worry about that now. Let's give them some light resistance and retreat to the tunnels. We need them to follow us in before we can spring our surprise."

This encampment was created differently from where Lar and his group were housed. At Neb's urging, Wald and his men had enclosed most of this cave's opening, only leaving two small rectangular passages for people to walk through.

During an emergency, Neb wanted to be able to seal off the entrances, trapping some of the attackers inside the cave to wander hopelessly through the tunnels. His people would escape to well-hidden areas outside and defenders would double back.

Neb waited for about ten minutes before giving the order to retreat. One by one, his people disappeared into the cavern. Standing just inside the darkened entrance, Neb shot three Tanlians through the head with his Earth hunting rifle. He wanted to make the other attackers angry enough to follow him inside; it worked.

¶ ¶ ¶

Riss Nels and the other seven camp leaders heard the alarms and got their people to safety. After determining their camps were not yet under attack, the leaders acted quickly. Splitting up into two groups, defenders from these camps rushed to the aid of Lar and Neb. Wald and his men had drilled hidden safety trails through the mountains so the colonists could reach one another in an emergency.

The group heading to help Neb's camp found the hunter and his followers already had the Tanlians trapped. Some of the attackers had followed Neb and Drever into the caverns and had been slaughtered in the dark passages by the defenders.

Other Tanlians had found their way out of the tunnels, only to suffer a heavy barrage of every known man-made weapon. Arrows, bullets, energy pulses, and sonics came screaming into their midst, killing them one by one. Everywhere the Tanlians scrambled, there seemed to be colonists lying in wait, ready to pick them off.

One large Tanlian moved with ease through the rocky terrain. Riss recognized him as one of the Syndicate woman's guards, the man who had sat across from Neb. *Obviously he's not one of them*, Riss thought, his face in a tight grimace while taking aim with his energy pulser.

Twice he missed the darting figure, who cut down colonists with efficient skill. The Tanlian carried two long knives that were practically swords. Another figure caught his eye moving parallel to the Tanlian. The second man was taking care to stay out of the large man's sight.

Grabbing his mag-viewers, Riss glimpsed a familiar red-headed figure snaking through the rocks following the large Tanlian. Both men disappeared from Riss's view. He wanted to signal Neb and tell him the enemy's location, but he did not want to chance exposing his friend. Too far away to help, Riss helplessly watched the deadly drama unfold.

Neb had seen Masat scrambling through the rocks, gutting any defender he faced. Most of his men were hunters, such as himself, not skilled in combat techniques. The large man must have killed seven or eight of Neb's people.

Neb carefully made his way to an overhang about twenty meters away and lay in wait, as if he was hunting a grazer. Lying on his stomach, the hunter watched the Tanlian inch his way closer.

Not realizing Neb was nearby, Drever also was hunting Masat. The Tanlian managed to slip away every time he took aim. It was easy to mark the attacker's progress by the screams of his dying victims. Drever carried an old Earth shotgun, good for close-range shooting with its spray-pattern shot. Holding up the shotgun's barrel so he could make his way through the rocks, Drever peeked around one large boulder; nothing.

As he made his way through a narrow opening, Masat sprung at him. Drever tried to swing the gun around, but the Tanlian knocked it out of his hands and stabbed him through the chest. Drever collapsed, chocking in his blood.

Masat pulled his knife out of Drever's chest and had straightened up when he felt a hot stab in his back. Pain shot through his body. In shock, he looked down to see an odd point sticking out of his stomach.

"You've killed enough of my friends Tanlian," a voice said above him. Masat clumsily shuffled around and looked up to see a red-haired man holding an ancient weapon. Neb took careful aim and let his second arrow fly. The big man swayed after the arrow passed through his neck, a look of surprise on his face and fell in a heap.

¶ ¶ ¶

Ismala N'pofu had reluctantly allowed her brother, Shadra, to join the Tanlians in their hunt for colonists. She now sat at the ship's console, listening in horror to the slaughter taking place on the planet. The Tanlians were not doing the killing, but were being slaughtered one by one.

Shadra had followed a Tanlian party of about twenty men into the caverns that supposedly housed Lar Vonn and that annoying Wald Bergmann. He had hoped for a chance to kill one or both of the colonists. No longer would he be known back home as just Ismala's brother, but he would be famous as a killer of the despised Alliance people.

The hunting party had turned into a fight for survival for Shadra and the others. Two Tanlians had run into one of the cave shelters after hearing a noise only to be blown apart by a fierce explosion. Screams could be heard down the tunnels. When his group rushed to the sounds, they found a dead Tanlian or two lying on the cold stone floor, blood pouring out of knife wounds. No colonists' bodies were found.

Growing more nervous with each passing meter, the Tanlian party decided to turn back and take their chances outside. Shadra did not argue, but trailed the others, keeping to the shadows. His group slowly made its way out of the tunnels where they were greeted by sunlight streaming into the entrance. All but Shadra rushed out and were greeted by a fusillade of energy blasts from outside and behind.

A group of colonists had appeared out of hidden alcoves and gotten behind the Tanlians. All the attackers, except for Shadra, were dead in a matter of a few seconds. Desperation seized Ismala's brother as he hung back in a doorway, wondering what to do.

A lone figure stood in the cave entrance talking on a communicator. Shadra crept close. The voice was familiar. Lar Vonn was talking with the other colony leaders, assessing the battle. It was clear the colonist was happy. He laughed, relieved his people had repelled the attack.

Listening to Lar, Shadra could tell the Tanlians had all been killed. The security chief mentioned one of the big men who had escorted the Syndicate woman. Masat was killed, too, he realized. Shadra was shocked. The Tanlians had expected a few losses, but these colonists had no missiles, no flyers.

How could this have happened? His situation seemed hopeless. If Shadra gave himself up, he would return home a disgrace. He may even lose his family name if the clan fathers so deemed. The best he could hope for would be to find work as a common laborer.

"Alliance rat!" Shadra called out fiercely, stepping out of the shadows and brandishing two knives.

Surprised, Lar spun around and aimed his energy pulser at the oncoming man. "I see you survived," the security chief said with disgust. "I suppose you want to plead clemency so you can return home safely."

"You hide behind your weapon," Shadra said as he walked steadily toward the security chief.

"You can choose life," Lar said frowning, putting down his pulser and pulling out his knives.

Shadra drew close and posed in a combat-ready position. The two men warily circled each other. Shadra attacked first, feinting with his left and slashing with his right. Lar managed to block the move, spun, and attacked, but was repelled as well.

A somber crowd of colonists soon gathered at the entrance to watch the deadly duel. Lar and Shadra feinted, slashed and parried with each other. The clash of metal on metal and the grunts of the fighters echoed through the tunnels.

Shadra had been successful with his thrusts and parries. He had drawn blood several times, hearing Lar gasp in pain each time he was successful. Lar's knives were clean. He could not penetrate his opponent's defenses.

Growing weary and feeling his skin becoming soaked with his blood, Lar plunged at Shadra, hoping to surprise and overpower the other man. The security chief's attack was successful, the two men grappled for a few seconds and separated.

Shadra stumbled backward into a wall and slowly slid down to a crouch. One of Lar's knives was inserted to the hilt in his stomach. The colonists let out a cheer until Lar stumbled around to face them. A half-smile was on his face, but his eyes were dazed. A knife was stuck firmly in his chest and blood was streaming out.

Leaping forward, Martje caught Lar before he collapsed, easing him to the ground. Wald walked over to Shadra, pointed his energy pulser and fired point blank. He then hurried to where Lar lay, knelt and clasped his friend's hand.

Breathing in gasps, Lar looked up and whispered, "We did it again." He smiled and slowly his grip relaxed on Wald's hand.

"You will not be forgotten. Your blood will strengthen our people. I will proudly bear the child I have conceived," Martje whispered in his ear. She then closed his eyes with her fingers and rocked him. The only sounds that echoed through the tunnels were sobs from the mourning colonists.

18

The color flowed out of the face of Tanlian comm operator Trellon Stotzen. Eyes wide, he turned to Ismala N'pofu, who was holding her face in her hands, shaking her head. The surviving collector pilots on the surface had reported the humiliating defeat. They listened with horror as their shipmates died.

As if to confirm the news, a woman with a deep voice signaled through Masat Ebber's communicator: "All your men are dead, Tanlians and a Syndicate man. If you do not believe me, how else could I be on this channel? We can give you a count if you wish. The bodies will soon be burned."

Trellon gulped, his hands shook. The junior officer did not know what to do. Ismala walked over to him and placed a hand on his shoulder. "I suggest you recall the collector ships before the colonists find them." Giving a quick nod, Trellon contacted the pilots and ordered them to return to the ship.

"Tanlians we demand you cease hostilities," the woman on the surface cut in again. "We now have destroyed one of your ships and killed all your attackers. How much more proof do you need that we can defend ourselves? Tell the Syndicate woman we now consider ourselves at war with her people."

Trellon looked around the control center and took a roll of his people. Twenty-two Tanlians, including two returning pilots, were left. There were barely enough bodies to fly the ship back to Tantalum 2.

"How will you be treated upon your return?" Ismala asked Trellon.

The young officer thought for a moment and shook his head. "It will be humiliating that we returned alive and left the others on the planet. They may execute us as an example of failure." This was his first deep-space mission, and he realized it might be his last.

Ismala leaned over Trellon, asking permission to broadcast a message throughout the ship. "Tanlians, we all have suffered a terrible loss this day," she said, fighting back a sob. "I understand your lives may be in danger if we go back to your home world. Return with me to Kenyata directly and I promise you a safe future. You could become valuable members of Kenyata's space fleet. The Tanlians need never know. We will alter this ship to look like one of ours."

Navigator Adan Longor interrupted Ismala on the comm. "Do not heed this woman, fellow Tanlians. It is our duty to return home. She will make a valuable hostage."

Smiling, Ismala glided behind the navigator as he continued exhorting his comrades. Adan did not see the flash of metal or have time to react as Ismala slashed his throat with an expert stroke. He slumped over his blood-soaked console.

"Brave Tanlians, there are now twenty-one of you left," Ismala spoke into the comm, her voice was emotionless. The navigator's comments were unwelcome. My offer stands."

Trellon, shaking even more, asked for a show of support from his shipmates. As soon as Adan's body was taken away and his station cleaned, a new navigator set a course for Kenyata.

¶ ¶ ¶

Taryl Bryann's aides had never seen her meditate this long. It had almost been an entire day and night. They gently offered the Seer water, which she sometimes accepted. But she continued to stare into space. Throughout the day, her expression changed from studious to somber to horrific. Toward evening, tears pooled and trickled down her pale cheeks. Even Larinia's crying could not break her concentration.

By the dawn of the second day, she broke out of her meditation. Looking exhausted and saying nothing, she ate a few more bites of food, checked on Larinia, and curled up to sleep. Another day had passed before Taryl stirred from her slumber.

"Kindly assemble the colony for second meal," she told her aides. "I have news of the others." She said no more until everyone had gathered in front of her shelter.

The colonists had been gathered for about half an hour. They murmured in anticipation. Word had spread the Seer was going to tell them about the others across the mountain. Many hoped it was good news, that the two groups would be reunited.

All grew quiet as Taryl's aides emerged from her shelter, like acolytes leading a procession in one of Earth's old worship houses. The Seer stepped out. Though a small woman, she commanded their attention. Her long red hair shone in the midday sun. It was accentuated by her white flowing robe.

"I bring sad tidings of our fellow colonists across the mountain," she said, pausing to take a dramatic look at the crowd.

"The others have fought a terrible battle with the Tanlians. Many have been killed, both Tanlian and colonists." Some of her listeners wailed. Others bowed their heads in grief. "After the battle, the mother ship left orbit. I fear we can no longer help the others."

Taryl stood before her audience. She could tell they were shocked and saddened. They did not know she had told them only parts of the truth, that most of the dead were Tanlians and the ship had left in defeat.

Sensing a pivotal moment, Taryl continued with great sobriety. "We all have lost loved ones and friends in the past few days," she said, looking at the ashen-faced Franca, who was standing in the front row. The other woman looked at Taryl and whispered, "Lar?"

Taryl nodded sadly. "Uri Navrakov and Lar Vonn have given their lives to protect us. The Tanlians have no plans to return. We are safe for the time being, but we must stay vigilant." Taryl turned with a dramatic swoosh of her robe and returned to her shelter. As she passed, many of the colonists bowed their heads and made other signs of reverence.

¶ ¶ ¶

The message could not have been more devastating to Jamison Gresser. The GEMS woman's message had been clear. Tanlians had attacked Verde Grande and apparently killed or kidnapped all of the colonists.

The director of Colonization Alliance of Independent Nations scrolled through the list of names of all those brave people: Captain Hector Nandez. Security Chief Lar Vonn. Wald Bergmann. Taryl Bryann, the Seer. Two thousand in all were reported lost.

Jamison even had received confirmation of Ismala N'pofu's identity from the Galaxy Exploration and Minerals Syndicate, which repeated her offer to trade the troubled planet for a new world being bioformed. As he feared, the CAIN Council had shown great interest and most likely would vote to accept the offer.

It is time to leave this business, he thought to himself. *Only one more job to finish*. Buzzing his friend, Per Vosberg, Jamison told him his plans.

"I agree. It must be done." Per said. "Recall the auto ship. It is traveling to Verde Grande for nothing," said the chief of Universal Mineral. "I'm so sorry, Jamison. We all have lost so much on Verde Grande. I'm in the mood for a trip. I have never visited Earth."

Jamison nodded, looking at his friend in the viewer. "I was born there, but left when I was twenty. That was almost fifty years ago. I'd say it was time for two old colonists to go home."

CONTACT

1

Darya Vonn sat very still in the tall grass, intently watching a bee pollinate the flower of a fruit tree. The petite young woman recorded the scene with an etcher on a thin piece of cloth stretched across a small piece of smooth wood.

Her eyes seldom left the bee as her hand deftly captured every detail, from the hairs on the insect's body to the grains of pollen stuck to its legs. The drawing filled the entire cloth, many times the size of the real bee. The swish of footsteps moving through the grass did not disturb her. She heard them, but she was not concerned.

"I come soon, Raaf," the artist said to her visitor without looking away from the bee. She did not break her gaze and her hand continued its graceful motion.

"Darya, didn't you hear mother call for second meal?" an annoyed male voice said from a few meters away. "Ah, drawing flowers again. You can come back after the meal."

The young woman did not react. She continued drawing for a few moments, then slowly turned to look at her impatient twin brother, who was standing with his hands on hips. "Not flower, bee," she said slowly, and then held up her drawing.

Raaf had seen dozens of his sister's drawings. The details in her artistry always amazed him. Walking closer to her, he took the drawing and stared in admiration despite himself. He looked at the bee and then at her drawing.

"You certainly see things most of us don't notice. I'm not sure this will sell at market like your drawings of flowers," Raaf said, playfully mussing her long blond hair. "Come. Mother has the meal ready." He turned and walked away, still holding her sketch. He knew it was no use arguing with her. She would come when she was ready.

"My drawing!" Darya called after her departing brother.

Raaf stopped and held it up. "Come to meal, then you can have it back. You know Mother hates it when you forget to eat."

Darya cocked her head as she watched her brother head back to their village. She looked back to study the bee again, her hand twitching slightly as if it were seeking the sketch cloth. A few minutes later, the bee eventually flew away. Only then did she rise from her spot to join her family.

"Oh, Darya are you ever going to learn to come when you are called?" Marna said gently after her daughter found her way back home. "I made your favorite: lamb stew with honey sauce."

"Yes, I like," Darya said, holding out her hands expectantly for her plate. She began eating without further conversation.

Tursym smiled at his daughter. "Raaf showed us the drawing. Very good, but it may not sell," he said. "The valley folk love your drawings of flowers."

Darya scrutinized her plate in almost the same way as she had watched the pollen-gathering insect. "I liked the bee," she said without looking up.

Marna cast Tursym an angry glance. He shrugged and returned to his meal.

Raaf frowned at his sister. He hoped she had not put his parents in a bad mood. "I have news," he announced. Marna and Tursym put down their eating utensils and looked at their son, but Darya continued to enjoy her meal.

"My circle has chosen its first mission," he said and paused for a moment. "We are going to climb Mount Barrasca."

Ever since that first Tanlian attack when the colony's defenders had formed a circle to defend against the assault, young Nuven men had bonded in small groups. These groups, often comprised of relatives or close friends, were called circles.

The words were barely out of Raaf's mouth when Marna jumped up, tipping over her chair with a crash. "No, not my son, not that!" she cried. Her face flushed with anger.

Tursym shifted in his chair, an annoyed look on his face, but he said nothing. Even Darya stopped eating. She stared thoughtfully at her brother.

Raaf tried to placate Marna. "We will be fine, mother. We are all good climbers. It is our turn to try. Our ancestor, Lar, made a blood oath he would find the others." Marna stomped back and forth across the room with her arms tightly folded against her body. The normally congenial woman was upset beyond words.

She stopped by her mate's side and gestured toward Raaf. "Say something, Tursym. Please talk him out of it," she pleaded.

Tursym shook his head when he looked at her, but pride shone in his eyes. "It is every Vonn's dream to cross Mount Barrasca and find the others. He is of age," he said in a hushed tone. "I would have gone at his age, but a Tanlian attack wiped out half our village. I was never able to mount a climbing expedition after that."

Marna threw up her hands in frustration. "People have died trying to cross that mountain. Some have disappeared and their bodies were never found," she wailed. "Most of the climbers who did return were half-starved or deathly ill."

Raaf walked over and hugged his mother as she sobbed into her hands. "I promise we will take every precaution," he said soothingly. "This is something we've all wanted to do since we were children."

Marna reached up, cupping his face in her hands and looking into his blue-green eyes. "But you are still a child. You are my child," she said as tears streamed down her face.

Raaf took her hands in his and gently kissed them. "My circle all has Vonn blood, and we all have seen eighteen harvests. We want to be the ones to reach the other side. The ancestors have waited too long." Marna backed away from her son, collapsing in a chair. She knew she could not talk him out of it, especially if her mate would not help her.

"When do you plan to leave?" Tursym asked. He was frightened for his son, but he also felt a surge of pride.

Raaf paused, taking a deep breath, "We plan to leave in two days." He winced as his mother doubled over as she wept, her body shaking with each sob. Tursym tried to comfort his wife with a hug. He knew the next few days were going to be difficult for her.

Shifting uneasily at the discomfort he was causing his mother, Raaf glanced around the room. He was startled to see Darya smiling at him. This was even more unsettling because his sister seldom showed emotion. When she did, no one knew why. It could have been caused by something she saw hours or even days before.

"What is it Darya?" Raaf demanded, not bothering to mask his impatience. Even Marna managed to stop sobbing and looked with surprise at her daughter.

Darya stood up and pointed to the mountain. "I go, too," she exclaimed. "I find the voices." Darya's three family members stared at her in shock.

The silence was shattered with Marna's scream. "Oh the ancestors! Not you, too!"

This time it was Tursym's turn to object. "No daughter, you cannot go with Raaf. It is too dangerous," he said, sitting down next to Darya and patting her gently on the shoulder. She did not react, but continued to eat her meal contentedly.

Tursym was not surprised by Darya's impassiveness. Ever since she had been a youngling learning to walk, her family suspected she was different. As a child, Darya was content to sit and watch others for hours on end without moving. She learned to walk and talk much later than her robust twin brother.

Early on, Marna suspected Darya was a "quiet one." For unknown reasons, one or two Nuven children were born with this trait every generation. This suspicion fueled the fear that Darya would be dealt with according to Nuven tradition. Their culture expected the families of these quiet ones to mercifully euthanize them.

This unpleasant task always fell to the father to carry out. The Nuvens considered these children to be unproductive members of their society, weaklings who could not fend for or protect themselves.

However, when he set out to fulfill his duty, Tursym had been unable to kill his pretty three-year-old daughter. He had carried Darya into the mountains to find a quiet place to lay her to rest on a funeral pyre. Tursym set his daughter down on a large rock and picked up a fist-sized stone.

Trying to ignore his churning stomach, Tursym was determined to strike a quick, fatal blow to the child's head. He did not want her to suffer. A bird landed a few meters from them and started to scold the intruders.

Darya laughed and pointed at the twittering fowl. "Papa, bird. It's pretty." As she turned and smiled, a breeze ruffled her long blond hair. Tursym stared in astonishment. He dropped the rock and didn't notice it clatter down the mountain.

These were the first words Darya had ever spoken. The little girl slid down the rock, picked up a stick, and began drawing in some loose sand. Still stunned, Tursym peeked over her shoulder and saw she was drawing a perfect image of the bird.

Moved beyond words, he watched her for almost half an hour, then picked her up and carried her home. He was determined to care for her no matter how much work it would be or the criticism he would receive from the other villagers.

Now, Tursym tried to convince his grown daughter not to accompany her brother to the mountain no Nuven had been able to scale. Taking her face in his hands, he gently turned her head so she looked him in the eyes.

"No, Darya. The mountain is too dangerous. You cannot go," he said slowly, hoping she would understand. The family never knew if she comprehended what they said or if she chose to understand.

Mimicking her father's gesture, Darya put her hands on his face and smiled. "Darya remember to come home, Papa. Voices call from there. I want them to stop," she said, patting his cheek. Then she returned to her meal as if nothing out of the ordinary had happened.

Marna shook her head while she dabbed at her eyes. "Voices again. She hasn't talked about them in two harvests. I thought she was over that," she groaned.

Oblivious to the protestations of her family, Darya looked up at Marna and held out her plate. "More please, Mama."

2

The watcher broke from her trance and stretched to loosen the muscles in her legs. She was stiff from having been in a meditative cross-legged position for more than three hours. A young aide offered her a goblet of water, as was the custom when a Tarylan Seer came out of a trance.

Eraphia frowned at the interruption, but took a few hasty gulps then hurried down the hallway to report her troubling vision. High Seer Yseni listened to the report with keen interest. Despite barely being of age, the young woman was an experienced Seer.

So far, Eraphia twice had been the first sentinel Seer to detect Tanlian marauders. She had helped deter them from entering Verde Valley and guided them toward the unfortunate others on the other side of the mountain.

Yseni frowned. “Very curious. You say there are eleven hunters starting the trek up Mt. Kiken?” The descendants of the colonists in the large valley called themselves Verdans. They had named their side of the mountain “Kiken.” It meant “danger” in old Earth Japanese.

Eraphia nodded, “Yes, High Seer. I took my time when I felt their presence. The hunter I saw through looked at his group many times. I was able to reach all of them except the female.”

Yseni did not like the change in pattern. For the past two centuries, the Nuvens, which the others on the opposite side of the mountain called themselves, had ventured up Mt. Kiken in groups of ten. All of them were always men. The Seers had been successful at confusing the climbers into seeing things that were not there.

Many times the Nuvens were forced to give up, convinced the fog they thought they saw made the mountain impassable. A few stubborn climbers tried to venture into the imagined fog, but a misstep sent them tumbling to their deaths or serious injury. While regrettable, these incidences helped spawn the belief among many in the hunter society that the mountain was too dangerous to climb.

The Nuvens on the other side of Mt. Kiken were not the only people the Seers monitored. The psychic women also monitored those among their own people who wished to climb and reunite with the "lost ones."

Despite the Seers' best efforts, the story of these lost people from the colony seeder ship *Colonia Nueve* had become the stuff of legend among the common Verdan folk. Children were told of the others' sacrifice when the Tanlians had attacked for the first time. Many youngsters fantasized about climbing the mountain to "rescue" their long-lost comrades.

In an effort to control these overzealous adventurers among their own people, the Seers established the tradition of "blessing" the climbers. In doing so, each climber unknowingly became bonded with a Seer.

The Verdan climbers met the same fate as their Nuven counterparts. The terrible imagined fog and seeming impassible ravines always drove them back to their valley, dejected and defeated. Despite this record of failure, it seemed every generation produced more young Verdans wishing to attempt the dangerous but heroic trek.

These numbers of new climbers had started to put a strain on the Seers' ability to keep their minds open to sense any Tanlian attack and to monitor those annoying Nuvens, who also insisted on scaling the mountain. And now, a change in the hunters' pattern was not a good sign. More troubling was the fact that the talented Eraphia had been unable to reach the eleventh member, a woman.

It was unusual for the Nuvens to travel with a woman during a dangerous climb such as this. The Seers never had trouble reaching women in the hunter society. Yseni wanted to know who this female was and why she could not be reached.

"Until we learn more about this group, we will use standard procedure for the climbers," the High Seer ordered. "Pick the ten best Seers to follow the males and control them when possible."

Eraphia bowed, but could not mask her confused look. Yseni smiled, "Don't worry. I have a special task for you, my dear. I want you to continue to try reaching the woman. So far, no hunter has been immune to our 'sight,' no matter if they are men or women. Remember, it is vital that all the members of that climbing party be convinced the mountain is too dangerous for them to continue."

Eraphia nodded. "Yes, High Seer, I understand. I will try my best." Bowing, she paced out of her superior's chambers, fully intending to carry out her orders.

Yseni rose from her chair and walked to her window. She gazed at the comings and goings in Fortress Bryann, but her mind was occupied by this strange incident. The High Seer was so deep in thought she did not hear another person who had entered her chambers.

"What is it, Yseni? You look troubled," a soft voice said behind her. Startled, she began to scold the intruder, but chuckled when she saw it was Zasha, her old childhood friend and confidante.

"Do you remember maybe ten harvests ago or so one of our Seers discovered a Nuven girl we were unable to reach?" the High Seer asked.

Zasha nodded. "Yes, a young girl, a strange one to be living among the hunters. We deemed her to be harmless. What is it? Why do you mention her?"

Yseni repeated what Eraphia had told her about the newest group of hunters attempting to climb Mt. Kiken.

Zasha frowned. "Oh my, a woman with a group of hunters, and unreachable as well! It must be that girl. But why did they bring her with them? This is very out of character for the others," she said. "I understand why you look so worried. However, Eraphia is one of our most gifted Seers. She certainly will be able to reach her."

Yseni reached out and clasped her friend's shoulder. "If Eraphia cannot reach the hunter woman, I want the most talented Seer to try. Those climbers must be stopped."

"Of course. I will give her every chance before I step in," Zasha said, gazing out the window. "I do not want to discourage her. Eraphia has shown great promise so far."

Yseni shook her head while the ramifications of an unreachable hunter coursed through her brain. "If this woman is truly unreachable, we have no other alternative than to have our guards kill the group. They must not discover the pass and find us. That would put all Verdans in danger from the Tanlians."

Zasha was stunned. Never before had the Seers been faced with such a quandary. The hunters had always been turned away. But, to deliberately send out a troop to kill them was a shocking thought.

"Surely we don't need to resort to those measures," Zasha entreated her friend. "If the hunters find their way here, then we can protect them as we have done our own people."

Yseni shook her head. "No. If the hunters leave their valley then the Tanlians will grow suspicious and be more determined to find where they escaped to. Besides, we have been killing the hunters ever since we settled Verde, though maybe not by our own hands. They have served as our sacrifices to the Tanlians. As unpleasant as it is, the safety of our society depends on the hunters staying in their valley."

3

The young Nuvens had been climbing for eight days and now were leaving the tree line. Even though the oxygen was growing thinner the higher they trekked, the climbers kept a constant steady pace. This endeavor came naturally to them. Raaf Vonn's group had the benefit of having descended from a long line of climbers.

They were unaware every time an ancestor strained himself during a climb that the preceding generation was born with the ability to more easily withstand the stress, thanks to the adapator genes they inherited from their clone ancestors. Much to the surprise of Raaf and his circle, Darya kept up. The young woman never complained and even had to be reminded to take necessary sips of water from her canteen when they took breaks.

It was midday when the group neared the summit. The day had begun as bright and sunny, but now the young men were complaining about the darkening skies and the infamous cloud bank that had stopped so many parties of climbers before them.

Raaf and his circle slumped on nearby rocks and cursed their luck. Darya stopped, too, but looked puzzled. "Time for break again?" she asked. "Darya not tired. Want to go."

Her brother shook his head. "No, Darya, the clouds look threatening. It is getting too dark. We will pitch camp and see what morning brings."

Darya cocked her head, trying to understand his words. She gazed up the mountain then turned back and looked at Raaf. "I see no clouds. We can go now," she said matter-of-factly, then set off up the mountain. Raaf muttered an oath as he rose to fetch her.

Darya's reluctance to take orders and her lack of ability to comprehend basic survival skills were the reasons he had not wanted her to accompany them. However, just as he reached her, she stopped and clasped her hands over her ears. She whirled around, an uncharacteristic frown on her face.

"What is it, Darya?" Raaf asked, forgetting his displeasure with her. His sister looked up at the sky and shook her head violently. Then she looked plaintively at Raaf.

"Make the voice stop, please," Darya moaned. "Sky not cloudy. Sun is bright. Why does she lie?" Raaf gently put his arm around her and led her back to the group. His circle brothers looked at her quizzically, but went about the business of making camp.

They all had grown up with Darya and were familiar with her unusual abilities and shortcomings. As surrogate brothers, each one of them gladly would have defended the eccentric girl if the need arose.

"Let's rest and eat," Raaf said to her. "Maybe the air is making you dizzy. We will try again in the morning." Darya stumbled over to a rock and sat down. She swayed back and forth with her hands still over her ears.

Every few moments, she would mumble, "No, no, stop. No clouds, no clouds."

Ganick Nels, one of Raaf's circle brothers, looked over at the poor girl. "Will she be able to continue?" he asked, concerned.

Raaf shrugged. "I've never seen her like this before. It must be the altitude. If she continues like this, I may have to take her back down the mountain until she feels better."

Juban Caleria, another circle brother, looked at the sky and shook his head in disgust. "If we cannot continue, we all will be escorting her down the mountain. We cannot climb if we cannot see where we step. The weather is just as all the climbers have described it."

Much to his relief, Raaf saw Darya sitting peacefully, watching a small rodent scurry nearby. She no longer mumbled or clasped her ears. His sister looked up. She looked tired, but smiled. "Voice stop. Darya hungry. Eat, please."

Ganick and the others laughed, relieved to see she was feeling better. Fearing a storm from the ominous-looking clouds, the group found protection under boulder juttings to make camp. Not much more was said as they broke out the rations, ate their fill, and settled in for the night.

In the morning, Raaf and his brothers cursed when they woke up to a thick fog. They had trouble seeing and shouted to locate each other. Darya was the only one who did not respond. Raaf called her, growing more concerned with the unnerving silence with each passing moment. He stumbled over to her bedroll, but found it neatly rolled up. She apparently had awakened and cleaned up according to the usual practice.

Fearing she had wandered off and gotten lost in the fog, Raaf shouted her name as loudly as he could. He tried to search the area, but his eyes could not pierce the gray, misty shroud that swarmed over his eyes.

Raaf's circle reconnoitered. They fanned out, taking careful steps in an attempt to cover a large area. Each one took turns calling for Darya and then to each other. Without benefit of the sun, the circle could not tell how much time they had been searching. Several brothers were growing hoarse.

Fearing they would lose each other, the circle called all its members back together. With no sign or sound from Darya, they reluctantly made their way back to camp. Famished, the other circle brothers ate in silence while Raaf sat hunched against a rock. He was exhausted and too sick with worry to eat anything.

"She might have wondered off after her toilet and is waiting for us to find her," Ganick said, trying to ease Raaf's fears. Raaf rocked back and forth on his haunches and grunted an irritable "maybe" in response.

The others were almost finished with their meal when a soft scuffling sound made them stop. The young men drew their knives as a precaution and stared into the gloom. A familiar voice cut through the fog. It was so close, a startled Raaf jumped up and hit his head on an overhang.

"Darya hungry, too. I eat now, please." Raaf crept toward the voice and almost bumped into his sister before he saw her standing in front of him.

"Darya, where have you been? We've been calling for you for hours," he said, relieved, but a little angry. Ganick scrambled over and offered her some food. The other brothers also surrounded her, curious where she had gone. The young men could barely contain themselves as she took great care in finishing her meal.

"Why Raaf and others not climb today?" she asked in her usual emotionless voice. "You act strange. Is Raaf sick?"

Her brother was dumbfounded. "You left, but we couldn't find you in this fog."

Darya looked at him and shrugged. "I can see. Darya go for walk after I tell voice to stop. I find path in mountain. It's pretty."

Raaf gasped. "You can see? How? A path in the mountain?"

Darya said nothing, but pulled out her sketchpad and began to draw. Even in the murky imagined grayness, the circle brothers watched as she traced a mountain and then her sharpened charcoal stick created a gentle gap that sloped down the mountainside.

The young men stared in wonder at the extremely detailed drawing. No one accused her of making up the scene because they all knew Darya only drew what she saw. She was incapable of imagination or interpretation. Raaf did not understand how his sister was able to do such a thing or if she had found a gap through the mountains. Now it was time for the strong twin to trust the weaker one.

"Show me," he said, taking a deep, trembling breath.

Darya smiled. "I show Raaf." She took her brother by the hand and led him into the dense fog. The other circle brothers watched the two siblings disappear. Too stunned to say anything, they sat down to wait and to hope Raaf and Darya would be able to return.

4

Eraphia slumped backward, exhausted. Two nearby aides barely caught her before her head hit the floor. The Seer's clothes were drenched with sweat. Her hair looked as if she had just stepped out of a bath.

Zasha hurried over to the young woman. She had never seen a Seer look so bedraggled when coming out of a trance. "What is wrong, Eraphia? Why are you in such a state?" the older Seer asked, while the aides toweled her off.

Eraphia took several long drinks of cool water. She blinked for several moments to compose herself and focus her eyes. "The hunter woman is hard to reach," she murmured, panting from the exertion of reaching such an unusual mind. It was a labyrinth of complexities she had never encountered.

"I can only see faint glimpses through her," Eraphia whispered. Then a slow smile formed as she stared at Zasha. "But I made her stop finally." Eraphia grinned at the somber group of Seers who had gathered around her. "I cannot control her vision, but she seems confused."

Zasha was pleased. "Excellent, my dear. The other Seers tell me they are in control of the male climbers. The hunters all believe the cloud bank is making the mountain impassable. If the woman can be stopped, the men will grow discouraged, too. It does not matter what she sees as long as they turn back."

The older Seer knelt by Eraphia. "Take some nourishment and get some rest while the hunters sleep. You and the other watchers must be prepared to control the climbers when they awaken. We need the fog to chase them back down the mountain."

Eraphia nodded. The Seer felt certain she could at least keep the hunter female bewildered enough to make her and the other climbers want to return home. However, she did not tell Zasha of the strange experience from her attempt at contacting the unusual woman.

Eraphia had flashed a brave smile when the older Seer complimented her, but she could not repress the memory of hearing the female climber plead with her to stop. The words were barely a whisper, but the contact sent a chill through her.

Zasha cheered on all the watchers, then left to report the good news to the High Seer.

Eraphia tossed and turned in her sleep. She awoke almost once an hour to check if the other watchers had seen the hunters awaken. All was quiet, however. Only a lone sentinel Seer sat in a trance. At the first sign of activity from the hunters, this watcher would alert the other Seers so they could hurry to make contact.

Shortly before dawn, Eraphia at last fell into a deep, fatigued slumber. Even then her dreams were filled with plaintive pleas for help. The young Seer was jolted awake by the vivid dream. She sat bolt upright, breathing heavily from the disturbing vision.

Eraphia's unconscious mind had drifted into the watcher state. It reached out for the female hunter the Seer had worked so hard to contact just hours before. Blinking heavily, Eraphia took deep cleansing breaths in an attempt to bring her mind under control, but the same vision — that of a young, blond woman with a vacant expression — stared back at her.

Terror seized the Seer momentarily, but she fought for control. It was to no avail, however — the vision would not go away. "Stop, go away," Eraphia gasped, pawing the air in an attempt to brush the face away.

A voice in her head almost made her heart stop with fright. It echoed through her brain. "Why you tell me there are clouds when I see sun? Raaf and others see clouds. Do other voices lie to them?"

The Seer was trembling uncontrollably. The terror she had fought back before now swept through her whole body. Never before had she or any other Seer been controlled by another.

"You are not real. I am dreaming," Eraphia sobbed. Her cheeks were flushed and wet from tears of fright streaming down them.

"I will not listen to you," the calm voice said. "Stop lying. Stop. Leave me alone. I will tell the others you lie."

The Seer tried one more feeble attempt to sever contact with the vision. Dread stung her heart as she realized who was speaking — the female hunter. "How can you do this? It is not possible," Eraphia moaned, rocking back and forth faster and faster in her bed.

Now the vision of Darya smiled. "I not afraid of you. I climb mountain and tell others what I see. I go now."

The Seer gasped as the vision blinked away. Eraphia felt like a blanket had just been thrown over her head. A suffocating feeling threatened to choke her. "No, stop. It's not possible!" she screamed over and over again.

Moments later Tarylan aides rushed into her room. They were stunned to find the Seer shaking uncontrollably, her body in a tight fetal position. Less than a half hour later, a concerned-looking Zasha and frowning High Seer stood over Eraphia. The unresponsive young Seer stared straight ahead. She whispered something unintelligible from time to time.

"What in Mother Verde happened to her?" Yseni demanded, shaking her head in disgust.

Zasha shot her friend an angry glance. "Even you could show some compassion for one of our finest Seers," she scolded only loudly enough for the High Seer to hear. "Apparently the strain to reach the hunter female took a higher toll on her than we were aware of."

Yseni glared at Zasha. "This talented Seer of yours has failed. Find someone else to make contact with that hunter female or undertake the task yourself."

Zasha was about to snap back a reply when gasps and moans filled the meditation room. Frantic aides were rushing back and forth, trying to comfort the other ten Seers who were being startled out of their trances.

"What is it? What in Mother Verde is happening?" Yseni barked. After conferring with the aides and speaking to several of the Seers, who were in a state of shock, a pale-looking Zasha turned to the High Seer.

"Our Seers have lost contact with all the hunter climbers. Apparently, the female is leading them through the gap."

The color also left the High Seer's face. She turned clumsily to one of the aides. "Bring me the captain of the Tarylan guards. I have a mission for his men."

5

Raaf stumbled and tripped over every other stone in his path as Darya led him by the hand up the mountain. His frustration grew with his clumsiness and failure to see through the fog that swirled before his face. However, his sister walked gracefully, as if she could see perfectly where she was going. This feeling of helplessness was new to the athletic young man, who had excelled at any physical activity.

Growing impatient at his inability to keep up with his sister, Raaf took a long stride and promptly cracked his shin on a rock. With a yelp of pain, he let go of Darya's hand, tripped over another stone, and fell to the ground, skinning an elbow. Cursing his misfortune, Raaf rubbed his wounds. He glanced up to see Darya sitting nearby, a half-smile on her face.

The young man started to scold his sister for her amusement at his expense when he stopped and blinked in surprise. Raaf could see his sister perfectly as she sat nearby. A strange feeling swept over him as he realized the fog had lifted. Bright sunlight reflected off Darya's blond hair. His vision was totally clear as he stood slowly and looked around. The sky was a bright blue. He could see for hundreds of meters away.

"What happened to the fog?" Raaf asked incredulously, forgetting about his injuries.

His sister looked at him as if he were a youngling. "No fog. Darya can see. Can Raaf see now?"

He nodded slowly, still not understanding what had happened.

"Good. I show you now," Darya said, rising and continuing up the mountain. Being able to see perfectly, Raaf strode along beside her.

However, after walking for several minutes, the young man noticed fog was starting to settle in again. Looking up at the sky in puzzlement, Raaf took his eyes off the path and stepped on a stone wrong, causing his shin to throb slightly. As soon as he grimaced in pain, the fog was gone again. Raaf stopped in bewilderment.

Darya halted, too, and waited for her brother.

"The fog came and went again," he said, pausing, trying to understand what was happening.

His sister shrugged slightly. "No fog. I can see."

Raaf started to argue when a thought came to him.

"You could always see, couldn't you, Darya? You said you saw no clouds or fog," he said grinning, appreciating his epiphany. "We thought you were dizzy from the altitude, but in fact it must have been the others and me who were affected. Getting hurt must have made my mind focus. Somehow you are not affected."

Darya cocked her head. She did not understand exactly what he said, but she was pleased he was no longer bothered by the fog. "Did you tell voices to stop, too?" she asked.

Raaf looked at her quizzically, but shook his head no. "Perhaps that is how the altitude affected you," he shrugged, and then smiled. "The others and I saw what wasn't there and you heard what wasn't there. Now I will see no more fog and you will hear no more voices," he said, rising and gesturing for Darya to continue to show him the way.

Brother and sister walked for less than an hour when they reached the summit. However, instead of being a peak, the mountain angled downward. Raaf stood in wonderment. The gap gently cut through the giant mountain range. He could just make out the tree line on the other side, many kilometers below.

With a shout of glee, Raaf picked up his sister and swung her in a wide circle. Darya swayed a bit from the unexpected dizzy ride, but smiled from the exhilaration.

"We did it, Darya! We did it! We found the way across the mountain. Maybe we can even find the others," he said smiling broadly, clapping at their good fortune. After drinking in the view one last time, Raaf turned to Darya. "Come, let us lead the circle brothers here."

¶ ¶ ¶

Juban Caleria was slumped against a rock taking a nap when someone shook him awake. Before he could get his bearings an unseen hand slapped his cheek sharply, causing him to fall. In a fury, Juban jumped to his feet, drew his knives, and looked for the attacker. However, the only person he saw was Raaf, who stood several meters away, grinning at him.

Juban started to protest when he realized he could see Raaf perfectly. Darya stood beside him with an amused look on her face, too. "Where, where is the fog?" Juban stammered, looking around in amazement.

Hearing the commotion, the other circle brothers sprang to their feet, but stared helplessly into space as if they were blind.

"What is happening?" Ganick Nels demanded. "Raaf, is that you?"

Raaf greeted the others then winked at Juban. "They will thank me for this later, I hope."

Eight more slaps rang out, followed by pained protests and colorful oaths. One by one, the other circle brothers stood looking at each other in plain view. A few grumbled while they rubbed their cheeks, but all were astounded that the fog had lifted.

Raaf grinned and gestured for his brothers to follow. "Come see what Darya has found."

6

Agusto Harn was shocked at the High Seer's orders. She wanted him and a select troop of his Tarylan guards to pursue and kill a hunter party that had found its way from across the mountain range. Yseni tried her best to convince Agusto these strangers were a danger to Verdan society.

The Tarylan captain had always carried out the High Seer's orders without question. But he also was one of many Verdans who believed in the legend of the lost ones. The story of how a small band had sacrificed themselves to save a larger group of colonists from marauders was still told in Verdan homes. Even the powerful Tarylan Seers had not been able to erase this memory from the collective Verdan consciousness.

"With all due respect, High Seer, couldn't these people be the ones predicted to find us according to the prophecy?"

Yseni was prepared for this reaction. Zasha had warned her any word of strangers appearing from across the mountains would trigger such questions.

"Ah, my loyal Agusto, if only that were true," she said, exhibiting a benevolent smile. "My most gifted Seers have watched these strangers very carefully. It is our judgment that these invaders are not the lost ones we hoped would join us one day, but they are descended from the marauders who landed and killed them."

Agusto's eyes widened with surprise. "Descendants of the marauders? Our brothers from the Earth ship were wiped out?"

Yseni lifted her arms up in a helpless gesture. "Apparently so. These strangers bear no resemblance to our fellow Verdans. We fear their mission is to spy on us and return with greater numbers to attack our people."

The Tarylan captain was astounded at this revelation, but he did not question what Yseni told him. Every Verdan knew the Seers possessed extraordinary abilities understood by no one except these mysterious women, who were descended from Taryl Bryann, the savior of Verde.

"I will gather my best men," Agusto said with fierce determination. "We will protect our people from these intruders and also carry out revenge for killing our lost brothers."

The High Seer fought back the urge to smile. The captain's reaction was more than she had hoped for. The other Tarylan guards would be much more zealous for this mission. Yseni managed a perfunctory nod. "Very good, Captain. I have faith you will do your duty."

Enthused by the honor bestowed on him, Agusto started to take his leave when the High Seer stopped him. "Forgive an old woman's memory, but I forgot to mention there is another unusual situation with these strangers." Agusto started to blurt a clumsy compliment about her youthful appearance, but stopped himself, coughing with embarrassment.

Yseni smiled. "Don't worry, Captain, all women enjoy receiving sincere compliments, even Seers." Her tone then changed. "Remember, Agusto, your orders are to kill all of the intruders."

He bowed. "Of course, High Seer. I understand.

She held up a finger as a caution. "You and your men may find it difficult to carry this out. The intruders travel with a young woman. A beautiful, innocent-looking female, I'm told."

Agusto was startled by this revelation. To his knowledge, no Tarylan guard had ever arrested a woman, much less killed one. He frowned but said nothing.

"My Seers believe this woman to be a sorceress. She is the one who is leading the strangers here. If this female is allowed to live, she may return to her people to lead others to us."

The captain nodded. "I will select men who will carry out any orders. How much time do I have until the intruders reach our valley?"

Yseni shrugged. "We believe they could reach our outer settlements in about eight or nine days. They are traveling fast."

Agusto bade a brave farewell. "My men and I will make you proud, High Seer." But his stomach tightened at this unusual order. "Where will I find men who will carry out such a deed?" the captain muttered to himself as he marched out of Yseni's chambers.

¶ ¶ ¶

Eret Drumlin and Yev Serrat watched in terror as the executioner checked the sharpness of his knife on a blade of grass. The two were tied to separate poles. They were gagged and their hands and feet were bound in tight, painful knots. Even their heads were bound so they could not jerk away and cause a mess when their sentence was carried out.

The two Tarylan guards had been found guilty of raping a young barmaid. The men had spent their off-duty night indulging in the strongest ale they could find. When it came time to close, Eret and Yev refused to leave the small tavern. The poor girl had tried to usher the guards out of the building, but the two drunks had attacked her.

The next morning, it had not taken long for their fellow Tarylan guards to track down the two men after receiving full descriptions from other patrons at the tavern. In their stupor, Eret and Yev had stumbled back to their barracks. The two were arrested. Verdan judges wasted no time in issuing their death sentences after witnesses confirmed their identities.

Crimes such as this were unusual on Verde. But when perpetrators were caught, they were dealt with harshly. Due to the influence of the Seers, penalties for committing crimes against women were severe.

Eret stared wide-eyed and tears streamed down Yev's face as their sentence of death was read aloud. The executioner stood nearby, his gleaming knife in hand, preparing to carry out his orders.

The judge had just finished the reading when the gate to the small enclosure swung open. The executioner swung around to confront the intruder, but was stopped by a sharp command.

Agusto Harn strode over to Eret and Yev and pulled out his knife. Recognizing the Tarylan captain, the two convicts clamped their eyes shut, fearing he had come to personally carry out their execution. However, Agusto grimaced then cut off their gags.

"You two have one chance to live," the captain said, his lips curling into a snarl.

"I am picking a select group of Tarylan guards to carry out a dangerous mission. Intruders are headed for Verde Valley and must be killed. One of the strangers is a woman. She, too, must die. If you two accept and carry out the mission, you will be awarded your freedom as long as you never enter Verde City again."

Frowning, Agusto stepped back and folded his arms. "You have one minute to decide." Eret and Yev needed no other convincing. With sobs of gratitude, both swore their allegiance to the captain and the mission.

Agusto shook his head in disgust. "If I had another choice I would rather see your blood being spilled for your crime." The captain proceeded to cut them loose. While doing so, he whispered the same threat to each man.

"If you try to escape, we will find you and kill your families in front of you, and then we will allow the barmaid's brothers to kill you very slowly." The two men nodded solemnly and left with Agusto to join the rest of his men.

7

The Nuven climbing party had made excellent progress as they followed the gap in Mount Barrasca that Darya had discovered. Even when they stopped to mark their trail by carving signs on trees or building markers out of small rocks, they proceeded quickly, driven by an excitement about what lay ahead of them.

On the morning of the seventh day, Juban Caleria poked at the leftovers of the previous night's meal, a combination of rabbits and birds they had hunted and prepared for third meal. "I'm getting tired of eating rodents," he complained. "When can we go hunting for grazers that will yield some real meat?"

Raaf Vonn scowled at his circle brother, but said nothing. He, too, was hungry for a more substantial meal. "Let us break camp and keep moving until second meal. If we find nothing of interest before then, we can split into hunting groups and bring back something more to our liking."

Juban and the others nodded their approval and broke camp to continue their journey. The young Nuvens had been traveling for about two hours when the tree line stopped unexpectedly. They stared in wonder at the vast valley that stretched out as far as they could see.

"Have we found the other valley?" Ganick Nels whispered, not daring to say it aloud for fear the scene would melt away.

Before anyone could answer, strange bellowing from far away caught their attention. Ganick scampered up the largest nearby tree to find the source of the strange noise. The others stared up at him impatiently, waiting for his report.

"It's a herd of grazers. Hundreds of them. Maybe more," he shouted. Ganick climbed down, shaking his head at the wondrous sight. "I've never seen anything like it. The grazers are just over the next ridge. They are large and all colors — red, white, brown, black, even spotted."

Raaf and the others exchanged excited smiles. Such a large herd would mean they would be enjoying a fine meal. It did not take long for the Nuvens to reach the herd. With instincts honed from two centuries of subsistence survival, they approached the strange animals downwind so the herd would not be alerted to their presence.

Darya hid herself along the ridge. The young woman would not take part in the hunt, but she had already pulled out her sketchbook and was recording the scene in her usual extraordinary detail.

When the group drew near enough to take a look, they gasped at the size of the beasts, which were grazing peacefully in the long grass. The animals were noisy and appeared to be unconcerned about their safety. Bellows rang out constantly. They were very different from the silent deer and mountain goats the Nuvens were accustomed to hunting.

Mothers called to their young and sometimes were answered by a bleat. Lower-pitched rumblings also rang out from even larger animals, which appeared to be males.

"Remember, we only need to take a grazer that will feed us for the next meal," Raaf whispered to the others.

Ganick nodded and surveyed the herd for an animal that would fit their needs. After a few moments, he whistled softly to the others and pointed out a black half-grown grazer that was eating at the edge of the herd. Without exchanging further words, the circle automatically broke into three groups.

The first two groups of three led by Ganick and Juban slowly made their way around either side of the young grazer. The grass was so long, the hunters' crouching approach went undetected. The remaining four men led by Raaf formed a semicircle and edged its way forward. The hunters closed in on the oblivious calf as it wandered about looking for tender morsels of grass.

Using soft, birdlike chirps, the hunters called back and forth to alert each other of the grazer's movement. At the moment all groups had signaled affirmative, a loud, sharp whistle sounded.

With a whoop, the six hunters who had cut the grazer off from the rest of the herd sprang out of the grass and ran toward the animal. It snorted in surprise, turned and ran toward Raaf and his men, who waited with their bows drawn and ready. When the animal drew near enough, the four archers sprang up and unleashed their arrows. All the missiles hit their intended mark.

Even with four arrows in it, the young grazer bellowed painfully and tried to bolt away. Terrified by the attackers and pain from the arrows, the animal tried to limp back to the herd, but another covey of arrows from Ganick's men hit it. The grazer stumbled to its knees. It desperately tried to rise, but the arrows had done their job. With a last painful gasp, it fell twitching on its side.

Raaf and the others triumphantly ran toward their prize. The hunters had barely lowered their bows when an angry bellow erupted behind them. Juban's group twirled around and barely had time to dodge out of the way of a larger grazer that charged into their midst. Caught unprepared, the other hunters had to retreat quickly as the angry mother charged over to her baby.

The female grazer bellowed loudly and stomped her foot in the grass when she reached her offspring. She sniffed her unresponsive calf and bellowed over and over again. By this time, Raaf and his nine circle brothers had reconnoitered nearby. The Nuvens had never seen a grazer react this way. Deer and mountain goats always fled for safety when hunters felled a herd mate. Survival was always the first instinct with the wild animals.

However, this mother now protected her fallen offspring. She called loudly, tossed her head up and down angrily, and trampled a ring of grass encircling her calf. The hunters formed a line and charged the grazer, yelling loudly and waving their arms in an attempt to drive her off. Instead of fleeing as expected, the mother lowered her head and charged the Nuvens.

For the first time in their lives, the hunters had to run from an animal. The grazer ran after one hunter, then turned and chased another until all the Nuvens had retreated to a safe distance.

"What kind of an animal is not afraid of being attacked?" panted Ganick, who had barely avoided being trampled by the angry mother.

Raaf shook his head. "These animals must have never been hunted. She is unafraid of us."

Juban frowned and stood with his arms folded across his chest. "We need to dress that dead one quickly or the meat will go bad. There is only one way to solve this. We have to kill the mother." Even though they were frustrated and hungry, the other Nuvens started to object.

Juban's suggestion contradicted the first rule of the hunt — never kill more than absolutely necessary. Dropping this mother grazer would rank as an obscenity in their eyes. Wounding her with an arrow or two also was unthinkable because the beast probably would suffer painfully before she died.

While the other hunters were arguing loudly, Ganick slipped away and slowly approached the grazer, who stood snorting near her dead calf. Instead of wielding a bow, he pulled a sling out from his belt and placed a palm-sized rock in the pouch. His circle saw what he was doing and stopped arguing. Ganick was the only one among them who was proficient in using this ancient weapon most Nuvens had given up on in favor of the more-efficient bow. The other nine fell in a few paces behind him, holding their bows at the ready, just in case Ganick was unsuccessful.

The mother grazer bellowed a warning then charged Ganick, who braced himself and spun the sling with dizzying speed around his head. With a snap of his wrist, a stone struck the animal in the snout with a dull smack.

She stopped and shook her head painfully. The grazer stomped her hoof as a warning but held her ground. Ganick reloaded his sling, twirled it again, and hit the grazer between the eyes. This time she bellowed in pain and backed up as blood dripped down her nose. The confused animal shook her head and retreated to her calf. Ganick followed and fired another stone, which caromed off the top of her head. She snorted at her baby once more then turned and trotted back to the herd.

Ganick smiled at his compatriots. "We will eat well tonight."

8

"Who could have done this?" A little boy wailed to his father as he pointed to the site where his favorite calf had been slaughtered and then cooked for a meal. Meat scraps were strewn about the area. About thirty meters away, the hide had been scraped clean and was stretched out on the ground, held tightly by pegs pounded into the earth. The father and son had been checking on the grazer herd when they made the gruesome discovery.

"I have never seen anything like this before," the father, a ruddy-faced man, said as he tried to comfort his son. "Didn't these people know all they had to do was ask for food if they were hungry?"

Another man shook his head sympathetically as he strode around the area, examining the strange scene. He knelt to feel the ashes, finding them barely warm. "It is as if these people hunted the beast then cooked it here as in the old times before our herds grew large enough to provide for us," Agusto Harn said. "Apparently, whoever killed the calf plans to return to collect the hide. Otherwise they would not have taken the trouble to clean it and stretch it out to dry."

The first man nodded. "It is very fortunate for us a troop of Tarylan guards were close by. Normally, it would take us at least two days to travel to Verde City to report this crime."

Agusto smiled and clasped the older herdsman on the shoulder. “We were on maneuvers when one of your villagers found us. It will be our duty to find these criminals and bring them to justice.” The Tarylan captain turned to face one of his men, who had approached a moment earlier. “Well, Sergeant, have you found their tracks?” Agusto asked, his eyes glinting in expectation.

The younger Tarylan saluted. “Yes sir, their trail is hard to read, but apparently they are following the line of foothills down the valley.”

Agusto returned the salute. “Gather the troop quickly. We need to find these interlopers before they can escape. It appears they are possibly three or four hours ahead of us.” He bade farewell to the herders and smiled as he strode away. *What luck to have stumbled upon a trace of the intruders we are hunting,* he thought.

The Tarylan captain had expected it to take at least a week to find the strangers who had somehow found their way over the mountain. It was obvious these strangers were not familiar with Verdan laws and customs or they would not have killed the calf without permission.

Agusto and his men tried to follow the strangers' path, but they were slowed by the hard-to-find tracks. The Tarylans had to stop often and backtrack when the trail seemed to disappear. Apparently, the strangers were not traveling single file, as was the norm for Verdans. The tracks would spread out almost nine or ten persons wide for half a kilometer or so and then change arbitrarily to a different pattern, making it difficult to follow.

Growing frustrated with his troop's slow progress, Agusto sent three scouts to fan out and sprint ahead in hopes of finding the strangers. It was midday and he feared they might not catch the others before nightfall. Three long excruciating hours passed as the Tarylans slowly followed the trail. The shadows of late afternoon were growing long when one of the scouts returned with good news.

When the young man regained his breath, he reported seeing a small band of people traveling at a quick pace. The scout had followed the group for several kilometers and watched as they routinely changed into different formations while they continued their journey.

Satisfied he had found their targets, the Tarylan signaled to a fellow scout and ordered the other man to follow the group while he returned to the troop.

"Excellent work," Agusto crowed, slapping the scout on the back. "Now we can go double time, catch up to these criminals, and perhaps take care of our business before nightfall." The other Tarylans grinned in anticipation as they hurried to catch up with their fellow trooper, who was trying to keep the strangers in sight.

After another long hour of double time, the troop spotted their scout, Vitor Pratern, crouching at the top of a hill. He signaled them to slow their pace and take cover when they neared his position.

"Where are they?" Agusto asked, panting from his run.

Vitor, who was Agusto's nephew, grimaced as he pointed to a small grove at the edge of a foothill.

"Sir, the strangers disappeared into those trees less than half an hour ago. They have not come out nor have I seen any movement. I suspect they are bedding down for the night."

Agusto nodded in agreement. He looked with pride at his sister's son.

At first, the captain had been reluctant to add the tall, gangly youngster to the troop. But the youth's skill in long-distance running had proven to be invaluable.

"Night is falling, but at least we know where they are," Agusto said, smiling. "They are trapped. We will surround them during the night and take them when they move in the morning."

The captain turned to his men. "The Seers will be pleased that we have brought this dangerous situation to such a quick resolution. They will be pleased with all of you."

Looking up and down his troop, his eyes rested on Eret Drumlin and Yev Serrat. The reprieved criminals stared with savage intensity at the grove.

"Remember, men, the rewards will be substantial for successfully carrying out this mission," Agusto called out. The captain nodded curtly at Eret and Yev. They both nodded, fully understanding what their reward would be for completing their deadly assignment.

9

The sun had barely cleared the mountain range when the Tarylan troop crept its way into the grove where they believed the intruders were bedding down. Agusto Harn planned to have his men catch the slumbering strangers and kill them quickly. With javelins and clubs poised for combat, the Tarylans eased through the trees, stopping often to listen and look for signs of the intruders.

Halfway through the grove, the troop found nothing. The only sound came from twitters and odd whistles of birds in the trees. At last they came upon a depression in the ground where a campfire had been made, but it had long since died out.

The strangers they sought were nowhere to be found. A quick inspection of the campsite only gleaned a few scraps of food. The Tarylans continued their sweep through the grove, but found nothing. When they reached the opposite side of the grove, the men lowered their weapons, seeing only the steep embankment of a foothill looming before them.

Agusto exhaled angrily. The intruders apparently had crept away in the middle of the night. The captain shook his head in disbelief. His men had kept watch on the grove all night. They hadn't seen or heard anyone emerge from the trees. The troopers, who had been primed for battle, now grumbled with disappointment.

As if to mock the Tarylans, the trees suddenly came alive with the sounds of birds awaking for the day. Agusto turned and signaled for his men to make their way back through the grove. This time, the troopers did not bother to disguise their movements. They noisily chattered and strode through the trees, eager to reach the edge and try to find the intruders' trail.

The Tarylans had not made it as far as the abandoned campsite when one of them called out an alarm. Ten figures quietly emerged from behind trees only about twenty meters in front of them. Agusto swore under his breath at being surprised. The strangers obviously had been watching and waiting for the Tarylans.

One of the intruders, a young man with blond, curly hair, stepped forward a few paces. He smiled and raised both of his hands in a strange gesture. Seeing the young man wielded no weapons, Agusto carefully returned his javelin to its holder on his back, turned to his men and warned them in a hushed tone to be ready for his signal.

Both men slowly advanced until they were only a few meters apart.

"I am Raaf Vonn of the Nuven people," the young stranger said proudly, touching his chest. Agusto just shook his head curiously, unable to understand. After two hundred years of separation, the Nuven dialect was very different from the Verdan tongue, which had evolved from a blend of Old Earth languages.

Raaf seemed unperturbed, however, and repeated himself. The Tarylan captain smiled, stepped forward and feigned a helpless gesture. Hoping to catch the young stranger off guard, Agusto snatched the knife fastened behind his back and thrust it savagely at the younger man.

Raaf instinctively sidestepped the clumsy attack. In one smooth, quick motion, he snatched his own knife from his belt, whirled toward the Tarylan and plunged it into the attacker's neck. Seeing their captain collapse, all but two of the Tarylans shouted in unison and rushed toward the waiting Nuvens. However, a hail of arrows struck the attackers, felling about half their number.

The remaining troopers flung their javelins in desperation, but hit nothing. The two groups met in a clash of bodies, knives, and clubs. Even though the Tarylans were older, they were no match for the Nuvens, who were descended from generations of people who had to fight for their very existence.

As ordered, Eret Drumlin and Yev Serrat hung back, looking in vain for the young woman they had been ordered to kill. However, after seeing all their comrades fall at the hands of the strangers, the two surviving Verdans tried to flee for their lives. The two escapees failed to get far. Another batch of arrows easily cut them down.

Raaf shook his head in disgust at the useless loss of life. "I thought the others would be happy to see us," he said to Ganick Nels who stood nearby.

Ganick shrugged. "They obviously must mistrust strangers. Perhaps they thought we were Tanlians."

Raaf started to answer when he was interrupted by a shout from Juban Caleria.

"One is still alive." The circle surrounded the fallen Verdan, a thin, harmless-looking youth about their age. Juban stood with the sling in one hand and a knife in the other. He pointed at an ugly gash in Vitor Pratern's forehead. "He still lives. I missed his temple. Shall I finish him?"

The young men looked at each other, not knowing what to do. However, Darya interceded on behalf of the injured youth. Raaf's sister had been hiding in a tree during the fight. She now scrambled down and rushed to Vitor's side. "He is hurt, Raaf," she said looking at her brother.

Raaf gestured helplessly. "I think Darya has made the decision for us. Killing him now would disturb her greatly. Besides, he doesn't look like much of a threat." The others agreed. Bandages were made by ripping the dead Verdans' clothes and applied to Vitor's wound. A stretcher was put together to carry him.

Ganick frowned. "It looks like he will live, but what do we do with him?"

Raaf thought for a moment. "We came here to contact the others. Perhaps they will be friendlier if we bring back one of their young men." The circle marched through the valley for almost an entire day without seeing any signs of other people. As dusk was approaching, flickering lights from a small village could be seen.

It was nightfall when the Nuvens approached the edge of the village with caution. Raaf and the others would have waited until daybreak to approach the strangers, but the wounded man needed attention. He had not regained consciousness.

After making sure no one saw them, the circle silently approached a large cabin and placed Vitor's stretcher near the door. The Nuvens melted into the shadows and waited. Juban stepped forward, placed a stone in his sling, twirled it and let the missile fly. The stone hit the door with a loud crack.

After a moment, the door flung open. A man peered out and called to others when he saw Vitor in the stretcher. In less than a minute, the wounded Tarylan had been picked up and taken inside. The first man from the cabin strode outside and looked around. He shouted several times.

The Nuvens could tell he was calling out questions by his tone, but they did not understand his words. Finally, the man called out something familiar, "Allo? Allo? Is anyone out there?"

The Nuvens smiled at each other. "Is he saying hello; our greeting?" Juban asked excitedly.

Raaf nodded. "Finally a word we recognize. Perhaps there is hope to talk to these people." A scratching sound drew his attention to Darya, who stood beside her brother. Sketch pad in hand, she gazed intently at the village while her hand effortlessly glided across the paper, recreating the cluster of houses perfectly.

Raaf smiled. "I know a way we can communicate with these people." He playfully tugged his sister's hair. "You've already proven to be a valuable part of this troop, Darya. I think you're going to help us again." She stopped drawing for a moment to gaze in puzzlement at Raaf. Darya reached out and pulled his hair and then returned to her work.

10

Fortress Bryann had never seen such an uproar of wailing and screams. Seers were fainting and others were huddled in groups of three or four, speaking in hushed, worried tones. Aides and med techs were rushing from room to room to check on the more serious cases.

Some of the watchers who had been monitoring the Tarylan troop, which had been sent out to exterminate the intruders, had come out of their trances in a state of hysteria. As one, the Seers watched with horror through the troopers' eyes as the strangers quickly and efficiently killed their men in the grove.

Several of the Seers groaned and writhed in empathetic pain as the hunters' arrows dropped their fellow Verdans. One Tarylan guard was pinned to a tree by two arrows piercing his stomach. He weakly struggled to free himself then watched helplessly as his fellow troopers fell, until his vision slowly blurred then went black.

The women witnessed in shock the bloody scene until all the Tarylans' life forces faded away. Nothing this traumatic had ever happened in the Verdan Valley since the Seers had anointed themselves protectors of their people.

When the watchers came out of their trances, some became violently ill, others screamed in terrified agony, and a few crumpled into helpless heaps from the strain of the experience.

One of the recovering watchers managed to mumble to several aides the fate that had befallen their troopers. The attendants quickly spread the tragic news and soon an uncontrollable wave of despair swept through the fortress.

Even normally stoic High Seer Yseni grew pale and appeared shaken when she heard the disturbing news. She hurried back to her quarters with her stomach churning violently.

Only the even-tempered Zasha kept her wits as she bustled from watcher to watcher to check on their conditions. She found other cool-headed Seers to help carry the traumatized women to the infirmary then broke up small groups of frightened gossipers, ordering them to return to their duties.

After getting the situation under control, the exhausted elder Seer trudged to Yseni's quarters to see what assistance the leader might require. To her surprise, the High Seer was speaking in an agitated tone to five Tarylan captains. Yseni didn't halt her tirade even when Zasha approached the group.

"All of them must die," Yseni hissed. "These strangers have killed sixteen of our bravest men. We have underestimated their prowess and skills. But this shall not happen again. I want every able-bodied Tarylan guard used to find and kill these enemies of the Verdan people."

The grave-faced captains saluted respectfully and left to gather their troops for the campaign. Yseni was wild eyed with fury when her eyes fell on the waiting Zasha. "My orders stand. I will not be talked out my decision," the High Seer growled at her friend.

Zasha just shook her head. "I did not come to argue with you, Yseni. But it will be much harder to keep it secret that there are strangers in our valley. If word spreads, many of our people will think the prophecy of the others is being fulfilled."

Yseni snorted with disgust. "It is too late to worry about such things. These intruders must be eliminated from our presence before they do more harm to our people."

Too tired to argue, Zasha only nodded, bid farewell, and wearily shuffled to her quarters for some much-needed sleep.

She hoped the next group of Tarylans could find the strangers and kill them before word spread among the populace.

The five captains carefully scrutinized the map of Verde Valley. Pursuing and finding strangers in their midst was a new experience. No protocol existed that could help them decide what to do.

After the other four Tarylan officers had voiced their strategies, senior Captain Wojaht Gafla traced the areas on the map where the intruders could have traveled. He drew dozens of routes. The biggest unknown was the exact location of the infamous grove where Agusto Harn and his troopers had been slain.

"It will be difficult finding such a small group in the area we need to cover," Wojaht said, cupping his chin with his hands. "They could easily slip past us if we stay in five large groups. But if we employed small scouting parties, say three men apiece, then we could cover a large area very quickly."

With the other four captains in agreement, it was decided to send out twenty groups of three men each to scour as much territory as they could quickly cover. The remaining troops, a strike force of forty men, would slowly make its way up the central valley.

In Wojaht's plan, if a scouting party found the intruders, one of the troopers could alert the strike force, while the other two continued to monitor the strangers' movements. The captains were more than willing to hunt down the murderers of Agusto and his men. However, they begrudgingly respected their opponents' fighting skills.

They were confident the eleven people they were hunting would be no match for such a large force. Suspecting her Tarylan officers would balk at killing a young woman, Yseni changed her orders regarding the "witch," who traveled with the intruders. The High Seer ordered the young woman to be captured and brought back to Fortress Bryann where she could be interrogated.

11

The old woman trudged out of her house, intent on her daily early morning trip to the village's communal well. However, she stopped and stared in amazement at the artwork that covered the well. In awe, she shuffled back and forth, inspecting each sketch that perfectly depicted every cabin in the village. When she spotted the drawing of her home, the old woman shook her head in disbelief then reverently took it down to admire it.

Not long after her arrival, many of the other villagers emerged from their cabins to go about their morning chores. It didn't take long for a crowd to gather around the well after word spread about the unusual drawings.

One ten-year-old boy tried unsuccessfully to squeeze between bodies of the adults pressed together as they viewed the marvelous illustrations. Frustrated, he paused to watch a bird flit around the top of the well then spotted something curious on the inside of the roof.

"Look, there's something hanging from a rafter!" the boy yelled. One of the taller villagers boosted himself up on the edge of the well and retrieved a scroll. After jumping down, he carefully unrolled it as the others crowded around to view the drawing.

"Mother Verde, it's the wounded boy who was brought here last night," a woman said, pointing to the perfect likeness. "And look, he's being carried by some young men."

A short, round little man practically put his nose on the piece of paper as he inspected it. "Do you recognize any of these men?" Osmar Nezdan asked, looking from villager to villager. The shaking of their heads answered him.

Again looking closely at the scroll, he spotted a young woman in the background of the drawing. The girl in the picture had a slight build. However, her face was indistinguishable, a curious oddity compared with the perfect details in this and the other artwork.

After finally getting a chance to see the scroll he discovered, the boy voiced his disappointment the surprise didn't contain more exciting secrets. Growing hungry and bored with the adults and their chatter, the boy pushed through the crowd in search of first meal, but stopped short, staring wide-eyed at the smiling strangers standing only about ten meters away.

He recognized the eleven people immediately. They were the ones who appeared in the drawing. The strangers wore perfectly fitted animal hides and leather boots. This was a sharp contrast to the tunic-style cloth garments worn by most Verdans. The young men had long flowing hair and short beards, which set them apart from the well-groomed villagers.

"Elder Osmar, look at this!" the trembling youth squeaked with fright. Glancing behind him, the boy saw no one was paying attention. "Elder Osmar!" he shrieked after taking a deep breath.

This time the villagers turned to see what all the fuss was about then a collective gasp escaped from the crowd.

Raaf Vonn took a few steps forward, said "Hello," and held out more drawings. Osmar smiled broadly as he approached the strangers. Something in his gut told him this was going to be a rare moment. He stopped within a few meters of the group, laughed with delight, and said, "Allo, welcome to our village."

Raaf did not understand the villager's words, but sensed this friendly man meant no harm. He stepped forward and presented the drawings to Osmar.

"We are Nuvens. We have finally crossed the mountain to find you," Raaf said then turned and pointed toward Mount Barrasca. Osmar was shocked to hear a language he did not understand. Verdans had spoken the same dialect for generations. The elder shook his head sadly then finally looked at the drawings Raaf had given him.

Osmar's face paled as he studied the etchings. The realization of what these drawings showed almost made him faint. "Can it be? Can it be?" he muttered over and over.

The old woman, who first discovered the drawings, took the new etchings from Osmar to look for herself. Unafraid, she shuffled to the group of strangers to get a better look at them. She stared hard at the drawings then approached each Nuven and touched him gently as tears ran down her cheeks. Each stranger gently cupped her hand in an alien but comforting greeting.

The last person she welcomed was Darya, who was sitting on an overturned bucket and feverishly drawing. Cocking her head to one side, the crone looked to see what the young woman was working on.

Seeing herself appear on the sheet of paper before her eyes, she cackled with delight. "By Mother Verde, the prophecy has come true, the lost ones have found us," she crowed clapping her hands with delight.

In awe, the other villagers slowly made their way to greet the strangers. Even though they could not understand one another, soon Nuvens and Verdans were slapping each other on the back and laughing at their good fortune.

During the celebration, Osmar could not shake a troubling thought. While sifting through the drawings, he found the one that showed the strangers bringing the wounded Verdan youth to his doorstep. Seeing Osmar frown, Raaf walked over to check what was troubling the other man. The Nuven shook his head sadly and called for Darya, who was the center of attention after it was discovered she was the extraordinary artist.

After freeing herself at last, Darya sauntered over to her brother. "Give him the other scroll, Darya," Raaf told her gently.

With great deliberation, she pulled out a roll of more drawings and handed them to Osmar.

The Verdan elder could not contain his surprise as his eyes drank in the new illustrations. They showed in great detail the skirmish in the grove that led to the deaths of the fifteen Tarylan guards and wounding of the youth who lay recuperating in his home.

Osmar patted Raaf on the shoulder. "This is a great day, my friend, but I fear you may be in dire trouble if these drawings are true."

12

The youth moaned in pain as he tried to move in his cot. His head still throbbed sickeningly. It even hurt to try to open his eyes. Someone was speaking, but his mind had trouble focusing on the words. His entire attention was devoted to the fire that burned in his skull.

He winced slightly after a wet cloth was placed over his head. The cool sensation relieved the pain just enough for him to try to open his eyes again. The voice returned at the same time he felt a hand clasp his shoulder reassuringly.

"Trooper Pratern, wake up," a woman soothingly implored him. "Can you tell us what happened to you and the other Tarylan troopers sent to find the intruders?" *Intruders? Tarylan troopers?* Those words sounded familiar to Vitor Pratern.

Suddenly a flash of memory swept through his brain. He relived the battle scene at the grove — his fellow Tarylans were screaming in pain and falling to the ground. Arrows were protruding from their bodies.

With a gasp, Vitor opened his eyes. Even this effort made him dizzy, but he forced himself to focus on the somber faces gazing at him. He tried to talk, but could only manage a hoarse croak.

"Ah, he's awake. Welcome back, trooper," the voice said. Vitor now could see it belonged to a smiling woman sitting at his bedside. "Quick, give him some water. The poor boy is trying to talk."

A pair of unseen hands lifted up his head slightly, while the woman at his side allowed him to take a couple of slow, thirsty sips. Even this small amount of water tickled his throat, making him cough. The movement sent another spasm of pain shooting through his head. His eyes rolled back at the reaction.

Focusing again on the nearby woman, Vitor recognized her as a Seer. "Forgive me. My…head…is…on…fire," he sputtered, his face wincing in pain. Each word jarred his brain a little more.

"Take your time, young Pratern," Zasha said as she sympathetically patted his hand. Vitor asked for more water and successfully gulped it down.

"Our troop searched the grove the intruders had camped in overnight, but we did not find them in the first sweep," he said slowly, trying to remember the events as they unfolded. "We were on our way back through the trees when the others appeared out of nowhere."

Zasha leaned forward. Her eyes gleamed with intensity. She was no longer smiling. "What did Captain Harn do?"

Vitor closed his eyes at the painful memory. "The captain tried to lure one of the intruders to get close, then he pulled his knife, but the stranger blocked his attempt and killed him. The rest of the troop then rushed the others, but many were hit with arrows."

Vitor stopped and frowned. His memory seemed to stop in the middle of the fight. "How many other troopers are left alive? I can't seem to remember anything else after that. What happened to me?"

Zasha shook her head. "You are the only one of Captain Harn's troop who survived. We don't think you were wounded by an arrow. It appears you were struck by some other kind of weapon."

Vitor's eyes grew wide at the terrible realization that he was the lone survivor. Another stabbing pain sent a shiver through his body. The youth attempted to lift his hand to feel his head, but he could only move his arm slightly. He resigned himself to the fact it hurt to move any part of his body.

"How did I get here? Did you rescue me?" Vitor mumbled, fighting to refocus his blurring gaze. Exhaustion was sweeping over him.

Seeing he was tiring, Zasha leaned over him. "Someone brought you here. Apparently some Verdans found you and treated your wounds."

Vitor struggled to stay awake, but he couldn't keep his eyes open. "Who?" he whispered, but passed out before he could hear the answer.

Zasha sat back. "That is what we want to know, too, young man." An angry snort erupted behind Zasha.

"Well, he wasn't much help," said a frustrated High Seer Yseni. "Do you think he was telling the truth?"

Zasha shrugged. "I don't think he's capable of lying in his state. He has a deep cut in his skull and probably has a severe concussion."

Yseni paced around the infirmary, her hands folded tightly around her chest. "Why in Mother Verde would our people transport a wounded man to our troopers' encampment and then leave without reporting where they found him?" she fumed. "I don't like this turn of events at all. It smells of traitors."

Zasha looked up and nodded. For once she and Yseni were in total agreement.

¶ ¶ ¶

"Are you sure no one saw you with the injured Tarylan?" Osmar Nezdan asked. The four young men smiled at their good fortune. All assured their village elder the plan had worked perfectly.

Posing as suppliers to Captain Wojaht Gafla's large strike force, the village men easily slipped into the encampment at dusk with their horse-drawn wagon. While others bustled around them, they carefully placed the blanket-covered Tarylan in a tent where he would be found.

They then steered the horses to the edge of the camp, unfastened the team, quickly watered the animals, mounted and rode off, leaving the rickety old wagon behind. On the way out of camp, one of the villagers approached a passing Tarylan trooper to tell him they thought they heard someone moaning in one of the supply tents.

When pressed for more information, they just shrugged and told him the general direction they thought they had heard the noise come from. After the trooper left to investigate, the four villagers rode off into the night. They rode hard, but stopped often to make sure no one followed them.

Hearing their story, a wry smile broke across Osmar's face. “Good work, men. Now we've given the troopers another puzzle to think about. Perhaps we've earned enough time to guarantee no harm comes to our new friends. I trust you left the note with the wounded man as we planned?”

The four grinned and nodded in unison. This was the biggest adventure they had ever partaken in. They made sure every detail was carried out in full. The note claimed that Verdans hauling supplies had found the wounded trooper near the grove where the Tarylans had attempted to attack the Nuvens.

The writer claimed he didn't want to be questioned due to an unscrupulous past, but was concerned for the safety of the trooper. Information in the note also gave great detail where the bodies of the other Tarylans could be found. This had accomplished the desired effect Osmar had hoped for.

As Osmar started to walk away, he stopped for a moment, looking concerned. “Oh well, I suppose losing a wagon is a small price to pay to protect our guests, eh?” The four young men guffawed at their miserly elder then set off in search of ale to brag about their exploits.

¶ ¶ ¶

After the discovery of the wounded trooper, a furious Captain Wojaht ordered the strike force to march double time to find their lost comrades. He sent the unconscious wounded trooper back to Fortress Bryann for treatment.

The Tarylans stared in shock at the sight. Fifteen of their fellow troopers lay dead before them in a perfect line. The slain men were respectfully laid out, arms crossed over their chests, their weapons placed by their sides. The blood-stained bodies had not been looted or mutilated, except for the obvious wounds that had killed them.

Several arrow shafts still protruded from a few of the fallen troopers. Never in recorded Verdan history had such a fate befallen Tarylan troopers.

These protectors of the Seers had never been in a battle with an unknown enemy. Troopers occasionally suffered injuries when the rare malcontent resisted arrest. Barely a handful of Tarylans had died in the line of duty in the Verdan Valley since it was settled two hundred years ago.

The normally fearsome Wojaht Gafla struggled to fight back tears as he knelt beside the body of Augusto Harn. His good friend looked peaceful, except for the large gash in his neck. The two captains had grown up together, products of the most respected Verdan bloodlines — Seer mothers.

Wojaht and Augusto had been hand picked at fourteen harvests to start their Tarylan training. Both had earned their captain's ranks through hard work and devotion to duty.

Finally, after saying a silent prayer to Mother Verde in honor of his friend, Wojaht rose and commanded his men to place the bodies of the fallen troopers in a wagon to be taken back to Fortress Bryann for a heroes' burial.

"I want every village within three days' march of here thoroughly searched," Wojaht growled to his waiting lieutenants. "We have permission from the High Council of Seers to do whatever is necessary to avenge the deaths of our brave comrades."

The wide-eyed officers saluted and backed away, determined to carry out their leader's orders. As they started to withdraw, the captain called them back.

His grief had been replaced with an anger that made his body tremble.

"Report any Verdan who may have helped these intruders. Any traitors will be dealt the same sentence as the strangers — death!"

13

The little man sat hunched over a dilapidated desk, scrutinizing an old document. The yellow parchment crunched as he ran his fingertips across it ever so lightly while struggling to interpret the almost-forgotten language.

Two men stood patiently in the doorway watching the seated fellow study the paper while mumbling to himself. Focused on his work, he did not notice when the visitors rapped on his door then opened it. Hearing someone clear his throat behind him, the man in the chair impatiently waved at the noise without looking up.

"Yes, yes, Kunser. I know it's time for third meal, but I'm in the middle of something fascinating here," he said, not bothering to mask his irritation at being disturbed. "I'll be along shortly. Go on without me."

One of the two men chuckled then admonished the reader. "Ah, cousin, are you still forgetting to eat? Some things haven't changed since you were a youngling."

Startled, Rajeef Nezdan swung around in his chair to see who dared to disturb him. He was quite the sight, with large bushy gray sideburns that swept down his face and curled under his jowls. His unkempt curly light brown hair stuck out in all directions.

"By Holy Mother Verde is that you, Osmar?" he asked, a look of shock on his face. Osmar Nezdan laughed and approached Rajeef, holding his arms out. The cousins greeted each other with a warm hug.

"This is a sight I thought I'd never see, Osmar Nezdan finding his way to the College of Ancient Arts and Languages," Rajeef said, chuckling and poking his rotund relative in the stomach.

Not to be outdone, Osmar shook his head in mock sadness. "Ah, but cousin it is you I fear who has gotten lost. It has been nine harvests since you've been back for festival. Have you forgotten the way to the village where you were raised?"

Rajeef stared, his mouth wide open. "Nine harvests? That cannot be! I'm sure it's only been five, no maybe six harvests at the most since I've been home."

Osmar guffawed. "Corya is twenty harvests. She was bonded two harvests ago and has presented me with a beautiful granddaughter."

Rajeef sputtered at the realization. "But, but little Corya? She was only seven, no, no, maybe eight harvests when I last saw her. Oh my, my, that can't be. Nine harvests?"

Osmar nodded, chortling at Rajeef's absentmindedness. "You have not changed, cousin. Remember how you would be so intent on reading a story you would forget to eat for a whole day? Your mother always worried we would find you withered away under a tree with a scroll still clutched in your hands."

Rajeef blushed at the memory, then nodded. "Yes, my colleagues would attest to my being slightly absentminded." Neither cousin had noticed the third man walk in quietly behind them. He picked up the scroll Rajeef had been studying and began to easily read it aloud.

"On this day, let it be known to the witnesses and parties involved that Taspard Najparti has fulfilled his obligation of three thousand goldens and now is rightful owner of the ale house known as Taspard's Inn, three hundredth sector and ninety-second crossroads, Verde City. Why, it's nothing but a bill of sale," the young man said, laughing. "This is what you were studying so seriously?"

Rajeef whirled around, stunned at hearing someone speak the ancient tongue so fluently. He then noticed the stranger's odd animal-skin clothes and long hair. Osmar put his arm around his cousin's shoulder.

"Please forgive an outlander's manners. Let me introduce you to my friend, Juban Caleria. He and ten others have traveled a great distance to find us. The only problem is we are having trouble understanding one another. I thought you might know of a good translator."

Drawing close to Rajeef's ear, he whispered. "The prophecy has come true, cousin. The lost ones have found us." Rajeef looked at Osmar, then at Juban, who continued reading other bills of sale with great amusement. Then Rajeef fainted.

¶ ¶ ¶

Raaf Vonn and his nine circle brothers sat patiently on benches as they listened to Rajeef try to translate their cryptic Earth Espan-Anglo into the Verdan tongue, which had evolved from a blend of mostly Anglo, Chinese, German, Japanese and Hindi.

Verdan Corya Nezdan and Nuven Darya Vonn had proven to be invaluable. Both were accomplished artists — Corya as a painter and Darya as an illustrator. The two young women would draw an object to help explain what their fellow Verdans or Nuvens were trying to say.

Although Rajeef was an accomplished scholar in the old languages, even he stumbled often when trying to translate. The two parties started simply, identifying common objects such as trees, household objects, colors and animals. The process was agonizingly slow because even their common words were pronounced differently or the meaning had changed over the centuries.

Corya and Juban proved to be quick studies. They often were the first ones to grasp a meaning and explain it to the others.

However, many of the finer nuances of each other's tongue were proving to be difficult to grasp. After three days of intense lessons, the Nuvens and Verdans could only greet each other by name, remark at the pretty bird and ask for food or drink.

During a welcome break, Juban strolled to the well. He was looking forward to splashing some cool water over his throbbing head. Seeing an old woman drawing water ahead of him, he sat down to wait his turn and rubbed his temples in an attempt to relax. After taking her bucket off the crank, she turned around and uttered a curse.

"Young master, strangers come. Danger to you. They be Tarylan troopers," she said in a low hiss. Juban blinked in surprise at being able to understand her, but before he could utter a word, she thrust the bucket his way and commanded him to follow her.

A quick glance confirmed the old woman's warning. Three riders wearing the same gray uniforms as the men the Nuvens had killed were making their way through the street. The strangers stopped to talk to everyone they saw.

Juban grabbed the bucket and quickly followed the old woman into her home before the riders could question them. The two watched the Tarylans ride past, but it was obvious the troopers were searching for something.

After the strangers were out of sight, Juban shook his head in wonder as he accepted a loaf of bread and a mug of cool water from his hostess. "How can you speak my language and the others cannot?" he asked between mouthfuls.

She raised her eyebrows in surprise. "The others do not understand you? What have you been talking about for all these days?"

Juban just shook his head in amazement. He could understand her even with the Verdan accent. "We have been trying to learn each other's language, but it has been difficult," he explained. "May I have the honor of your name, good lady?"

A cackle erupted from her, half-cough, half-laugh. "Bless Mother Verde, no one has called me good lady as long as I can remember. Pardon, young sir. I am Sarlen Alator. My family has always spoken old Espan-Anglo.

One of my ancestors insisted his line keep the tongue alive so we could speak to the lost ones when they found us, according to the prophecy." Sarlen flashed a toothless smile and playfully pinched Juban's cheek. "And so young master, you have found us. I am honored to speak with you."

Juban shrugged. "Why did you not come forward to speak to us before this?"

She looked at him with a smug smile. "No one asked me." The Nuven started to laugh at the irony of the moment when someone loudly banged on the door. Sarlen darted to the window and gestured for Juban to hide.

Opening the door a crack, she peeked out and demanded to know who was bothering her. Juban could not understand the Verdan words, but he could tell the strangers must have come back and were going door to door.

He heard Sarlen snarl, "No," and slam the door shut. She called for him. "The Tarylans are asking for you and the others. Quick, go out the back window and warn your friends."

But before he could move, Sarlen swore violently as she peered out her window. Looking over her shoulder, Juban saw the three troopers talking to a young boy who was excitedly nodding and pointing to Osmar Nezdan's cabin, where the other Nuvens were gathered. One of the troopers leaned over and patted the boy's head, and then the three riders wheeled their horses around and left at a hard gallop.

Juban waited a moment to make sure they did not return and bolted out the door to alert his fellow Nuvens. Halfway down the street, Juban met Raaf and Ganick Nels, who were racing toward him. Raaf tossed a bow and quiver to Juban and gestured for him to follow.

"They won't get far on those animals. It's almost nightfall." The Nuvens quickly set out in fast-paced pursuit of the Tarylans.

Halfway through the night, Osmar Nezdan was awakened by a rap on his door. Opening it a crack, he saw the three Nuvens who had set out in pursuit of the Tarylan scouts.

"Have no fear of being reported by those men," Raaf said. Oscar shook his head to show he did not understand. Raaf's hair was matted down from sweat and his face was streaked with dirt. Osmar thought he saw bloodstains on his clothes.

The young man held up three fingers and with his other hand swiped it across his throat. Osmar let out a heavy sigh and nodded. The three somber Nuvens then bowed to the elder and departed for their beds.

14

Wojaht Gafla scowled as he read the scouting reports. There had been no sightings of the murderous intruders or even rumors of sightings. He murmured an oath when he was informed scout party seventeen had not reported in.

"Three days since seventeen has returned to camp?" the Verdan captain asked the nervous-looking lieutenant.

Koriz Arillo saluted. "Yes, sir. Seventeen is one day overdue." The young officer hated to disappoint his captain. Wojaht had given four lieutenants responsibility for commanding the twenty groups of scouts. Koriz had been honored to have been given the assignment.

"Well, Lieutenant what are you going to do about this truant group? We need these scouts to report on time or else we won't know what area has been covered."

Koriz nodded. "With your permission, sir, I propose taking a trooper each from sixteen and eighteen to find the missing party. These men are familiar with the surrounding territory and should be able to make good time."

Wojaht drummed his fingers on his makeshift desk, a large wooden plank set atop two sturdy logs, that was set up for him wherever the strike force camped for the night. "I hate breaking up our scouting parties. Lt. Arillo, I want you and whichever trooper you deem fit to find the missing party," he ordered.

"Move quickly. Just question each village elder. Missing Tarylan troopers cannot be that hard to find."

Relieved at being given the chance to redeem himself, Koriz saluted briskly and hurried out of the tent to prepare for his mission. Wojaht waited a few seconds, looked at his aide, and then let out a hearty guffaw.

Lt. Uson Stadova shook his head sympathetically. "A bit hard on Lt. Arillo, perhaps?"

The captain chortled. "Ah, Arillo doesn't know this is the seventh or eighth party that has failed to report on time. The three other lieutenants have had to pull a scouting rotation. It's Arillo's turn."

¶ ¶ ¶

Trooper Hubart Avery could not believe his bad luck. He and his scouting party had just returned to the strike force camp late in the evening after two hard days of riding and no success. It was barely past first meal, when his lieutenant ordered him to find a fresh mount and be ready to go on a fruitless search mission without the customary half-day rest.

He was now cursing his misfortune at having grown up in a village on the border of sectors seventeen and eighteen. "With all due respect, sir, those missing troopers are probably drunk and have found girls," Hubart said.

Koriz stood with his arms crossed. "Captain's orders. He wants those men found. Be ready to leave within the hour, trooper."

Hubart saluted. "Yes sir, within the hour."

¶ ¶ ¶

Osmar Nezdan welcomed the two troopers and listened politely as Lt. Arillo explained their mission. "Yes, Lieutenant your men traveled through here maybe two days ago. They asked the villagers something about strangers, but found nothing here then rode off."

Koriz sighed. It was the same answer he had heard in the last three villages. "Did you see the direction they were traveling or hear where they were headed?" the exhausted officer asked as he leaned against his froth-caked horse.

Osmar smiled. "Why, yes. I believe one of the villagers heard them say something about taking a swim in Lake Nandez."

Hubart groaned. "Lake Nandez? That's a half-day's ride from here."

Osmar shrugged. "Yes, that sounds about right. You will have plenty of light to travel tonight. Luna Primo is full and Luna Nino will be almost half-full."

The lieutenant shook his head at the thought of riding more that day. Hubart slumped in his saddle, also exhausted from their hard ride. "Our horses need water and rest, as do we," Koriz said.

Osmar nodded. "Of course. Help yourselves to the well, troopers. There are troughs nearby to water your horses, too."

"Ah, water and some grazing sounds good for the horses, but I could use a bit of ale and perhaps a meat pie," Hubart said, perking up at the thought of sitting down on something that wasn't moving.

The elder shook his head. "I'm sorry, troopers, but our tavern is closed. The keeper had business elsewhere for a few days. You are welcome to rest yourselves and your mounts at the well."

Koriz mumbled a thank you and led his horse toward the well. Hubart dismounted and looked expectantly at Osmar, but the elder just smiled, wished him good luck and walked away. The trooper stared at Osmar, then turned to follow his lieutenant. Something troubled him about this village.

The townspeople were quietly going about their business, basically ignoring the Tarylans. The usual curious mob of children was missing.

While they were attending to their horses, Hubart quietly got Koriz's attention. "Something is wrong here, sir," he whispered. The lieutenant raised his eyebrows, but said nothing.

"It is tradition in these villages to invite strangers into their homes to feed them if other means are not available. We Tarylans are always treated as honored guests, but these people are acting oddly aloof."

Koriz nonchalantly looked around as he watered his horse and washed the caked sweat from its coat. "Perhaps we need to observe this place from afar," he said quietly. "Let's ride out, then double back." Feigning gratitude for the "hospitality," the two troopers took their time and rode out of the village.

Ganick Nels stared from a hidden vantage point on a rooftop. "The older trooper was acting strangely," he said to Raaf Vonn who crouched next to him. "He was looking as if he lost something, then spoke quietly to the other man."

Raaf agreed. "We will follow them until we're satisfied they will not come back. I hope we do not have to kill more of them."

Ganick shrugged. "It may be too late to stop the killing. These Tarylans seem intent on finding us."

Raaf grinned. "Perhaps we don't have to kill them." He then gestured for Ganick to follow him.

Koriz and Hubart rode away from the village for about half a kilometer and then turned around and eased their way back in an effort to approach without being seen. The troopers tied their horses to a tree in a draw and slunk forward, hoping the night would hide them.

"You take the far end and I will work around the other side," the lieutenant ordered. "Meet back here when Luna Major has traveled three hours."

Hubart grunted an affirmative and slunk off to find a spot where he could observe the villagers. Koriz darted from tree to tree as he neared the village. After racing to the last tree before entering the village, the lieutenant heard a soft rustling behind him. A quick glance assured Koriz nothing was there, but when he turned back around, a figure flashed forward, knocking him down. The young officer tried to get up, but a sharp crack to his head quickly quelled his attempt to escape.

¶ ¶ ¶

Both Tarylans were unceremoniously revived by buckets of cold water poured over their heads. Hubart awoke with a start and tried to fight out of his bonds. Koriz sputtered and coughed as if he had just been saved from drowning.

"Now, now, troopers, no harm will come to you," Osmar Nezdan tried to reassure them. "Quiet down so we can talk to you." Blinking through the drops of water on his face, Koriz saw the village elder, an old woman and eleven young adults, about his age, wearing strange garb, mostly animal skins.

A sickening feeling swept through him as he realized who these people must be. "I command you to release us immediately," he shouted. "You are interfering with official Tarylan business."

Seeing they had no bargaining power, the more pragmatic Hubart tried to convince the lieutenant to quiet down. The trooper was a bit more roughed up than his officer. Hubart had been attacked, too, but he had put up a respectable fight until finally being overpowered. He sported black eyes and a cut lip after the tussle.

The old woman shuffled over to Koriz and slapped his cheek, much the same way a mother might discipline an unruly child. "Be quiet, young man, and listen to what our guests have to say," Sarlen Alator scolded him. The stunned officer stopped struggling and slumped back in his chair.

Sarlen patted him on the head. "Good pup. There you go. Now, I want to introduce you to Raaf Vonn of the Nuven Valley. He and his people have finally crossed the mountain to find us."

Hubart perked up at her words. "They crossed Mt. Kiken?" he asked reverently. "Mother Verde are you telling the truth?"

Sarlen smiled, "Yes, it's true. They call the mountain Barrasca. Ah, this one appears to have been raised by a good Verdan family who remembered our ancestors' promises to welcome the lost ones home."

Chuckling, she told the Nuvens what Hubart had said. With a nod from Raaf, Ganick walked over to Hubart, pulled out one of his knives and cut the Verdan free. The two former combatants grinned broadly at each other and embraced in friendship.

Raaf stood up, spoke briefly, and stared sternly at Koriz. The lieutenant looked puzzled then turned to Sarlen. "What did he say?"

The old woman shook her head then jabbed the lieutenant in the chest with a sharp fingernail. "He says his people have been trying to cross the mountain for two hundred years. And when they finally find us, we try to kill them. Why?"

15

Zasha impatiently thumbed through the pile of papers. Each sheet plaintively begged for an audience with her superior. As confidante and personal secretary to the High Seer, it was Zasha's responsibility to pick out the most compelling problems Yseni could reasonably resolve.

The petitioners had been waiting in the courtyard of Fortress Bryann since first meal had finished. The Verdans had an efficient court system where rulings between two disputing parties were decided by a jury of their peers based on some of the more progressive societies on Old Earth. However, a party on the losing end of a ruling had the right to appeal.

All final decisions were made by the High Seer or the Council of Seers, depending on the gravity of the case. Any request not deemed worthy of the Seers' consideration automatically reverted to the court ruling.

Through the past two centuries, the Tarylan Seers had used their mysterious gift of "sight" to permanently entrench themselves as the religious leaders of Verdan society. The Seers were cognizant of their responsibility, but over the years, various High Seers found it beneficial to hand down judgments that would empower them even further among their fellow Verdans.

Zasha was bored by the array of complaints in front of her. Nothing she saw so far warranted intervention by Yseni or the

Council. The requests ranged from land disputes and disagreements with inheritances to petitions of leniency from relatives of incarcerated criminals.

The Seer was about to reject every request when a wide-eyed guard approached and held out another hand-written document. "Sergeant, you know better than to give me a late request," Zasha snapped.

The guard blushed with embarrassment but did not retreat. "With all respect, Seer Zasha, you may want to address this one," he said, then bowed. Surprised by his impertinence but intrigued, Zasha snatched the paper and sighed loudly to show her annoyance. Within moments, however, the color drained from her face as she read the request.

Slowly putting down the sheet, she beckoned the guard to come closer. "Is this true? Can you verify this?" Zasha whispered, dreading his answer.

The Sergeant nodded slightly. "I can identify the Tarylan trooper. We have served together." Zasha slowly rose and for the first time this morning looked out over the gathered crowd from her second-story balcony perch. She scanned the people below. All were anxiously awaiting for word on their requests.

"Where are they?" she asked continuing to stare at those milling around below her. The guard stepped forward and pointed out a group standing in a far corner, keeping to themselves. "You were indeed correct, Sergeant. Please escort those people to the council chambers at the highest security level. The High Seer will be very interested to meet with them." The sergeant bowed and strode out.

¶ ¶ ¶

Yseni tried to appear nonplussed when she met with the group. However, earlier when she heard the news about these visitors, the High Seer had flown into a rage. "These people are standing in our fortress under the protection of adjudication?" she shrieked, her face turning red. "How did they get past Captain Wojaht's troopers?"

Zasha shrugged. "Apparently they had the help of several Verdans. There's nothing we can do about it now. You need to meet with them and determine our next move."

Yseni howled with disgust and threw a half-full pitcher of water across the room, where it exploded into a dozen pieces and soaked one of her tables. "Get an aide to clean that mess up," she ordered then stomped off to prepare herself for this most unlikely meeting.

Now a bit more composed, Yseni tried to force a benevolent smile as introductions were made.

"Thank you for meeting with us, High Seer. We are humbled by this opportunity and beg your indulgence and wisdom with this, ah, situation," Osmar Nezdan intoned in his best politician speak.

The High Seer nodded slightly and gestured for him to continue. She could not take her eyes off the two young men who stood slightly apart from the others. Something about those two unsettled her. They were the only ones in the room who were not in awe of their surroundings. Instead, both stared at her with a fierce intensity.

Osmar then introduced his cousin Rajeef, Sarlen Alator, Tarylan trooper Hubart Avery and lastly himself. He then walked over to the two youths and beamed proudly.

"High Seer, it is my privilege to present you with the first visitors to Verde Valley in two hundred years. Raaf Vonn and Juban Caleria are from what they call the Nuven Valley." Raaf and Juban stepped forward, gave slight bows, but kept their eyes on Yseni.

Barely able to contain himself, Osmar clapped delightedly, nudged between the two young men and draped his arms around their shoulders. "Your Eminence, these are children of the lost ones. They have sacrificed much and undertaken a great journey to find us."

Yseni and Zasha rose from their seats at the quarter-moon-shaped council table, spread their arms out in the traditional Verdan greeting and bowed. Unimpressed with the gesture, Sarlen shuffled so close to Yseni that the High Seer could smell the old woman's onion-laced breath. Zasha glanced nervously at the Tarylan security guards, who stood with their javelins at the ready.

"The prophecy has come true," Sarlen squawked in her raspy voice, pointing at Raaf and Juban. "We should be celebrating their return, but instead they've been hunted like wild animals." Osmar mumbled an apology for Sarlen's rudeness as he took the old woman by the arm and led her back to the group.

Yseni stared at Hubart Avery and ordered him to come forward. "Trooper, explain yourself. Why are you with these people?"

Hubart bowed. "High Seer, I believe what the old woman says is true. The lost ones have found us. It is our duty to welcome them."

Yseni angrily stabbed a finger at Hubart. "Trooper, you are a Tarylan, sworn to follow orders as given by the Seers," she snarled. "I command you to surrender. You will be put on trial for your actions."

Hubart was shocked by Yseni's reaction. As a mere trooper, no Seer had ever spoken to him. Now the High Seer was ordering him to surrender. He heard a voice that sounded like his, but it seemed to come from a great distance. "With all due respect, I am a Verdan first, and it is my honor to welcome back our lost brothers."

Realizing the voice was his, Hubart felt his heart leap into his throat. He bowed again and rejoined the group, although his knees felt like they would buckle from the strain.

Fearing the meeting was spiraling out of control, Osmar politely asked to speak again. "It appears there has been a great misunderstanding which we need to rectify, High Seer," he said. "Apparently, some of your Tarylan troopers have mistaken our guests as intruders."

Yseni shrugged. "A misunderstanding of grave proportions, indeed. Sixteen Tarylan troopers were attacked by unknown assailants, and fifteen were killed. That is more than a misunderstanding. It is murder."

Osmar threw his hands up helplessly. “High Seer, we believe the Tarylans may have attacked first, leaving the Nuvens no recourse but to defend themselves.”

Yseni glowered, folding her arms across her chest. “That may be most difficult to prove, my good man.”

Osmar shook his head. “With due respect, we may able to provide irrefutable proof, High Seer.”

Yseni stole a quick worried glance at the stoic Zasha, who sat nearby. Sarlen said something in a strange tongue that prompted Raaf to pull a roll of papers from a tube strapped around his neck. The Nuven slowly approached Yseni and handed her drawings made by Darya.

The High Seer and Zasha could not contain their amazement at the detailed drawings that recorded the attack in the grove. Yseni nodded and handed the drawings back. “Impressive, but this only tells one side of the story,” she said matter-of-factly.

Osmar smiled. “Yes, indeed, but we have another witness, High Seer. One of the Tarylans was wounded and treated in my home.”

Before Zasha could stop her, Yseni nodded impatiently. “Yes, the young trooper is recovering here. We thank you for caring for him, but what does that prove?”

Osmar nodded. “Good, good, then the trooper undoubtedly has told you what he said to us as he drifted in and out of consciousness — that the Tarylan captain in the grove attacked first.”

16

Wojaht Gafla slowly put down the piece of paper. The Tarylan captain was stunned by the orders from the High Seer. In terse language, Yseni apprised him of the situation and then issued specific commands for his plan of action. She told him of the unexpected visit by the party of Verdans and so-called Nuvens, who had pleaded for thc ccssation of hostilities against the visitors.

Wojaht had to reread the next passage due to the incredible plan it laid out. Lt. Koriz Arillo and Trooper Hubart Avery had been captured by the Nuvens. But now Hubart was cooperating with the intruders and traitorous Verdans. Koriz was being held hostage in Osmar Nezdan's village in sector seventeen.

Although the Tarylan officer had been loyal to the Seers his entire life, the next command made him ill. The High Seer was very clear. Wojaht was ordered to march his strike force into the village, rescue Koriz if possible, and kill all the Nuvens and any sympathetic Verdans who attempted to thwart his troopers, especially the traitor, Hubart.

If Koriz was killed, his death would be unfortunate, but justifiable. All surviving adult Verdans from the village then would be arrested and tried for their complicity in this most serious chain of events. The captain sat back and combed his hands through his thick black hair. Never before had he or any other Tarylan officer been faced with such a dramatic situation. The Tarylans had been trained to be a policing force, not warriors and certainly not murderers of their own people.

"What is it, Captain?" asked Lt. Uson Stadova, who had never seen such a look of consternation from his superior.

Wojaht sat silent for almost a minute then gave Uson a somber look. "We have our orders, lieutenant. We are to proceed to the third village in sector seventeen, hopefully rescue Lt. Arillo, kill the intruders and anyone else who tries to interfere."

The captain paused and winced at his next command. "Trooper Hubart Avery has fallen in with the intruders. He is considered a traitor and is to be killed on sight."

The color drained from Uson's face as he listened. "Sir, Avery? Kill anyone who tries to protect the intruders? Even our fellow Verdans?"

Wojaht glared at his junior officer. "Lieutenant, you have my orders. Now relay them to the rest of the troop. I want this strike force armed and ready to march immediately after first meal. Dismissed." A grave-faced Uson saluted and left to deliver the most unpleasant order he had ever been commanded to carry out.

Knowing the reaction his fellow Tarylans would have to the captain's orders, Uson announced anyone challenging and reacting unprofessionally would have their daily rations cut by half. Even so, after hearing Uson, the other troopers looked at each other in disbelief. Loyal though they were, they had never been directed to carry out such bloody duty.

"I can believe Arillo got himself captured, but Avery a traitor? Now, that doesn't sound true at all," a grizzled sergeant mumbled to those nearby as they walked toward their tents. "Who are these intruders if Avery has fallen in with them?"

The other troopers echoed his sentiments. They all knew Hubart, the happy-go-lucky prankster. He was as good a fighter as many had seen, but he also was the first one to buy a round of ale for his fellow troopers.

Later that night, after the other lieutenants had retired to their tents, the rank-and-file troopers met in secrecy. Arguments erupted back and forth between individual groups as they wrestled with the almost unimaginable task before them.

Many of these Verdans had signed on to be Tarylan guards for the prestige and high wages. These men were more than happy to carry out protective duties among the general Verdan population.

The lucky ones were chosen to stand guard at Fortress Bryann while the Seers went about their mysterious business. It was not unusual for the younger Seers to bestow delightful "special" favors upon the Tarylan guards. But now they were charged with possibly attacking a Verdan village and maybe executing one of their own.

Just as the arguing reached a heated crescendo, a familiar voice called from the darkness. "Brave Tarylans, I wish to approach under truce of parlay."

The old sergeant held up his hand to quiet his fellow troopers. "Who goes there and why should we honor such a truce?" he shouted back. "We don't know who you are or how many others are out there."

The only response was laughter, then the mysterious voice replied. "Is that Sergeant Onji Haiko? You always were a suspicious old snapper. By the Tarylan code I have sworn to uphold, I pledge only two of us wish to approach."

Onji frowned and looked at the other troopers. "Whoever is out there knows me and is or has been a Tarylan. That voice is familiar, but I can't recall who it is. Now, lads, all in favor in pledging truce let me hear you." A loud chorus of ayes rang out and only a smattering of nays.

"You and your companion may approach under protection of parlay," Onji called out. "Lower your weapons and we will do the same."

The mysterious stranger agreed. Just a few breaths later, two shadowy figures walked slowly toward the wary Tarylans. One of the strangers cheerfully greeted Onji, who stood rigid with his arms crossed across his chest. However, his demeanor changed when he saw who now stood before him.

"By Holy Mother Verde! Trooper Avery is that you?" the sergeant sputtered. Momentarily forgetting protocol, as well as his orders, Onji gave Hubart a welcoming bear hug. Finally remembering the awkward situation, the sergeant choked out an embarrassed cough and backed up several steps to inspect Hubart and his companion.

"Avery, what has happened?" Onji asked, holding up his hands in a helpless gesture. "Tarylan command has identified you as a traitor. You are not to be treated, ah, well."

Hubart nodded. "I suspected that had happened after our meeting at Fortress Bryann."

The old sergeant shook his head in disbelief. "You've been to the fortress? What meeting? Why have you been branded a traitor?"

Hubart smiled. "All good questions, my friend. I hope I can answer them to your satisfaction. First, however, let me introduce you to my new friend, Ganick Nels, a better fighter than I. He and his people are at the center of a dangerous misunderstanding." Onji and Ganick stared at each other, not bothering to mask a mutual distrust.

"Better fighter than you, eh? This sounds like a story worth hearing," the sergeant said, beckoning the two to sit by the roaring campfire.

Hubart chuckled. "If we live through the next few days, this will be a story your grandchildren will be retelling for many harvests, Onji."

17

"Don't be nervous, don't be nervous," Rajeev Nezdan whispered to himself as he paced back and forth in a large hallway. He stopped momentarily in front of two closed giant wooden doors to mop sweat from his brow with a sleeve.

Looking at his companion, Rajeev tried to feign confidence, which had fled him ever since they entered the Hall of Justice. The professor of ancient languages had never visited this most respected building in Verde City, much less argued a case, which he was about to attempt.

Juban Caleria smiled at his new Verdan friend. He did not quite understand what Rajeev had in mind, but the Nuven trusted this eccentric little man. Something important was going to happen behind those doors. When Rajeev asked for Juban's assistance, the young man agreed, sensing the adventure may help him and his fellow Nuvens' plight.

Rajeev jumped as a latch clanged. The two giant doors swung open, revealing a well-lit but small auditorium. A formally dressed bald man somberly gestured for Rajeev and Juban to enter and follow him.

The two men were led to straight-back chairs in the center opening of a U-shaped table filled with distinguished-looking men and women. Juban looked around curiously. This room was similar to the council chambers in Fortress Bryann, but he sensed no animosity from the people looking back at him.

A small woman with flowing gray hair arose from the outside center of the table. She gestured for Rajeev and Juban to approach.

"Rajeev Nezdan, this is the first time in Verdan history that a professor of the School of Ancient Languages has requested an emergency meeting of the Assembly," she said, smiling. "I must admit, my fellow members and I are intrigued. However, you failed to identify your companion. This is most unusual."

Comforted by her words, Rajeev took a trembling breath. "I thank you for granting a hearing. Forgive me. I am no orator, but only a mere researcher who is more content in the company of scrolls than people."

Turning to Juban, Rajeev managed a smile as he patted the youth's shoulder. "Before I introduce my friend, I must know if the truth-sayer is here. It is important that my, er, our testimony be validated."

A somber-looking young woman silently left her seat at one end of the table and walked toward the two men. She was dressed in a simple gray gown. A long braid of red hair was wrapped neatly around her head.

Not knowing or caring about this foreign etiquette, Juban grasped Rajeev by the arm. "That woman looks like others in the fortress," he managed to say in broken Verdan. "I no trust, what you call, ah, Seer."

Gasps of surprise escaped from several of the seated Verdans, who had never heard their language spoken with such a strange accent. Sensing Juban's concern, Rajeev forgot about his nervousness.

"No, no, my friend, this woman is no Seer. She is here to help," he said, measuring his words slowly to help Juban translate. "You must trust me. Let her touch you when you speak."

The truth-sayer stood before Juban. She looked curiously at the youth, then turned to Rajeev. "He speaks in a strange tongue. Does he understand what we say?"

Rajeev shrugged. "He understands some words, but not all." The truth-sayer nodded, but appeared not be surprised. The other Verdans sat in stunned silence. She smiled at the professor and asked him to translate.

"Many years ago, a young girl was born to the Seers. She did not share their mysterious ability, but Mother Verde blessed her with a special gift, that of truth-saying. As the young girl grew, her gift became valuable to the people of Verde. She was able to help in disputes. The Seers allowed her to leave because she was not one of them, but the Verdans honored her and she thrived. She was my ancestor."

The truth-sayer smiled. "We share the red hair with the Seers, but little else." After hearing Rajeev's slow translation, Juban nodded his approval.

Turning back to the table, Rajeev cleared his throat, reached out to the young woman and let her grasp his hand. A strange feeling of purpose filled him. This was the moment he had spent his life preparing for.

"Honored members of the Assembly, it is my privilege to introduce Juban Caleria of what they call the Nuven Valley. He and others have survived a dangerous journey over Mt. Kiken to find us. They are the children of the lost ones."

The seated Verdans erupted in shouts of surprise, which were quickly quieted by the gray-haired woman who pounded the table with a large gavel. She eyed the truth-sayer, who still held Rajeev's hand.

"Judge Soretti, this man believes he is telling the truth," the truth-sayer said showing no emotion. She then stepped around Rajeev and held out her hand to Juban.

Encouraged by the professor, Juban reluctantly took the strange woman's hand. Making such informal contact with a stranger was foreign in Nuven culture. Instead of recoiling at her touch, he found it to be warm and comforting.

"My friend speaks the truth, honored ones," Juban said in his native tongue, then waited for Rajeev to translate. Encouraged by a few smiles from those seated, he continued.

"Three weeks ago, eleven of us left the Nuven Valley in an attempt to climb the mountain we call Barrasca. My people have been trying to find a passage here for two hundred harvests. Many have died trying, but we are the first to find you," he said, flashing a proud smile.

After Rajeev translated again, the truth-sayer nodded slightly and confirmed both men were telling the truth. Then in a rare show of emotion, she knelt and kissed Juban's hand. "You and the others have overcome many obstacles to reach Verde Valley — many more dangers than most of us can even imagine," she said.

Blushing with embarrassment, Juban shrugged and gently helped the truth-sayer to her feet. "It is with great pleasure I greet you, my cousin," he said in Verdan, stealing a quick glance at Rajeev, who nodded approvingly.

With tears welling in her eyes, Judge Soretti asked Rajeev what would be a proper Nuven greeting. The professor beamed as he demonstrated, holding up his open hands at shoulder height.

"This gesture signifies you are unarmed and mean him no harm," he explained. Silently, each Verdan judge stood and greeted Juban, who smiled and responded in like manner.

"This is a great honor you have bestowed upon us, but why did you call for this emergency meeting?" Judge Soretti asked. "Such an august occasion certainly merits a formal greeting by Verdan officials."

Rajeev sighed and nodded. "I pray that it would be that simple, but a terrible misunderstanding has developed between the Nuvens and the Seers."

Judge Soretti sat up rigidly, the smile melted from her face. "A misunderstanding with the Seers; how so?"

Rajeev gestured for Juban to show the judges Darya's chronological drawings of the Nuvens' journey, including the fight at the grove where fifteen Tarylan troopers were killed.

After several minutes of carefully studying the drawings, Judge Soretti called for order. "How did this happen? Why did the Tarylans attack them?"

Rajeev shook his head. "Apparently the Tarylans mistook the Nuvens for intruders, possibly Tanlians, those marauders who attacked the first colonists all those years ago. Juban and his people swear they are telling the truth. Why would they carry a wounded trooper for a day to find help for him and then stay and make contact with my cousin's village?"

He then told the judges of the unsuccessful attempt to plead the Nuvens' case before the High Seer.

"I find it troubling the Seers and their Tarylan guards consider the Nuvens dangerous," Judge Soretti said. "I fear we can do little to help."

Juban had been following the conversation the best he could. He did not fully understand everything that was said, but he sensed it was not going well. "With all due respect, the one dream my people have fostered for generations is to reach this valley," he said, clutching the truth-sayer's hand.

Juban took his time to look each judge in the eye. The Nuven knew this was a rare opportunity to argue his people's cause, and he was determined to succeed. Juban may not have been the strongest warrior, but he was descended from a long line of superb storytellers. He stopped often to let Rajeev catch up with the translation.

"We have endured terrible attacks from Tanlians. Men, women, and children have died over many harvests, but we have survived. I do not know why these terrible things have not befallen you, but I swear by my ancestors this is true."

Rajeev held up his hand for Juban to stop for a moment. As best he could, the professor explained the Nuvens' ancestor worship. "When a Nuven swears by his ancestors, this is as holy a pledge as appealing to Mother Verde. They consider their dead ancestors holy because without their heroic efforts to fight for their survival, the Nuven people would have perished."

With tears running down his cheeks, Juban knelt before Judge Soretti and held out his hand. She clasped it gently. "I implore you honored ones to help my people," he said, choking with emotion. "Thousands of my people have been waiting all their lives to join you in this wonderful valley. Have we not sacrificed enough?"

Rajeev dabbed his eyes and translated in a faltering voice. When he finished, the truth-sayer stood before the judges with both hands over her heart.

"This Nuven is speaking the truth. I will inform my fellow sisters of this momentous event. It appears the prophecy has come true. We will argue the Nuvens' case with the Seers, if you request it."

Judge Soretti shrugged. "I wish we could help, but the Seers have the Tarylan guards."

A tall, sandy-haired man in a dark blue uniform stoop up. "That is true, Judge Soretti, but as commander of the Verdan Enforcers, we may be able to provide a stalemate to the Tarylan guards. Many of my men may relish the opportunity to offer protection to the Nuvens and their Verdan sympathizers. Our domestic protection forces have been bullied too often by these elite troops. Besides, my enforcers number in the hundreds, far more than the Tarylans."

Judge Soretti tapped her gavel. "The Assembly will meet and discuss this. You present us with a great many problems to resolve."

In a rare gesture, she reached out and touched Juban's cheek. "Whatever happens, my young friend, may Holy Mother Verde and your ancestors protect you and your people."

18

Wojaht Gafla fumed as he stalked through the encampment of his Tarylans after second meal. Every few seconds, he barked at squads to clean up their tents or singled out a trooper for being sloppily dressed.

The Tarlyn captain was furious his plans to attack the Verdan village, which sheltered the murderous intruders and traitorous Verdans, had been delayed. He and his men had been prepared to march and engage in battle, but they had been ordered to wait.

At dawn the day before, he received a communique from High Seer Yseni that she and other select Seers wished to observe the elimination of the intruders and orchestrate arrests of Verdans where necessary.

A shout from behind him drew his attention. Wojaht whirled to see what the commotion was about. “Captain Gafla, sir, the Seers have arrived,” said a breathless Lt. Uson Stadova as he sprinted up to his superior officer and saluted.

“About time they honored us with their presence,” Wojaht snarled. His heart was racing in anticipation of this dangerous mission, and these women were slowing him down. “Stadova, alert the other lieutenants. Tell them to have their men ready to march within the hour. Let's get this mission under way.”

All the way back to his tent, Wojaht shouted commands for his troops to be armed and ready. Half the encampment was preparing to march before the other junior officers received their orders.

Out of the corner of his eye, Wojaht watched as the delegation of Seers was escorted to his tent. Ignoring the women momentarily, he continued talking to a group of lieutenants until he was satisfied they understood his orders.

"High Seer, I trust you are well," the captain said nodding brusquely, far different from his usual ceremonial bow from the waist. "My men will be ready within the hour. You and the other Seers should take positions behind the strike force for your protection. Lieutenant, please escort our guests to a place of safety," he said to Uson who had just scurried over.

Without waiting for her reply or dismissal, he nodded again and disappeared into his tent to prepare for the march, leaving a very nervous Uson to face the Seers alone. Yseni stood with a look of shock. She had been expecting the captain's usual groveling, but being treated with such disrespect unnerved her.

Zasha touched the High Seer's shoulder. "Ah, so now we see the mood of our troops before they go into battle. He and the others are anxious to engage the enemy. Can you blame them?"

Yseni frowned, but nodded in agreement. "You may escort us to our positions," she said coldly to Uson, who bowed so deeply his nose almost touched his boots.

After a hard two-hour ride at full gallop, Wojaht and his men pulled to within sight of Osmar Nezdan's village. The captain signaled for the troop to stop and rest. While the captain was taking a long gulp of water, a worried-looking Uson approached with the three scouts who had been watching the village for the past two days.

"Yes, Lieutenant, what have our scouts found? Are the intruders still in the village?" Wojaht asked while wiping his mouth across his sleeve.

Uson cleared his throat. "Ah, Captain, it seems the population of the village seems to have at least doubled. The scouts report many riders have arrived within the past two days. With all the commotion they cannot tell if the intruders are still in the village."

Wojaht shook his head in disbelief and pointed at one of the scouts. “Are you saying the village has received reinforcements? From where? Who are they?”

The scout saluted. “Sir, it appears many of the riders are Enforcers by their uniforms. They have taken up positions around the village.”

The captain stared in disbelief at what he just heard. “Enforcers in the village? Why would they be here?” Wojaht shouted, his face flushing with anger. This was an unbelievable revelation. Enforcers had never challenged Tarylan guards in carrying out their duties.

Only in a rare instance would an Enforcer confront a Tarylan guard, such as in a drunken brawl where Verdan citizens were injured or property was damaged.

“Renegades. That's it. They must be renegades,” Wojaht said. “Someone in the village must be related to a few officers or bribed them.” Turning to Uson, the captain ordered him to find out who was leading the enforcers.

The lieutenant shook his head. “No need, sir, we already know. Commander Kaj Striff is in charge.”

Wojaht stood dumbfounded with his mouth open. “Are you telling me the commander of the entire Verdan Enforcer division is leading those traitors?” he hissed.

The veins in the captain's neck bulged ominously, looking like they would explode at any moment. “Striff, eh? I might have known he would turn traitor. He's taken every opportunity to challenge Tarylan jurisdiction since he was appointed commander.”

Wojaht remembered with irritation the arrest of two Tarylans — Eret Drumlin and Yev Serrat — who had raped an innkeeper's daughter. Striff had led the investigation and arrest of the two men.

The Tarylans were tried and sentenced to death by civil Verdan court. Only a reprieve by the Seers carried out by Capt. Agusto Harn had spared the two men. For some reason unknown to Wojaht, his fellow captain had requested the killers for Harn's now ill-fated mission.

When Striff had discovered the reprieve, he had lodged a formal complaint, with the blessing of a Verdan Councilliary, to the Seers. Of course the High Council of Seers had rejected the commander's complaint and reprimanded him and the Assembly for challenging their ruling.

"Mother Verde, is Striff trying to take vengeance for being humiliated in public?" Wojaht muttered. "What a fool. The commander now will have more to contend with than being embarrassed."

Now that he had time to assess the situation, the captain flashed a sly smile. "Lt. Stadova, please inform the High Seer and her companions that their assistance is needed with a problem."

Within a few minutes, Yseni and Zasha listened with disbelief as Wojaht explained the situation with the village. "They are all traitors. Can't you just attack and wipe them out?" Yseni demanded.

The captain threw up his arms. "If it were that simple, yes, High Seer. But we seem to be outnumbered now, counting the Enforcers, intruders, and who knows how many villagers will offer resistance."

Yseni turned to Zasha, who for once only shook her head in disbelief. She whirled around and addressed her officer. "You are the military leader here, Captain. Do you have any suggestions?"

Wojaht smiled. "Yes, I do High Seer. I think we should request a truce to speak with Commander Striff and even the village leaders."

Yseni frowned. "What would that accomplish?"

The captain's laughter startled Yseni and Zasha, who exchanged nervous glances. "With all due respect, High Seer, you seem to have forgotten your influence on these simple Verdans. A severe reprimand on your part or threat of extraordinary punishment may drive a wedge between these factions."

Yseni smiled and was about to speak when another scout sprinted into their midst and conferred with Lt. Stadova.

"Well, what is it?" Wojaht demanded.

Per protocol, Uson bowed to the Seers then saluted his captain. “Sir, Commander Striff and the village elders have requested a truce. They are willing to meet immediately.”

Wojaht slapped his side, grinning widely. “Ha, the cowards are already prepared to beg for their lives.” With the High Seer's approval, the captain ordered Uson to arrange the meeting.

19

Much to the amazement of the Seers and Capt. Wojaht Gafla, a large tent had been pitched. Inside, two rows of parallel wooden tables ran the length of the tent, only separated by a few meters.

It was not the accommodations, but who was waiting that stunned the Tarylan party. Instead of a ragtag collection of simple villagers and the suspicious intruders, lining the table was an assemblage of the most respected citizens of Verdan society.

The Tarylans were greeted by five members of the Assembly, as well as Osmar Nezdan, Rajeev Nezdan, what looked to be several village elders, Nuvens Raaf Vonn and Juban Caleria, Enforcer Commander Kaj Striff, trooper Hubart Avery, and the most unnerving — three truth-sayers.

Even the usually unflappable Seer Zasha looked shocked. High Seer Yseni fought to keep herself from gasping like a frightened youngling. The seated party rose in unison and bowed as the Seers and Wojaht entered the tent. This gesture calmed Yseni for the moment as she and her entourage took their seats at the opposite table.

The High Seer took her time as she and the others were waited on with goblets of cool water. Her thoughts raced wildly. Such a confrontation was unheard of in Verdan society. She studied her fellow Verdans who sat across from her. Much to her dismay, they showed no fear.

"What is the meaning of your presence here? You are interfering with Tarylan business by my orders," Yseni snapped, hoping to unnerve a few of the others. "If you withdraw now and turn over the intruders to Capt. Gafla, I may be persuaded not to seek retribution."

Judge Soretti rose from her chair. "With all due respect, High Seer, we ask that you halt your actions against the Nuvens. After hearing testimony from these visitors, which has been verified by truth-sayers, the Assembly unanimously agrees our visitors are the children of the lost ones. It is our duty to welcome and protect them."

Not waiting for Yseni to answer, Wojaht roared in protest. "These barbarians have attacked and killed fifteen Tarylans. The High Seer has justly ruled what their fate should be."

Commander Striff stood and faced his Tarylan counterpart. "It appears Capt. Harn and his men attacked first, leaving the Nuvens with no choice but to defend themselves. What transpired was a tragic misunderstanding."

Wojaht pounded his fist on the table. "How dare you accuse a decorated Tarylan officer of such an action! You were not there. We have lost fifteen brave men. I am here to mete out justice."

Kaj nodded. "I will grant you thirteen of those men should be justly mourned. However, two in Harn's party were convicted murderers and were about to be executed until the captain mysteriously stopped it."

The Enforcer commander stopped as a wry smile crinkled his lips. "Actually, we should thank our Nuven friends for carrying out this unpleasant duty, which was approved by Verdan law. I am curious Captain, why did Harn need those two men?"

Wojaht's face was bright red with fury now, but he did not have an answer for Kaj. He had not been privy to his friend's orders.

"I do not know why Capt. Harn required their services," Wojaht sputtered. "Perhaps he knew he was going on a dangerous mission and did not want to endanger more good men than necessary."

Trying to gain a foothold in this debate which so far was going disastrously for him, the captain raised what he thought was his most irrefutable argument. “We can all guess what Harn's motives were, but the fact is we were not there and do not know what happened for certain.”

Much to the Tarylan's surprise, Kaj shook his head and smiled. “Ah, Captain, but we do have people here who were there and have given sworn testimony validated by a quorum of truth-sayers. Even our respected Seers are bound to honor such a judgment.”

At Yseni's signal, Wojaht slumped back to his seat, but he continued glaring at the Enforcer commander. Kaj stared back with equal distaste until the Tarylan officer finally looked away in frustration. Yseni was gathering her thoughts to speak when one of the truth-sayers stood.

“With all due respect, High Seer, we understand the survivor of the skirmish at the grove is recuperating at Fortress Bryann. Perhaps a truth-sayer could talk to him and determine if there are discrepancies in the Nuvens' story.”

Yseni's throat tightened with fright at that proposal. Even the Seers with all their power and privilege were duty bound to abide by a determination of a truth-sayer judgment. *Damn that agreement our great grandmothers signed*, the High Seer thought.

All those harvests ago, the High Council of Seers agreed to comply by any decision reached by truth-sayers. In exchange, the truth-sayers promised never to reveal their distant cousins' secret — the gift of the sight.

Sensing her friend's predicament, Zasha arose. “We appreciate your kind offer, truth-sayer, but the young man has suffered such a serious wound that he continues to wander in and out of consciousness. Unfortunately, during his lucid moments, he has been unable to recall what happened at the grove.”

The truth-sayer studied Zasha for a moment. A slight inflection in the Seer's voice and ever-so-slight eye dilation interested her. “I see, Seer Zasha. I would be honored if you would allow me to verify your statement.”

A cold chill swept through the Seer, but Zasha forced herself to smile. "That will be unnecessary. My word has never been challenged. I believe I have not been called to judgment. I am only stating the situation as I know it."

Showing no emotion, even though she noted even more dramatic dilation and voice distortion, the truth-sayer bowed. "As you wish, Seer Zasha."

Yseni had had enough of her plans being thwarted. She stood with her usual dignified air. "As I recall, truth-sayers can only determine what their subjects believe to be true. Am I not correct?"

Zasha smiled. Many did not realize the High Seer was a clever debater. Judge Soretti and the truth-sayer nodded.

"Our Seers have not felt the presence of the lost ones for many years," Yseni said, giving only a slight hint of the Seers' abilities. "It is our opinion the colonists in the other valley were wiped out centuries ago by the Tanlians — the same ones who attacked the first Verdan landing party, which was rescued by the sainted one and our ancestor, Taryl Bryann."

At the mention of the "sainted" one's name, all the Seers kissed the palms of their right hands and covered their hearts.

Rajeev had been translating all that was said to Raaf and Juban. He raised his eyebrows in surprise at what Yseni had said, but repeated her statement word for word.

Raaf sprang up and pounded the table in anger. "She lies! This woman lies! My ancestors came from the same sky ship that brought you here, too," he shouted in Nuven.

Rajeev coughed nervously, but translated what Raaf had said. The professor gently put a hand on the Nuven's shoulder to guide him back to his seat, but the young man refused.

Yseni smiled patiently as she gestured toward Raaf. "Our Seers believe the Tanlians were stranded in your valley many generations ago. They wiped out most of the lost ones, but spared a few of the women. After many generations, these Nuvens, as they call them themselves, took up the belief their ancestors came from the Earth sky ship. That is why we sent Capt. Harn and his squad to investigate, because we were wary of their intentions."

Yseni clucked sympathetically as Juban and Rajeev fought to restrain Raaf from making another outburst.

"As you can see, these young men honestly believe they are descended from the lost ones, but most of their bloodlines come from those blood-thirsty marauders. And look what they did to poor Capt. Harn and his men. They probably misunderstood a harmless gesture and killed our Tarylans."

Yseni paused and stole a quick glance at those across from her. Encouraged by the looks of doubt that shadowed some of their faces, she sat back down with a regal air.

After a long, uncomfortable pause, Judge Soretti addressed the group. "The High Seer's statement gives us much to contemplate. However, she said the Seers 'believe' these events had happened. Without facts or historical records, any case will be difficult to prove. I also am encouraged that the Seers believe the Nuvens to be descended from female ancestors of the lost ones. Therefore they are indeed children of the lost ones, despite the question of their male ancestors."

Despite Yseni's skill as a debater, Judge Soretti was regarded as possessing the finest mind in Verdan society. The other Verdans were smiling and nodding at what they considered to be legal, according to their law — relation through any lineage was acceptable.

Yseni could not believe what she had just heard. The High Seer had just delivered the performance of her life only to be undermined by a legal interpretation.

Sensing she was losing her argument, Yseni formulated a desperate plot. Rising, she gestured for her party to follow her lead. "Ah, Judge Soretti, I appreciate your wisdom. I ask our hosts' permission to allow us to reflect and discuss what we have heard. May I suggest a half hour?" Seeing no objections, Judge Soretti granted the recess.

Once outside the tent and well away from the others, Yseni called a still-fuming Wojaht to her side. "Captain, are you still loyal to your Tarylan oath?"

Wojaht bowed. “Of course, High Seer. I am your servant, as are the men who follow me.”

Yseni sighed with relief. “It is a joy to find a loyal Verdan. Now, Captain, what we do here will determine the destiny of Verde. My orders will sound unusually harsh, but difficult decisions must be made today.”

Wojaht bowed. “I will carry out your orders to the best of my ability.”

The High Seer smiled like a proud mother. “Good. Now listen to me well. I want your men to attack this tent and kill everyone in it but the Seers.”

The captain stared in disbelief, trying to comprehend what he had just heard. “But High Seer we all came under a parlay truce. By Verdan law, everyone is guaranteed to be protected.”

Yseni grabbed him by the collar and pulled him nose to nose with her. “We Seers are the Verdan law. The others will endanger our society by allowing those intruders safe passage. Do not fear any repercussions. We will blame the Nuvens. We will say they became enraged by our decision and attacked the others.”

Wojaht felt sick to his stomach, but said nothing as he listened to Yseni's plot.

“Make sure that bothersome Commander Striff is killed,” she said. “If we are lucky, his fellow Enforcers will feel compelled to avenge him. If not, kill his men during the confusion. Go now. I will make an excuse. Perhaps I will say you are telling your men to stand down and are preparing to return to Fortress Bryann.”

Wojaht nodded. “I will do as ordered, High Seer, but how can we ensure you and the other Seers will not be harmed during the attack?”

Yseni paused, then smiled. “Call out Agusto Harn's name loudly when you attack. That will be the signal for the others and myself to take shelter.”

For the first time in many hours, the captain smiled. “With pleasure, High Seer.”

20

Wojaht Gafla did not divulge the goal of the terrible mission to the Tarylan troopers or even to his four lieutenants. The captain did not want to give his men too much time to think about the ramifications of breaking Verdan law and turning them into murderers.

Sergeant Onji Haiko listened with great interest, but did not find fault with falling into ranks to form an honor guard for the Seers according to the captain's orders. Thinking a peaceful solution must have been reached, Onji saddled up with his fellow troopers and rode toward the tent. When the Tarylan strike force reached within a half kilometer of the parlay tent, Wojaht ordered his men to halt. He turned and faced his troopers with a determined look.

"Fellow Tarylans, what we do here today will be an act of great importance and necessity. The future of Verde Valley lies in our hands. I demand your full obedience."

Onji scowled as he leaned forward on his mount. He sensed something was very wrong. These were not the orders for an honor guard. The captain rode up and down the ranks, looking each man in the eye. He paused briefly when he passed Onji. The sergeant sported a strange expression, but Wojaht was too caught up in the moment to bother with this underling.

Returning to front and center before his men, Wojaht delivered his orders. "Men, we have been searching for the killers of Capt. Agusto Harn and his men for weeks now. Well, we have found them and the traitors who protect them. On this day, the Seers are entrusting us to protect our fellow Verdans and avenge our murdered comrades. We need to act now or we may never get such a chance to kill our enemies gathered in one spot."

Wojaht raised his hand. "Prepare your weapons. On my signal, we will attack the tent and kill everyone in it but the Seers. The High Seer and her party will seek protection under the tables."

The captain had turned his horse and was preparing to lead his men toward the tent when he was startled by a voice calling from the ranks. "Captain, sir, I request to speak."

Wojaht whirled around and shouted, "Who dares this outrage?"

Onji slowly guided his mount out of the ranks. "Sir, I request to know if Trooper Hubart Avery is in that tent."

The captain was startled by the sergeant's audacity. "Yes, Avery and other Verdan traitors await us in the tent, including two of those murderous Nuvens," Wojaht said, frowning. "We have been ordered to eliminate all the enemies of Verde. Now fall back in rank, Sergeant, or you will lose all your privileges."

A somber Onji regarded his officer for a moment then unstrapped his javelin pouch from his back and let it fall to the ground. "Sir, I do not believe Trooper Avery or the other Verdans to be traitors. I cannot carry out your orders. Effective immediately I am resigning from the Tarylan Guard."

The veteran of seventeen harvests of Tarylan duty knew his rights. By law, a guardsman could not be punished if he resigned. Onji turned his horse, rode off a short distance, and waited.

Before a shocked Wojaht could respond, the majority of his troops also dropped their javelin bundles and announced their resignations. They parted ranks and joined Onji. The captain was stunned beyond words. He spun around to see who was left in his strike force.

Only fifteen young and very nervous-looking troopers remained, including his four lieutenants. All the veterans had left to join Onji. Such a mass resignation during active duty had never occurred in recent memory. Wojaht felt helpless and abandoned.

Even in this desperate moment, the captain knew these troopers were within their rights to voluntarily leave when they wished. Resignations were rare among young and healthy Tarylans. Realizing he could no longer threaten these men, Wojaht frantically tried another tactic.

“Men, I understand your reluctance, but the Seers have assured me this unpleasant task must be done to secure the safety of our fellow Verdans. If you rejoin our ranks, I promise all of you will be rewarded with extra pay and privileges.”

Onji took a quick survey of his companions. No one flinched. “I'm sorry, Captain, but we have made our decision. We will not take part in this business.”

Without waiting for Wojhat's response, Onji and the others turned their horses away from the strike force and left for home.

Feeling furious and betrayed, the captain screamed after them, “Traitors! You are all traitors. I will see you are punished for your cowardice.”

Onji stopped and spun his mount around to face his former officer. “Captain, if you call me and my brothers cowards again, I will challenge you to a formal duel. As a Verdan citizen, that is my right. I don't think you are willing to fight me, Wojaht Gafla!”

The stunned captain smoldered, but said nothing else as he watched his former troopers make their exit.

¶ ¶ ¶

Before re-entering the tent, Yseni gathered the other Seers around her. “I have arranged with Capt. Gafla to take care of this troublesome situation.” Zasha, unaware of what had been planned, cast a suspicious glance at her friend.

“I cannot allow these murderous Nuvens and traitorous Verdans to flaunt our laws and threaten our society,” Yseni said in a hushed but threatening tone. “Be warned. Gafla is coming with his men to remedy this problem. Take protection under the tables when you hear Agusto Harn's name called out."

Zasha shook her head at the High Seer's audacity, but dared not challenge Yseni in front of the other women. She gestured toward the tent. "What do we do say to them until our troopers arrive?"

Yseni smiled. "Why, I intend to give them everything they ask for in the spirit of reconciliation. Do not be surprised at what transpires in there. It will be meaningless very shortly."

With a flourish, the High Seer whirled around and marched toward the tent, confident her plan would work. Zasha's stomach churned nervously as she and the other Seers followed their leader inside.

As before, the Verdans and Nuvens stood and bowed as the Seers took their seats. Yseni smiled benevolently and raised her hand, the formal gesture in Verdan society when one asks permission to speak. A surprised Judge Soretti glanced around the table, then granted the High Seer permission.

"I first must apologize for the absence of Captain Gafla," she said. "I felt his presence was an obstacle to negotiating a peaceful settlement. He has returned to his men while they prepare to stand down."

Seeing the expressions of surprise across the table, Yseni paused for dramatic effect. "The other Seers and I were very impressed with your eloquent arguments and moved by the passion of your beliefs. We now are convinced the Nuvens' intentions were misunderstood and acknowledge them as the children of the lost ones."

Rajeev gasped, not quite believing what he had just heard. However, he continued translating to Raaf and Juban, whose smiles grew wider and wider as they understood what had just transpired.

"This is most gratifying news, High Seer," Judge Soretti said smiling. "I cannot speak for the others, but I am greatly relieved and grateful for the wisdom you have demonstrated." Without any prompting, the other Verdans let loose with a chorus of cheerful ayes.

Zasha was impressed by the High Seer's performance. It appeared the others were falling fully into Yseni's trap. Everyone but the truth-sayers were smiling warmly. She noticed all three showed no emotion, but stared at the High Seer. Watching those women made her uneasy.

I will not mourn those witches when Gafla's men cut them down, Zasha thought, smiling genuinely for the first time. Seeing the Seer's reaction, one of the younger truth-sayers looked surprised, then smiled back. Zasha had to fight to keep from laughing at the other woman.

"You asked us here to negotiate," Yseni said. "You will find we will be most accommodating."

Judge Soretti carefully unrolled a scroll. "We respectfully ask the High Seer and her council to consider these requests."

Yseni encouraged her to continue. "Please read them."

The judge nodded and began. "The Nuvens offer their sincere apologies for the loss of your troopers and ask for cessation of hostilities by the Tarylans."

The High Seer bowed toward Raaf and Juban. "We accept their apology and so order all hostilities to cease."

Judge Soretti continued. "After Raaf and his party return to their valley, they believe many Nuvens will wish to cross the mountain to settle in Verde Valley. They want your blessing to do so."

Yseni looked up and down the row at her council members. Of course as puppets, the other Seers readily endorsed the Nuven request. "We gladly give our blessings to welcome the children of the lost ones."

Judge Soretti read the last request. "Once settled in Verde Valley, the Nuvens wish to be considered Verdan citizens with all the rights and privileges."

By now, Yseni had been hoping to hear Wojaht's signal, alerting her and the other Seers to take shelter. She was growing anxious for the bloody solution to their troubles to begin. Yseni shrugged. "This request should be considered by the Verdan Assembly, not just the High Council of Seers."

Judge Soretti smiled. "The Assembly already has approved the request."

Trying to mask her irritation, the High Seer again surveyed her council, who agreed without argument. "Ah, wonderful, we are in agreement then," Yseni purred. "I will be most anxious to properly greet the Nuvens who choose to settle here. They will be a welcome addition to Verde Valley."

An ecstatic Juban stood up to speak. "Please forgive my clumsy Verdan talk. My fellow Nuvens wish to thank the Verdans who help us. We are grateful for the most kind blessings by the Seers. We are, ah, happy not to fight your warriors."

Juban looked to Rajeev for approval. Before the professor could respond, however, the Verdans at his table erupted into hearty applause. Not to create suspicion, even the Seers politely clapped.

"Wonderful, wonderful. That was most gracious," Yseni said, doing her best to smile at Juban. She kept waiting to hear Wojaht's alarm, but nothing came. "Well, what is next?" the High Seer asked.

Judge Soretti stood and handed a scroll to an aide. "This is the agreement I have just read and you have agreed to. The Verdan Assembly has signed it and we request the signatures of the High Seer Council to make it binding."

Stalling for time, Zasha asked to study the document. After several minutes, she handed the document to Yseni, who also took her time reading it. With still no sign from Wojaht and her heart beating so hard from anticipation, the High Seer tried to keep her hand from trembling as she signed the document, then passed it among her council members. Each Seer took her time signing, but the Tarylan troopers never appeared. After the scroll was handed back, the other Verdans and Nuvens started to personally thank the Seers.

Sensing her leader was about to explode in a rage, Zasha begged for their understanding. "It has been a most momentous occasion and indeed a taxing day," she said, trying to mask her disappointment. "Please forgive us, but we require time to rest and meditate. There will be another day to celebrate what we have accomplished here."

Barely able to contain her shaking nerves, Yseni nodded to the others, rose, and hurried out of the tent, followed by the other Seers. The High Seer had barely left the tent when she saw a subdued Wojaht Gafla standing alone.

Yseni stomped over to her captain, grabbed him by the collar like a mother with an unruly child and dragged him with her until they were well out of earshot of the tent. Before he could say anything, Yseni released him angrily and slapped him across the cheek with all her strength. The force of the blow made him take a couple of steps backward.

"Where are your men? You were supposed to have attacked the tent long ago," she hissed, still not daring to be heard by the other Verdans.

Wojaht straightened himself, then told her of the mass resignations by Sergeant Haiko and the others. "I beg your forgiveness, High Seer, but only fifteen youngsters and four untested junior officers were left. We would have been barely able to attack the tent, much less take on any Enforcers."

Yseni shook her head violently and strode away with Zasha following closely behind. After several minutes, the High Seer stopped and fell to her knees. Zasha knelt beside her in an attempt to offer comfort.

Rocking back and forth, Yseni looked at her confidante. "Mother Verde, what have I done Zasha? What have I done?" She burst into tears of rage. "I — I have just opened Verde Valley to the people we have worked to seclude from us for two centuries."

21

The Nuvens were not prepared for the throngs of people who welcomed and cheered them in Verde City. News of the agreement, signed by the Verdan Assembly and High Council of Seers, officially welcoming and recognizing the Nuvans as the "lost ones" spread throughout the city faster than salacious gossip during a religious service.

At Osmar Nezdan's suggestion, the Assembly announced that the children of what the Verdans called "the lost ones" would be honored with a parade through Verde City. Osmar thought such a public event would satisfy many Verdans' curiosity about the Nuvens.

Thousands of people would be able to catch a glimpse of the visitors, then would be content to go about their daily lives, allowing Raaf Vonn and the others to explore the Verde Valley in relative peace.

A large open-air carriage, drawn by six giant white horses, carried the Nuvens through Verde City. The streets were full of curious Verdans, sometimes six people deep as the driver carefully maneuvered through the crowd. Young children sat on their fathers' shoulders and older youngsters pushed their way to the front of the line and stared wide-eyed as the Nuvens passed by.

Every Verdan had grown up hearing stories of the lost ones who had sacrificed themselves to the Tanlians when the first colonists landed. Now the descendants of these heroes had miraculously traversed what everyone had believed to be the impassible mountain.

The legend was true. The prophecy was fulfilled. The Nuvens were proof of it. However, the children of the lost ones were feeling anything but heroic during this surreal journey through the strange and wondrous city. The mass of people as far as they could see made the Nuvens nervous and anxious.

Raaf and the others had grown up in relative isolation. Over the generations, their ancestors learned to avoid large groups to avoid making easy targets for the Tanlians, who could attack at any time. The young Nuvens tried to put up a brave front by forcing themselves to smile and wave.

Sensing the visitors did not understand the Verdans' reaction to them, Osmar and his cousin, Rajeev, rode in the carriage to reassure their new friends.

Even poor Darya, usually unflappable and impervious to what went on around her, was terrified by the noise and crowds. She slunk down in the carriage with her hands over her eyes and huddled next to Raaf.

The city was a startling sight. The Nuvens had never seen so many buildings clustered together. Their native shelters were rough affairs, log huts built to blend in among groves of trees and carefully placed well away from other homes. Many Nuvens still lived in the ancestral caves.

"If we are attacked now, there would be nothing we could do to prevent it or defend ourselves," a worried Ganick Nels said, when he caught Raaf's attention.

Noticing the Nuvens' growing agitation, Rajeev tapped Osmar on the shoulder. His cousin, however, was oblivious to the visitors' discomfort. Osmar was relishing his moment of glory. "Cousin, we need to get them out of here now!" Rajeev yelled over the shouts of the crowd.

Osmar gave him a puzzled look, then laughed. "Don't worry so much, cousin. We have waited two hundred years to see the lost ones return to us. We owe a duty to our fellow Verdans."

Rajeev shook his head and looked over his shoulder. Even the affable Juban had stopped waving and was glowering with impatience. Knowing he had to act quickly, the professor leaned over and landed a sharp elbow into Osmar's ribs, making him double over in pain.

"I meant it when I told you we need to get them out of here now!" Rajeev shouted. "Look at them!"

Osmar grimaced, but finally glanced at the Nuvens. He did not need a truth-sayer to tell him the visitors' mood. Leaning over to the driver, Osmar told him to make haste from the street and return to the inn where they were staying. A rider seated next to the driver raised a bugle and blew loudly to alert passers-by to get out of the way of the fast-moving carriage.

"We leave now," Rajeev told a relieved Raaf. Knowing they were escaping the masses of admirers, the Nuvens now smiled and waved.

¶ ¶ ¶

The next morning at first meal, Osmar cheerily informed the Nuvens of the agenda he had arranged for them for the next few days: tours of schools, talks with craftsmen and tradesmen, and numerous banquets with countless Verdan dignitaries, all of whom were posturing to meet them.

Ganick Nels frowned as he listened to the plans. It had been more than a lunar cycle since the Nuvens had arrived in the Verde Valley, and he had spent most of the time inside small cabins hiding from Tarylan troopers or now surrounded by people in this bustling, strange city.

He watched impatiently as his fellow Nuvens shook their heads and graciously accepted the itineraries. "Enough. I have had enough of this," Ganick growled as he stood with arms crossed tightly across his chest. "I have not hunted for weeks. I do not care to see more of their buildings. I want to see the valley."

Raaf started to admonish him, but stopped after seeing the intensity in his circle brother's eyes. He had seen that look many times and knew Ganick could not be persuaded to change his mind.

"Very well, Ganick, but you will need to travel with someone who will see to it you don't get lost," Raaf said. "I am not going to spend needless time searching for you."

Ganick started to protest, but was interrupted by Rajeev. "Now, now, I may have a solution," the professor said in his improving Nuven. He disappeared out the door, but returned quickly with two men by his side.

"These brave Verdans have volunteered to accompany Ganick," Rajeev said with a smile as he presented Hubart Avery and Onji Haiko. The two former Tarylan guardsmen, along with most of the others who had resigned with Onji, had volunteered to be a security detail for the Nuvens.

After hearing of Ganick's request, Hubart and Onji jumped at the chance to hunt with thc Nuven, who had since become their friend.

"We will look after this poor, lost Nuven," Hubart smirked in broken Nuven. He and Onji stood side by side, grinning wickedly.

Ganick laughed. "We will soon see if these city dwellers can keep up with a hunter."

¶ ¶ ¶

The three men hunched over the campfire, snacking on the hare and pheasant that were roasting on the nearby spit. In between mouthfuls, Onji sighed as he rubbed his sore feet. Hubart looked at his friend and nodded in sympathy. He lay stretched out and massaged his sore calf muscles.

Ganick grinned, but said nothing as he munched on the bird's roasted breast. He had demonstrated his archery skill by bagging both with arrows. Seeing the Nuven's amusement, Hubart faked a growl and flung a bone at Ganick, who easily caught it with one hand as he continued his meal.

"Well, Nuven, it looks like you were correct," Hubart said. "It's only been two days, and we can barely keep up with you. Poor Onji has blisters on both feet, and I fear I've pulled something in my leg."

The two Verdans and Nuven had learned enough of each other's dialect that they could understand each other fairly well.

Ganick finished gnawing on the breastbone and tossed it at Hubart, who had to dodge to avoid being struck on the head. "Ah, I know you two are fierce warriors, but I fear you would not be able to keep up with some of the old women in my village," the Nuven said with a smirk.

Onji snorted and glared at Ganick. "Did he just call us old women?"

Hubart shook his head. "Easy, old friend. I think he said old women in his village can move faster than the two of us. It would be difficult to disagree with him."

Ganick shrugged. "Do not feel badly. I understand why Verdans have no need to hunt except for your amusement. You have herds of tame grazers to harvest whenever you need food. Nuvens have to hunt for all our meat and search for fruits and edible plants. Even younglings of six harvests are required to help gather food."

The two Verdans listened with respect and continued their meal. During their short time with Ganick, they had learned much about the hardscrabble life the Nuvens had had to endure. Hubart and Onji were impressed the Nuvens had survived, much less thrived in such difficult circumstances.

Neither man voiced an opinion, but the same thought had occurred to both — would the Verdans have fared as well as the Nuvens under similar circumstances? Even though he had joked with his friends about keeping up with him, Ganick understood the two Verdans needed a rest from the pace they had been keeping.

"Before we made camp for the night, I spotted more terrain I wish to explore tomorrow," the Nuven said. "Perhaps you both would enjoy resting and letting your wounds heal. I would be back before nightfall."

Hubart started to protest, but winced in pain when he moved his leg. Onji grunted and continued rubbing his aching feet.

"As former Taryln troopers, we should be insulted we cannot accompany you," Hubart sighed. "However, reality has taught us a difficult lesson. Enjoy your journey."

Onji scowled. "Be sure you return at nightfall, Nuven, or we will be forced to search for you."

Ganick grinned. "Yes, it would be embarrassing for you both to return home and have to admit you've misplaced one of the children of the lost ones." The two Verdans glared at the Nuven momentarily, then all three men erupted in laughter.

¶ ¶ ¶

Ganick was on his way when first light barely could be seen through the dense tree cover. It felt exhilarating to be on his own. Even though he enjoyed Hubart's and Onji's company, it had been too long since he had enjoyed such joyous solitude.

The Nuven skillfully scrambled over boulders and nimbly jumped over crevasses, much like the mountain goats in his native valley. After about two hours of hard climbing, he perched on the top of an unusually large boulder to refresh himself with a quick sip of water from his canteen.

Ganick closed his eyes, enjoying being bathed in the warm sun. As he started to move from this serene spot, something snorted nearby. The Nuven saw a huge, antlered buck eyeing him from not more than thirty meters away.

The male deer stood on three legs. One of his front legs was raised, partially curled under his body. It was preparing to strike a rock as a warning to other nearby deer.

Ganick wished he could snatch an arrow from his quiver and string it, but he knew the buck would escape before he could raise his bow for a shot. Taking a deep breath, he knew killing such a magnificent beast would be a needless act. Even if he did score a fatal shot, the animal most likely would bolt away from fright and pain.

It would prove to be a difficult task to follow the blood trail and find the carcass. Besides, Ganick had no easy way to carry the meat and he wasn't near a village where the venison could be put to good use.

Calming himself, the Nuven rose from his sitting position. As expected, the buck struck the rock with its raised hoof and bolted a short way off. From experience, Ganick knew the deer would stop and look to see if it was pursued. He quickly leaped to another boulder and sprawled on top of it, lying perfectly still.

The Nuven could see the buck standing between two trees a short distance away. It stared where Ganick had been sitting and then slowly searched the area. After several minutes, the deer walked a few paces, stopped and looked back, then continued this pattern up the mountain.

Ganick only moved when the animal had disappeared from sight. Crouching low, he scurried from boulder to boulder, stopping often to scan the area for the buck. Even though he was barely twenty harvests old, the Nuven was a veteran hunter. He circled around where he had last seen the buck and crept up another large rock.

Ganick broke into a satisfied smile at the sight below him. The buck and four does were peacefully grazing in a small ravine. The vigilant male would stop after every mouthful of forage and check for danger.

The Nuven admired the animals for a while, then realized he needed to move to stretch his aching muscles. Ganick sprang to his feet. As expected, the deer leaped away after seeing the motion from above. Instead of hurrying out of the ravine to safety, the does and buck jumped between two giant boulders and disappeared.

Ganick stared after them, wondering why they chose that route. He scurried over to where he had last seen the deer and saw a large fissure about three meters off the ground. Even the Nuven had to work to scale the incline. Once he had pulled himself up, Ganick found the crack opened up large enough to allow him to walk through it.

A quick glance at the ground told him this was a well-traveled route. Deer feces were everywhere. Some were fresh and others were decaying with age.

Ganick walked through the fissure for a minute or two when he stepped out into the other side and gasped at the view that greeted him. Stretched out before the Nuven was a beautiful little canyon.

Standing at the entrance of the fissure, he estimated the gorge was barely two kilometers wide, but it stretched out beyond his sight. Ganick could see the mountain looming on the other side, but it was a respectable distance away.

The ground on this side was only a short hop down from the fissure. Amazed at his discovery, Ganick explored the canyon. Trees lined a stream than ran the length of the ravine. The remainder of the area was covered by lush grass and wildflowers.

The Nuven smiled as he surveyed the area. After a quick search, he spotted a giant oak in the middle of the canyon. The huge branches made it an easy climb. At almost forty meters high, he stood in the crotch of two limbs and surveyed the area. The canyon was similar to the hundreds of small ravines found in the Nuven Valley.

After climbing down, Ganick moved with a determined purpose. Reaching into a pouch at his side, he pulled out two small bags filled with seeds his father had insisted on giving him before he departed on this adventure.

Kneeling, the Nuven stabbed the ground with one of his knives. The soil that stuck to the blade was black and moist, a good sign.

Ganick spent the remainder of the day stabbing the ground intermittently and sprinkling several seeds from both pouches near each other. He planted the seeds up and down the stream, as well as in choice areas throughout the canyon.

With the sun starting to set, Ganick headed back toward the entrance. With a little luck he would be able to make it back to camp, where Hubart and Onji waited for him, before nightfall. As he started to pass back through the fissure, he turned to admire his discovery one more time.

"What a perfect place to grow my family's honey fruit," he said to himself, then turned and hurried away.

22

Raaf Vonn and the other climbers exchanged wide grins when they successfully navigated Mt. Barrasca's gap and found their way into familiar territory. Even Darya started humming as she recognized the landmarks that meant they were close to home.

Stopping suddenly, Darya turned to her brother, a serious look on her face. After all they'd been through together, the troop stopped as one. They had learned to trust her implicitly, so when she halted, the other Nuvens also stopped.

"What is it, Darya?" Raaf asked. He and the others scanned the area for danger, but saw nothing.

Darya gazed at Raaf. "I miss Mama's cooking. Time to go home." The other Nuvens broke into howls of laughter at her serious announcement. The troop had been gone for almost three lunars, and this was the first time Darya had given any indication she missed home.

Raaf shook his head in disbelief, then playfully mussed his sister's hair. "Yes, Darya, we should be home for last meal. I'm sure Mama and Papa missed you, too — even me."

The happy troop continued their journey at an eager pace. They laughed and joked about the heroes' welcome they would receive when reaching home. They were the first Nuvens to successfully cross Mt. Barrasca, discover the mysteriously hidden gap to Verde Valley, and make contact with the others who, until now, only existed in legend.

Only now did the troop realize the magnitude of their achievement. The members chatted excitedly about the opportunities of a wonderful new life in the peaceful, bountiful Verde Valley. Knowing their fellow Nuvens would demand proof of their adventure, the troop had agreed the best way to convince their people was to present them with live examples — two young Verdans, who had eagerly volunteered to make the trek back home with them. No Nuven climbing party had ever returned from an attempted climb of Barrasca with more members than it set out with.

The climbers were traveling at a steady pace, a bit slow for the Nuvens, but grueling for the inexperienced Verdans, when they reached the mourning rock. The giant pinnacle had an unusually flat surface. The names of climbers who never returned were etched into it.

When they stopped to pay their respects, according to tradition, Juban Caleria cried out in surprise. "Oh no, look at the newest names on the rock. They think we died on the mountain!"

The climbers quickly gathered and gazed where Juban was pointing. All their names were freshly etched into the surface. At the base of the rock were flowers and memorabilia of each climber.

"They think we're dead, but we left them messages along the route that we found," Juban groaned as he sifted through the personal items left by their families. "My favorite hunting knife. They left this to honor me."

Darya recognized her drawing of the bee on the flower, the last one she finished before embarking on the climb. She held it up and looked at Raaf, puzzled. "This is mine. Why is it here?"

Her brother patted her shoulder, "Mama and Papa left this as a gift."

Darya shrugged. "I not understand," but she put it back exactly where it had been placed.

Raaf looked at the others. "We have to hurry back. Our families think we're dead. I can't imagine their grief." Without pausing, he barked out orders. "Ganick, we need someone to guide our Verdan friends and keep an eye on Darya while the rest of us make haste back to the village."

Ganick Nels started to protest, but stopped. He understood the Verdans and Darya could not keep up with the frantic pace Raaf and the others would maintain while they raced back home.

"Agreed," he said with a nod. "We will travel as fast as possible. May the ancestors protect you."

Raaf took Darya gently by the face, so she would look at him. "Ganick will bring you home. I have to hurry back."

Darya smiled. Satisfied that she understood, Raaf turned and left with the other Nuvens at a hunter's sprint. The Verdans were amazed at how quickly Raaf and the others disappeared into the forest line. They apologized to Ganick for slowing him.

"It is an honor to protect and guide you to our home village," he said, gesturing for them to continue their journey.

¶ ¶ ¶

Raaf and the others kept up a steady but quick pace through the forest as they hurried home. He envisioned shouts of relief and tears of joy from the villagers when they finally greeted them. However, as the troop crested the last ridge that led to the village, they stopped and gazed with horror at the sight of dozens of smoke plumes snaking into the sky. Breathing heavily from their trek, the troop stared wide-eyed at the scene.

"That, that can't be funeral pyres for us, there's too many," Juban stammered.

Still gasping for air, Raaf wiped the sweat from his face, took a quick gulp from his canteen, and sprinted at full speed toward the village with the others on his heels. The troop was moving so quickly, a lookout did not recognize the running men and blew his alarm horn. Nearby, a woman screamed in fright. "Intruders!"

Not wanting to cause a panic, Raaf halted, tried to catch his breath, and called out the village welcome. Before the signal was barely out of his mouth, ten men with drawn knives surrounded the troop. Instinctively, Raaf and his troop held out their hands to show they carried no weapons. The other men advanced cautiously.

Finally, a voice called out. "Look! It's the climbers! They've returned!" Shouts of greetings filled the air as Raaf and his troop were surrounded and thumped on their backs by the well-wishers.

Raaf grasped one of the other men on the shoulder. "What happened here? Why are there so many funeral pyres?"

Sakir Purvill shook his head sadly. "Tanlians. It was the worst attack I've ever seen. They dropped explosives in many of the villages. Hundreds were killed. However, many of us were able to escape to safety in the caves. When they landed to harvest the survivors, we surprised and killed many of them. Only a few escaped back to their ships."

Raaf stared in disbelief. "Tanlians did this? We should have been here to help."

Sakir shook his head. "You cannot change the past. Many are still alive. We are Nuvens. We always survive. But what of you and your troop? Did you get lost?"

Raaf started to answer when he was interrupted by a screaming woman running toward him with her arms held out.

"Oh, the ancestors, you are alive!" Marna cried, hugging her son so tightly he could barely breathe. After a few moments, she looked around. Fearing the worst, she grabbed his arms. "Where is Darya? Why isn't she with you?"

Raaf calmed her with a hug. "Darya will be here soon. She is coming with the others. We saw our names on the mourning rock so a few of us rushed home."

Other hysterical shouts of joy were heard as relieved parents welcomed the climbers home.

Raaf grinned as he watched, then looked around. "Where's Papa?" The color melted from Marna's face. She hugged her son and wept bitterly.

Sakir patted Raaf's shoulder. "Your father died fighting the attackers. He saved a group of young girls from being dragged into a collector ship and killed three Tanlians while doing it."

Raaf sunk to his knees, sobbing. Of all the people he wanted to tell of his triumph, his father would have been the proudest.

Marna stroked her son's thick curly hair. "What happened to you and the others? We gave you up for dead."

Raaf wiped away tears as he looked at his mother. "We did it. We crossed the mountain. Darya somehow could see through the fog, and we all followed. We found the others, Mama. They are waiting for us in a beautiful, peaceful valley."

23

Yseni scowled as she read the report. The numbers of Nuvens pouring into Verde Valley was startling, much more than even the most pessimistic of predictions. “Can this be correct?” the High Seer growled as she tossed the parchment in disgust on her table. “It won’t be long until they equal the Verdan population.”

The nervous Tarylan guard shifted on his feet. He was not accustomed to being scolded by the most powerful woman on Verde. “By all accounts this is just an estimate because groups of Nuvens scatter quickly into unsettled areas as soon as they enter the great valley,” he said.

Yseni looked up; her mood looked even darker. “What do you mean by estimate?”

The guard winced as if he had just been whipped. “It’s hard to count them all,” he murmured. “They pass through at all hours of the day and night. We, ah, we feel there could be many more than this number.”

The High Seer stood up and angrily gestured for the man to leave, which he gladly obeyed after a quick perfunctory bow. Yseni leaned down on the table and took another look at the startling numbers.

“Well, are you going to tell me how many Nuvens we have welcomed to the valley?” Seer Zasha asked as she watched her friend’s cheeks flush with anger.

Yseni glared at the other woman, but said nothing. She slid the parchment down the table for Zasha to read.

"My goodness, these accounts vary," Zasha said as she scanned the report. "So it could be anywhere from five thousand to seven thousand with hundreds more arriving every day. I had no idea there would be so many."

The High Seer stomped around her room in frustration. She was not afraid to show her displeasure in front of her childhood friend. "They are like insects swarming to rotten fruit," Yseni snapped. "It won't be long before there are no Nuvens left in the hunter valley."

Zasha tried to comfort the High Seer. "That's not what I am hearing, Yseni. The Tarylan guards we have stationed at the mouth of the gap to 'welcome' the Nuvens have told us many hunters have chosen to stay in their valley."

Yseni just shook her head. "The Tanlians will grow discouraged with much fewer hard-to-find hunters scattered through the mountains. I fear their curiosity will eventually lead them here despite our best efforts to stop them."

Zasha sighed, knowing her report would only darken Yseni's mood. The High Seer glanced momentarily at the other woman then remembered why she was there. "Ah, forgive me, Zasha. I was too upset by the migration numbers. I forgot about your convert report. At least with all these new people, there will more to worship Mother Verde."

Zasha dreaded the expected reaction. Even though she had known Yseni all her life, the woman was still the High Seer and prone to violent mood swings.

She spoke soothingly, hoping her tone would soften the message. "It appears the Nuvens are as adamant about their ancestor worship as we are about Mother Verde. So far, less than a hundred have indicated any interest in converting."

The High Seer turned and glared at Zasha. "Out with it. How many are there? You have never been reluctant to tell me the truth."

Zasha tried to prepare herself for the ensuing storm of emotion that was about to erupt. “To date, thirty-seven have committed their lives to Mother Verde.”

Yseni was struck speechless — quite the opposite reaction Zasha had been expecting. She shuffled toward her chair and slumped down. “The Nuvens have been escaping here for six lunars now and only thirty-seven are converting to worship Mother Verde? This is the best you and the other elder Seers have been able to accomplish?”

Zasha shrugged. “You cannot force a conversion. Most of the Nuvens are very proud of their heritage and protective of their beliefs. The few we’ve been able to convince are craftsmen who are interested in trading with us. I suspect their intentions are based on improving their lot in life rather than a change in belief.”

Yseni covered her face in her hands and moaned. “I knew it was a mistake to allow those first Nuvens who found us to return alive. Our way of life will be threatened by those pagans as well as the Tanlians who will come looking for them.”

¶ ¶ ¶

No smiles were evident as the High Council of Seers stared at the construction site. The walls of a temple were taking shape from the giant slabs of rock being placed with great expertise by Nuven stonemasons with the eager help of Verdan workers.

“How long has this been going on?” Yseni asked the captain of the Tarylan guards.

The man shrugged. “About five lunars, perhaps a bit longer.”

The High Seer frowned as she stood with her hands on her hips, then she snapped, “Bring me the Verdan foreman now.”

Daman Bafer and another man approached the group of Seers. “What an honor it is to see the High Council of Seers. How can I be of service?” Daman, the Verdan, said while bowing.

Yseni waved him over. “The High Council was not aware another temple to Mother Verde was being built. Why were we not consulted?" she asked, her eyes glinting with displeasure. "Who is this Nuven?"

Daman was surprised at her tone. Only now, as he looked from Seer to Seer, did he notice the women were not admiring the activity. "Forgive me, High Seer, but we are not building a temple in honor of Mother Verde. The Nuvens have asked for help to build a temple where they can worship their ancestors in peace and feel safe from the marauders who they say have been attacking them for generations."

Daman gestured for the other man to join them. "High Seer, it is my honor to introduce Cantero Bergmann, the most gifted stonemason I have ever worked with. I am told his ancestor helped save the Nuvens from the marauders after they were separated from the first colonists."

Cantero, a small man with wide muscular shoulders, gave a slight bow. He regarded the Seers for a moment then turned to survey the flurry of workers. Pride shown in his strange blue-green eyes at the progress being made.

"The other Verdans and I tried to tell the Nuvens we have never seen these Tanlians they are so fearful of, but were honored they asked us for our help," Daman said. "We Verdans are whole now that the lost ones have returned to us. The prophecy has come true. It is our duty to help them."

Yseni stared at Daman, but he looked back at her with the confidence of one who believes in his mission. The High Seer gave a slight nod to acknowledge what he had told her. "Ah yes, the prophecy. Of course the High Council and I are delighted the prophecy has been fulfilled. Thank you for your time, foreman. And, thank your friend for his efforts."

Relieved at being dismissed, Daman thanked them for their attention and gestured for Cantero to follow him back to the work site. The Verdan was puzzled by the Seers' curious reaction, but did not let it bother him as he and his Nuven friend returned to the important task.

Zasha shook her head as she approached Yseni. "I see the story hasn't died despite our best efforts."

The High Seer snorted with disgust. "We have protected our people for two centuries now, but they still have clung to that ridiculous myth that the lost ones from the colony ship that brought us to Verde would rejoin us."

Zasha held up her hands in a helpless gesture. "As much as we dislike the latest events, it appears the prophecy has come true."

Yseni was about to snap back a retort when she noticed one of the Tarylan guards standing by himself. The young man stood with his arms crossed. He glowered with a simmering anger as he watched the building of the Nuven temple.

"Who is that Tarylan? He looks familiar." she asked.

Zasha smiled. "He is probably the only Verdan who hates the Nuvens more than you. Remember? That is Vitor Pratern, the lone guard who survived the skirmish with those first Nuvens who found their way to our valley."

The High Seer nodded as she remembered the troop she had ordered to intercept and kill the Nuven climbers before they could contact the Verdan population. However, the Nuvens proved to be fierce fighters. Of the sixteen Tarylans who attacked the newcomers, only Vitor survived.

He was knocked unconscious by a blow to the head during the struggle. The Nuvens decided not to kill the thin, harmless-looking youth, but carried him to a nearby village to be cared for.

A sly smile curled on Yseni's lips as she walked over to Vitor. The Tarylan was so entranced in the activities he did not notice her presence. "I am not pleased with what is happening here," the High Seer whispered in his ear.

Startled from his brooding thoughts, Vitor bowed and mumbled an apology for not seeing her. But Yseni clucked at him sympathetically. "No need for that, my courageous Vitor. It appears we are of the same mind regarding the newcomers."

Vitor blushed at the attention. He was honored the High Seer knew his name, much less took the time to speak with him. "Yes, High Seer. I am troubled at seeing these people."

Yseni smiled. "You have permission to speak freely. I am eager to find brave Tarylans who might be willing to help with the problem of these invaders." Her words acted as a key to the door holding back his emotions.

"These vermin should not be allowed to be here," Vitor said, his lips curling into a snarl. "They dishonor Mother Verde with their strange religion." He looked at Yseni. "How may I help you, High Seer?"

Yseni sighed. "If only there were more Verdans who felt as you do. Perhaps we could persuade these Nuvens to return to their accursed valley."

Seeing she was serious, he bowed. "I know of many Verdans who believe as I do. We feel these Nuvens threaten our way of life. They do not respect us or our ways."

The High Seer stroked his hair and ran a finger across the half-moon scar on his forehead. "My grandmother told me stories of the Sankari, heroes from the old Earth country of Finland, that would right the wrongs done to their people. Go, young Vitor, and find as many brave Sankari as you can convince to follow you. But do it secretly. I fear too many Verdans will not understand the importance of our cause. The High Council would support such warriors if they could be found."

Vitor trembled at her touch and words. Much to her surprise and delight, he grasped her hand and kissed it. "I pledge my life to this cause, High Seer," he said dropping to one knee.

24

The village elders gazed at the sad sight of the three slain children stretched out before them. They looked peaceful, almost as if they were in a deep sleep, but these young Nuvens would never awaken.

The attackers had targeted only the boys among a group of children who were fishing and playing in a mountain stream. Their sisters were unharmed, but the killers had terrorized the girls by chasing them through the woods

"My poor son is dead and my daughter is so frightened she has not eaten for three days," Amatti Zent wailed as she stroked the boy's thick brown curly hair. "We came here to escape the Tanlians, but these Sankari are much worse." Amatti's mate tried to comfort her, but she pushed him away.

"The attacks are getting worse," she shouted. The crowd behind her called out the names of loved ones and friends who had been killed by these mysterious attacks. Someone behind Amatti yelled, "We want to return to the Valley of Heroes. We were safer there. We knew how to fight the Tanlians."

The crowd stopped shouting as an old man rose slowly from the elders' table. Even Amatti was quiet as she watched him shuffle over to the body of her eleven-year-old son. With great effort, the elder knelt and tenderly kissed the forehead of each boy. Tears ran down his craggy cheeks and made his long white beard glisten.

His knees cracked as he stiffly stood up to face the crowd. “I do not understand these attacks,” Josid Vonn said in a hoarse voice. “We have beseeched the Tarylan Seers for help, but they claim ignorance of these killers.”

In a surprisingly stronger tone, much the way an orator would fluctuate his voice to keep an audience’s attention, Josid continued. “We Nuvens have every right to live in Verde Valley. It would insult our ancestors if we gave up and returned to the Valley of Heroes. We never gave up trying to climb Mount Barrasca. Dozens died trying until my niece and nephew found the way here twenty harvests ago,” he said, pointing to a stoic Raaf Vonn who sat listening at the elders’ table.

Josid glared at the crowd. No one said a word as he turned and looked at the other elders. “Our people need protection from these cowardly Sankari who attack our villages in the middle of the night and kill innocent younglings. We need to return to the old ways of protecting ourselves.”

Raaf raised his eyebrows as he listened. He finally understood what his kinsman was saying. “Uncle, we need more Defenders to protect our people. Only a handful, besides myself, left the Valley of Heroes to settle here.”

Josid nodded. “Exactly, Raaf. That is why I am asking you to take your sons and the sons of the other Defenders back to the Valley of Heroes. They need to be trained in the old ways. When you return, try to beseech as many young Defenders as you can to come back with you. Tell them their people need them.”

Raaf regarded his uncle for a moment, then rose to address the crowd. “I will take my two sons and daughter and gather as many other younglings as are willing to travel back to the Valley of Heroes. I am partly responsible for why many of you are here, so I will help however I can to protect our people.”

¶ ¶ ¶

Detta's eyes filled with tears as she kissed her three children goodbye. Raaf's mate did not object when he told her of his uncle's request to take younglings back to the Valley of Heroes. Her reaction had surprised him. Instead of worrying for her children, she was proud they were asked to aid their fellow Nuvens.

"You are a Vonn. It is your blood duty, a well as our children's, to protect our people. This murder of innocent Nuvens must stop."

Detta cupped her hands on each of her children's cheeks and smiled lovingly as she looked deeply into their eyes. Even though they did not closely resemble each other, the same pairs of blue-green eyes stared back at her.

"Mama, I can't wait to see the Valley of Heroes," crowed twelve-year-old Grig. "When we return, we will be great warriors!"

Seventeen-year-old Nyrthka tousled her youngest brother's hair. "It will be many harvests before you grow into a great warrior, little mouse," she said, laughing.

Fifteen-year-old Xander just shook his head at his siblings' antics and looked expectantly at his father. The middle son was quieter and more intense than his more personable siblings.

Even though he said little about the trip, Xander's eyes glowed with excitement about the adventures that awaited them. Already a proven hunter and expert archer, he was eager to test himself during the Defender training.

Raaf looked at his children. "Kiss your mother goodbye. It may be a few harvests until you see her again. We still need to see your grandmother and aunt . . . "

Before Raaf could finish what he was saying, a blonde woman glided through the doorway. Darya brushed past her brother and stood before the three younglings. The youngsters stopped clowning and stood quietly as their aunt gently touched their hair, a rare show of emotion for her. They had learned early on to respect their eccentric kinswoman.

"She understands you are returning to our home valley," a voice said from the doorway. Raaf turned and warmly welcomed his mother. "Well, give your grandmother a hug, you young warriors," Marna said, smiling. "Just promise me to return safely. It seems I am destined to always watch my kin leave me."

As Raaf was bidding his mother farewell, Darya tugged on his sleeve. "Yes, Darya, what is it?" he said.

She pointed out the door. "You go home. I come, too." Raaf was stunned, but how could he argue with the woman who had discovered the passageway to Verde Valley.

Darya reached over and grasped Nyrthka's hand. The young woman was startled, but she did not pull away. "I take Nyrthka to see Papa's stone," she said in her usual emotionless tone. "Xander and Grig come, too."

Detta stepped over to Marna and put her arm around the older woman. "We will wait together for all of you to return to us," she told her mate and children.

Raaf nodded and gestured for his three children and Darya to follow. "Come then, we have to fetch more younglings. It will be a long and hard trek for everyone."

Turning back one final time, Raaf gazed at his mate and his mother. "I will do everything in my power to bring them back safely to you. When we return, they will be able to guard our people from any attacker."

Even though her eyes glistened with tears, Marna smiled. "Yes, my son. It always seems our people need Defenders to protect us."

Raaf nodded. "Defenders in Verde Valley will be a welcome sight."

25

Vitor Pratern flashed a wicked smile as he surveyed the small Nuven village. The first light of dawn was just seeping through the trees, and no one could be seen moving. The Sankari leader and his men were anticipating their first raid in four harvests.

The secret campaign to drive the Nuvens back to their home valley stalled when the newcomers abandoned their outlying villages and gathered in their temple or smaller but well-defended fortresses. Single raids against the Nuvens now were useless. The Verdan plotters were unhappy their plan had failed, but took some satisfaction the Nuven sprawl into their territory had at least been halted.

However, two lunars ago, without warning, the Nuvens once again ventured out and were re-establishing their villages throughout the valley with surprising speed. This new migration caught the Sankari by surprise. The secret units almost were in the process of being disbanded when the Nuvens left the security of their temples.

Now Vitor and his men crept up on the village, much like predators preparing to launch themselves on a helpless victim. The Sankari plan was to kill all but one of the villagers — a witness who hopefully would help spread terror through the Nuvens — and burn their shelters to the ground.

By their best estimate, there could barely be more than thirty people in the village. The sixteen Sankari expected to cut that number in half after their first sweep through the cabins. After that, the confusion of the attack would work in their favor as they swarmed through the village, cutting down anyone attempting to fight back.

Vitor raised his hand to signal for the attack to begin, but he never completed the motion. A deadly whoosh sliced through the air. The Sankari captain watched in horror as the man next to him gasped in pain, his hand clutching helplessly at the arrow in his chest. He took two tumbling steps forward, then collapsed dead.

Seven Sankari had been hit and were now sprawled on the ground, either fatally wounded or dead. The memory of the deadly attack in the grove after the first contact between Verdans and Nuvens flashed through Vitor's mind.

"Take cover behind the trees," he yelled to his men. They were at a loss about what to do. This was a new experience; Sankari had never been attacked before. As the attackers watched, ten shadowy figures slowly made their way toward them.

Vitor drew a long knife and growled with hatred. "They are nothing but Nuvens. We need to avenge our brothers," he called out.

Another admonished him. "Only nine of us are left alive, and there are at least ten of them. We need to retreat now."

"Sankari don't retreat," Vitor yelled. "Who's with me?" All but one shouted in agreement. Now that the initial shock of the attack had worn off, the other Sankari were filled with rage and thoughts of revenge.

When the ten figures from the village drew near, Vitor and seven of his men rushed the Nuvens. A lone Sankari hung back, the one who had wanted to retreat.

Bodies flailed at each other, but the skirmish ended quickly for the Sankari. Only Vitor was left. He and Xander Vonn measured one another warily then charged.

Their knives clashed. Metal on metal rang out as each combatant tried to break through the other's defenses. Panting heavily from his exertions, Vitor's frustration gnawed in his guts until he exploded in a frantic rush at Xander.

The young Nuven easily ducked the attack, sidestepped his opponent and landed a sharp kick to the Sankari leader's knee. Vitor howled in pain and collapsed. He tried to rise but his injured leg crumpled.

Bracing himself with his good leg, Vitor lunged again at the approaching Defender. Xander blocked the strike and drove his knife into the Verdan's chest. Vitor choked out one word — "Nuven" — then rolled onto his side, dead.

The lone Sankari squinted through the early morning shadows, trying hard to see who survived. Terror filled him as he heard only Nuvens speaking to each other. With his worst fears realized, the surviving Verdan's only thought now was of survival. He bolted from behind his tree and ran.

From behind him, he heard a shout. "One escapes! Nyrthka, you are closest." The Sankari heard the sound he was dreading. Someone was chasing him. Fleeing for his life, he tried to put as much distance between him and his pursuer as possible.

The escapee leapt over downed trunks and zigzagged through the forest in a desperate attempt to escape. Adrenaline and fear propelled his body to keep going as the sounds of the pursuer got closer.

After almost an hour of this mad dash, the Verdan's lungs felt like they were going to explode and his clothes were drenched in sweat. Knowing he could not keep up this frantic pace much longer, the Sankari knew he had to take a chance to save his life.

Scurrying through a ravine, he bolted up a downed trunk and quickly took cover behind a large tree on the other side. His only hope was to catch the Nuven by surprise and wound or kill him. The Verdan warrior fought off the overwhelming urge to cough and gasp.

Several minutes passed, but the Sankari only heard the sounds of the forest. However, he knew the Nuven was out there, probably waiting for him to move or make a deadly mistake.

The Verdan looked up briefly at the sound of rustling overhead, but dismissed it as one of those bushy-tailed rodents.

As soon he looked away, a body hurtled from the branches above, knocking him to the ground. The force of the blow pushed him several meters away, giving him time to leap to his feet. Before him crouched a somber-looking young woman.

The Nuven barely looked old enough to be an adult. The Sankari sneered at the sight of a female but his expression melted into a shock as an arrow whizzed through the air, burying itself into a tree only centimeters from his head.

Nyrthka mimicked her opponent's sneer then flung her bow and quiver to the ground. She brandished two imposing-looking knives. Verdan and Nuven circled each other warily. Neither made the first move.

In a surprising move, Nyrthka took a few steps backward and sheathed her knives. She had been studying her opponent intently and saw only a fearful resolve in the other to defend himself.

“Why do you Sankari want to kill us? We came in peace. We have never harmed your people.”

The Sankari’s eyes were wide with surprise. He studied his young opponent warily but did not let his guard down. “Your people want to settle here, but you do not respect our religion or learn our language. You live away from us and build your own villages.”

Nyrthka shook her head. “Our ancestors sacrificed themselves so your people could settle here in peace. It is our right to be here, too. We are as committed to our religion and language as you are to yours.”

This was the first time this Verdan had spoken with a Nuven. Even though they were in a face off, the young woman’s sincerity impressed him. “Your words may be true, Nuven, but one of us will die here today, and nothing will change.”

Nyrthka regarded the Sankari for a few seconds, sheathed her knives and slowly backed away. “Go and tell the others like yourself that Nuven Defenders are now prepared to protect our people and our property.”

The Sankari also retreated but kept his eyes fixed on Nyrthka. He was shaking with relief at not having to fight for his life. “I will give both your messages to the other Sankari. I cannot guarantee hostilities will cease. Too many have sworn oaths against your people."

Nyrthka stopped and cocked her head. "Both messages?"

The Sankari nodded. "Yes, I will tell them why you fight." Both warriors gave each other a respectful nod and continued backing away from each other. "I pray we do not have to face each other again," the Verdan said, lowering his knives.

Nyrthka smiled. "If we do, fight well Sankari."

WAR

1

The steward inspected the ten young men standing at perfect attention before him. None blinked as he paced in front of them, stopping often to examine each one. This day was to be their last and most difficult test. The youngsters, all 18 or 19 harvests old, would pass or fail as a group to become the most revered of Nuven warriors — a Defender circle.

With a shrug to indicate he was unsure of their worthiness, the steward stepped aside. Hundreds of quiet onlookers watched from seats in Temple Darya's small arena. Two veteran Defender circles had been standing nearby, watching the trainees going through the usual tests of archery accuracy and hand-to-hand knife fighting.

The older Nuvens laughed and joked as they neared the group of younger men from all sides. It appeared they were going to welcome them to their ranks. Without warning someone screamed, "Defenders! Kill them for the honor of Mother Verde!" The approaching warriors drew knives and rushed toward the trainees.

Instinctively, the young Nuvens closed ranks in a protective circle, each facing outward as they prepared to take on the attackers. The circle did not budge from the onslaught. Each member defended himself, repelling one attacker after another. In a secret code, the circle brothers called out to each other with warnings and encouragement.

The group moved in unison to fight off the attackers. The young warriors would spin clockwise, then at a signal, would reverse counterclockwise or go forward or backward as the necessity of the fight dictated.

One by one, the older Defenders threw themselves furiously at the young men in an attempt to break through the circle to gain access to their vulnerable backs. If the circle was breeched, the attackers and the test would stop. The young warriors would be congratulated for their efforts, but they would fail to become Defenders.

However, the circle proved to be impenetrable. It constricted and expanded as needed to withstand the assault. In a surprise move after one of the members called out a signal, the circle tightened to where each member was shoulder to shoulder. It spun forward with surprising quickness, cutting a swath through the older Defenders.

Once free of the attackers, the young warriors stopped and charged the Defenders, forcing those who had not been repelled to form their own defensive circle.

At this turn of events, a giant gong boomed throughout the arena, stopping all fighting. The combatants stood panting from their exertions. No one had been injured other than the occasional black eye and bloodied nose. The fighters wielded unsharpened wooden knives to prevent fatal wounds.

A tall, white-haired elder ambled toward the young men. A smile lit up his face. The old Defender moved with a grace that belied his age. It was rumored that he had seen more than 80 harvests. However, he loved to joke that he could only remember 70 harvests.

At an order from their steward, the circle formed a straight line and again stood at attention. The young fighters' bodies glistened with sweat and a few streaks of blood.

"Magnificent, simply magnificent," the elder proclaimed then broke into a proud laugh as he walked down the line, patting each young man on the shoulder. "We have never witnessed such a feat during a test," he said, waving to a small group of elder Defenders in formal attire who stood behind him. "You managed to turn a defensive stand into an attack. Brilliant."

Turning, he gestured for the circle's steward to approach. "Witt Peyser, you are to be commended for the training of these skilled Defenders. They have succeeded beyond our expectations." Then said in a whisper only Witt could hear, "I'm proud of you, grandson."

The steward bowed. "Thank you, Elder Xander. These youngsters have taken to their training with an energy and dedication I have not seen before. I am proud of them."

Although still at attention, the young men beamed with pride. This was the first time they had heard their steward offer them such high praise and to do so in front of one of the Defender elders was a great honor.

Xander Vonn looked back at the men behind him. Seeing them all smiling, he turned toward the Defenders who had just tested the young men. "What say you? Is this circle worthy of joining the ranks of the Defenders?"

One by one, each of the older Defenders raised his arm with a thumb pointing toward the sky and shouted "aye." Soon the arena was filled with a raucous cheering of "Aye! Aye! Aye!"

Holding up his hands for silence, a grinning Xander addressed all those in the arena. "By unanimous decision of the Council of Defenders, as well as the warriors who have tested your mettle today, we proclaim you Defenders, protectors of all Nuvens."

Turning toward the new Defenders he asked, "What name has your circle chosen?"

As one, the ten young men stepped forward, drew their knives, clashed them together and shouted in unison, "Circle Sankarikiller." A surprised hush fell over the onlookers and older Defenders in the arena at the audacity of these young men.

Xander folded his arms, gazing at the newly anointed warriors. Seeing their fierce conviction, he thrust his right arm into the air. "So be it. You have been born and bred for this purpose. May you make your ancestors proud and live up to your name. Welcome, Circle Sankarikiller."

The arena erupted in a roar of approval as the new Defenders were swarmed over, this time by well-wishers.

¶ ¶ ¶

Egan Pozos flashed a giant smile as he slapped his circle brother on the back. The two new Defenders had proven to be particularly vicious during the test. Many of the veterans had targeted them because they were smaller than their circle brothers.

"We did it, Aron. We're Defenders," Egan yelled, relishing their accomplishment. "This is what we have worked for since we were younglings. And the others were worried we would be the ones to fail."

He pointed at one of his circle brothers. "Did you see how I had to help Tanzer when he got knocked down? He almost let that Defender through the circle."

Aron Nels nodded and laughed. "That was a pretty hard kick to the head you gave that Defender. I think he's still a bit woozy."

Egan chortled as he looked at a large bruise on Aron's forehead. "What about that Defender you laid flat with the head butt? I think you broke his nose." Before the two could enjoy their moment further, their eight circle brothers surrounded them.

A somber Tanzer Unota walked over to Egan and looked at him nose to nose. However, he could not maintain his pose for long. "You two were targeted by the other Defenders, but proved to be our best fighters. Well done, and thank you for helping me when I fell." He smiled and clasped Egan's shoulder.

Before they could react, Egan and Aron were hoisted on their brothers' shoulders and paraded triumphantly around the arena, drawing even more cheers from their well-wishers.

2

The silence was heavy. All the members of the High Council of Seers frowned as they read the report from their spy in Temple Darya. Until now, the campaign to undermine the Nuven influence in Verde Valley had been going well. The Sankari, secretly encouraged by the Seers, had managed to keep the Nuven fervor at bay with their attacks on their temples and, in some cases, isolated villages.

Only Temple Darya remained unharmed. However, the Nuven mother temple also was the most well built and heavily fortified. Now another problem had surfaced — a strange new warrior group of Nuvens who called themselves Defenders.

"The audacity of these vermin calling themselves Circle Sankarikiller," High Seer Rufina said, while she crumpled the report and threw it to the floor.

Another Seer stood to address the High Council. "Forgive me, High Seer, but it is more worrisome to me about the second part of our watcher's report. Besides these new Defenders' foolish bravado is the fact they were unreadable. This is very troubling."

Rufina nodded in agreement. "Lanella is correct as always," she sighed, ignoring smirks from some of her sister Seers seated at the crescent-shaped table. "We have never seen this before in the Defenders. This new circle could prove to be most difficult for our Sankari."

Seer Abitha stood. "Until now, the only males who were unreadable to us were a few of our Sankari and Tarylan guards, who were sons of Seer mothers. How have they achieved this?"

Rufina dismissed Abitha with a disgusted snort. "It is too late to worry how the barbarians have accomplished this. We have been at an impasse with the Nuvens for months now. This new circle could put us on the defensive."

Lanella, eager to prove her worth to her elders and earn a seat on the council table, again requested permission to speak. "We need more than the occasional watcher among the Nuvens, especially with the threat of this unknown circle. I propose we offer them assistance."

Rufina scoffed at the younger woman. "Why should the Nuvens accept help from us? We have ignored their pleas for help so far by claiming we have no influence over the Sankari."

Lanella flashed a sly smile. "Perhaps a particularly vicious attack on one of the Nuven villages might change their mind. They may be more receptive if it appears the Sankari are stepping up their attacks against them."

Rufina and the other council members stared in wonder at the audacity of this young Seer. Her bloodthirsty solution surprised them. Until now, the Seers were satisfied with attacking temples in an attempt to keep the Nuvens at bay. So much the better if Nuven warriors, especially Defenders, were killed. They sanctioned an occasional attack against a village, but only to scare the barbarians.

"How vicious of an attack would this be?" Rufina asked.

Lanella shrugged. "To be effective, there would have to be no survivors. Every shelter burned. Every possession destroyed."

Abitha stood up. Her face paled at the reality of what Lanella was proposing. "Their women and children? The Sankari would kill them, too?"

Lanella regarded her coldly. "This will have to be an attack so effective that it will make every Nuven shake with fear. They will be very grateful when we offer our assistance."

Rufina paced back and forth in back of the room. Her arms were crossed against her chest. She stopped to gaze out of one the windows that looked out over the fortress's courtyard. The High Seer wondered what her predecessor would do with this new threat. She was new to her leadership duties after the death of Yseni.

"This conflict with the Nuvens has gone on too long. If we are to crush their expansion and stop their barbarous religion from spreading, we must take drastic measures. I propose we act on Lanella's idea. What say you, council members?"

One by one the Council of Seers voted aye. Only Abitha objected.

¶ ¶ ¶

Vatan and Alim sat quietly in the huge pine tree they had shimmied up. They could hear their father calling for them on the forest floor. He sounded angrier with every shout. "Boys, it's getting dark. Answer me now!"

It seemed like he was directly under their tree. But he kept moving, looking for his wayward sons who had run out to play before finishing their chores.

"Maybe we should go down," whimpered ten-year-old Alim.

Twelve-year-old Vatan grabbed his brother's arm. "No, you know what he does to us when he is this angry. We won't go down until Mother calls. She will be so worried, she won't let Father use the switch — maybe not so much, anyway."

Alim wiped away a tear. "We should have done our chores."

Vatan tried to spot his father in the darkening forest. "I've never seen him this angry. Maybe the beating won't hurt too much if we promise never to run away again."

Their father was making his way under the tree again. He had not calmed down much by the sound of his voice. "Vatan and Alim, if you don't show yourselves, you can stay out here all night and be food for the …"

His voice was cut off, and then the boys heard something heavy fall to the ground. The two younglings looked at each other. Sensing something was wrong, they started to climb down when strange voices made them freeze in position.

"Good throw, Tarko. I thought his yelling would rouse the whole village," a deep-voiced stranger said with a Verdan accent. "Are the others in position?"

Another man answered. "Thank you, Captain. He made an easy target when he stopped so often. Yes, sir. All troops report they are ready."

The first man grunted an acknowledgment. "Good. Give the signal. Let's be quick and get this business over with." A short blast from a horn startled Vatan and Alim. Moments later they heard bodies crashing through the forest.

Almost instantaneously, screams from their village pierced the early evening air. From their vantage point, the boys could see fires from the shelters shoot into the sky. The terrified brothers clung to their limbs as they watched their little mountain village burn into the night. The screams and shouting didn't last long.

An eerie silence hung over the forest as the heavy smoke from the village filled the sky, making it difficult for Alim and Vatan to breathe. The youngsters had no way of knowing how long it had been after the attack when they heard those frighteningly familiar voices return through the forest as they left the village. Some of the men were laughing.

"I thought them Nuvens would put up much more of a fight than that, captain," a Verdan called out.

The first man answered. "We caught them completely by surprise. Burning them out made it easy. Lucky for us there were no Defenders or else we would have lost more men. Tarko, what were our casualties?"

The gruff-voiced man started to count aloud. "So far, six dead and eleven wounded, Captain. I counted about fifty villagers, though many more died in the cabins we burned."

Choking from the smoke, the leader called for his men to retreat. He coughed. "We've done our job. I'd say we sent the Nuvens a clear message."

Vatan and Alim fought back sobs and coughs while the strangers returned from where they came. Shaking with fright and cold, the boys stayed in the tree until the first rays of morning filtered through the forest.

Even though some smoke still hung in the air, birds started singing, a signal the strangers were gone. After climbing down, they found their father lying face down on the forest floor, a javelin wound in his chest.

Alim let out a wail and threw himself on top of his father's lifeless body. Vatan shook from his sobs then turned and ran toward the village, frantically shouting, "Mother! Mother!"

The sight that greeted Vatan made him drop to his knees in horror. Nothing was left of his village. Every cabin, barn, and the communal hall were smoldering ashes. A pile of bodies lay in the middle of what had been the market square. Most of the villagers sustained javelin wounds. A few had body parts hacked off.

Vatan covered his eyes, vomited and screamed in anger. Trembling, he rose to search his family's cabin, looking for his mother and baby sister. The ashes of his family's home were still smoldering, but he could make out the form of his mother on what had been the floor. She was holding something, probably his sister.

"Mother?" Vatan whirled around after hearing Alim's sob behind him. The younger boy's face was sickly pale as he stared at the awful sight. Tears dripped down his chin.

Vatan put his arm around Alim. Seeing his frightened brother stoked a strong desire to protect his sibling. "Mother died trying to protect Nadia. No one in the village is alive."

Alim shuddered between sobs. "Why did they do this? We weren't hurting anyone."

Vatan shielded his brother away from the grisly sight. "I don't know. They must have been Sankari. We can't stay here. They might come back to look for survivors."

Alim looked at his brother with wide eyes. "Wh, where can we go?"

Vatan pointed down the valley. "Uncle Kelfar's village is only four kilometers away. We can be there in a couple of hours if we hurry." Taking his younger brother by the hand, Vatan led him away from their destroyed home, toward the safety of their kinsman's village.

¶ ¶ ¶

The Nuven elders looked at each other with surprise. Never before had the mysterious Seers offered their assistance, even though the elders had sought their help in ending the unprovoked Sankari attacks.

"We are honored by your offer, but are somewhat surprised. Why now?" asked Chief Elder Marco Enriks.

High Seer Rufina raised her eyebrows at the Nuven's candor. She was not accustomed to being spoken to in such an informal manner, but remembered this barbarian had not been raised to respect her.

Forcing herself to smile, she tried to allay Marco's suspicions. "My sister Seers and I have grown worried over the terrible fighting between you and these Sankari. We were especially saddened by the tragic destruction of that village and all its inhabitants."

Rufina stopped and held out her arms to the Nuvens. "We have tried to stop the Sankari's unwarranted attacks on your people, but have failed to convince these zealots to cease. We offer this resolution to hopefully stop the bloodshed."

Marco and the other elders seemed satisfied and even pleased with Rufina's explanation. The Nuven elder looked at his counterparts who had accompanied him to Fortress Bryann. They looked to be in agreement.

Marco stood and bowed to the High Seer. "The Nuven elders humbly accept and welcome your offer of assistance, which we pray will end these unprovoked attacks upon our people. It is our wish to peacefully coexist with our Verdan brothers."

Rufina was impressed with his eloquence and attention to Verdan formality. *Perhaps there is hope for these barbarians yet,* she thought, but forced herself to follow through with the Seer's plan.

"Very well, Elder Enriks. Each of the ten Nuven temples will be assigned six Seers. It is our hope our sisters will be able to discourage future attacks by the Sankari and hopefully lead to a peaceful resolution."

Marco raised his eyebrows. "We are most appreciative of your offer, High Seer, but why so many?"

Rufina scowled. This Nuven was trying her patience. She did not like having her orders questioned. The High Seer fought the urge to scold Marco. It was her duty to convince these elders of the Seers' good intentions. The only way their plan to destroy those bothersome barbarian temples could succeed was to plant Seers inside and gain the Nuvens' trust.

"Why, my dear elder, six Seers is the least number needed to ensure one can be on watch at all hours day and night," Rufina said. "Of course, one Seer can be on watch up to six hours, then she requires sustenance and rest. This will guarantee a fresh Seer will be able to serve you at all times."

Marco, an older man with silver-streaked thick hair and a salt-and-pepper beard, stared at Rufina while he considered her explanation. After a few moments, he smiled. "Of course. We can't expect one young woman to bear all the responsibility by herself. Even our Defenders need their rest and meal breaks."

All the Nuven elders stood and bowed to the High Council.

"We will treat the Seers you send us with the utmost respect," Marco said. "We will protect them with the same fervor as we would our families."

Rufina stood and bowed to the elders. "Our Seers look forward to serving our Nuven cousins. We appreciate your offer of protection."

3

The young man was troubled by the scene playing out in front of him. Many people in a long line were hugging and slapping his cousin, Aron Nels, on the back. Some of the well-wishers were laughing. However, others were crying, including his mother, which upset him.

Tevan Nels did not understand many of the words the old ones were saying to Aron. However, he knew the meaning of good-bye, which everyone was repeating over and over again. This was not good. Tevan did not like that word. The last time Aron said it to him, his cousin left for so many days that Tevan had lost count. He was always sad when Aron went away.

Few others let him tag along with them the way Aron did. The two would go for walks and laugh. Actually, Tevan did most of the laughing just because he was so happy to accompany Aron.

When it was his family's turn to greet Aron, Tevan's mother gave his cousin a big hug and a kiss on the cheek. Thella said many words which he did not understand, but he recognized "my precious boy" and "good luck." Tevan was surprised to see tears in his father's eyes when he warmly clasped Aron's shoulder. Again, he heard "good luck."

Now it was Tevan's turn to see Aron. The two looked at each other and smiled. "Mama, Papa say good-bye. Aron go away?" Tevan asked, concern flickering in his blue eyes.

Aron nodded, while giving his cousin a bear hug. "Yes, I have to go Tevan, but I will come back. I promise."

Tevan shook his head violently. "No Aron go, please!" The young man then got excited and started babbling incoherently, which he was prone to do when words failed him.

Tevan's embarrassed father tried to remove him from the line, but Aron gently stopped him. "No, Uncle. Let him stand by me for a while. It may make him feel better."

As a boy, Aron was often bothered by his cousin who never matured mentally past a young child. But as they two grew older, Aron had grown protective of his gentle childlike kinsman. Aron did not remember the incident that changed Tevan's life.

One summer, the two boys were playing hide and seek in a giant fruit tree. Both younglings were four harvests old. Tevan had scrambled high up the tree and was laughing at Aron, who was too frightened to pursue him. As boys are prone to do, they soon started throwing fruit at each other.

The throwing match got heated when both plunked each other on the head. Tevan stood up on his branch to get better leverage, when he lost his balance and fell crashing through the foliage. During the fall, Tevan's head struck several large branches and he hit the ground with a heavy thud. Miraculously, no bones were broken, but the little boy lay unconscious for several days.

Tevan recovered physically, but his mind was irreparably damaged. He was forever frozen with the mind of a child, even though he grew into a good-looking young man with blond hair and broad shoulders.

Now when Aron gestured for him to stand next to him, Tevan laughed with delight and proudly greeted everyone, too. The day ended with a somber farewell. A platoon of new recruits assigned to Temple Darya stopped to collect Aron. Some were archers and support troops, and the other nine were his circle brothers. The officer in charge stepped forward and called for Aron Nels to join them.

The young Defender hugged his father and mother, Lawryf and Noria, then bade his brothers farewell and waved to the crowd. Tevan watched as his cousin joined the strangers. The platoon marched away, heading for Temple Darya. The young men strode in front and were followed by a long line of supply wagons.

Much to his parents' surprise, Tevan did not put up a fuss when Aron left. Instead, he turned and walked in the opposite direction. Thinking he was pouting, his family let him go, believing he wouldn't wander too far. However, Tevan moved to the far edge of the crowd to watch the wagons, which looked like a parade.

Many in the crowd followed the platoon for a while, calling farewells and well wishes to Aron and the other young men. Tevan was left standing by himself. Those familiar words — good-bye and good luck — rang in his ears.

He finally understood Aron was leaving. A gut-wrenching wave of emptiness overwhelmed him as the wagons passed by and the crowd walked away from him. Tevan shook his head with grief. As the last wagon slowly rolled past, Tevan started to follow it. *Aron go away*, he thought. *Wagons go with Aron. Tevan want to go with Aron.*

In a surprisingly quick motion, Tevan jumped onto the back of the wagon and wiggled underneath the tarp covering the supplies. He had made up his mind. If Aron was going, he was, too. Tevan peeked out of a hole. Many of the people were standing and calling good-bye as the platoon proceeded down the road. He giggled. It was his best joke yet that he was playing on Aron.

¶ ¶ ¶

The swaying of the dark, tarp-covered wagon soon rocked Tevan to sleep. He awoke hours later to the sounds of men talking and food cooking when the troop and wagon train had stopped for the night. Tevan climbed stiffly out of the back of the wagon and stretched. Following the smells and voices, he wandered over to a group of men standing in line and joined them without being noticed.

The others paid little attention to him. To them, he was just another wagoneer who had arrived late. Tevan followed their example, picked up a bowl, took a mug of water and eagerly accepted the food the cooks dished out.

After he finished eating, Tevan timidly scouted the area, but he could not find Aron. Many campfires were scattered throughout the clearing where the troops had stopped for the night. Being afraid to wander too far, a saddened Tevan returned to the safety of his wagon. He listened to the men he had dined with, but understood little of what they were saying. After about an hour, the stowaway crawled back under the tarp and slept for the remainder of the night.

The camp came alive with first light. Tevan awoke to the sounds of men readying the wagons for the next day's journey. Again, he got in line for first meal without being questioned.

A hectic scene greeted Tevan when he returned to the wagon. An old man with a huge belly was having difficulty hitching up the four horses. Two of the animals stood patiently in the harnesses, but the other two were being cantankerous. Each time the driver had almost backed the second team into place, one of the pair would spook or bite the other, causing them to bolt nervously away.

The old man was growing more agitated with every failed attempt. He was yelling insults at the horses, making them even more skittish. Tevan understood the man's words. He had heard them many times when his father and brothers had difficulty with their horses. When this happened, they would call for him to calm down the animals, which he gladly did.

The driver glanced over to see Tevan watching him. "You there, are you a handler? I could use some help here," he called gruffly. Recognizing the word "help," Tevan happily lent his assistance.

Saying nothing, he took hold of the team and walked the pair around the wagon once. Tevan stopped and whispered soothingly to the horses, then turned them and walked them around the wagon in the opposite direction. Lining up the pair to its traces, Tevan patiently backed the horses into position. The wagon was ready to travel at last after he and the driver finished harnessing the animals to their saddle trees.

The sweating, bald man shook his head and stroked his white mustache, which cascaded past his chin. “Never seen anything like that, but you got the job done. My thanks.” Gesturing toward the wagon, the driver said, “You’re welcome to ride with me, son. I could use the help.”

Tevan nodded and smiled. “I help and ride.”

After guiding the wagon to its place in the supply train, the driver thumped his chest. “I’m Gristo Poller. We’ll get along if you don’t talk much. I don’t like needless chatter.”

Imitating his companion, Tevan thumped his chest and introduced himself. Not talking came naturally to him. The young man could spend hours without uttering a word, perfectly content in his own world.

Gristo nodded. “Nels, eh? That sounds familiar. I’ve heard that name before. Wasn’t one of those new troopers that joined us yesterday a Nels?” Not understanding, Tevan just smiled and shrugged. The driver grunted. “Never mind, probably a long-lost cousin. I’ve heard that name in other villages, too.”

Recognizing the word “cousin,” Tevan nodded. “My cousin Aron say good-bye. I say good-bye.”

The driver sighed. “I see. It’s never easy leaving family. I understand that.” The two rode for the rest of the day in contented silence, except to note an occasional bird or rabbit that was flushed by the passage of the wagon train.

¶ ¶ ¶

Usso and Thella did not miss their son for several hours after Aron left with the troop. The farewell gathering had taken place at the Nuven temple that was close to their home village. Tevan had walked home from the temple by himself many times. His parents knew his moods. He would hide for hours when sad, but always returned when he became hungry or was frightened by nightfall.

This time, however, Tevan did not return home. Usso and Thella frantically searched everywhere that night. Their other two sons also helped look, but they could not find him. Early the next morning, the whole village fanned out and retraced every possible route Tevan could have taken back from the temple.

After another day, other nearby villages were alerted to look for what they assumed to be a lost and confused young man. Again, all the searches turned up fruitless. By evening of the second day, word of the Sankari attack that had burned down the remote village and killed all but two of its inhabitants had spread among the Nuvens.

The search for Tevan was reluctantly abandoned as concerned villagers made plans to protect themselves from a possible surprise attack. Thella and Usso refused to sleep that night. They kept a candle burning in every window in their cabin hoping Tevan would find his way home. The next morning, Thella reluctantly extinguished the candles and said a prayer to the ancestors to protect her innocent, missing son.

4

The scout rode his horse so hard toward the troop, it appeared he would ram through the marchers without stopping. At the last moment, the young man yanked the reins so hard the animal reared up on its hind legs.

Horse and man were heaving from exhaustion and gaminuteg for air. The animal was covered in froth and the man was soaked from his and the horse's sweat. Exhausted from a day's nonstop ride, the scout collapsed when he dismounted.

Calling for water, Witt Peyser rushed over to the young Nuven. "By the ancestors, son, what is it? You almost killed yourself and your horse." Arri Grion took a big gulp of water and choked. The steward admonished him to take sips, but waited patiently for the rider to get his breath.

After a few moments, Arri gasped out his urgent message. "Steward, a Nuven village five days' ride from here has been wiped out by Sankari. Only two younglings were left alive."

Witt frowned. "A whole village? Everyone killed? That is a new tactic by those bastards. But what has that got to do with us? We are too late to help."

Arri shook his head while taking another gulp of water. "Sir, I saw a Sankari party less than a day's ride from here. They were traveling slowly because they had wounded." Witt's eyes narrowed into fearsome-looking slits. Before he could bark out an order, someone spoke behind him.

"Steward, let Circle Sankarikiller pursue those Nuvens," said a somber Tanzer Unota. His circle brothers stood behind him, all nodding in agreement.

Witt turned back to Arri. "How many Sankari are there?"

The scout thought for a moment. "I counted about twenty-some, sir. Half their force split off and left this group with the wounded."

The steward shook his head. "That is too many for an untested circle. We may have to let these murderers go."

Aron Nels knelt before Witt. "With all due respect, sir, we have been tested by the best warriors on Verde. Let us pursue the Sankari. The villagers will never be avenged if we let them slip away."

Witt snorted. "You have never spilled blood nor had your blood spilled in battle. Killing a man is very different from pretending to kill him." The circle of young Defenders stood up with their arms folded against their chests. Ten pairs of eyes focused fiercely on their steward. None of the warriors exhibited any braggadocio, just a quiet confidence.

Witt rose and inspected his charges with a new respect. He had watched this circle grow up. They were the most talented fighters he had ever seen. Shaking his head as if he couldn't believe what he was about to say, the steward told the circle to mount up. But before doing so, he growled out orders.

"I am in charge of this mission. If I determine it is too dangerous or we are outnumbered, you will obey me. This is not the way I had planned for you to experience your first battle test. However, you are correct, Aron. The Sankari may escape if we don't try to stop at least some of the murderers."

In unison, the circle shouted, "Yes, Steward! Understood!" The ten young men ran to one of the armament wagons and hastily grabbed weapons.

¶ ¶ ¶

Osald Bettinga was not happy about being left behind to bring the wounded home. The Sankari lieutenant felt he was being punished for suffering the most casualties during the attack on the village.

In a show of bravado, when the horn sounded the attack, Osald led his men in a headlong rush into the village. The arrogant young officer wanted to claim the most kills. Unfortunately for his troop, the large building they chose to barge into was filled with men who had just returned from a successful hunt. The villagers were still carrying bows and arrows, plus spears and knives.

The Nuvens quickly defended themselves and forced Osald and his troop to retreat. Only a barrage of javelins from another Sankari troop saved them. Despite many being wounded, the villagers fought frantically but were overwhelmed.

Only after Osald's troop reconnoitered after the battle did he realize four of his men had been killed and another five wounded. Captain Erlan Telfeer was furious with the lieutenant. After the attackers had killed everyone in the village and burned it to the ground, Erlan ordered Osald to safely escort all the wounded home. This would prove to be a slow and tedious trip, which infuriated the junior officer.

During their return journey, Osald's troop came upon a gorge, which meandered in the general direction they were traveling. Traveling through the small valley could get them home faster. Negotiating a route around it probably would add another half-day to their journey.

Osald ordered two scouts to explore the gorge to ensure its safety. About an hour later, the scouts returned to report there was no sign of danger. "Good news at last," the lieutenant muttered to himself. With a wave, he ordered the Sankari party forward.

A small stream cut through the ravine. Thick stands of trees and brush covered the sides. An hour after the Sankari had entered the gorge, they heard strange bird calls from both sides. A few of the Sankari looked up, but most kept trudging along.

A sudden shrill whistle pierced the air. Before the Sankari could react, a hail of arrows rained from the trees. All the arrows found a target; more than half of the Sankari fell wounded or dead. The survivors of the first hail of arrows tried to escape, but the Nuven Defenders furiously attacked, bringing the remainder of them down.

An arrow had struck Osald in the shoulder. He, too, attempted to escape. However, a body hurled itself from behind a tree, knocking him off his horse. Landing with a heavy thud, the Sankari officer tried to rise, but his shoulder was on fire with pain. Looking up with horror, the last thing Osald saw was a knife flashing toward his throat.

¶ ¶ ¶

The skirmish did not last long. Witt Peyser's Defenders carried out their orders perfectly and fought with veteran skill. They quickly dispatched their foes, including the wounded Sankari. The steward wiped Osald's blood off his knife and stood up to survey the battle scene. All ten of the young Defenders stood together, smiling at their steward. None had been injured in the fight.

"We have never seen you move like that, sir," said an impressed Egan Pozos.

Witt shrugged. "I've spilled Sankari blood many times. I have not forgotten how to be a Defender." Looking at the dead Sankari, he ordered the circle brothers to take any worthwhile weapons but leave personal belongings.

"We are not scavengers or the barbarians the Sankari accuse us of being. Respect the dead. Let their fellow Sankari take them home to their kin."

Before leaving the site of their first real test, Witt ordered his men to attention. This time, the steward did not frown. Much to the circle brothers' surprise, he saluted them. "Circle Sankarikiller you have performed with great skill and bravery. I am honored to serve with such fine Defenders."

¶ ¶ ¶

Two days later, when Osald's troop did not return with the wounded, Erlan Telfeer led a search party to find the truant Sankari. The captain shook his head with disgust when his scouts led him to Osald and his slaughtered men. A quick examination of the bodies told him what he had expected — the troopers who had not been killed by an arrow had died from slashed throats, the telltale sign of Defenders.

One of the scouts tentatively approached Erlan, handing him a pouch with a note inside. "This was on the lieutenant's body," the scout said, then he quickly stepped back. Frowning, the captain opened the small leather pouch and pulled out a note written in perfect Verdan script.

"These men paid the price for the unwarranted attack and murder of innocent Nuvens. Our only regret is that all the cowardly Sankari were not here to die with their brothers — Circle Sankarikiller."

"Defenders! Damn Defenders!" the captain bellowed, his face red with fury. He unleashed a torrent of obscenities, crumpled up the note and stomped on it.

After returning to Fortress Bryann, Erlan Telfeer's peers found him guilty of negligence. The Sankari captain was executed as a lesson to all that a victory by the Defenders would not be tolerated.

5

The execution of Erlan Telfeer did not appease Rufina. The High Seer was still furious over Circle Sankarikiller's surprisingly easy ambush and the ensuing slaughter of half of the captain's troop.

The exercise that had started out to strike terror in every Nuven heart through the extermination of a remote village had turned into a brazen act of revenge by those mysterious young Defenders. Instead of being disheartened, the barbarians now had new heroes to give them hope.

"We need to place our Seers in the Nuven temples immediately," Rufina said, slapping her hands loudly for emphasis.

Even the normally eager-to-please Lanella could not offer her solace. "We are testing our watchers as fast as we can, High Seer. It has been difficult finding sixty sisters with the gift who can carry out this mission."

Rufina snorted. "It is taking too long. The Nuvens grow bolder with every passing day." Pausing for a moment, Rufina barked out an order. "We don't need six Seers blessed with gift of sight in every temple. Send six of the most talented to Temple Darya where those cursed new Defenders are stationed. For the other nine minor temples, send a Seer and five good spies. The Nuvens won't know the difference."

Lanella bowed. "Yes, High Seer."

Rufina stopped her when she turned to leave. "I want you to lead the mission at Temple Darya. You are the only one I can trust to carry out what must be done."

The younger Seer smiled with pride. "You honor me, High Seer. I was going to ask permission to lead one of our parties."

Rufina nodded while she considered another idea. "Yes, yes, Lanella, I was expecting you to volunteer. I would have been surprised if you had not done so. However, I will choose the other five who will accompany you. They must be perfect for this assignment. I want Seers who are as beautiful as they are gifted."

Lanella lifted her eyebrows in surprise, but said nothing. Rufina smiled at the younger woman's reaction. "You are savvy in many things, Lanella, but not in the ways of men's desires. With the selection of the right women, one or more of those young Defenders may fall under the spell of our Seers."

Lanella considered the plot and smiled in agreement. "It will be done, High Seer. The candidates for Temple Darya will be sent to you for selection."

¶ ¶ ¶

Verinya's heart sank with every selection. She had been one of fifteen young women who had been summoned before the High Seer for selection to accompany Lanella to Temple Darya. Now, four had been chosen by the High Seer, who paced back and forth in front of the group, critiquing them as if they were commodities in a marketplace. Rufina had asked all of them personal questions, such as how many lovers they claimed and if they were adept in seduction.

The High Seer frowned as she regarded the final eleven. This choice was proving to be difficult. She liked two candidates. One was a tall beauty with a full figure that most men would fight their brothers for the chance to sleep with. But she looked similar to the other comely Seers Rufina had selected for their beauty and sexual expertise.

The other woman was petite and fair skinned. She looked much younger than her years. Her innocence was not an act. This Seer had only had one sexual encounter, a hurried act with a drunken Tarylan guard. Rufina studied the young women she was considering. She asked both to stand at either end of the line with the four women she had selected to accompany Lanella.

The High Seer smiled with approval. The petite Seer stood out. Her youthful look was even more exaggerated when compared to the others. Perhaps one of the Defenders also would notice the refreshing difference.

"Verinya, you are chosen to accompany Lanella's group to Temple Darya," Rufina announced. The High Seer placated the disappointed taller woman. "Your beauty and talents will not be wasted. You may have your choice of leading a Seer group at one of the other temples."

The Seer who was not picked looked surprised, then beamed with pride at the confidence Rufina had shown in her. She ran over to Verinya, gave her a warm hug and wished her well. Verinya was shocked at being chosen. She was joining the elite group selected to ferret out the secrets of Defenders at Temple Darya.

Lanella thanked the young women who were not chosen to join her group and assured them they would be dispersed among the other Nuven temples as well. Turning to her select group, Lanella ordered them to be ready to leave at first light for Temple Darya. She wanted her Seers in place at the temple as soon as possible.

The five young Seers bowed to Rufina and Lanella and scurried away to make preparations for what they assumed would be the adventure of their lives.

6

Manor Stillinger and the other Sankari captains stared at the diagram of Temple Darya. Their spies had provided amazingly detailed drawings of the Nuven fortress. Apparently, very few areas were forbidden to strangers. All accesses to the temple were noted, as well as watchtower schedules and guard postings.

Even the locations of armories, food pantries, stables, and archer barracks were included. One of the most important details was missing, however — where the Defenders were housed.

The Sankari spies were unable to discover where the Defenders spent their leisure time or slept. It seemed these elite Nuven warriors somehow melted into the walls of the temple at will. Apparently, there was no one area for the Defenders. They dined in the commons with all the other temple dwellers. Their schedules were erratic. These warriors came and went as they pleased. It was never a surprise to see Defenders occasionally manning the watchtowers, providing security for the gates, or patrolling the perimeter of the temple at all hours of the day and night.

The Verdan spies also were unable to find out one key piece of information — how many Defenders were stationed in the temple. All the informants tried to guess, but each tallied a different number. The counts ranged from about fifty to as high as one hundred.

Manor shook his head in disbelief as he read the dispatches from the spies. All presented good arguments for how many Defenders they thought were in the temple, but the numbers were different.

"How can this be?" Manor grumbled as he paced back and forth across a room in Fortress Bryann. "Our spies agree on everything else in minute detail, but they have no clue how many Defenders there are."

Stanis Shalov, one of the older captains, shrugged. "We have known for many harvests the Defenders follow no set pattern. Those of us who have faced them in battle know how unpredictable they can be," he said. "This campaign against the Nuvens may not have gone so well if we hadn't had help from the Seers."

Manor threw up his hands in frustration. "No one is debating the vermin's fighting skills. I don't understand why all the Defenders can't be identified and counted."

Stanis smiled at his younger peer. "Perhaps the vermin don't wish to be counted. Their leaders may suspect we have spies in their midst. If I was them I, too, would make such an assumption. Look at the reports from our people in the temple. Sometimes the Defenders appear in casual dress and other times they are in full battle gear with their faces covered."

"So what?" Manor said, not masking his impatience.

Stanis casually leaned back against a wall as he thought. "Perhaps our spies are seeing the same Defenders twice or even more times in different gear. What a clever subterfuge. Give the appearance of many more men than you actually have."

The younger captain acknowledged that Stanis's theory was sound. "Even so, it still does not tell us how many Defenders are stationed at the temple."

Stanis reached for the spies' dispatches and studied them carefully. "Numbers two and five both describe the features and characteristics of the Defenders they have identified. Their counts are only off by two — either forty-four or forty-six. The other spies go on about the mysterious masked Defenders they cannot recognize. Numbers two and five are reluctant to count these unknown Defenders."

The other captains at the table voiced their agreement. Stanis stood up. "Soon we will have even more eyes in the temple when the new Seers arrive. Let us see what numbers these watchers will provide."

Manor smiled as he accepted Stanis's proposal. However, it did not solve their main objective. "Even when we determine how many there are of the vermin, it still does not help us with how to breach the temple. This stronghold is almost as impenetrable as Fortress Bryann."

Stanis examined the temple's blueprint, which had been copied on a huge canopy that hung on the wall in front of them. "You speak the truth, Manor. It is unfortunate so many of our grandfathers volunteered to build the intruders a temple they could feel safe in. If we had an army with all of its resources and weapons we could be successful, but even some of our people are speaking out against us."

The Sankari had been fighting a secret war against the Nuvens for more than seventy harvests. They fought at the behest of the Seers, who feared the Nuvens and their religion, which was attracting too many Verdan converts.

Many Verdans were outraged by the attacks on the Nuvens, whom they considered to be the lost ones from the storied early days after the planet was settled. Many entreaties were sent to the Seers begging for a resolution of the violence.

Temple Darya was solid and well fortified. It was designed so a few Defenders could withstand a prolonged attack by a large enemy. The temple was built into a mountain. It had its own water supply from two waterfalls. Massive amounts of food and supplies could be stored for long periods in its subterranean caves.

Even though the Verdans had tried to assure the Nuvens that they would be protected and safe in their new home, the new immigrants demanded a safe stronghold be built. The Nuvens were fleeing an enemy they called Tanlians, who they said had preyed on them since their ancestors landed on the planet.

The Verdans were puzzled by these stories. They had only been attacked once in their history. The first colonists had repelled the marauders, who had never reappeared.

Manor impatiently addressed his peers. “We have to find a way to penetrate that temple. It won’t make any difference how many hidden eyes we have in there if we can’t destroy it and kill the Defenders.”

The young captain grew tired of sitting in the room with the other Sankari leaders and talking but finding no solutions. He needed fresh air to think. Manor strode out the fortress gate and headed toward the nearest glider launch site.

After climbing the nearby mountain for almost two hours, he reached his favorite takeoff point, an outcropping over the Nandez River. Two fellow flyers helped him find a well-built glider to his liking. A check of the wind currents determined it was safe for a launch. Without a second thought, Manor sprinted off the ledge and flung himself into the air.

The glider banked downward for a few seconds, which was normal. The Sankari turned into the wind and swooped upward almost as fast as he had dropped. Manor smiled as he found an air current to his liking and steered the glider to ride along with it. This was one of the few activities where he could find peace — soaring over the Verdan valley much like a bird of prey.

How boring our lives would be if one the first colonists hadn’t built a crude glider and leapt off into the unknown only to find he could soar effortlessly over the valley, the captain thought.

With no destination in mind, Manor flew over Verde City and then headed down the valley, grinning as children in small villages shouted and waved as he soared overhead. As he followed the river, a detestable site came into view — the newest of the Nuven fortresses, Temple Vonn. Manor started to bank away, but curiosity tugged at him.

In a bold move, he glided above the temple and circled it. The captain could plainly see people going about their business. He banked closer until he was only about thirty meters above the nearest guard tower. Three guards walked out of the tower onto the wall's walkway and watched him with amusement. One even waved. The other two did not threaten him or call out a warning.

Manor banked as close as he could and still ride his current. "Greetings, cousins," he called out in the friendliest Nuven greeting he knew. "Your temple looks impressive from here."

Now all three guards laughed and waved."Greetings to you, too, cousin," one of the men shouted. "You are welcome here. We will be happy to share a mug."

Manor was stunned by the gesture of friendship, then smiled as the solution to his problem spread out in front of him. "Thank you, I will be back to take you up on your offer," the Sankari officer shouted as he banked away and glided toward Fortress Bryann.

7

The new troops were still a half-kilometer away from Temple Darya when crowds of well-wishers rushed out to them. Word of Circle Sankarikiller's victory over the Sankari, who had slaughtered an entire Nuven village, had quickly reached the temple.

The young Defenders were given a hero's welcome as they and their fellow troops marched the remaining distance to the Nuven fortress. They beamed with pride when they entered the temple to even more raucous cheering and blaring trumpets. Even Witt Peyser couldn't suppress a proud smile as they marched through the throngs of admirers. It had been many harvests since there had been such an overwhelming Defender victory over the hated Sankari.

Instead of traveling the usual route to the temple barracks, the troops were obliged to follow a snaking path through the admiring throng, which circled the temple and emptied out into the large center courtyard. When they finally stopped and were assembled, Xander Vonn strode toward Witt.

Before the steward could react, the Defender leader saluted Witt, then clasped him proudly on the shoulder. Stunned by the gesture, Witt returned the salute, then waved toward Circle Sankarikiller, who stood in the front line at the insistence of their fellow troopers.

In a rare show of emotion, the elder patted the young warriors on their shoulders, telling each one, "Well done. We're proud of you." Turning toward the crowd, Xander called out: "These young Defenders have avenged a terrible crime against the Nuven people and now the Sankari know they will be dealt with just as savagely."

The crowded courtyard erupted in a victorious cheer. A gesture from Xander indicated that the crowd should move, and when they did, they revealed dozens of tables set up with food and drink. Smiling, the elder said, "I imagine you young ones are hungry and thirsty after your long journey and adventure. We've prepared a banquet in your honor."

The members of Circle Sankarikiller stood looking wide-eyed at the festive tables and adoring crowds. A friendly bark from Witt got their attention. "Pups, you've just been invited to the table by an elder. I suggest you accept so all the others and myself can enjoy this feast."

Tugging on Aron Nels's sleeve, Egan Pozos dragged his circle brother out of the line and headed toward one of the teeming tables. The other brothers quickly followed, again to the cheers of the crowd, who eagerly swarmed to the food and drink.

¶ ¶ ¶

Six young women calmly viewed the cheerful proceedings with great interest from a watchtower directly above the courtyard. They applauded politely when appropriate, just in case any curious Nuven was watching their reaction. The watchers took special notice as the members of Circle Sankarikiller stepped out from the line of troopers and took their seats at the banquet tables.

"They are barely young men," Lanella sneered to her fellow Seers. "Those Defenders aren't old enough to be Tarylan guards, much less Sankari. I cannot believe they attacked and killed our warriors without losing a single member."

The other Seers nodded in agreement as they studied the young Defenders who were their source of concern at Fortress

Bryann. Nothing about the young men stood out. They could walk through any village or city on Verde without being noticed.

Lanella and the other five women sat cross-legged on the ledge and stared intently at Circle Sankarikiller. After several minutes had passed, Lanella uttered a curse. “Our spies were correct. I cannot see into any of them.” The frowns on the other Seers told her all she needed to know. These enemy warriors were indeed unreadable, a discomforting thought.

Verinya watched curiously as one of the young Defenders stretched awkwardly and looked around. He was the one who had been dragged out of the line by his circle brother. It was evident this Defender was uncomfortable with the attention from the crowd. He kept shifting on his seat and looking around nervously.

After twitching some more, Aron Nels turned and scanned the walls of the temple. It looked like he was searching for something. Scrutinizing the ledge on the watchtower, the Defender stopped with a startled look as he spotted the young women. Verinya watched with slight amusement, knowing he was looking them over.

Lanella started to mock the watching Nuven, when the other nine Defenders swung around in unison to look up at the Seers. “How in Mother Verde did they do that? I didn’t see him say anything or give any signal,” she said.

Aron had been nervous about something as soon as he sat down at the table. Despite all the well wishes, the Defender felt like he was being watched from afar. Of course he was being doted on by his fellow Nuvens, but something wasn’t right.

He looked around, even glanced up at the watchtower, where he spotted the young women who were staring at him and his circle brothers. Not knowing why the Seers were so intense, he signaled the others with a series of low hums, which told them exactly where to look. Without questioning him, his circle brothers all swung around to investigate.

Egan Pozos studied the young women for a moment, then let out a hearty laugh. “Well done, Aron. I see you’ve spotted six attractive admirers, but there are only six of them. Four of us are going to be left out."

The other circle brothers joined in the moment. Some of them patted Aron on the head, thanking him for spotting such a dangerous threat. A few others offered to help him capture "those fierce-looking females."

The other eight turned back to their food and drink. Egan looked for a moment longer and gave all six a lingering wink. Chuckling, he jabbed Aron in the side and returned to his meal.

Embarrassed by the circle's reaction, Aron frowned and glanced up again at the young women. Verinya was amused at the reaction of the other Defenders. Smiling coyly at Aron, the Seer thought she detected a shadow of a smile in return. The Nuven started to turn back to the table to continue his meal, but was interrupted by a young man who ran over to him and gave him a warm hug.

Startled by arms thrown around his neck, Aron instinctively grabbed for his attacker's limbs and raised an elbow for a savage backward thrust when Egan stopped him. "Don't hurt him, Aron. It's Tevan."

Aron stood up to see his cousin facing him, laughing with delight. He was too startled to say anything.

Tevan hugged his cousin again. "I find Aron. I find Aron," he repeated over and over again. "Aron say good-bye, Tevan say good-bye. Tevan come with Aron," the man-child said, laughing at his cousin's startled expression.

Aron glanced at Egan, who just sat shaking his head in wonder. The other circle brothers also voiced their shock at the surprise reunion.

"Tevan, how did you find me?" Aron stammered after seeing his kinsman standing in front of him. "Did you follow me? How?"

Aron took a step back to examine his cousin. Tevan appeared in good health and good spirits. He obviously had eaten and had access to water. Laughing, Tevan pounded Aron on the shoulder.

"Excuse me, sir. I think I can explain," said a pot-bellied bald man with a huge white mustache.

Tevan turned and smiled. “Gristo, look. Tevan find Aron. Tevan find Aron.” The stranger introduced himself as Gristo Poller, a driver of one of the platoon’s supply wagons. “Tevan helped me hitch up my team the second day on our trip out here,” a nervous Gristo said in a shaky voice, noticing the intense looks he was getting. “I thought he was one of our wagoneers. We got along because he didn’t say much and he was good with the horses.”

Aron nodded slowly, still trying to understand how Tevan managed to join the platoon.

“I suspect this one jumped in my wagon the day you joined the platoon, sir,” Gristo said. “He’s been talking about an Aron Nels saying good-bye. Now I know what he meant. He saw you standing in line after you marched into the temple. I couldn’t stop him.”

Aron was speechless. His body swirled with emotions. He had vowed to fight and die, if necessary, with Circle Sankarikiller, but now his nearly helpless kinsman stood before him. Tevan obviously would need to be cared for.

The Defender was about to scold his cousin, when the young man pointed at the table. “Tevan hungry, Aron. Eat please. Tevan hungry.” Aron didn’t answer. Too many questions swarmed his mind.

“Let the young man eat, Defender,” Witt Peyser said from behind Aron. The steward and Elder Xander had seen the commotion and walked over to investigate.

Aron gestured toward the table and Tevan quickly sat down and helped himself. Egan grabbed a pitcher and poured him a cool drink of water. Tevan nodded and managed a muffled, “thank you,” between bites. The other members of Circle Sankarikiller greeted Aron’s cousin with friendly waves and calls. A few reached over and playfully mussed his hair. Tevan grinned in return.

Aron bowed to Xander and Witt. “My apologies, elder and steward. Apparently my kinsman stowed away aboard one of our platoon wagons and followed me here. Please forgive him. He is a quiet one, just like a child.”

Xander patted Aron's shoulder in a fatherly manner. "Don't worry, Defender. We shall take good care of him and return him home as soon as possible. He is welcome in Temple Darya. We shall send word to his parents by courier that he is safe with us."

Overwhelmed by the kindness, Aron bowed and managed to utter an emotional "thank you."

The Seers were too far away to hear, but watched this turn of events with fascination. "Something is different about that blond young man who just sat down," Lanella said.

Verinya smiled. "He is not a Defender. I can see through his eyes." The other Seers gazed at her with surprise.

"Excellent, Verinya. Very good indeed," Lanella said smiling. "This could prove very valuable to us."

8

Rufina smiled despite herself. Manor Stillinger's plan was so devious and well thought out, it might just work. Many of the other members of the High Council nodded in agreement. The High Seer knew she could bully the few members who were sympathetic to the Nuvens into silence.

"Brilliant, Manor. The Nuvens will practically open their temples to us," Rufina said gleefully as she addressed the council. "Once and for all, we will stamp out this barbaric religious movement and re-establish the proper observance of Mother Verde," she said, angrily eyeing the few naysayers who dared not argue against the religion they had sworn to serve.

Manor accepted the compliment with a formal bow. The Sankari captain had been surprised by how cheerfully he had been greeted by Temple Darya's guards. They had sensed no threat from Manor. They had even invited him to land and share a drink.

The plan to attack and destroy the Nuven temples opened up in his mind as he glided over the structure and returned home to Fortress Bryann. He could turn the Nuvens' trust against them. Once the idea anyone flying a glider was an ally was reinforced among the barbarians, future access to their temples would be easy.

After flying over Temple Vonn, Manor could see a direct assault would be fended off easily. However, if the guards were preoccupied or taken by surprise, once inside, invaders could swarm through the Nuven temple and eliminate the Defenders. Rufina had been delighted when Manor first detailed his plan to her in private, even though he was at a loss about how to carry out his idea on a grand scale.

The Sankari needed to fool all the temples into falling for his plot in one coordinated assault. The plot might work with one or two temples, but the other Nuvens would be wary of their gliders. To accomplish such a feat, the Sankari would need thousands of troops to convince the Nuvens they were being threatened by an attacking force. The plan could be hindered because only a few hundred Verdans had sworn loyalty to the Sankari cause.

"We need a massive amount of recruits for a show of force against the Nuvens," the High Seer said. "That could prove to be difficult because, unfortunately, many Verdans seem to be sympathetic toward the barbarians."

Manor nodded. "Many of our people even supported the damn Defenders when they took revenge on our troops that burned down that Nuven village."

Rufina reluctantly agreed with him. "I don't even have the full support of High Council. A few Seers even think we should cease hostilities against the Nuvens. If these contrary Seers could be convinced, then so could many Verdans. If the Nuvens were more aggressive, it would make your plot so much easier to carry out."

Manor was silent for many seconds before a strange look clouded his face. "Can you tell me the names of the contrary Seers?" he asked.

Surprised by his request, Rufina complied, quickly naming the four most vocal Seers who were sympathetic to Nuvens. "Ah, Serna Holser. Wasn't she raised in a small, outlying village?" Manor asked, flashing a wicked smile.

Rufina nodded, puzzled at the captain's question.

"Perhaps I have a solution to winning over your troublesome Seers, as well as capturing the hearts of many Verdans," he said, carefully watching Rufina's reaction. "But, it may require, hmm, how can I delicately put this? It would require the sacrifice of a few to gain many followers to our cause."

The High Seer frowned, trying to understand what he was saying. "What do you mean it would require a sacrifice by a few? What does Serna's small village have to do with …" Rufina gasped as she finally understood Manor's plan. "Do we dare?" she whispered. "Serna's home fishing village only has about thirty people."

The captain smiled. "The village is smaller than the Nuven nest we burned. But, do you remember how upset people were at such an audacious attack on 'innocents,' as they were called."

Instead of being shocked and angry at Manor's suggestion, the High Seer found herself becoming excited at the proposition of carrying out such a devious plot. She did not relish the death of thirty innocents, but these people could be turned into martyrs, a cause that revenge-minded Verdans could grasp. This could be the turning point in the campaign to stop the spread of the Nuven religion.

In her excitement, Rufina found herself grasping Manor's shoulders. She could see he appreciated the attention. Instinctively, she massaged his tight muscles as she congratulated him for his cleverness. Although a warrior, Manor shivered at the touch of the most powerful woman on Verde. He basked in her attention, but was embarrassed by his rush of excitement.

The thought of their plan actually working stirred a slow, smoldering desire in Rufina that she had not felt in many harvests. Pausing for a moment, the High Seer felt Manor tremble ever so slightly.

She looked in the young captain's dark brown eyes and saw raw passion gazing back at her hungrily. Rufina let her mind wander. How many harvests had it been since she had taken a lover? Four? No, five at least.

Her last lover, a handsome young Tarylan guard, had misused his relationship with the High Seer for personal gain. When she found out he had amassed a large tract of land and built an ostentatious cabin after promising to grant favors, Rufina exiled him to an outpost in one of the far-flung settlements.

Touching Manor conjured up memories of that delicious physical act a man and a woman could enjoy in private. The

Sankari captain would be a perfect lover. He was handsome, accomplished, clever, and he harbored enough secrets to make him compliant to her whims.

Leaning over, she whispered softly in his ear. "Captain, there are other rewards I could bestow upon you for your cleverness and success. These rewards would be my special gift to you."

Manor took a deep breath and nodded. Although middle-aged, Rufina was still a striking woman. She was tall and voluptuous. Her long, red hair was just now showing streaks of gray. The power this woman represented coupled with the strong physical attraction he felt for her almost made him light-headed with anticipation.

The High Seer smiled, took Manor by the hand, and led him to her private chamber. At the bed, she quickly disrobed and gestured for him to do likewise. Rufina walked slowly around the captain, letting her naked body brush sensuously up against his body. Goose bumps exploded on his skin when her body rubbed against it. She noticed his breathing was getting heavier.

A lingering look at his loins was all she needed to see he was ready. She approached him from the back and ran her hands slowly up and down his body. It did not take much of a push from her to maneuver him to the bed. Manor looked up eagerly, but said nothing. This was the first time he had not been the dominant lover.

As she mounted him, the High Seer exhaled with pleasure. Then she proceeded to make up for five harvests of loneliness.

9

Tevan Nels loved to watch the merchants in Temple Darya peddle their wares. He would chuckle with delight as customers haggled with sellers, whether it was food, jewelry, or clothes. If a vendor singled him out and gestured for him to approach a booth, Tevan would blush, utter a polite no thank you, and hurry off to find another attraction.

Since he looked a bit tattered from wearing the same clothes for many days now, the garment sellers were particularly insistent when they spotted him. Embarrassed by the attention and not understanding why they called to him, Tevan hurried from one stall to the next and crisscrossed row after row of stalls.

Now lost and growing hungry because it was nearing second meal, Tevan stood helplessly, salivating in front of a vendor selling meat pies not unlike what his mother would have made for him. The vendor saw the hungry potential customer and held up one of the pastries.

"They're fresh, young sir. Made less than an hour ago. If you don't like what you taste I'll give your coin back. One silver will buy a pie and a mug of sweet cider."

Tevan nodded and searched his pockets, but only found three coppers. His cousin, Aron Nels, had been in a hurry this morning to go on maneuvers with his Defender circle and had forgotten to give Tevan his food allowance. Not understanding the merchant, Tevan held out the coins.

"I'm sorry, young fellow, but that's not enough. You need five coppers or one silver," the vendor said shaking his head, holding up two fingers.

Tevan licked his lips hungrily, shrugged, and started to walk away when he was stopped by a young woman who told him to wait. She handed over two silvers and ordered pies and drinks for both of them.

Even though he was shy with strangers, Tevan smiled and eagerly grabbed the pie and mug. The red-haired woman gestured for them to sit at a nearby table under a large shade tree. Delighted at his good fortune, Tevan tried to converse with his new friend between bites.

The young woman pointed at herself, repeating "Verinya" several times. Tevan tried to repeat her name, but could only manage something that sounded like "Vera." Seer Verinya smiled at his attempts and quickly understood his limitations. "That is good. I like Vera. You can call me Vera."

Tevan laughed when she said "Vera." He knew couldn't say her name correctly but was amused she mimicked him. Now the Seer pointed at her feasting companion and sweetly asked, "Who are you, my friend?"

Taking a big gulp of the sweet cider, he understood what she asked. Chuckling, he thumped his chest, "Tevan Nels." He reached out his hand for the traditional greeting his father had taught him to do when meeting strangers.

Verinya shook hands, noting the firm grip. "That is good. I am pleased to meet you, Tevan Nels."

Nodding politely to his benefactor, Tevan eagerly returned to his meal. She let him finish before asking more questions. "So, Tevan, my friend, do you know Aron Nels?"

The young man's eyes lit up and he laughed. "I find Aron. He say good-bye. Tevan say good-bye. Tevan find."

Verinya smiled when she saw his delight at telling his tale. "Who is Aron? Your brother?"

Tevan giggled. “No, no. Erral and Ivad brothers.” Verinya studied him for a moment. The Seer understood he had a limited vocabulary. Perhaps if she used the correct word, he would understand it.

“Ah, I see. Is Aron Nels your cousin?” Tevan shrugged at the unfamiliar word. Verinya tried again. Obviously the two were probably related, with the same family name.

The Seer tried to remember the Nuven word for relative. A girl cleaning off a nearby table politely interrupted. “Excuse me, but I couldn’t help overhearing. Perhaps the Nuven word you are looking for is kinsman.”

Tevan didn’t need any more prompting. He finally understood what Verinya was asking. “Yes, kinman,” he said, slightly slurring the word. “Aron my kinman.” Verinya thanked the girl. The Seer had the answer she suspected.

Tevan and his new friend spent the remainder of the day wandering through the rows of vendors. He was oblivious to the special treatment they received because his escort was one of the mysterious Seers.

Verinya smiled as she strolled with Tevan. He was genuine and innocent. The young man would tug on her sleeve excitedly when a trinket would catch his eye or thump her on the shoulder and laugh when haggling between a vendor and customer turned heated.

When they passed a clothier, a friendly woman told Verinya she would be happy to stitch some of the tears in Tevan’s trousers. The Seer took a step back and reviewed his clothes. Before he could protest, Tevan found himself being measured. The two women picked through the vendor’s wares to find proper-fitting trousers and several shirts.

The clothier had pitched a nearby tent where potential customers could try on clothes. Tevan complained a little, but minded the two women as they cajoled him into trying on different combinations of outfits. He was not shy about indicating if something didn’t fit right or a material was not comfortable. Even though he could not voice his concerns, his tone and gestures made it clear if there was a problem.

After about an hour of modeling and fitting, four new outfits were chosen. Verinya paid for them without haggling. The kind vendor offered a fair price after hearing about Tevan's plight.

As the time for third meal approached, Tevan and Verinya sauntered back to the temple's living quarters. The new companions were chattering away happily when Tevan spotted his kinsman. Aron had returned more than two hours ago and was growing concerned over his cousin's absence. He expected to see a very worried and upset Tevan, but instead his kinsman was cheerfully chatting with one of those mysterious Seers.

Forgetting his new friend, Tevan let out an excited yell and ran toward Aron, proudly holding up his package of new clothes. The Defender frowned, but his kinsman was oblivious to his displeasure. After happily chattering for a few moments, Tevan walked over and pulled on the Seer's sleeve until she followed him.

"Tevan like new clothes," he said, pulling out the outfits, making Aron approve of each one. "Vera help me." Without warning, Tevan turned and gave the Seer a hug. Instead of being insulted, she returned the hug and laughed with him.

Again, his kinsman had dumbfounded him. Before Aron and his Defender circle reached the temple, Witt Peyser had warned them of the Seers' presence. The Defenders did not understand the power these women had over the Verdan populace. They were mistrustful of these females who looked eerily alike with the flame red hair and coal-black eyes.

Now one of these Seers and his childlike kinsman were acting like old friends. Stepping forward, the woman introduced herself. "I am Verinya, one of the Seers sent to Temple Darya. I beg your forgiveness, but I saw Tevan was in some distress when he didn't have enough coins to buy second meal. It has been my pleasure to spend the day with him."

Aron looked at his cousin, shaking his head in embarrassment. "Oh, no, I forgot to give him coins for his meal." Against his better judgment, it was only right to thank the Seer for helping Tevan. "I am most grateful to you for helping my kinsman. Forgive my manners. I am Aron Nels. Tevan was overdue for new outfits. It was most kind of you.

Reaching into a pocket, Aron drew out a leather purse and started pouring coins out into his hand. "Please let me repay you for his clothes and food."

Verinya started to object, but stopped when she saw his intense expression. Remembering stories of Nuven pride and honor, she told him ten silvers would be fair compensation.

"For all the clothes and a meal?" Aron asked, surprised at such a bargain.

The Seer crossed her arms and returned his stare. "That will be most satisfactory, Aron Nels. I cannot remember having a more enjoyable day with such a charming companion."

"Fair enough," Aron said glancing at Tevan, who was grinning as he stood by his new friend.

As she accepted the payment, Verinya clasped Aron's hands. "It will be my pleasure to see Tevan and you again."

10

Hans Holser smiled as he and his brother, Deter, slowly but skillfully, guided their boat back to the dock of the remote mountain village. Fishing that day on the river had been bountiful for the brothers, as well as for their fellow Verdans. Their net teemed with the wriggling creatures. It had strained both men to haul their catch into the boat.

As usual, the village's womenfolk and children greeted the boats as they glided to their usual places on the dock. This catch would feed their families for many days, as well as fill wagons to haul to nearby villages to sell at market. When the men returned home, the entire village helped process the fish. Tables were set up for gutting and scaling.

Cleaned fish not kept back for that day's meal were quickly taken to the smokehouses, where the meat would be preserved. Some of the entrails were saved to make bait for the next fishing foray. The remaining guts were thrown into grinders. The end product filled baskets that were taken to the village gardens and dumped out for fertilizer. Nothing was wasted.

Ten men watched the scene with great interest from a hidden, rocky ledge. With such a large catch, they suspected the villagers would celebrate their bounty with a large communal feast, including music, dancing, and many mugs of their favorite ales.

The watchers were not disappointed. Less than two hours after the fishermen had landed, a dozen large bonfires were started. The delicious scent of fresh fish cooking filled the air, followed by raucous laughter. One of the ten men smiled as he stood and gestured for his companions to follow.

Hans already had downed two large mugs of Deter's homemade ale when he spotted the strangers who slowly approached the feasting villagers. Tapping his brother on the shoulder, both men rose from their seats to greet the visitors.

"Pardon our intrusion, cousins, but we could not help but smell this wonderful feast of yours," said a smiling, bearded man. "We would most happily pay to take part in your meal. My men and I have been traveling hard and would appreciate a good meal and lodging, if possible."

Deter, who had gulped three mugs of his brew, stumbled over to the smiling visitor. "We don't see many strangers in the village. Who are you? What brings you fellows here?"

Hans started to admonish his brother for his rudeness, but was waved off by the man who spoke. "Perfectly understandable. Forgive my manners. I am Lanzo Kroll, leader of my circle," he said, nodding toward the others. "We have been chasing some Sankari but lost them in the mountains."

Hans and Deter now were joined by a handful of their fellow Verdan villagers who were curious about the strangers. "Nuvens?" an elderly woman asked. "We've never seen Nuvens in this village before."

A wide-eyed boy of about ten harvests peered at the visitors in awe. "You've been chasing Sankari?" he asked excitedly. "Have you been in a fight?" Lanzo laughed and patted the boy on the head.

"No, youngling. We haven't gotten close enough to fight them. But we've been chasing them for days."

Hans stepped forward. "We have seen no Sankari. You are the only strangers who have visited our village for the past two lunars." Gesturing toward the ongoing feast, he invited the outsiders to join them. "We are celebrating a great catch. You are welcome to share with us and pay us what you will."

Lanzo nodded. "My men and I are most grateful for your generous invitation. We have worked up a tremendous appetite as well as strong thirsts," he said, winking at Deter.

Hans's brother slapped the supposed Nuven leader on the shoulder and led him toward the other villagers. "Thirsty, you say?" he said with a wink. "Let me offer you some of my special ale. That should take care of that thirst."

Lanzo smiled. "My men and I were hoping you might have something a bit stronger than sweet cider."

Deter waved for mugs of his brew to be served to the visitors. "My friend, this is better than any cider you've ever been served in the Nuven villages!" he shouted with pride. "Oh, and bring them fish, too."

It did not take the visitors long to join in the fellowship of the feast. After they had eaten their fill, the ten supposed "Nuvens" intermingled with the villagers and soon were laughing at their hosts' stories and sampling the various homemade ales. Much to Deter's delight, Lanzo declared his ale to be the best.

Busy with their revelry, the villagers did not notice that their guests drank very little. Most of the strong brews were sipped and then discreetly spilled or poured onto the ground. When their paths crossed during the festivities, Lanzo approached Hans, who now was relaxed and affable after eating and drinking his share.

"Pardon me, cousin, but someone told me this village was famous for something, or perhaps someone, but I cannot recall what it could be?" the visitor asked.

Hans smirked. "Someone famous from here, friend? I think not. We are simple fishermen. We are content to stay here, away from the troubles in the valley, especially that crowded, noisy Verde City."

Lanzo prodded his new friend. "Ah, that's it. Someone in Verde City."

Hans thought for a moment then smiled. "My sister, Serna, is a Seer in the city. Is that who you're talking about?" he said, laughing. "She has been gone for more than twenty harvests."

Lanzo's eyes lit up with great interest. "Yes, that's it. You must quite proud of your sister."

Hans shrugged. “Yes, it was an honor for her to become a Seer, but she has never been back since she left.” A beautiful young woman carrying pitchers of ale stopped nearby. One long reddish-blond braid was draped over her shoulder and the other hung down the middle of her back.

“Father, are you talking about Serna?” she asked, her eyes lighting up. “Oh, how I would love to visit her in Verde City.”

Hans leaned over, giving her a hug. “Maybe someday, Arista,” he said playfully, tugging the braid that ran down her back. “But for now, my girl, you’d better deliver those pitchers before someone gets upset with you.” Arista stuck out her tongue. She glanced at Lanzo, then blushed and giggled when he winked at her.

“I’m sure the Seer would be happy to host such a charming kinswoman,” he said with a smile as he watched the young woman hurry away. Hans shrugged as he took a big draw of ale. “Perhaps, but my sister does not know about Arista. Serna left before my daughter was born.”

Lanzo put his arm around Hans’s shoulder. “I have a feeling, my friend, that your sister will be very interested in your daughter.”

The two moons of Verde had risen and almost made their way across the night sky when the last of the villagers stumbled toward their cabins, which were built into nooks and crannies in the nearby mountain. The visitors turned down invitations to be lodged in various homes, explaining they preferred to stay together as a troop.

The villagers apologized for the lack of comforts and opened an empty storage shed for the “Nuvens" to bed down in. Lanzo was gracious, assuring his hosts the shed would be much more comfortable than sleeping on the cold ground in the mountains.

The leader even insisted he and his men help some of the villagers, who had celebrated too much, back to their homes. About an hour after everyone in the village finally settled down for the night, Lanzo made sure his disguised Sankari troop was ready to carry out its mission.

Each warrior had been selected for exhibiting a vicious nature. Most had spent time in prisons for crimes against their fellow Verdans, including assault and robbery. Even Lanzo, who once had been a promising officer, had been jailed for attacking a fellow Sankari over a game of chance. All the troopers had been promised amnesty for carrying out this bloody mission.

"Just as we practiced," the captain ordered in a low voice. "Go in pairs. The cabins are unlocked. Most of these drunks can be killed in their sleep. Do what you will to the women, but make sure they make no noise. Spare a few of the older male children. We want to leave a vengeful batch to be witnesses to this 'Nuven' attack. Remember, act like Defenders. Slit their throats and leave the bodies where they fall. The cabins must be left standing. We want plenty of proof that Defenders did this."

Lanzo looked at his men with a deadly glare. "Leave Hans Holser and his family to me. I have special plans for the daughter." The troop silently made its way toward the sleeping villagers. No one raised an alarm as they crept close.

Hans and his mate were sleeping soundly, snoring in a drunken stupor, when they were pulled savagely from their bed. Before the fisherman could defend himself, his nose was broken by a heavy blow. He passed out from the injury.

His wife never uttered a sound as Lanzo neatly slit her throat. Her blood gushed out and pooled around her limp body. Arista was dragged into the room by Lanzo's partner. The girl was gagged and bound, her eyes wide with terror.

The captain doused Hans with a pitcher of water to wake him up. The fisherman gasped in pain as he tried to focus on his attacker. While the sobbing Arista watched, Lanzo beat her father, demanding he tell them where the Sankari were hiding.

Of course, poor Hans could tell him nothing and endured more of the punishment until he slumped to the floor, dead. Not finished with his act, Lanzo grabbed the frightened girl and flung her to the bed.

As he tied her down, the Sankari leader looked at his companion and snarled, "The captain always goes first." When the two men had finished, they made sure Arista's bonds were loose enough so she could eventually free herself. The poor girl had fainted from the trauma of the attack.

To make their intentions seem deadly, Lanzo struck her head with the hilt of his knife. The blow was designed to leave a welt and ugly gash, but not be fatal.

The Sankari troop reconnoitered at the dock about two hours after they started their deadly mission. All the men waded into the river to wash off the blood that covered their clothes. Lanzo took one last look at the village which was eerily silent, except for the twitters of birds as they awoke for the day. After congratulating the troop for a job well done, the captain ordered them back into the mountains.

11

Witt Peyser banged open the door to the small barracks where the Circle Sankarikiller brothers had been dozing. True to their training, the Defenders half-rose from their cots, clutching knives, to see who dared to disturb them. One of the young Nuvens recognized Witt and yelled, "Steward in the room! Attention!"

The ten Defenders groggily stood up and saluted their leader. Witt chuckled to himself, but dared not let the circle see his humor.

"You've only been in the temple for a week and look how soft the lot of you have become," he said in his best growl. "Circle Sankarikiller has drawn the privilege of patrolling the Western villages. I was going to give you two hours to get ready, but now you've got one hour to get your gear ready and fetch some food. Meet me at southwest portal three."

The Defenders were now wide awake. They scrambled to grab their traveling gear and weapons, which had been prepared in advance. Aron Nels scurried about with his circle brothers, but a frown was etched on his face. Witt, who had anticipated Aron's mood, called the young man over.

"Defender, don't worry about your kinsman. I've seen to his care," Witt said reassuringly. "The third-level trainees have eagerly volunteered to see to his needs."

Aron saluted his superior. “Yes, steward. Thank you for telling me.” He started to leave, but stopped. “Sir, Tevan will need coins for his daily needs.”

Witt smiled to allay Aron’s concerns. “His allowance has been taken care of by three generous benefactors. I promise he will be well taken care of.”

Aron frowned. “Benefactors? I trust it is not the Seers. One has taken an interest in Tevan.” This time it was Witt who looked surprised.

“A Seer has been paying attention to Tevan? I was unaware of that. Hopefully it is out of kindness. No, it is not the Seers. The benefactors are Elders Nyrthka, Grig and Xander Vonn. They have pledged to support Tevan when you are busy elsewhere.”

Smiling, Aron was relieved he was being helped with the care of his kinsman. He could now give full attention to finishing his preparations.

The members of Circle Sankarikiller were ready by the portal at the scheduled time. A few were breathing hard from scrambling to get there. Every Nuven temple was built with dozens of secret portals to allow for emergency entries and exits.

The first Nuvens had insisted on this system to emulate the cave system that had saved their lives so many times from those mysterious off-world marauders, the Tanlians. The portals were cleverly hidden in architectural features throughout the temple. Only the privileged knew about these secret doorways.

Witt inspected the circle. To his satisfaction, they all were ready to go on their three-week tour to protect remote Nuven villages. Every Defender circle in all the temples shared in this responsibility of protecting the outlying villages, which could be in danger of a Sankari attack.

The circles visited each village in their protection area, staying for an undetermined amount of time. They entered unannounced and departed the same way, the same way Circle Sankarikiller was now leaving Temple Darya.

Much as they did when patrolling the temples, the Defenders established no pattern for the enemy to pick up on. Many times, even the villagers were unaware Defenders were among them. The warriors often posed as traveling merchants or artisans, just passing through.

¶ ¶ ¶

Rakir strained to see out the watchtower she was visiting in Temple Darya. The Seer thought she saw a group of men scurry out of an opening in the wall and disappear into the half-light of early morning. It was almost a full hour before first sun. The young woman took deep, meditative breaths to relax and project her sight onto the shadowy figures. But nothing came to her. Her mind was unable to connect with whoever was out there.

The seer shook her head, then frowned. Rakir was sure she had seen men departing. The fact she could not use her sight only confirmed what she suspected. The men must have been the unreadables — Circle Sankarikiller. Armed with her suspicions, it was her duty to report the departure to Lanella. Since arriving at Temple Darya, Rakir and the other Seers had tried to watch the comings and goings of this special group of Nuvens closely.

However, this mission had proved to be difficult. Unaccustomed to being unable to use their sight to gain an advantage, the Seers had to resort to physically spying and watching this circle of Nuvens. Even though Defenders had a reputation for being womanizers, this circle had gone out of its way to avoid the Seers. Almost every attempt to flirt with or attract them had failed.

Only Verinya had successfully contacted one of the Defenders, Aron Nels, when she helped the Nuven's helpless kinsman in the marketplace. Even then, the warrior had been polite but was wary of her. After hearing Rakir's report during first meal, Lanella turned to Verinya.

"Find your new friend and see if you can discover where that circle has gone. If we can chart those Defenders' activities, then we can learn more about them."

Verinya quickly finished her meal and left to search for Tevan. She knew he loved to visit the marketplace after meals.

The Seer would be able to learn something about the Defenders just by finding Tevan. It would be almost as telltale to find the childlike man without his warrior kinsman nearby.

As she walked slowly through the marketplace, Verinya searched with her eyes and ears. Oftentimes his hearty laugh could be heard echoing through the rows of vendors before he could be spotted. Finally resorting to using her "sight," Verinya found Tevan with a group of teenage boys. Much to her surprise, the group scuttled off when one of the youngsters spotted her.

Curious, the Seer patiently followed them, knowing Tevan would insist they stop to look at something interesting. She was not disappointed. The group had paused near a booth where the vendor and a customer were loudly haggling over a price. Verinya easily picked out Tevan's laughter from the noise of the crowd. This time the Seer made sure she kept other people between herself and Tevan's group.

Four teenage boys stood near Aron's kinsman. One paid close attention to Tevan, while the other three obviously were watching out for danger. Verinya smiled. One very important person was missing from this group — Aron Nels. The Seer had never seen Tevan with a group of boys before. They obviously were taking care of him.

Verinya suspected if Aron was unable to care for his kinsman, he must have made arrangements for these boys to take his place. The Seer felt she had her information concerning Aron's whereabouts, but first she wanted to have some fun with Tevan's young protectors. Without drawing attention from the group, Verinya sauntered over to a nearby vendor who was showing off brightly colored scarves.

Tevan shook his head, disappointed the vendor and his customer had finally agreed on a price. It was such great fun to watch the arguing, but from experience, the young man knew all he had to do was to wander through the marketplace to find more entertainment.

As Tevan and his new friends started to walk up the aisle, an old woman jostled him. "Take care where you step, youngling," the crony cackled.

Surprised, Tevan mumbled, "Sorry," and took a step back. His protectors looked at each other, unsure how to handle this problem. Ever since they were babies, the youngsters were told to respect an elder. The woman drew closer as if she were going to lecture poor Tevan then pulled down the scarf covering her head.

"Vera!" Tevan called excitedly, reaching out to give her a hug. His caretakers stood with their mouths agape. The Seer, who they had been trying to avoid, had easily slipped through their ranks. When Tevan finished hugging the Seer, one of the youngsters reached out to pull him away, but without success.

"Look Farro, Vera here," Tevan said laughing. He playfully swatted the Seer on the shoulder.

Verinya smiled sweetly. "It's good to see you, too, Tevan. Why, where is Aron?"

Tevan shrugged. "Aron not here. Farro come with Tevan."

The Seer gazed at Farro, who was blushing with embarrassment at having failed to avoid her. "I can't imagine why Aron Nels isn't watching his kinsman. He must be away from the temple."

Farro bowed clumsily. "He is busy with temple duties, so we are watching Tevan." The other three members of the group nodded. "Yes, temple duties," they murmured in unison.

Verinya reached out to take Tevan's hand. "I see. Well I would be happy to accompany this handsome young man through market. I will bring him back when he is ready," she said, flashing a smile.

Farro started to argue, but Tevan stepped close to the Seer. "Tevan go with Vera," he proclaimed loudly. Like old friends, the pair turned and walked up the row. Verinya laughed at her victory. She imagined the four younglings would be severely chastised once they returned to their quarters, plus she had her answer as to Aron's whereabouts; he obviously was not in the temple.

12

Arista Holser was slow to regain consciousness. She tried to open her eyes, but her head throbbed so hard any movement was painful. The young woman was thankful for the cool compress someone had placed on her forehead. She lay in a fetal position; her whole body throbbed with pain.

Strange noises started to seep into her subconscious. Noises that ordinarily would have alerted her that others were in trouble. Arista opened her eyes again, forcing herself to focus. It took her a moment to realize she was lying underneath the giant shade tree in her village's marketplace. Huddled around her was a cluster of youngsters about her age.

One of the older girls was on her knees, sobbing uncontrollably. Several other girls tried to comfort her, but they all looked to be in shock. All of their clothes were torn and splattered with blood. Three older boys sat cross-legged in the grass, nursing various wounds to their bodies and faces.

"Cousin, thank Mother Verde you were spared," a familiar voice whispered hoarsely. Arista turned her head to see Gustaf sitting close. Despite her condition, she gasped when she saw Uncle Deter's son.

One of his eyes was closed and swollen. His shirt was covered with dried blood that had poured from a terrible gash in his neck. Seeing Gustaf's wounds sparked the memory of those terrible events from the past night. Tears streamed down her cheeks as she recalled being dragged out of her room to witness her parents being brutally murdered and then her horrifying violation by the two killers.

Gustaf tried to blink away his own tears, but he was not successful. Arista shakily held out her hand, which he clasped tenderly. "I don't remember what happened last night after the celebration," he said softly. Obviously it hurt for him to speak. "I woke up barely being able to see. My throat was on fire."

He stopped and shook his head at the awful memory. Arista had never seen Gustaf so sorrowful and in pain before. Her strapping cousin was always eager to do a man's work to show off his prowess, but now he looked more like a lost and wounded little boy.

Choking back tears, he continued. "I tried to call for Mama and Papa, but they didn't answer. I crawled to their room and found them still in bed. Their throats had been cut. Their blood was everywhere." Arista sobbed as he spoke.

"I didn't know what to do, so I ran to get Uncle Hans, but found your parents …" Gustaf's voice trailed off. "I thought you were dead, too. Your face was all bloody. But you groaned a little when I was about to leave. I wrapped you up in a blanket and carried you out here." He gestured at the tree. "Some of the others saw me, and we all gathered here to help each other."

Arista squeezed her cousin's hand and propped herself up on an elbow to survey the scene. "There are only eight people here," she gasped. "Where is everyone?"

Gustaf looked off in the distance. "Dead. Everyone else in the village is dead. Stanis Osten and I checked every house. Everyone had their throat cut—well almost everyone," he said softly, remembering Arista's father, who had been beaten to death. The girl, who had been crying hysterically, had finally stopped. She lay in a crumpled heap on the ground. The other girls stroked her hair, trying to comfort her.

"Why? Why did they do this?" Arista asked shuddering. "We told them we had seen no Sankari, but the Defenders kept demanding Papa tell them and they kept hitting him and hitting him. Then they tied me up and they…" She curled back up and sobbed into her blanket.

"I know, cousin. I know. They attacked the other girls, too." Gustaf patted her shoulder while she cried. He did not know what else to do.

After an hour or so had passed, one of the older girls approached Arista. "Are you able to walk?" Irina Nodeu gently asked her. "We need to help some of the younger ones. We all will have to eat eventually."

Gustaf started to scold Irina, but Arista stopped him. "No, I can help," she said, pulling herself up slowly. Irina took one of the pieces of cloth she was carrying and wrapped it around Arista's head to cover the gash. Earlier she had applied a healing salve to Gustaf's wound. Now, she carefully placed another strip around his throat to aid healing.

Arista rose a bit wobbly, but steadied herself and looked at her cousin. "Gustaf, go the drying house and get us fish. We can cook them in the fire pits where we ate last night. I will try to help Irina with the others."

Gustaf eased himself up and slowly made his way to the drying house. A sharp pain jabbed his throat with every step, but he knew his father and uncle would expect him to help. The survivors ate in silence. Their solemnity was a stark contrast to the laughter and joyous event of the previous night when the entire village celebrated the fishermen's bountiful catch.

Arista and Irina made sure everyone ate something, even the poor girl who had been racked with hysterics earlier that morning. They managed to get her to eat a few bites and drink some water even though she stared off into space, a sad look frozen on her freckled face.

"What do we do now? Should we bury everyone?" Arista asked after the meal was over.

Gustaf sat deep in thought, resting his chin on his folded hands. "No, I think we need to leave and get help. We need to show others what happened. Besides, I don't think we should spend another night here. We can't protect ourselves if those Nuvens decide to return."

Arista could not help but look up at the eerily quiet cabins, where their family and friends still lay where they had been killed. Although small, the village had been a bustling place, where children played and people went about their daily lives — cooking, washing clothes, working in the gardens, or helping the fishermen with the catch of the day.

Irina agreed. “But how will we leave? Some of the young ones are hurt or unable to move very far.”

Gustaf pointed to the boats still in place where their fathers had docked the day before. “Maybe the Nuvens left us a way out of here. We can get everyone into two boats and make our way upriver to the next village.”

He slowly made his way to the docks. To his surprise, none of the boats had been damaged. Gustaf stopped at the boat his father and uncle rowed out every day on their fishing forays. The young man often had been allowed to accompany the older men while he learned the family trade.

Seeing the boat brought a flood of memories washing over him. He had been the strong one among the survivors so far, but clutching the side of the vessel made him think of his parents. Gustaf slipped into the boat and lay face down, sobbing loudly. He had not cried this much since when he was a little boy after his father told him he was too small to go fishing with them.

Two hours later, three boats quietly slipped from their home docks. Gustaf and Arista rowed one of the vessels, while Irina and Stanis helped guide the others. None of the youngsters said a word or looked back as the boats glided down river en route to the next Verdan village, which would be almost a day’s journey.

13

Farro had never been so ashamed in his young life. He and the other three Defender trainees stared at their feet, not daring to make eye contact with an angry Aron Nels and Steward Witt Peyser, who shook his head displaying his disappointment. Circle Sankarikiller had recently returned after two days on patrol and Aron had just learned about the Seer's daily forays with his cousin.

"All I asked you to do was to keep an eye on my kinsman and keep him away from that Seer," Aron said, glaring at the four youngsters. "I was gone for two days, and she outwitted you and even took Tevan from you. How did this happen?"

The Defender was the last person Farro and his future circle brothers wanted to disappoint. Aron and Circle Sankarikiller had become heroes to all the trainees after the young men had helped wipe out a Sankari troop, successfully avenging the slaughter of an entire Nuven village. The trainees had immediately idolized members of the new circle, who were barely four or five harvests older than themselves.

A trembling Farro took a deep breath and related in exact detail how the Seer had slipped past them that first day and contacted Tevan, who insisted on accompanying her. Much to their chagrin, Verinya had managed to intercept them almost every day as they tried to look after Tevan. It had seemed as if she'd known where they were going even though they changed the time of day and route.

"Please, Defender, do not blame the others," Farro said. "It was my plan that failed." Aron was impressed with Farro's leadership qualities, although he was still irritated the Seer not only had contacted Tevan, but also found out his circle had left the temple.

"Perhaps you should not be too upset with these young men, Defender," Witt said thoughtfully. "From Farro's account, this Seer seemed very determined to get to Tevan, quite different from an accidental meeting. Oh, and the trainees might be interested in how the Seer and Tevan met the first time. Hmm, I believe your kinsman was wandering the marketplace unescorted," he said, smiling at Aron.

The Defender shrugged and shook his head. His frown changed to a sheepish smile. "The Steward is correct in reminding me who was the culprit who first allowed the Seer and Tevan to meet — me," Aron said, pointing at himself.

Witt smiled. "Perhaps even the prowess of a Defender may not have prevented the meeting. It seems Tevan's friend has carefully planned her actions. I believe it's time to find out why she is so interested in the two of you."

Aron agreed and turned to the four youngsters, who all looked a bit more relieved. "My thanks, trainees, for looking after my kinsman. It was not an easy task I asked of you. Tevan is healthy and happy. I am grateful to you. May I call on you again for assistance with my kinsman when I am away?"

Beaming with pride, Farro did not need to consult with the other three youngsters. "Aye," they called out in unison.

¶ ¶ ¶

After first meal the next morning, Aron guided a confused but willing Tevan around the labyrinth of secret passageways that snaked through the temple complex. The Defender paused at one of the lookout points that was hidden on the outside wall by a statue of Juban Caleria, one of the original eleven Nuven heroes who crossed the treacherous mountains to find the Verdan Valley.

From their vantage point twenty meters above the marketplace, Aron and Tevan easily watched the activities below. Tevan giggled with delight as he peeked unseen at the vendors and shoppers. The Defender brought his kinsman here to watch for the Seer who was so insistent on being with Tevan.

Aron wanted to surprise the mysterious woman, hopefully to unsettle her enough so she might reveal her intentions. "Tevan, watch for Verinya. Tell me when you see her."

His kinsman chuckled. "Tevan look for Vera."

Aron knew his cousin had the mind of a child, but his eyes were sharp. He often spotted familiar people in a crowd long before others saw them coming. It was not long before Tevan chuckled softly, then tugged on Aron's sleeve. "Vera coming. Vera coming."

The Defender studied the crowd carefully, but could not locate the Seer. Knowing his kinsman was seldom wrong at finding people, Aron patiently kept scanning the area until he finally saw a red-headed woman at the far end of the marketplace.

He did not know how Tevan saw her from that far away, but congratulated him on his find. The two kinsmen watched Verinya make her way through one of the aisles among the vendors. As she drew near, Aron could see she was not seriously shopping. The Seer would stop at a vendor, casually examine the wares, but kept looking around, searching for someone.

Just as he was about to lead Tevan down to the marketplace to surprise her, the Seer stopped. An odd expression came over her face as she stood with her eyes closed. An uneasy feeling filled Aron as he watched Verinya spin slowly around. Her head raised in their direction. Her eyes were still closed when she smiled with recognition.

The Seer glanced up quickly at the statue that hid Aron and Tevan, then slowly made her way down the aisle. Aron had never seen someone act so strangely. She seemed to know where they were, even though her eyes were closed.

The Nuvens knew very little about these Seers, the keepers of the Verdan religion. Aron memorized her movements and expression so he could describe them to Witt later. With his surprise apparently spoiled, Aron and Tevan waited to emerge from one of the hidden exits in the temple wall. The Defender did not want to reveal this secret to the Seer.

As he watched Verinya, something Farro told Aron edged its way into his mind. The trainee said the Seer seemed to always know where Tevan was going, even showing up at a vendor's booth before they got there.

Just as Aron was about to lead his kinsman down one of the tunnels to the exit, Tevan started to giggle at a squabble between a vendor and a customer immediately below them. Aron smiled as he watched his cousin's delight with the scene. A movement out of the corner of his eye caught his attention.

Verinya had turned around and also was watching the argument. As she viewed the scene with amusement, Aron caught her stealing a look at their hiding place. Somehow she knew where they were hiding. It was as if she could see what they were watching.

Tevan grew bored when the vendor and his customer finally worked out their differences. He started to scan the marketplace for other interesting amusements. Aron keenly watched as Verinya also went back to her "shopping," at the same time as Tevan lost interest. The Defender looked from his kinsman to the Seer as he formulated an experiment.

Reaching into Tevan's pocket, Aron pulled out one of the handkerchiefs his kinsman always insisted on carrying with him. Smiling, the Defender folded it long-ways and placed it over Tevan's eyes. His cousin started to protest, but Aron gently quieted him. "Shh, Tevan. It's a game. Let's surprise Verinya."

Tevan tugged at his impromptu mask, but chuckled at the plot. "Surprise Vera? Yes, yes, surprise."

Taking Tevan by the hand, Aron carefully led him down a passage that ran the length of the fortress wall. His plan was to get ahead of the Seer. The Defender wanted to know if she would sense their presence again.

The two kinsmen stopped when they reached another lookout point. Aron peeked out and easily spotted Verinya making her way down the aisle. This time, when the Seer closed her eyes she looked puzzled. Again, she turned slowly in a circle, but she did not look up to where Aron was watching.

The Defender guided Tevan down some narrow, winding steps to the exit, which was hidden behind a giant sculpted bush. When no one was watching, the two young men stepped out into the marketplace behind the vendors.

Tevan complained about his blindfold, but followed obediently as they walked ahead of the slow-moving Verinya. Aron stopped at a large booth of a garment seller. He knocked on the back door and spoke briefly to the owner.

¶ ¶ ¶

Verinya had been pleased with herself when she had used her sight to find where Tevan and Aron were hiding and watching her. The Seer was now slightly troubled. For some unknown reason, she could not see through Tevan's eyes. Everything had gone black as if the young man had fallen asleep, but she knew that had not happened.

She was disturbed by not knowing where her watchers had gone. The Seer stopped at every vendor's booth to listen carefully. She easily could distinguish Tevan's guffaws out of a large crowd. However, she could neither hear nor see her friend.

When she paused to examine a merchant's goods, a familiar voice startled her. "Ah, pretty lady, may I help you find some beautiful garments?" She gasped with surprise as Aron and Tevan stood behind the kiosk's counter, holding up bolts of cloth.

She didn't miss Tevan's laughter this time. "Surprise, Vera!" he shouted with glee. "We surprise! We surprise." Even Aron displayed a self-satisfied smirk.

Verinya stood there dumbfounded. Being taken by surprise was a new experience for her or any other Seer. These women prided themselves in watching others in secret.

"Greetings, Seer. I understand you have been asking about me," Aron said, delighted in seeing her discomfort. "It seems you did not bother to look among the vendors for me. What a shame."

Verinya shook her head in disbelief. Words escaped her. The Seer was so rattled she did not notice Tevan scurry out of the kiosk. She jumped when he gave her an enthusiastic hug, which sparked another round of raucous laughter from him.

Tevan's hug actually helped Verinya calm down. She allowed an embarrassed smile to creep across her lips.

"Why, yes, Defender, I have been asking about you," Verinya admitted, then smiled when she saw his eyes narrow with suspicion. "My, are all young men so curious when a woman asks about them? I was told you Defenders are wise in the ways of romance. Perhaps this is not so?"

She then flashed Aron a sly smile, gently said good-bye to Tevan and strode away. This time it was Aron's turn to look dumbfounded.

14

Haral Kaut trembled with fatigue and hunger, but he refused to give up trailing the ten men who had murdered almost everyone in his village two days ago. The slender youth of sixteen harvests did not have a plan except to stay hidden from the murderers and keep following them. He hoped to find some sympathetic Verdans who would help him. He remembered the horrifying things that had happened.

On that terrible night, Haral had stumbled outside while half-asleep to relieve himself in the outside toilet. When finished, he heard strange muffled sounds from the cabin next door. Thinking his neighbor, Innes, was having a nightmare, Haral crept over to her window, hoping to get a peek at the lovely girl who was about his age. To his horror, he saw a large man holding her down, forcing himself on her.

Haral was about to shout a warning when the man pulled out a long-handled knife, the same kind the visitors displayed at the festivities, and took a deadly swipe across her throat. The attacker snarled with disgust as Innes's blood spurted out on him. The boy dropped to his knees in a reflexive gag. He stifled the urge to vomit, knowing the noise would alert the attacker to his presence. Even so, Haral heard the attacker run to the window. In a desperate attempt to hide, he dove into his mother's flower bed, hoping the bushy plants would shield him.

Moments later, he heard two gruff voices. "What is it, Kolo?"

"Thought I heard something when I was finishing with her," a second voice said.

After a long silence the first man said, "I don't see anything. It was probably just one of their chickens. Let's go. We're almost finished here."

Terrified, Haral tried to crawl through the flowers without making them betray him. Peering through one of the thicker bushes, he stared at Innes's window, fearing the murderer was just out of sight waiting for him to move. Knowing he wasn't helping anyone by hiding in the flowers, Haral snuck out and darted to his parents' cabin to alert them to the gruesome events that had taken place next door.

Instinctively, he carefully peered into his parents' bedroom window. Seeing nothing unusual, except for two figures in the bed, he softly called out for his father, but got no reply. This was not unusual because most of the village must be sleeping off the food and drink from that night's festivities. Haral crept around the cabin, but froze next to the wall when he saw a group of men gather close by. They spoke surprisingly loud for the late hour.

"Is it finished?" a familiar voice asked.

"Aye, Captain," the others answered in unison.

One of the men snorted. "These drunks were easier to kill than an old grazer. With the few pups we left and the bodies as proof, everyone will think Defenders did this. Let's leave this worthless place," the first voice ordered.

Haral recognized the speaker as Lanzo, leader of the so-called Defender circle who had wandered into the village that night and took part in the celebration. With his heart pounding so hard in his chest that it hurt, the youth forced himself to wait until the men had walked to the river, when he bolted into his cabin. He got no response from his parents when he rushed into their room.

Grabbing his father, he tried to shake him awake only to discover to his horror that sticky blood was everywhere. Now sobbing, he checked his mother only to find her lifeless body. Their throats had been cut, and blood was everywhere. He somehow managed to stifle a scream of anguish as he hugged his mother's bare feet.

Now in shock, Haral stumbled toward his brother's room. His sibling had suffered the same fate as their parents. The boy of twelve harvests looked eerily peaceful. He must not have awakened.

In a daze, Haral shuffled over to a basin of water and methodically washed his parents' blood from his hands. The sound of voices again snapped him back to awareness. Crawling on his hands and knees, the youth stayed in the darkness just inside the front door, which was standing wide open, as were all the other cabins in the village.

The killers were now walking out of the village. They were not hurrying. Obviously they had no fears of being detected. Hatred surged through Haral's heart as he watched the men head toward the same mountain path from which they had entered the village.

Something Lanzo had said etched itself into Haral's brain: *"Everyone will think Defenders did this."* What did he mean by that? Haral wondered. If Defenders hadn't done this, who were the killers?

A feeling of helplessness seized the trembling youth as he watched the departing group. Fearing the killers would get away unnoticed, Haral swung into action. The youth grabbed his father's hunting knife. He then quickly threw some dried meat and fruit into a pack.

Peering carefully out of the door to make sure he was not being watched, Haral sprinted up the path to follow the men. He felt he was his village's only hope for revenge.

¶ ¶ ¶

Now after trailing the killers for two days, Haral was growing weak and finding it harder to keep up with them. He slept fitfully when the killers did, but was fearful of losing them. His food had run out, and he had no water to drink for most of the second day.

Thankfully, the group decided to camp for the evening, which would at least give Haral a chance to rest. The boy crawled onto a small ledge and lay his head down on his folded arms with a tired sigh. Haral did not even notice the soft rustle behind him. Before he could defend himself, a pair of strong arms pulled him off the ledge. The boy tried to struggle, but he was subdued and bound without a sound.

Fearing one of the killers had somehow doubled back on him, Haral squeezed his eyes shut. He did not want to see the knife that would slit his throat. After a few terrifying moments, the youth opened his eyes. He was in the middle of a group of smiling men, but they were not the killers.

One of the men put a finger against his lips to indicate he wanted no sound from Haral, then untied his bonds and offered the young man a large canteen of water. The youth nodded that he understood and gratefully drank his fill. Returning the canteen, Haral eyed his captors. A chill ran through his body as he realized this bearded group of men must be Defenders.

"Who are you and why do you follow those men?" asked the man who had given him water. He spoke Verdan, but his words were heavily accented.

For some reason, Haral did not feel threatened by this group. These men were younger and had no malice in their eyes. Taking a deep breath, the young Verdan sobbed as he told the strangers about the tragedy that had befallen his village at the hands of the men he had been following.

He could not help himself when he finished. "Those men said they were Defenders. Even bragged about it during the celebration. Afterwards, though, they said the killings would look like Defenders had done it."

The new group frowned as one after hearing his story. "I can promise you the men you follow are not Defenders," said the leader. "We, too, have been following them the past two days after we saw them leave your village. We were curious about them and you. I am Ranar Matao," the leader said, handing Haral the canteen again. "My circle and I are saddened to hear about the killings in your village."

Haral nodded slowly. He had not allowed himself to think about losing his parents, brother, and most of his friends. His eyes welled with tears as he remembered. One of the other men smiled and gave Haral a large piece of dried jerky. They knew the youngster had had little to eat or drink for many hours.

Ranar reached over and patted Haral on the shoulder. "Tonight we will avenge your village. Defenders do not kill innocents who have done them no harm."

¶ ¶ ¶

Lanzo Kroll was awakened by a strange sound in the middle of the night. The veteran Sankari captain lay perfectly still, keeping his breathing even in case he was being watched. He listened carefully to all the night sounds. Nothing seemed out of the ordinary except for light rustling, normal for night rodents in the mountains.

Lanzo was about to relax when he heard the sound again — like someone gagging—then it stopped abruptly. His body stiffened at the familiarity of the noise — that slight gurgle when someone's throat was sliced open.

The officer rose slowly from his hiding place. Out of habit, he changed sleeping locations two to three times at night. He never wanted an enemy or one of his disloyal men to know where he was. Lanzo stared into the night from behind a cluster of rocks where he had bedded down. Large shadows moved silently from hiding places. The figures stopped and pounced on his sleeping men with deadly intent. The captain drew out his knife and crouched behind a large rock.

One of the shadows stopped to investigate the narrow wedge where Lanzo had bedded down. The Sankari leaped forward and sunk his knife into the other man's side with a savage thrust. The wounded Defender groaned with pain and fell backward from the attack. Lanzo pulled his knife out quickly and thrust it deeply into his foe's chest.

He rose to scramble away to a new vantage point, but the Sankari did not move fast enough. Two nearby Defenders heard the crash of the attack and their circle brother's moan. They jumped through the small opening and were upon Lanzo before he could raise his knife in self defense. Two knives jabbed into the Sankari's body.

Lanzo gasped and collapsed to the ground from his wounds. A hand grabbed the captain's hair, raising his head off the ground. The wounded man could feel the hot breath of the other man on his face. "Who are you? Why do you impersonate Defenders and kill innocents?" an angry voice asked in a Nuven accent. "Speak and we will treat your wounds."

Although he could not see the man, Lanzo knew who had attacked him — Defenders. "I am dead already," he rasped. "If you don't kill me, they will. Finish it." Before the Defender could raise his knife, Lanzo writhed in pain one last time then died with a soft gasp.

Ranar swore loudly and let Lanzo's head fall to the ground with a thud. A third Defender stepped through the opening and reported all the sleeping men had been killed.

"Now we'll never know who these impostors were," Ranar growled.

The Defender who helped kill Lanzo knelt down and examined the captain's knife. "This is a Verdan weapon. These men must have been Sankari, but why attack their own people?"

Ranar shook his head. "The Sankari must be getting desperate to blame such an atrocity on us. Let us hope we can convince the Verdans we were not responsible for the attack on that village."

The other Defender spoke up hopefully. "Perhaps we can plead our case to the Seers. They have seemed willing to stop the bloodshed."

Ranar nodded. "Perhaps they will."

15

The Verdan Chamber of Officials echoed with the shrieking woman's pleas for revenge. Normally, such a raw display of emotion would not have been allowed in the small amphitheater. However, this occasion was unusual due to the speaker and her cause.

Serna Holser, normally known for her tolerant nature, stood on the dais in the middle of the amphitheater. She was surrounded by two hundred Verdan leaders. The Seer shouted at the top of her lungs, demanding justice for a horrible crime — the murder of almost everyone in her home village. Beside her cringed a frightened blond girl, Arista Holser, her brother's daughter.

A group of ragtag youths sat in a circle around Serna and the girl. Many of them sported terrible wounds that were beginning to heal. The Council of Seers, led by High Seer Rufina, sat in somber silence behind the animated Serna. Their presence in the chamber was a first.

Normally, a handful of Verdan leaders were requested to appear before the Seer council. In the past, if the Seers wished to address the chamber on a specific issue, there would be one representative. The presence of the Seer council emphasized the importance of the message. Disregarding protocol, Rufina introduced Serna, then embraced her on the dais.

"Honorable leaders of Verde, I introduce to you Seer Serna. What she is about to propose to you has the complete blessing of the High Council of Seers."

Serna's face was fiery red even before she started speaking. In a choking voice, the Seer presented the eight young survivors of the murderous attack on their village by men they believed to be Defenders. The chamber was filled with gasps and murmurs of disbelief as the Verdan leaders saw what the attackers had done to the youngsters. Serna related the fate of the others in the village — most of them had been killed from slashed throats except for her brother who was beaten to death.

"As all of you know, I have long advocated a peaceful solution to the hostilities between the Sankari and Nuvens. But now Nuven Defenders have committed a terrible crime for which they must be punished. I ask your help in demanding these murderers be handed over to us for justice. My niece and these young ones will be able to identify the killers."

Serna paused and moved slowly in a circle as if to gaze into the eyes of every Verdan leader listening to her.

"If the Nuvens refuse to turn over these murdering Defenders, then I propose the complete surrender and abandonment of their temples. We cannot allow these shelters for their pagan beliefs to flourish. They undermine our true religion, the worship of Mother Verde. Any Nuvens, whether they be Defenders or not, who would oppose us should be executed as traitors!" she screamed.

Swept up by the emotion, the chamber erupted in cheers and shouts for action against the Defenders. One respected Verdan leader demanded the murderous Defenders be turned over immediately and all other Defenders be expelled from Verde Valley. His resolution was approved in the loudest unanimous vote of support ever heard in the august chamber.

High Seer Rufina gave an imperceptible nod to Manor Stillinger, who had accompanied her under the guise of representing the Tarylan guards. He flashed a quick smile to relate he understood. Their plan had gone much better than either had hoped. It would not take long for these Verdan leaders to return home and incite hatred and a call to action among their followers.

The Verdan population would rise up against such a horrible crime to an unsuspecting village. The fires for revenge would only be fanned further by the survivors of the unwarranted attack, the innocent girls who had been raped and beaten and the boys who would be scarred for life after they were left for dead.

¶ ¶ ¶

Grig Vonn was aghast at what he had just heard from the delegation of Verdan and Seer leaders. They had accused a Defender circle of an unthinkable crime: murdering all the adults in an entire Verdan village and leaving several mutilated younglings behind. The Nuven leader looked up and down the long oak table at his fellow elders seated on either side of him. Normally a stoic group, the others bore shocked expressions. Many shook their heads in disbelief.

Grig had listened sympathetically to the young girl and her cousin who described the attack on their village. The two youngsters, scarred from a recent attack, were accompanied by a stern-looking Seer. He had dealt with Serna before in attempts to resolve the hostilities between the Sankari and the Nuvens. Now the woman was angry and resolute in her call for the elders to hand over the offending Defenders.

Instead of arguing with the Verdan group, Grig barked an order to his aides. "I want all Defender patrol activities for the past month in front of me immediately." The elder leaned forward and asked the Verdan group the exact location of the village which had been attacked. Serna told him it was the farthest settlement downriver in Verde Valley.

"Downriver? Those are all Verdan settlements. We don't send our Defenders through your territory. We can hardly protect our own villages," Grig said.

Serna was not to be dissuaded. "Obviously, one of your circles decided to strike out at innocents who could not defend themselves."

An aide apologized for interrupting, then handed Grig a large folded map. The counselor unfolded the parchment and studied it carefully. With his finger poised just over the parchment, he traced many lines that ran to and from all of the Nuven temples. After a few moments of silence, the elder straightened up, a somber look on his face.

"According to all the records of our Defender patrols, only one circle has been close to the village," he told the Verdan delegation.

Even Serna seemed surprised by this admission. "Do you know who these murderers are?"

Grig looked at the coded information and nodded. "Yes, we know what circle was there. It is undetermined if they are murderers."

Serna snorted. "Perhaps these Defenders were acting on their own. It does not matter. We want these killers to face Verdan justice. Serious consequences will befall any Nuven who shelters these murderers."

Grig sat back in his chair and raised his hands in the air. "Our Defenders would never attack an unarmed village and commit the atrocities you describe."

Serna rose. The other members of the delegation followed her lead. "Your excuses matter not to me, Nuven," she hissed. "You have a week to find and release these villains to us or your people will face dire consequences."

Before Grig could offer a reasonable compromise, Serna and the others stormed out of Temple Vonn, named after his famous ancestor, Lar Vonn. All ten elders sat in stunned silence at this shocking turn of events.

"It may not matter if the murderers were Defenders or not," Xander Vonn said as he thoughtfully stroked his full, white beard. "As long as the Verdans are convinced Defenders attacked that village, our people may be forced to pay a terrible price."

Grig nodded in agreement. "I want every Defender circle to report their activities for the past two weeks. But I fear we may have to prepare for the worst if we cannot convince the Verdans our people are not to blame for the killings in that village."

16

Aron Nels checked his bow for stress fractures. He ran his fingers up and down the string, feeling for snags and weak spots. Then he grabbed his quiver of arrows. The Defender was eager to spend time hunting alone. It had been a long time since he had ventured out on his own.

He looked forward to the challenge of wandering the foothills around Temple Darya. It was not a mission of necessity to hunt for food, but he planned to bag any fat trophy he could carry home by himself. For once, no worries troubled him. Farro and a few other young Defender trainees were looking after his cousin, Tevan, while they worked in the horse corrals.

That troublesome Seer Verinya had not shown herself this day. Aron smiled as he strode toward the main gate. The early morning air was crisp, and the sky was a beautiful light blue with only a few clouds drifting overhead. Many people in the marketplace recognized the young Defender and greeted him as he made his way out of the temple.

Just as he reached the main gate, Aron saw Verinya and three of the other Seers examining bolts of beautiful cloth that a vendor had just pulled out for viewing. He frowned slightly at the sight but picked up his pace, hoping the young women would be more interested in their shopping than noticing a passing hunter.

Verinya glanced up as he approached and smiled. Much to Aron's surprise, a strange feeling gripped his stomach when the Seer noticed him. His first instinct was to ignore her, but he nodded in recognition and kept walking.

"Good hunting, Aron Nels. May your first arrow find its target," Verinya called out, using the Nuven greeting for good luck.

Aron stopped and exhaled slightly. It would be rude for him not to reply. He had to admit this Seer had studied Nuven ways. "Thank you, Verinya. Hopefully good fortune will be with me, especially with my ancestors' blessing," he said with a wry smile.

The Seer laughed at his reference to his religion and waved. He nodded again and strode out of the temple, hoping this would end the conversation. To Aron's relief, no one else called after him as he left the temple. He turned off onto the trail and headed toward the foothills. He walked along with a contented smile.

Only lovely silence greeted him. No eager cousin begged for attention, no circle brothers jostled him, no vendors called out, and no Seer stood in his way. After a little less than an hour, Aron was scrambling through the foothills with ease. He didn't see many creatures worthy of wasting an arrow on.

He was not taking care with his approach. The Defender was not stalking the way a hunter would if he was intent on feeding his family. He was just enjoying the outing. As the climb got steeper, Aron occasionally loosened a rock as he walked. He listened with amusement as the stones tumbled down, ricocheting off and crashing into bigger boulders.

A noise startled Aron when he stopped for a moment to rest and get his bearings. Somewhere behind him a few small rocks were jostled and sent tumbling. The sound was similar to when he accidentally jarred stones out of their places. Aron had stopped moving. He had not caused the noise.

The Defender instinctively took cover behind a large boulder. He waited patiently, listening for any further suspicious sounds. Hearing nothing other than the normal chirp of birds and scolding of small rodents, Aron moved silently a few meters up the base of the mountain.

When he reached a boulder with a flat top, the Defender scrambled up to a spot that offered an excellent vantage point. Whatever was below him eventually would have to move either up or down the rocky terrain. When it did, Aron would see who or what had made the suspicious sound.

After waiting far too long with the hot sun beating down on him, Aron was about to abandon his position when he spotted movement below. He forgot his discomfort and settled back down to wait. At first it was difficult to see what was moving among the rocks. Whatever it was, the creature moved slowly, not making a sound. Aron glimpsed movement from time to time — then nothing.

Only one creature moved like that — a human. Suspicious at being followed, the Defender carefully notched an arrow. If it was a Sankari troop, Aron could fire a deadly hail of arrows down on them once they came into view.

The Nuven was at home in the rocky terrain. If attacked, he would prove to be a deadly and elusive target. Aron relaxed a bit when his target came into full view. The person did not move threateningly, but stooped down every so often as if gathering something.

Now more curious than suspicious, Aron relaxed his bowstring and watched intently. Something was familiar about the stranger as the person drew nearer to where the Defender waited.

After a few moments Aron could see what the other person was doing — picking flowers. Long red hair swung in the gentle breeze. When the flower gatherer stood up, the Defender almost swore out loud.

Seer Verinya moved slowly up the same path Aron had taken. It was obvious she was no longer concerned about hiding. Every so often she stood up and stretched, turning her face into the sun and smiling at the pleasant warmth.

The Defender caught himself admiring the young woman as she carefully plucked the colorful, sweet-smelling wildflowers.

His interest stirred as he watched her weave a string of white flowers with large petals together into a small wreath and then place it on her head.

Aron smiled as he begrudgingly conceded he was attracted to the beautiful Seer. Curiousity about why she had followed him now crowded out his suspicions. When Verinya walked within twenty meters of his perch, she stopped and looked around, clearly searching for something or someone.

After waiting patiently for a few minutes, the Seer found a clearing between several boulders, sat down in the soft, long grass and started to pull out the contents of a basket she had draped across her shoulder. The spot Verinya chose to relax in was almost directly below the boulder where Aron was perched.

He watched as she uncovered the contents of her basket. The Seer removed a large blanket and spread it on the ground. Then she pulled out a loaf of freshly baked bread, a hunk of pale cheese, some fruit, and what looked like a bottle of fine ale.

The smell of the bread made Aron's stomach growl. He smiled mischievously when he remembered how startled Verinya had been when he and Tevan had surprised her in the marketplace.

Pulling himself slowly up into a crouching position, Aron was about to launch himself beside the unsuspecting Seer, when she cupped her hands to her mouth and called out: "Defender, I know you are watching me from somewhere. Why don't you join me for second meal?"

Aron briefly sank back down on his stomach, disappointed his surprise had been thwarted. He needed no further cajoling to leave his perch. He was sweating profusely from lying in the sun and he was hungry and thirsty.

In one fluid motion, he launched himself from the top of the boulder and landed with a soft thud only a few meters from where Verinya was sitting. She looked startled for a moment but said nothing.

"It's a beautiful day to pick flowers," Aron said with a smirk as he plopped down on the other side of the blanket. "I'm glad I could be a guide for you. If I'd known, I would have walked faster."

The Seer smiled. "Then I would have gotten lost and you would have had to rescue me."

Aron shook his head, but laughed at her cleverness. He then took a long draft from his water pouch. "Tevan is not here to amuse you. Why do you follow me, Seer?"

Verinya coolly met his gaze. "Your cousin does not amuse me, Defender. I truly enjoy his company. He is pure; a true innocent. I appreciate that."

Aron nodded. "Yes, he is an innocent. Sometimes that is a blessing. Sometimes it is a curse. You did not answer me, Seer."

Her eyes glinted with amusement. The candor and directness of the Nuven people was different from the reverence which the Seers were accustomed to receiving.

When common Verdans approached this honored class of women, they normally spoke in hushed, respectful tones. Many Seers would be insulted if they were addressed with such informality, but Verinya found it refreshing. That is why she enjoyed Temple Darya's marketplace so much. The Nuven vendors were unafraid to argue for a bargain, unlike the meek Verdan merchants who almost fought over the chance to give their wares to a Seer.

With a casual shrug, Verinya decided to be as direct. "Have you not guessed my interest after we last spoke?" She cut off a piece of cheese and bread and handed them to him.

Aron took a bite, but eyed her suspiciously. "I thought you were playing games with me."

Verinya smiled, took a short sip out of the bottle and passed it to Aron. He took a careful sniff, detected the sweet aroma of a fine Verdan ale, and took a hearty swig.

"We Seers do not play games when a male interests us," she said with unusual candor as she looked into his eyes. "Do I need to explain my intentions?"

Aron stopped chewing. It was his turn to be surprised. He had no experience with romance. Witt Peyser had made sure the circle brothers were well versed with the physical act of sex. He purposely exposed his young charges to willing young women in some of the villages.

The steward did not want his Defenders yearning for the tenderness of a lover. He wanted to keep them sharp. For a reward after arduous training sessions, they were encouraged to find willing girls to bed.

Aron blushed. He did not know what to say. Witt had warned him and his circle brothers not to associate with the Seers, but here he was sharing a meal with one of the mysterious women.

Verinya smiled sweetly and reached for the jug of ale. She took a much longer sip this time. “When you ask a question, do not be surprised when you get an honest answer, Defender.”

The pair ate in silence for a while, sharing the food and drink. Verinya asked what had happened to Tevan to leave him in his childlike condition.

Aron took another long draft and slowly started to tell her the story. The words came haltingly, but she listened patiently. When he finished, Aron frowned, thinking of the accident that had frozen his cousin into a childlike state.

Seeing his sadness, Verinya moved to his side. “Aron, it was not your fault that Tevan fell. You were young boys playing. His slip was an accident,” she said, holding his face in her hands.

The Defender was thrilled at her touch. The smell of the flowers in her hair was intoxicating. He pulled her hands to his lips and softly kissed them. She was so close he could feel her warm breath on his face. Their first kiss came naturally. They both leaned into each other, their lips melting together.

At first tentative, their embrace and kissing became more passionate. The pair gently drifted down to the blanket. The food was carelessly tossed into the basket. They were solely intent on exploring each other. Clothing was quickly pulled off as their bodies slid passionately together.

Aron and Verinya held each other tightly. Legs were wrapped around each other’s bodies as they rocked back and forth, gently at first and then faster and more urgent until their passion reached that sweet crescendo. Both were breathing heavily and drenched with sweat when they unlocked with reluctant sighs.

Neither had felt such a complete connection to another person before.

Aron rolled over onto his back, but locked his gaze on Verinya's face. She shifted on her side and laid her head on his chest. This moment was theirs to savor. Neither Nuven nor Verdan worried about their respective missions or how this would change their lives.

They had just experienced that sweetest of human experiences — the act that had bonded man and woman together for thousands of years in the past and would forever link them in the future.

Aron and Vernya luxuriated as they lay in each other's arms. After a short nap, their hands started to explore each other's bodies again. With the energy only found in youth, the two made love again and again until exhausted. They finally fell asleep. As the sun slowly set, the pair reluctantly returned home hand in hand until they reached sight of the temple.

After a long, lingering kiss, neither said a word as they parted. Aron watched as Verinya walked through the main gate, then he slipped into one of the temple's secret entrances.

17

No singing could be heard in Juso Reyna's inn. The normally jovial and boisterous crowd was somber. News of the slaughter of the fishing village had spread like a spring storm through Verde City and the smaller settlements. The inn's patrons were in a dark mood. They stood in small groups, talking in hushed, heated tones.

The volume of the crowd grew steadily as more ale was consumed, until the room reverberated with an angry buzz. This was the moment the two men in the corner had been waiting for. One of the two violently rose from his stool, sending it crashing to the floor. Many of the patrons paused to see what had caused the commotion.

"Something should be done to those killers!" the standing man shouted. "Babies were killed. Young girls were raped. Their parents all murdered in their beds by guests they had given food and drink to."

He paused, listening. The inn had gone silent. "In … their … beds," he repeated, emphasizing every word. "I don't care what other Verdans say. I think the Sankari may be right. Kill those damn Defenders, then send the rest of the Nuvens back to their cursed valley."

Several young men shouted their support. Others chimed in and soon the whole inn echoed with shouts of bravado and revenge. The man who had kicked over his stool climbed onto a table and called for silence.

"My friend and I leave in the morning to search for the killers," he said, gesturing toward his drinking partner. "We are joining Verdan warriors who have had experience fighting Defenders."

The speaker paused, eyeing the crowd. "I have heard a lot of brave talk in here tonight, but do any of you have the stomach to fight for Mother Verde?" Again, the inn erupted in shouts of bravery and promises from every young man present. The man on the table held up his arms for silence.

"I'm proud to see such brave young Verdans willing to fight for their fallen brothers and sisters. We'll leave immediately from here after first meal. Pack sparingly. Only bring food and weapons."

The speaker started to step down from the table but changed his mind and climbed back up. He looked around the inn solemnly as if memorizing each face. "My brothers, look around at your neighbors here tonight. Anyone not joining us tomorrow will be remembered as a coward."

With a wave, the man jumped from the table with a flourish, gathered his friend and strode out of the inn, slapping many young men on the shoulders. Shouts of promises and farewell followed the two men out into the night.

The two men walked for a while before speaking. The man who kept silent while his partner addressed the crowd in the inn glanced over his shoulder to make sure they were not being followed.

"That was impressive, Lieutenant," he said with a chuckle. "I think you recruited every Verdan capable of carrying a javelin to join us."

Torvild Zullon smiled. "Thank you, Captain. I am accustomed to leading worship."

Manor Stillinger grinned at his companion. "If all our people were half as successful as you were tonight, we soon will have an army of thousands to march on the Nuvens."

¶ ¶ ¶

The Defenders slowly made their way out of the mountains. They built the traditional funeral pyre and mourned their circle brother who had died fighting the murderous Sankari.

Haral Kaut recognized all the Sankari who had murdered the people in his village, including his mother and father. Pent-up emotions exploded in the youth when he saw the bodies of the Defender impostors. Screaming in a rage, Haral flung himself on Lanzo's body, pounding it with his fists until he collapsed from exhaustion. The young man was still weak from his journey after following the attackers.

The sympathetic Defenders made sure Haral didn't hurt himself during his outburst then gently guided him away from the scene. Ranar Matao knew it was imperative his circle deliver Haral quickly to the Seers in Verde City. The youth was the only one who had witnessed the Sankaris' admission they had posed as Defenders.

Without Haral to convince the powerful women that Sankari were behind the murders, then Defenders surely would be blamed. Ranar was troubled as they scrambled through the mountains. The killers had wanted Defenders to be blamed for the villagers' deaths.

Murdering their own people was such a desperate move. Ranar wondered how widespread the plan was to incite hatred against the Defenders, and maybe even all Nuvens. With these suspicions, the group avoided all the Verdan villages they traveled near.

For the first two days of their journey, Haral had trouble keeping up with the Defenders' fast pace, but now into the sixth day he strode along as if he were one of the circle. The group traveled in the classic Defender formation — every other man walked to the left or right of the one in front. They kept plenty of space between each other, but stayed within sight of the man in front.

Haral was placed in the middle so he could be helped from any direction. If danger arose, the circle could react to whatever direction the assault came from. The formation made it difficult for any foe to wipe out the group with a surprise attack.

Ranar stopped by a large tree when he came to a river that meandered through a heavily wooded canyon. A series of low whistles sounded behind him as his circle brothers signaled each other to take cover.

The Defender scoured the valley, looking for any suspicious movement. He watched for birds sounding alarms and listened for rodents scolding unwelcome strangers. Hearing nothing unusual, Ranar slowly made his way into the valley. The whistles sounded again, this time signaling an all-clear message.

The circle moved easily through the canyon. The Defenders and Haral zigzagged through the trees. When they came to a clearing where the river widened, they stopped again before venturing out into the open. Something bothered Haral about this site, but he could not determine the cause.

The circle entered cautiously, but they were greeted by nothing but silence. Birds and smaller creatures had called and squeaked as they traveled through the trees, but now there were no sounds.

Ranar had almost made it to the other side of the clearing when a suspicious movement caught his eye. Only a moment after he called out a sharp warning whistle, javelins swooshed through the air, striking trees, the ground, and felling three of the Defenders and Haral.

The surviving circle brothers leapt for cover as their attackers crashed through the underbrush in an attempt to surround them. The remaining six Defenders managed to notch arrows and kill a few of the attackers before the fighting turned to hand to hand.

Screams filled the woods as the Defenders fought bravely. Their knives expertly slashed out at the attacking Verdans, wounding and killing many. The much larger number of attackers proved to be too much. Every Defender was swarmed over by the furious Verdans.

Ranar was the last to die. He backed up against a huge tree and valiantly fought off his attackers until a javelin pierced his chest. The Defender gasped and fell back against the tree. With a shout of glee, his foes attempted to overwhelm him, but Ranar leapt into the crowd. His knives slashed open two more Verdan throats before he finally fell.

Manor Stillinger shook his head at the number of Verdans the Defenders had killed. Even when wounded, the Nuven warriors fought fiercely, killing almost three times their number.

Curious about the lone survivor, the Sankari captain strode over to Haral, who lay against a tree badly wounded by a javelin that had struck him in his side.The youth weakly waved for the Manor to come near. He was surprised to see the young Verdan.

"What were you doing with these vermin, youngster? Did they capture you?" Manor knelt to examine Haral's wounds.

The youth struggled to speak through the pain. "Defenders did not attack my village. They were impostors. These Nuvens killed them. They — they helped me."

Manor's eyes narrowed as he studied the young man. "It was your village that was attacked?"

Haral nodded. "Yes. These Defenders were taking me to the Seers to tell them the truth."

The Sankari captain knelt close to Haral. "Oh, don't worry, young one. I will tell the Seers what happened here. Are you the only witness to the impostors?"

The word "yes" had barely left Haral's lips when a knife savagely plunged into his chest.

18

The Nuven convoy paused as it crested a hill overlooking Verde City. Concern was etched on every one of the thirty faces as they watched heavy smoke billow over the southern edge of the city. Even from this distance they could see people streaming out in a desperate attempt to escape.

Elder Xander Vonn called for the attention of one of the Defenders who were escorting the Council of Elders. "Is that the Nuven section of the city that is burning?"

Ossin Needhan frowned as he watched. "Yes, Elder. It looks like the entire Nuven part of the city is on fire."

Xander shook his head at the tragic sight. "It looks like the Verdans didn't wait to hear our peace proposal. The Seers knew we were coming, but obviously even they don't have the power to control their people."

Ossin looked at his circle brothers and gestured for a second circle to approach. All the Defenders who had been chosen to accompany the elders to Fortress Bryann were looking at him intently. He knew what they were thinking even without asking.

"With your permission, Elder, the other Defenders and I want to help our kin who are in trouble down there," Ossin asked the tall, white-haired man. "Perhaps we can prevent any further loss of life."

Xander paused and looked at the eager warriors who were waiting for his approval. He had a terrible feeling only twenty Defenders would be unable to lend much assistance. The damage looked to be too widespread.

Only now did he regret not allowing more active Defenders to accompany the elders on their mission to try to ease tensions between the Verdans and Nuvens. Xander had not wanted to give the appearance of a powerful, armed force marching on the city and fortress.

Grig Vonn seemed to know what his brother was thinking. "It won't be twenty Defenders helping our people down there, it will be thirty," he said defiantly, throwing his long beard over his shoulder. "We Elders might be slower, but we are still Defenders."

Xander smiled at his brother. "Yes, we are Defenders and sworn to help those in need." With a quick wave for the others to follow, he spurred his horse into a dead run toward the frightened Nuvens who were fleeing the city.

As the Defender convoy drew near, it became apparent their fellow Nuvens were being attacked. Woman and children were running for their lives ahead of a battle line of men armed with crude clubs and knives. They were desperately trying to fend off a horde of Verdans who were wielding swords and throwing javelins.

Ossin rode up alongside Xander and shouted instructions. "Please, sir, help the women and children to safety. We will fend off the Verdans." The Elder frowned, but didn't challenge the Defender leader. Xander shouted a reluctant "aye" and signaled for the other elders to follow him toward the mass of escapees.

The twenty Defenders spurred their horses around the flank of the attackers and charged into several hundred Verdans screaming high-pitched war cries. The Nuvens who were defending their women and children shouted for joy.

Encouraged by the Defenders who were coming to their assistance, the Nuvens fought even harder and halted the attackers' advance. The onslaught of the charging Defenders on horseback caught the Verdans, most of whom were untrained in warfare, by surprise.

The horsemen swept through the attackers' ranks, killing and maiming many as they cut the group into two parts. Whirling around before their enemy could regroup, the Defenders charged again, causing the back half of the Verdans to retreat in terror back to the city.

Ossin took quick stock of his troops. Only three Defenders had fallen during the first two charges. The remaining seventeen plunged into the first half of the Verdan force who were now in a deadly standstill as they clashed in hand-to-hand combat with determined Nuvens.

The slaughter was on as the Defenders slashed and cut through the Verdan ranks with deadly efficiency. Emboldened even more by seeing the success of their rescuers, the other Nuven fighters grabbed weapons dropped by dead or dying Verdans and pressed the fight. A loud cheer broke out when the two groups of Nuvens met and the last of the Verdans fell. However, the gaiety was cut short with a warning shout.

From the gates of the city, a troop of Sankari charged toward them. Ossin checked the number of Defenders left able to fight — fourteen. Without being asked, six sturdy Nuven youths quickly mounted the horses left by the fallen Defenders and joined their ranks.

Ossin ordered the Nuven men from the city to retreat slowly and act as a buffer to give their women and children more time to escape. The Defenders and the other youths turned their horses and met the attacking Sankari at full gallop.

The two groups met in a deadly crash of horseflesh, metal, and human bodies. The six young Nuvens were knocked off their horses with the first pass, but only two Defenders fell. The remaining Defenders instinctively formed a circle to protect themselves. Ossin and the others fought bravely, but fell to the superior Sankari numbers.

With bloodlust still coursing through them, the surviving Sankari charged toward the escaping Nuvens. However, another group of horsemen raced to face the attackers.

Without a second thought, Xander Vonn, along with most of the other Elders and a few volunteers, met the Sankari head on. Surprisingly, only five of the Nuvens fell after the first charge. Xander and the survivors turned their mounts, fiercely called out the Defender war cry and bravely met their deaths.

Surprised by the tenacity of these old men and commoners, the Sankari were slow to regroup. As they started to steer their mounts toward the escapees, the attackers were jolted by a fearsome sight.

Armed Nuven men, almost a hundred strong, formed a defensive line between them and their escaping loved ones. They shouted defiant threats at the mounted Verdans.

With a loud oath, the Sankari captain gathered his surviving troops and ordered them to charge the Defenders. The Nuvens held their ranks while watching the oncoming horsemen with tense expectation

When the Sankari reached within thirty meters of the Nuvens, a tall woman with two white braids hanging to her waist stepped out in front and raised her hand. At Nyrthka Vonn's signal, a hail of arrows filled the air, raining down on the attackers.

The air was filled with the screams of wounded Sankari and horses. Not realizing most of their fellows had fallen, the few unscathed Verdan warriors continued coming. Turning toward her fellow Nuvens with an eerily confident smile, Nyrthka called out another order just as the horsemen were almost upon the Defenders. This time, a swarm of javelins cut down the remaining attackers.

The Nuvens swept upon the fallen Verdans. The wounded were killed without mercy. The usable weapons were gathered up and the surviving horses captured.

Nyrthka searched through the bloody battlefield, picking her way among the mangled bodies of Verdan and Nuven alike. She finally stopped when she found her brothers lying next to each other.

Xander Vonn lay sprawled out in the grass, his hand still gripping the javelin that had pierced his chest. Grig's face was frozen in a fierce grin of a triumphant warrior. Both brothers died gazing at the other.

Stifling a sob, Nyrthka knelt by her siblings, tenderly closed their eyes and prayed. "May our ancestors welcome you into their midst. You both lived honorable lives and died as any Defender would wish to, protecting your fellow Nuvens. I will miss you my brothers. I fear we could use your wisdom and leadership in the days ahead."

"May the ancestors welcome you, brothers," a deep voice intoned behind her. A hundred other voices repeated the response. Nyrthka, the lone surviving Elder and only woman to achieve Defender status, arose. Shaking her head sadly as she viewed the carnage, Nyrthka and the others turned to join their fellow Nuvens.

19

The young women gathered around their sister Seer like excited schoolgirls desperate to hear a secret. Even the normally dour Lanella could not contain her curiosity about what had happened during Verinya's daylong adventure with the Defender Aron Nels.

Not accustomed to such attention, Verinya only shook her head with faked disappointment and let out a heavy sigh. While she trailed Aron up the mountainside, the Seer imagined what she would tell the others upon her return to Temple Darya. She fully expected to boast of snaring the Defender with her charms.

Verinya had been excited to have the chance of being the first Seer to seduce one of these mysterious, unreadable Nuven warriors. But against all her training as a Seer, Verinya was resolved not to tell the others about the private moments she had spent with Aron.

A bond had been created during that beautiful afternoon of lovemaking. No words had been spoken, but their souls had blended together, just as their bodies had during their time together.

When relaxing on the blanket and enjoying her afterglow, Verinya was startled by a vision of someone tracing her face gently with a hand. Without opening her eyes, the Seer realized she was watching herself through Aron's eyes. The Defender was lovingly touching and caressing her.

Forcing herself out of the vision, Verinya opened her eyes. Aron greeted her with a heartfelt smile and soft kiss on her lips. There was no mistaking his devoted expression.

Now after returning to the temple, her fellow Seers pressed her for details. "I'm afraid to admit the Defender had to rescue me," she said, frowning, in an attempt to feign disappointment. "I was able to follow him up the mountain for a short time, but he moved so fast I could not keep up."

The other Seers gasped with surprise, then a few giggled at her apparent embarrassment. Lanella frowned. "Verinya, you got lost, didn't you? Oh, don't tell me the Defender helped you back to the temple."

This was the reaction Verinya had hoped for. The Seers would assume the worst, and she would only have to confirm their suspicions. Verinya nodded shyly. "Yes, I wandered through the foothills for many hours before the Defender found me when he was coming home. I was very tired and thirsty."

Lanella glared at Verinya for a moment, let out an exasperated huff and walked away. The four other Seers waited until Lanella was out of the room, then peppered Verinya with questions and laughed at her story of being saved by the Nuven she was trying sto educe.

"Well Verinya, at least you have gotten closer to any Defender than we have," Rakir said, her eyes sparkling as she smiled. "I don't think being rescued by one of them was exactly what Lanella was hoping for."

Verinya shrugged. The less she said, the more likely the others would fill in the details of the story with their imaginations. After a while the other Seers grew tired of badgering her. They hugged her sympathetically and brought her some food and drink, which she was grateful to consume after her "exhausting" experience.

¶ ¶ ¶

Aron's circle brothers stared at him in disbelief. He had returned to the temple with no fresh game after a day of hunting in the mountains. If it were any other Defender, they would have understood. They all had hunted with Aron and knew of his prowess. If an unlucky grazer or fat rodent wandered across his path, the animal was destined to become the next day's meal.

Egan Pozos studied Aron carefully. It was clear he was not telling them the whole story. "If you did not bag anything, then what in the name of the ancestors were you doing out there?"

Aron shrugged. "I didn't see any game that interested me today." He then flopped face down on his cot. One of his arms dangled loosely over the edge.

Egan was not satisfied. "If you didn't drag anything back with you, then why are you so tired?"

Aron half-raised his head off the cot, squinted at Egan then plopped back down with a tired sigh. A hearty laugh made him tense up.

"You didn't go hunting, did you?" Egan shouted. "I suspect you've been wenching." When Aron didn't move or respond, his Defender brothers exploded in laughter and pelted him with dried fruit and hunks of cheese.

"And to think we were getting worried about poor, shy Aron not bedding one of the local girls," Egan said, guffawing. "There's only one thing that can tire a man out like that, my brother, and we've all experienced that."

Aron's circle brothers demanded to know which merchant's daughter had been the "lucky" girl, but he refused to move, let alone answer them. The others soon started to speculate, hoping to pester a confession from him.

They accused him of sneaking off with the tavern owner's toothless oldest daughter — the one who made it known she wanted to bed a Defender. Aron just groaned and shook his head. Not placated, they then suggested he had been with the baker's sister, a large, round woman who proudly displayed her prominent bosom with low-cut blouses.

Aron raised himself up on one elbow. "Yes, I was with both of them at the same time. Now are you happy?" His circle brothers laughed at his joke, then grew tired of questioning him. It was evident Aron was not going to reveal a name, at least not this night.

¶ ¶ ¶

Before they returned to Temple Darya, Aron and Verinya promised each other they would wait three days before seeing each other again. Both were well aware they were taking a huge risk to be together.

If the Elders discovered Aron had been with a Seer, he knew they would take severe steps to dissuade him from seeing her again. Although the Seers would have encouraged Verinya to keep seeing Aron, they would have demanded she cultivate him for valuable information.

This had been the longest three days Aron had ever spent. It seemed as if time stood still. He longed to be with Verinya. She was in his every thought. To make matters worse, Tevan went to the marketplace daily and always met Verinya. He would come back chattering happily about her.

Aron tried to keep himself busy with patrol duty and sparring sessions with other Defenders, but his thoughts were constantly of her. Verinya was not faring any better. She gladly met Tevan, who was always delighted to see her, but she longed to be in Aron's arms.

Three days later, when Tevan came back from the marketplace, he had a surprise. Giggling, he pulled something from his pocket and handed a small package to Aron. The Defender opened the small box and saw a note. It was not signed, but the message was clear. It contained directions to a secret rendezvous.

Seeing Aron's smile, Tevan laughed and thumped his kinsman on the back. "Vera say you like. She gave me sweets."

Aron nodded at Tevan. "Yes, you did well, Tevan. Thank you."

That night after last meal, Aron found Verinya in a secluded corner of the temple's large garden. The two wasted no energy with words, but embraced as if they had not seen each other for three lunars. Due to the darkness, the lovers could not see each other well, but their hands and lips reacquainted themselves with each other.

It was the middle of the night until they were finally satiated. As they departed with a passionate kiss, the lovers vowed to wait only a day until their next meeting.

19

The crowd swelled behind the youth as he solemnly pulled the two-wheeled cart behind him that carried his fallen friend. At first the Verdans came out of their homes or shops to investigate the curious sight. Most stopped chatting or stopped in stunned silence when they saw the haunted expression on Gustaf Holser's face.

The young man with the terrible scar that curled around his neck from ear to ear was well known throughout Verde City. He was one of a handful of survivors of the vicious attack that killed most of the inhabitants in his small fishing village.

Many young men respectfully fell in step behind Gustaf when they learned who he pulled. Those following him were only too eager to repeat the tragic tale. Passersby were told a troop of Sankari and Verdan loyalists had attacked a Defender circle. The gossipers said when the Nuven warriors found out there was no hope, one of them killed their hostage, Haral Kaut.

The dead youth also came from the fishing village. Gustaf apparently did not know his friend had survived the village massacre. When told of the murder, Gustaf picked up Haral and started to carry him through the city. A sympathetic Verdan offered the cart when the youth started to stumble from exhaustion.

He tenderly placed his slain friend in the cart and continued his journey. No one knew where Gustaf was headed, but they followed without question. Shouts of revenge and chants soon echoed through the crowd. The Verdans' anger seemed to grow with every step. The pride of many in the city still stung after the humiliating defeat by the handful of Defenders a few days earlier.

The Nuvens had thwarted a mob that was intent on attacking their kinsmen as Sankari-led troops drove them from the city. Dozens of Nuvens had been killed, but the Defenders had managed to scare off or kill even more of the inexperienced Verdan attackers along with their Sankari leaders.

Most of the Nuvens who had been driven from the city escaped to the safety of their temples. Now the Verdans had a sympathetic symbol they all could rally around: Haral, the helpless hostage who they believed was brutally slain by Defenders.

The crowd grew by the hundreds as Gustaf strode through the streets, seemingly energized by the calls for revenge. The youth finally stopped when he found himself at the foot of the altar of Taryl Bryann in the center of the city.

Panting from his exertion, Gustaf finally put down the poles of the cart. The crowd quieted to an eerie silence. Not even a bloodthirsty, riotous mob dared to be disrespectful near Verde's most holy shrine.

Two men stepped forward. They picked up Haral's body and made their way up to the top of the altar, all one hundred steps of it. Some in the crowd gasped at the audacity of the men climbing the altar, an honor usually reserved for Seers conducting worship.

When they reached the top, the men placed the body on the edge so all could still see it. In a display of grief, Gustaf sat on the step just below where Haral lay and put his head on his dead friend's chest.

No one in the crowd noticed Manor Stillinger's delighted smile when he turned toward his companion. The Sankari captain had not foreseen such a reaction. With a nod, Torvild Zullon stepped up and exhorted the crowd to remember the name of Haral Kaut. He pointed to the mourning Gustaf Holser and retold the story of the tragedy of his village.

When he finished, Torvild thrust his arms dramatically up to the sky as if seeking divine guidance. The crowd was silent as he held his pose. Lowering his arms slowly, Torvild descended a third of the way and stopped. "Who are responsible for these deaths?" he shouted.

The crowd took up the chant. "Defenders. Defenders. Defenders."

Torvild held up his arms for silence. "What is the penalty for these crimes?" he shouted in a rage.

"Death! Death! Death!" the mob shouted over and over again. Torvild did not stop the chanting. Instead he let it build to a terrifying crescendo that echoed across the square. He signaled again for silence and patiently waited for the chanting to subside like a wave rolling back into the river.

"My fellow Verdan loyalists, the Sankari cannot fight the Defenders alone. They need our help. We must join forces to help them force these vermin out of their temples so justice can be done."

Shouts of "aye, aye, aye," greeted him in fierce unison, but it subsided as all eyes stared at the top of the temple. Following their gaze, Torvild and Manor turned to see Gustaf now standing, surveying the crowd.

His voice still hoarse from his injury, the youth shook his fist angrily and shouted, "Justice! Justice!" Thousands of his sympathizers roared and took up the new chant.

When the shouting subsided, Torvild again addressed the onlookers. "Tomorrow after first meal we march on all the Nuven temples to demand they hand over the Defenders. If not, we will attack and destroy them." The mob shouted with approval. It was late into the night when the angry Verdans finally broke up and headed home to rest and prepare for the next day's task.

20

Tevan Nels chattered happily as he and his kinsman prepared their mounts for the long journey that would take him home to his worried parents. More than a lunar had passed since Tevan had stolen away in a cargo wagon in an effort to follow his kinsman. Now after the luster of his adventure had worn off, the young man missed his parents and begged to go home.

This was the moment Aron Nels had been waiting for. The Defender was close to his childlike cousin, but the responsibility of caring for him daily was becoming tiring. Also, his secret love affair with the Seer Verinya was constantly on his mind. Even though Tevan and Verinya were close, it was becoming difficult to maintain the masquerade of aloofness expected of him toward a Seer.

Aron frowned as he helped Tevan pack. The Defender had wanted to travel light, only taking the two horses he and Tevan would need to make the trip home.

However, his cousin had accumulated so many treasures, presents from Verinya and trinkets useless to others, but which Tevan had collected, that they would need a third horse to carry all of it. The extra mount would come in handy for hauling their camping gear and food for the trip.

As Aron and Tevan were making the final checks on their supplies, the other nine brothers of Circle Sankarikiller approached to bid them farewell. Tevan shouted when he saw them and darted over to greet the group.

Evan gave each circle brother a hug. The younger Defenders smiled and playfully mussed his hair. Egan Pozos looked away for a moment, wiping something from his eyes. Tevan had grown close to the circle. It was hard not to like the young man who would laugh and call out their names whenever he saw them.

After the goodbyes and well wishes for a safe journey were said, Aron and Tevan led their horses out of the stable and walked through the marketplace toward the front gate. Many merchants called out heartfelt farewells to Tevan as they passed. Most of them had grown accustomed to seeing him wander through their midst hoping to see an argument between them and a customer.

Several of the merchants had enjoyed his reaction so much, they would even start a ruckus just for his amusement. His laughter would make even the busiest shopper look around and smile. Despite himself, Aron smiled when he saw the others' reaction to Tevan's departure. His cousin smiled and waved good-bye.

When they reached the gate, Aron was about to mount up, but was stopped by Tevan's shout, "Vera!" The Seer smiled warmly when she heard him call out. Aron's cousin walked over to her with a great smile. "Tevan go home, Vera. I go see Mama and Papa. Aron take me."

Verinya smiled and stroked his cheek. "I know you have to go, Tevan. I will miss you, my friend."

Tevan nodded and put his head on her shoulder. "I miss you, too, friend."

Verinya took him by the hand and led him back to Aron. With many onlookers watching them, including two other Seers, she admonished the Defender to take care of Tevan. Aron nodded to her politely, not daring to meet her eyes lest he give away how he felt, and mounted his horse. Tevan followed his example and also mounted.

Staring straight ahead, the Defender spurred his horse past the temple's front gate. Tevan followed, but kept calling good-bye and waving until they were well down the road. They traveled in silence for several hours, which was unusual for Tevan because he loved to chatter almost incessantly. Aron knew his cousin was conflicted about leaving, but returning him to his parents was best.

The kinsmen made good time the first day, halting only briefly to eat and take the necessary toilet stop. They rode until dusk and made camp amid a small grove of trees. By now, Tevan had returned to his jovial self, remarking about everything they saw during their trip so far, everything from a fleeing rabbit to hawks circling high above them.

Aron was relieved when his cousin finally fell asleep only after being assured for the tenth time that yes, indeed, Tevan soon would see his Mama and Papa.

The Defender was half-awake as he listened contentedly to the birds chirping and calling to each other as first light was beginning to peek through the tree branches. A few meters away, Tevan snored lightly as he lay curled up in his bedroll. Aron pulled his head up slightly and smiled at his cousin. A tuft of blond hair was the only part of Tevan's body that could be seen.

The chattering of the birds grew louder as the early morning light grew brighter with each passing moment. Aron stretched and reluctantly thought about leaving his warm nest when a sound followed by an eerie silence made him freeze in place. Without warning, birds exploded from their roosting places with a unified whoosh of beating wings. The few birds that stayed called out sharp warnings to each other.

The Defender knew something was approaching that did not belong here. Growing up as a hunter, Aron had learned to listen to any changes in his surroundings that might indicate danger. Now the hairs on the back of his head stood up. Fully awake, he found his knife belt and slowly eased into a crouching position.

To his dismay, Tevan started to stir and mumbled in his sleep. Aron crawled over and gently put his hand over his cousin's mouth. Tevan woke up with a start, looking wide-eyed. "Shh, be quiet, don't move," Aron whispered. "You have to lie still. We're playing the hide game. Strangers are looking for us."

Tevan blinked, giggled softly and nodded that he understood. Relieved for the moment, Aron peered through the thicket of branches he had put together the night before. Nuven hunters always camouflaged themselves when bedding down.

A slight movement through the trees caught his attention. Whatever it was, stopped for a moment then slowly approached. Aron could faintly make out the soft rustle of footsteps. Two other shapes moved cautiously from different sides of the grove.

He reached for his bow and quiver of arrows while staring intently through the branches, looking for the intruders. A flash of out-of-place color moving nearby caught his eye. It was a red scarf worn by Sankari. The closest Verdan moved cautiously from tree to tree, looking for something. Aron scanned the area for the other two men, but they had moved out of sight.

The Defender crept out of his hiding place. Finding a large tree that would shield him, Aron notched an arrow and inched his way around the trunk. Only thirty-some meters away, the Sankari stood partially hidden behind a tree, but the man had not spotted Aron. A soft, lilting whistle aroused the Sankari's curiosity, making him move from his shelter to investigate.

The Verdan never got a chance to throw his javelin. An arrow pierced his chest before he saw his attacker. Sagging against the tree in shock, the Sankari stood for a few moments before his knees buckled, sending him sliding down the trunk. Only then did the dying man catch a glimpse of Aron, who was now moving through the trees looking for his companions.

The Defender glided through the trees, stopping for long pauses to listen and look carefully before continuing. His search was soon rewarded. To Aron's surprise, he spotted the other Sankari walking together back toward where they thought their companion must be looking. The two men must have given up their search and now were going to find their cohort.

Aron studied the situation. He knew he could not kill one of the Sankari without warning the other, but there was no way to avoid it. The Defender raised his bow and waited for a clear shot. Again, he pursed his lips and issued a high-pitched whistle.

Both Sankari turned as one. Before they could react, Aron's arrow sliced through the nearest man's neck, causing him to stumble briefly, then fall face first to the leaf-covered ground.

Aron reached for another arrow, but the surviving Sankari fled, dodging through the trees and making himself a difficult target. With a loud whoop, the Defender gave chase, hoping the fleeing man would stumble or fall, or even better, turn to face him. The Sankari did not stop. His only intention was to escape.

Aron followed his prey to a ravine where the Sankari leaped onto a horse and spurred away. After noting the direction his enemy was heading, the Defender sprinted back to where Tevan lay hidden.

Seeing Aron running toward him, Tevan crawled out to meet his cousin. "Tevan, ride to the temple quickly. Find Egan. Tell him Sankari attack. I have to chase a bad man. Go now."

Tevan started to protest, but he understood Aron's message. Without another word, the two ran to where they had hidden their horses for the night. Aron mounted and looked back at his cousin. A solemn-looking Tevan nodded.

"Good, Tevan," Aron called as he mounted his horse. "Now ride to the temple, fast. There may be more Sankari." The Defender did not worry about his kinsman riding alone. Tevan was an expert horseman and had an almost eerie sense of direction. He never got lost.

Aron rode in the general direction of where he had seen the Sankari escape. After charging hard for several minutes, the Defender guided his mount up a steep hill. He had barely reached the top when a lone horseman galloped out of the woods to his right. The red scarf gave the rider away.

Aron set out after the Sankari. Once his enemy was in his sight, he had no doubt his smaller, faster horse that was bred for hunting would catch up to his enemy's bigger, slower mount.

To Aron's advantage, the Sankari did not realize he was being pursued until the Defender was only a hundred meters or so away. The Defender wondered why the Sankari seemed to be riding almost leisurely instead of being concerned about a pursuer.

Casting an almost nonchalant glance behind him, the Verdan discovered with terror that the Nuven who had killed his two companions was chasing him down. The Sankari sunk low in his saddle and whipped his horse into a full run. Even racing at full speed, Aron knew the other horse was no match for his mount, so he kept up a steady gallop.

When the fleeing Verdan crested a steep ridge he began to scream for help. Curious, Aron urged his horse on a little faster, but pulled up when he reached the top of the ridge, making his horse rear on its hind legs in surprise.

Below him, spread out throughout the valley was a Verdan army of several thousand men. Their pennants flapped in the breeze. Colorful tents dotted the ground like the first flowers of spring poking their heads through the grass.

Aron was stunned at the sight. He had never seen such a large gathering of the enemy. The screeching Sankari whom the Defender had been chasing was drawing attention from his fellow Verdans. About a dozen men rode out to meet him.

Without waiting to see who was following, Aron reined his steed around and spurred him into a full run away from the army. The Defender knew Verdans with fresh horses would soon be chasing him.

Even hunting horses needed to rest occasionally, so Aron had to put as much distance as he could between himself and his pursuers. His only recourse was to ride toward the temple and hope his sturdy little mount could make the journey before collapsing from exhaustion.

¶ ¶ ¶

Verinya awoke from her trance gasping with fear. The Seer already missed Aron, so the only way she knew to be near her lover was to use her gift to see through him. Ever since Verinya and Aron had made love that first time, a bond between the two had been created. She had achieved what the other Seers desperately wanted — to be able to use the sight on one of the mysterious members of Circle Sankarikiller.

With trepidation, she had watched as Aron killed the first two Sankari as they stalked Tevan and him. She breathed a sigh of relief when Aron rode out to chase the surviving Sankari but gasped when he crested the ridge to discover an amassed army of Verdans obviously preparing to attack Temple Darya. The Seer was startled at discovering her people's plans. She had not been told of the pending attack.

Verinya trembled with fear and anger as she paced about her small room, unsure what to do. She feared for Aron's life and desperately wanted to do something to help him. The young woman splashed water in her face and sat on her cot in an effort to calm herself and weigh her options. She must choose whether to try to save the man she loved or assist the plot in destroying the Nuven temples and chasing the unbelievers back to the valley from which they had come only a few generations ago.

The Seer took a few cleansing breaths, then arose. She could not second-guess herself — her decision would affect many lives, especially her own. Verinya scurried out of her quarters and hurried to the marketplace. She paced up and down the aisles, looking for a familiar figure among the shoppers.

At last she spotted a familiar Defender. Egan Pozos was leaning over a counter, flirting with a vegetable vendor's very buxom daughter. The two were giggling at one of Egan's bawdy jokes when Verinya grabbed him by the arm. Startled, the Defender frowned and started to pull away when he saw the Seer, but stopped when he recognized her.

"Aren't you the Seer who befriended Tevan? What do you want of me?"

Verinya leaned close and whispered, "I have news of Aron and Tevan. I fear they are in danger."

Egan looked at her with surprise, but escorted her away to a secluded corner, away from the crowd. "How do you know this? What danger?"

Verinya glanced around, but to her relief, she saw no recognizable faces. "Please believe me. The other Seers would have my head if they knew what I am going to tell you."

Egan crossed his arms. He did not trust her, but concern and curiosity kept him from walking away from this mysterious woman. He gestured for her to continue.

"Seers sometimes have the ability to see what others see," Verinya said, not daring to tell the Defender the entire truth, but just enough to convince him to act. "Since I have grown close to Tevan, I occasionally can see what he sees. It's not constant, but more like flashes of sight."

Egan did not try to mask his surprise. His eyebrows raised in a look of disbelief.

"This morning, Tevan and Aron were in danger of being discovered by three Sankari as they slept. But Aron awoke, killed two of them, and set out to chase the other."

Egan started to smirk. "Then that third one is as good as dead, too." The look on her face stopped him. "There's more, I take it. What is it?"

Skipping some of the details, Verinya told the Defender about Aron's discovery of the invading Verdan army and his desperate race to escape a troop of Sankari. "Aron sent Tevan back. Both could be caught and killed."

Egan took her by the shoulder and looked into her eyes, which were moist with fear. "You are a brave woman to tell me this. Thank you," he said, gently squeezing her shoulders. "You said they both are in danger. Are you concerned only for Tevan?"

Verinya blushed despite herself. Egan smiled. "Your secret is safe with me. You have my word of honor as a Defender." He turned and ran through the marketplace to find his circle brothers.

¶ ¶ ¶

Aron kicked his heels into his horse much harder than he had ever done before. He slapped the animal vigorously on the shoulder with his reins. His mount now was visibly huffing and puffing. Its ears were flattened on the back of its head and foam flew out of the mouth. The horse's sides glistened with sweat, but it kept running at Aron's urging.

However, the Defender could tell the horse was slowing little by little. Courageous as the beast might be, Aron knew it would not last the entire trip back to the temple. Aron had glanced back several times during his frantic escape. It looked like a troop of Sankari were pursuing him.

Searching the countryside, the Defender spied a cluster of trees atop a rock-covered hill. If he was to be caught, Aron was determined it would be in a place of his choosing.

Guiding the horse to the spot, Aron grabbed his bow and rolled off his horse behind the tree. The well-trained animal attempted to stop, but the Defender whacked it savagely on the rump to make it continue running.

Out of breath and soaked with his and the horse's sweat from riding so hard, Aron tried to stand, but his legs cramped, causing him to fall with a groan. Grimacing, he stretched his limbs and stumbled to his feet.

The pursuing Sankari were drawing near enough that hc could hear the pounding of their horses' hooves. Without looking, Aron notched an arrow, swung out from behind the tree, and fired at the leader. His aim was off, but the arrow struck the Sankari's horse in the neck, causing it to fall, spilling its rider headfirst with a sickening thud. The Sankari's body quivered slightly, then lay still.

With a quick breath, Aron had another arrow on his bowstring and fired again. This time he was on target. The second Sankari screamed with pain, grabbed at the arrow in his sternum and toppled off his horse.

Not knowing what they were facing, the surviving troop swerved quickly away to regroup. Even though it was only a short reprieve, Aron slumped to the ground in exhaustion. The Defender squinted, trying to count how many Sankari he faced. He counted at least ten, maybe more. The Sankari's next attack likely would be fatal for him. He knew they would mount an all-out assault.

Most likely they would wait until just after sunset, encircle him and creep in. In the dark, his bow would be useless. It most likely would come down to hand-to-hand combat.

Aron was not the only one who was exhausted. The Sankari all had dismounted. Some sat in the grass staring at the stand of trees that sheltered the Defender. Others stretched out on the ground. It was already late afternoon. The sun would be setting in an hour. The Sankari, too, were conserving their strength for the final attack.

Aron leaned back against his tree. He was grimly planning how to send as many Sankari as he could to their ancestors when a familiar birdcall caught his attention. Glancing over his shoulder, he saw an amazing sight. His circle brothers were advancing quickly to where he was hidden. He rose slightly and waved.

The other Defenders dismounted and crept up the opposite side of the hill to him. After making sure he was well, the others surveyed the situation and saw the resting Sankari. Without a word, Circle Sankarikiller, minus Aron, mounted their horses and charged the Verdans. The Sankari were caught by surprise.

The Sankari mounted their steeds in an attempt to escape, but they were ridden down and dispatched with Defender efficiency. The skirmish was over quickly.

When all the Sankari were accounted for, Egan and the others swarmed their exhausted brother. Aron struggled to his feet and hugged each one of them. They assured him Tevan was safe. The circle had found him making his way to the temple.

"How did you know I was in trouble?" Aron asked.

Egan smiled and winked. "Some fortune teller must have had a dream. She slipped me a note. It's a good thing she wasn't drunk."

His Defender brothers exploded in laughter at his joke. Their levity was cut short when Aron told them of the advancing army. After allowing him a few more minutes of rest, the circle mounted the horses and headed back to warn Temple Darya of the impending danger.

During the ride back, Aron motioned for Egan to pull close. "Fortune teller?" Aron whispered not bothering to mask his suspicion.

Egan smiled and met Aron's worried look with a smirk. "Yes, a red-headed one, seemed quite concerned for you. Not to worry brother, all those 'fortune tellers' look alike to me. Don't think I could pick her out of a crowd." The two rode back together without saying another word.

21

Rufina became ill when she broke out of her trance. The High Seer had been watching with great pleasure through one of the Sankari who had been pursuing Aron. It appeared the Verdan warriors had the Defender trapped. All they had to do was wait for the right moment, surround the Nuven, and kill him.

However, the surprise attack by a Defender circle and subsequent slaughter of the Sankari caused Rufina to awaken in shock at the sudden turn in events. The Seer was tracking the oncoming Verdan army, which was about two to three days' march from Temple Darya.

Her curiosity at the commotion in the camp when a lone rider appeared over a ridge to peer at the Verdans switched to anger at seeing one of those young Defenders from the temple.The last thing she saw through the Sankari was a frantic attempt to escape on his horse. The Verdan didn't get far.

Rufina's picture turned upside down when her Sankari fell from his horse. The High Seer saw a flash of sky, then the ground seemed to rise up to grab him. She couldn't feel his pain from the arrow that stuck out between his shoulder blades. The Sankari's vision started to blur. Rufina glimpsed a mounted Defender standing over him then her sight went black.

The Seer rocked back and forth for a few moments to compose herself. The Defenders who had rescued Aron now knew about the threatening Verdan army. She had to warn her fellow Verdans that they had been discovered. If the Nuvens had time to prepare, it would make the attack on Temple Darya and its sister temples much more difficult, perhaps even impossible.

Rufina knew it would be impossible to send a messenger. A rider would not have enough time reach the army. The High Seer rose from her chair to gaze out her window, watching the bustling marketplace below. Rufina's attention was drawn to a sister Seer who had stopped to inspect a nearby vendor's wares.

This gave her an idea, but she shuddered at the thought. Rufina could attempt to connect with the Seer who traveled with the advancing Verdan force. Such an effort could prove to be difficult. Contact between Seers separated by great distances had been attempted, but it was rarely successful.

Most Seers were naturally immune from being "visited," as they liked to describe it. The women were not telepaths. They could not send mental messages to each other. Over the generations, they had tried to develop the telepathic trait so it could be passed from mother to daughter, but with little luck. If such Seer-to-Seer contact was attempted, both women would have to be receptive.

Rufina sat down at her table with a worried sigh. In front of her lay an unfinished report to the Council of Seers at Fortress Bryann. She picked up a parchment and studied it. With a grim smile, she reached for a clean sheet of paper and began to write slowly. Her hand swept across the page. When her message was complete, the High Seer took a deep breath, cleared her mind, and stared at the paper.

¶ ¶ ¶

Seer Giann was concerned about the twelve Sankari riding in pursuit of the Nuven who had discovered the Verdan army during its march to Temple Darya. After questioning the Sankari scout who had been chased back to camp by the Nuven, Giann suspected the lone rider to be a Defender. The interloper had killed two other Sankari scouts and had almost ridden down the third when he discovered their force.

It was almost sunset now, and there had been no word from the Sankari party. The troop had been gone for more than five hours now, which should have been enough time to catch and kill the Nuven. The Seer sat in her tent trying to use her "gift" to see through the eyes of one of the Sankari.

Giann had been preoccupied with other duties when the troop set out. This made it difficult because she did not know the Sankari she was trying to find. The young woman took deep breath after deep breath. Her mind reached out, but she was unable to reach the missing Sankari.

Frustrated, Giann shook her head and tried again. This time a slightly blurred vision floated before her eyes. She saw two hands holding up a parchment with words written on it. Letting herself relax, the Seer focused on the vision. The words on the parchment slowly came into focus. Giann gasped with surprise, almost breaking her trance. With renewed determination, she let her mind grasp the message.

Not daring to break her trance, the Seer reached out and fumbled for a parchment and writing utensil. In an awkward motion resembling the clumsy attempts by a child learning to write, she scrawled a few words.

Still in her trance, Giann tried to focus on the parchment she was holding. She kept her gaze locked onto her writing for several long minutes until her words faded away as if in a mist. This time, the second vision was much easier to understand. "Message received, Rufina."

Giann came out of her trance. She was shocked at the realization of what had just happened — Seer-to-Seer sight contact. The message she had received was more important than her own comfort. The young woman's head pounded from the extra exertion, but she made herself rise on wobbly legs and set out to find the officer in charge of the Verdan army.

Rufina broke off her trance and smiled with satisfaction. She, too, tried to rise, but the room swayed dizzyingly before her eyes. The Seer shivered and realized she was wet with perspiration. The effort to contact Giann had taken more energy than she realized.

Like a drunk lunging for a comfortable place to sleep it off, Rufina stumbled to her cot. She clumsily stripped off her soaked garments and curled up under a warm blanket, exhausted but content that she had accomplished her mission.

¶ ¶ ¶

An incredulous Manor Stillinger, recently promoted to general, listened to Giann's account of her contact with Seer Rufina. The gruff Sankari leader normally would dismiss anyone else with such a wild tale, but Manor knew better than to question a Seer.

The Tarylan officer cursed his luck at being discovered by a wayward Nuven, then swore loudly when hearing Defenders had slaughtered his Sankari. Manor started to bark orders at two nearby captains when a commotion to his right stopped him.

Giann had fainted and fallen to the ground with a heavy thud. A nearby med tech rushed to her side. A Seer showing weakness in front of men was unheard of. Even Manor was shocked by the incident. The med tech shouted for a stretcher.

As Giann was gingerly lifted onto it, Manor walked over to her. He had not noticed how pale the Seer had looked when she delivered her message. The young woman now looked even paler and her lips were turning blue. Manor grabbed the med tech by the arm. "You will be able to help her, will you not?"

The med tech frowned. "She does not look good, sir. Please excuse me while I attend to her."

Out of respect, Manor waited until the stretcher bearers had taken Giann away. He turned again to his captains. "I want the troops to be ready to march at first light. We have to assume Temple Darya knows of our plans. There will be no surprise attack now, but we still must advance to the temple."

The general strode over to a table covered with maps of the area and detailed blueprints of Temple Darya. His concentration was interrupted when someone coughed softly behind him.

Manor turned to see who dared intrude upon him. The med tech who had come to Giann's assistance stood in the doorway, looking very uncomfortable. His face was as pale as the Seer's had been.

"What is it? Why aren't you with Seer Giann?" the annoyed general demanded.

The med tech cleared his throat, not daring to make eye contact. "I regret to inform you, sir, that the Seer is dead."

22

Witt Peyser and Aron Nels watched from one of the parapets of Temple Darya as the threatening sight spread out below them. Several thousand Verdan warriors blocked the temple's access to the valley.

The two Defenders did not know the same scenario was being played out at the other Nuven temples. The other nine temples were more susceptible to attack. Only Temple Darya, the first Nuven religious fortress to be built in Verde Valley, backed up to a mountain.

Aron felt frustrated because he could do nothing about the threat gathering on the plains below him. Growing restless, he scanned the temple walls. His gaze fell on the tower that housed the Seers. A lone familiar figure stood on the balcony — Verinya.

Their eyes locked onto each other for a lingering moment. Not knowing if he was being watched, Aron tilted his head ever so slightly and mouthed a silent thank you. Verinya smiled, then stepped aside to let two other Seers join her.

Aron's warning about the advancing army had been correct. No one had questioned the Defender after his circle brothers had rescued him from the Sankari who had tried to chase him down.

Tevan Nels had found his way back to the temple before Circle Sankarikiller had returned from its rescue mission. All the frightened man-child could utter coherently was Aron had told him to return to the temple because there was danger. Not even the sympathetic Seer Verinya could glean any more information from the confused young man, who almost had ridden his horse to death as he hurried back to safety.

Now, just as the Defender elders had feared, the Verdan army had marched to the temple, leaving them barely a day to prepare for an unprovoked attack. All the merchants and other Nuvens not bound by oath to protect the temple fled to the safety of the mountains.

Without being asked, all the merchants gave their produce and other food items to those who stayed behind. The temple was well stocked with supplies. Two waterfalls ran into a network of cisterns, supplying plenty of water. Much to the Defenders' surprise, the six Seers insisted on staying. The women said they thought they could help suspend the hostilities.

The bridge that spanned the deep ravine that ran along the temple's perimeter was dismantled. The pieces were stored in the hope they could be used again. Giant beams securely held shut the front gate and the other hidden entrances.

Witt and the other Defender elders watched as a small troop rode toward the temple. One of the Verdans surveyed the ravine and shook his head in disgust. Manor Stillinger had feared this would happen. Without the bridge, any successful attack on the almost impenetrable temple would be nearly impossible.

The Sankari general rode to the edge of the ravine and shouted his conditions to the waiting Defenders.

"As leader of these Verdan loyalists, I order every Defender to leave this temple and return to the Valley of Hunters. Your refusal to hand over the murderers of innocent Verdans has brought this upon you. If you comply peacefully, you and any other Nuvens with you will not be harmed. You have my word."

Manor looked up and down the temple walls. Hundreds of faces stared impassively down at him. After a brief pause, the general received the answer he expected.

"You threaten Temple Darya without due cause," Witt called down. "We have every right to man this temple and protect it. You have been lied to, Verdan. Defenders do not kill innocents.

Attack if you must. You only will lose many men in your futile attempt."

Manor started to leave when a female voice stopped him. Curious, he spun around. "Major, I am Seer Lanella. I and five others were sent here to assist Temple Darya. We wish to prevent any deaths on either side. Please let us work out a truce."

The general shook his head. "With all due respect, Honored Seer, we are here at the request of the united communities of Verde Valley. This matter has nothing to do with the Seers," he called back sternly. I highly recommend that you and the other Seers leave the temple immediately before any harm comes to you. Or are you being held hostage?"

Lanella reassured Manor that she and the others had chosen to stay. Manor shrugged, reined his horse around, and headed back to the army. With his back to the Nuvens, a large smile spread across his face. He would be content to lay siege. Even though the Nuvens felt secure in their temple, the Verdan strategy was falling into place as planned.

¶ ¶ ¶

A little over a week had passed during the siege without either side exchanging an arrow or a javelin. The Verdans seemed content to wait in an apparent effort to starve out the Nuvens. The inhabitants of Temple Darya were not worried. They had an almost unlimited supply of food and all the water they needed. In the mountain stronghold, the Defenders had gathered vast stores of grains, as well as dried and smoked meats in cool, subterranean caves.

Just as dawn was breaking on the tenth day, the temple inhabitants were awakened by large crashes that shook the walls. Sentries in the towers sounded alarms as the crashes continued with alarming regularity.

Rushing to the top of the walls, the Defenders discovered the source of the noise: catapults. The Verdans were launching large stones from machines used centuries ago on old Earth. However, none of the stones made it over the top of the walls. The missiles struck the temple with great force, but the walls stubbornly held.

The temple had been built by expert Nuven stonemasons who had two centuries of experience in warding off attacks from a fierce and determined enemy who could strike without notice at any time — those mysterious space raiders, the Tanlians. The crisscrossed walls were three and four layers thick.

Much to the dismay of most of the Verdan army, the temple stood undamaged from the missiles hurled at it. The machines had to be kept a great distance from the temple because Nuven archers could fire their arrows a deceptively long distance, and they were amazingly accurate.

The first few stones unleashed by the catapults caused a hailstorm of arrows from the temple in response. The first unprotected catapult crews were killed within a few minutes. A few pieces were jarred loose from the temple, and the walls were scarred where stones had slammed into them, but they stubbornly held. Even the huge wooden doors of the temple's main entrance held.

Other than being annoyed and sometimes frightened by the barrage, those in the temple were unharmed. After three days of the steady pounding, the Verdans stopped. The only thing they managed to accomplish was to partially fill in the ravine with the large projectiles.

A day later, the catapults again hurled large objects against the walls, but this time there was no noise or jarring reverberation. Huge bales of grass and straw flew through the air and bounced harmlessly off the temple, but slowly large mounds started piling up the walls.

At first, Witt watched, puzzled, then he understood what was happening as the piles grew larger. As he suspected, when the mounds had grown to almost half the length of the wall, the Verdans shot flaming balls of wood into the piles.

Heavy, black smoke poured over the walls and spread through the temple. However, most of the Nuvens had escaped to the safety of the caves, where the smoke did not reach. A few Defenders kept watch and protected themselves as best they could with damp cloths over their faces. They rotated the watch every few minutes so no one would succumb to the heavy smoke.

The fire burned and smoldered for more than a day, when a heavy rain extinguished it prematurely. The Nuvens cheered their good luck, and the Verdans grew even more despondent at their failure to dislodge their enemy from the temple.

23

On the morning of the fifth day after the Verdan attempt to smoke them out, the Defenders of Temple Darya watched with grim curiosity as another army appeared to join the Verdan siege force. The newcomers seemed to keep a small distance between themselves and the first army. After a short time, the newly arrived force turned and marched toward the temple.

Egan Pozos squinted into the sun at the oncoming group. Something was familiar about the banners that fluttered in the wind as the army grew nearer. The Defender blinked and rubbed his eyes to make sure he was correct.

With an excited whoop, he called to the temple's Defenders on the ground. "It's the flags of the other nine sister temples."

Anyone who could manage it raced to the parapets to get a look. As the troop drew nearer, it was clear Egan was correct — the flags of the other nine Nuven temples were displayed along with a strange banner no one recognized.

One of the Seers called. "It's the flag of the Tarylan guard. They are marching with the Nuvens."

Witt Peyser quickly signaled for the shouting to stop. It was unheard of for Nuvens to accompany Tarylans, the hand-picked protectors of the Seers. The steward of Circle Sankarikiller suspected a trap. However, Witt was relieved to see Defender elders from each of the nine temples. Shouting familiar greetings, the Nuvens among the newcomers tried to reassure the Temple Darya Defenders the siege was over.

Witt and the other Defender elders were discussing who they were going to send to negotiate with this new army when they were interrupted by Seer Lanella.

"Forgive my intrusion, good sirs, but perhaps I can be of assistance. Please allow me to accompany you to talk with them. I will be able to tell if my people come in good faith."

The elders eyed her with suspicion. Lanella flashed a comforting smile. "I know you do not trust Seers, but we have not given you any cause to doubt us. We stayed here with you during the siege and now I offer my assistance to assure the safety of Temple Darya."

The Nuvens agreed to include her. Not even Witt could argue how this young woman could hinder the negotiations. In less than a half hour, Witt, four elders, and Lanella were lowered in a rope lift from the top of one of the temple's walls.

When they reached the ground, they were warmly met by Defender Elders from the other nine Nuven temples. Lanella was formally greeted by someone she called High Seer.

A small man with a long flowing blond mane approached Temple Darya's Elders. "The Seers are here to help," said Reynald Caleria, Defender leader of Temple Vonn. "All of our temples were under siege, such as yours, but the Seers halted the hostilities."

Witt was incredulous. "How did they do that? The Verdans were determined to avenge the villagers they accused Defenders of killing."

Reynald shook his head. "Temple Vonn is not nearly as well fortified as the mother temple. Our walls were almost breached. We were preparing to fight to our last when the Seers saved us." The elders from the other Nuven temples echoed the same story.

"The truth has been found out about who murdered those villagers," Reynald said. "It seems a band of renegades was responsible. A Verdan troop discovered them trying to loot another village and kill the people there."

Witt stepped forward. "Who are these bandits? Verdan or Nuven?"

Reynald shrugged. "The Sankari said they killed six Nuvens and four Verdans. They have been trying to catch this band for four harvests. The bandits were just murdering thieves."

Temple Darya's elders looked shocked. It was unusual for Verdans and Nuvens to join forces in such grisly business.

High Seer Rufina stepped forward, introducing herself. "Elders of Temple Darya, I give you my word that those responsible for the murders of those innocent villagers have been killed. It is most unfortunate that undesirables from both our peoples have caused so much grief. Hostilities have now ceased at all the temples," she said gesturing toward the Verdan army, which now had scattered and was moving away from the temple.

Witt scowled. "Forgive me, High Seer, but all the hostilities have ceased? Have you also convinced the Sankari to stop their unwarranted attacks on our people?"

Rufina smiled benevolently. "Yes, we finally were able to garner a promise from those wayward Verdans to cease their attacks. They now recognize the futility of their actions."

Trumpet blasts drew the attention of the group to the Verdan army. The calls were not sounding an attack; rather, they were mournful, a retreat. No flags were being brandished nor men calling out.

The army was breaking up into disorganized groups and leaving the area. The catapults were abandoned. Witt didn't bother to mask his stunned expression as he watched the Verdans leave without either side claiming a victory.

Reynald laughed, slapping him on the back. "You and the Defenders of Temple Darya have inspired awe in us all. Now it's time to enjoy the peace we all deserve."

24

Manor Stillinger strolled through the construction site in one of Mt. Kiken's huge caverns. Even the stoic Tarylan general was impressed by what he saw.

Dozens of new black-winged gliders were lined up on one side, awaiting pilots to test fly them before being released to a storage area, where they could be fetched later when needed. Hundreds more were in the final stages of being completed.

Long wooden tables, lined by Verdans intently working on the gliders, stretched into the cavern as far as Manor could see. He did not bother suppressing a pleased grin. Part of his scheme was coming to fruition.

Manor picked up one of the new gliders to examine it. He nodded approvingly at the workmanship. The general found no loose fittings or flaws in the woven material that stretched over the wings.

"Can I help you, sir?" asked a burly, bald man.

Manor turned and smiled. "Ah, foreman, your workers have done an impressive job here. The gliders look sturdy and ready to fly."

Kelz Ajolla beamed at the compliment. He knew the general was a man of few words and meant what he said. "Thank you, sir. The last of the gliders you ordered are being completed now.

The test flights have gone very well, too. Only a few minor flaws have been found, and no flyers have been lost."

Manor nodded absentmindedly while studying the glider he held. It had been many lunars since he had flown. He missed that rush of excitement when leaping off a ledge, followed by the exhilaration of being lifted by an air current. Nothing could compare to the feeling of freedom one experienced when flying.

"Where's the launch site?" the general asked Kelz. Assuming Manor wanted to watch a test flyer, the foreman smiled and told him to turn left out the cavern's entrance, and then follow the cut-out incline to a large ledge. Manor nodded, hoisted the glider over his shoulder and set out.

"No general, not that one. It hasn't been tested yet!" Kelz cried out in surprise.

The general winked at the foreman, who had now turned white with fright. "How many times does one get to take a maiden flight? Besides, I've looked over this glider. It looks to be perfect."

Kelz tried to change Manor's mind, but the general would not be convinced. "Sir, a few of our test flyers have crashed, but they are experienced and don't take unnecessary chances."

Manor reached out and gave Kelz a playful slap on his sweaty cheek. "Don't worry, foreman. I have flown many times. Besides, life can be so dull if you don't take a chance once in awhile. This whole project you've been working on for lunars now is one giant chance," he said gesturing toward the workers. "To achieve an ambitious goal, one has to step out into the unknown."

The general turned and walked out of the cavern, carrying the glider. Kelz's protests rang in his ears for many minutes after he had left.

¶ ¶ ¶

Rufina was enjoying the warm summer evening on her rooftop patio atop Fortress Bryann. She half-reclined on a padded lounger. Her eyes were shut as she enjoyed the cool night breeze on her face. A strange whoosh of air caused her to blink with surprise. She half-rose and searched the sky, but nothing stared back at her except Verde's two moons and the constellations.

The High Seer had just settled back down again when a stronger gust of air startled her. As she looked up, a shadow passed overhead, blocking out the light from Luz Primo.

Too frightened to call out, Rufina watched as the shadow pulled around again and dove for the patio. Something heavy landed with a solid thud, followed by a familiar laugh. Rising, the High Seer slowly walked toward where the shadow had set down.

"Who dares intrude on me?" Rufina demanded, unable to disguise her fright.

A laugh rang out again. The Seer now recognized her visitor's voice and stopped to compose herself, but her heart still raced from the excitement. "Manor Stillinger, is that you?" she snapped, this time with more authority in her voice.

The Tarylan general chuckled as he walked out of the shadows. "Greetings, High Seer," he said bowing with exaggerated formality. "I personally wanted to demonstrate how well our new gliders are performing."

Rufina started to scold him, but couldn't help admiring the man's bravado. "Very impressive, General. Even when I was looking, I could not see you flying overhead. The gliders are as invisible as you predicted."

Manor walked slowly toward her. He was still breathing heavily from the excitement of his flight. The glider's maiden flight had been spectacularly successful.

The Tarylan leader had launched himself off the takeoff ledge and was immediately swept up by a strong updraft. He grew bored with flying over Verde City. Spotting the lights of Fortress Bryann gave him an idea.

Without the Tarylan guards noticing, Manor drifted overhead, amused at his secret vantage point. Swooping around the fortress, he spotted Rufina in the moonlight, relaxing on her large patio.

The High Seer was now scolding him for scaring her, but her words did not sting. Ever since Rufina had taken him as a lover, he had been able to tell her intentions by her tone and body language.

Without saying another word, Manor embraced her. Rufina exhaled softly and returned the hug. It had been many lunars since the two had been together. The preparations for the attack on the Nuven temples had taken up all their waking moments.

The High Seer started to massage Manor's back, when he bent over and picked her up. Rufina only let out a soft gasp as she enjoyed being in the snug security of his strong arms. The general carried her to a lounger and gently set her down. The last time they had been together, Rufina had controlled the lovemaking. Now it was Manor's turn.

The High Seer watched with growing excitement as the general stripped off his clothes. She also started to slowly disrobe, but he stopped her. Before Rufina could say a word, Manor grabbed her garments and tore them off in one swift motion. The thrill of their plans falling into place to defeat the Nuvens translated into a night of violent lovemaking.

The next morning, both were exhausted and sore from the previous night's activity. An unusually relaxed Rufina watched as Manor leaped off her ledge with his glider, caught a gust of wind and soared overhead. He circled the patio twice then headed back to return the glider to poor Kelz, who was probably sick with worry.

25

Aron and Verinya embraced with the frantic passion of lovers separated for too long. They held one another tenderly and reveled in each other's touch. Neither would have objected to having this rare time together stretched out for many hours, even days. Almost no one at Temple Darya noticed when the couple snuck off together.

Despite being in the middle of a crushing hug from a baker's daughter, Egan Pozos managed to smile when he saw the Seer follow his circle brother off to their rendezvous.

All the Nuvens broke into a wild celebration as soon as Witt Peyser and the other Defender Elders returned with the news the Verdan army had disbanded, ending the siege. The reaction was the same at the other nine Nuven temples. Cheering and dancing broke out in the courtyards and hallways.

As a token of peace, the Seers from Fortress Bryann had brought dozens of bottles of their best wine to share with their Nuven brethren. The celebrations lasted for days at the ten temples. Even other Nuvens who lived nearby, including many of the vendors, joined in.

Tents were pitched outside the temples when the number of celebrants grew too large for the structures to accommodate. Large bonfires sprang up as the singing, dancing, and storytelling lasted well into the third night.

Aron and Verinya escaped to the safety of a small, out-of-the-way storage room. The Defender locked the door, then ensured their privacy by sliding several large wood planks crosswise through brackets on either side. It would take an army to interrupt them now.

He had managed to commandeer an unused cot, flasks of water, and even a jug of ale. She had gathered some cheeses, breads, dried meat, and fruit in a basket. They intended to be alone as long as their supplies and bodies could hold out.

The lovers had never been together longer than an hour or two. Now they had time to sleep in each other's arms after a vigorous session of lovemaking, wake up hungry, dine and satisfy their passion all over again.

After the third day of their private bliss, Aron ventured out of the room to investigate the goings on of the temple. Much to his chagrin, the celebrations had ended. The tent city outside the walls had been dismantled. Repairs were being made everywhere, including the bridge that had been torn down over the ravine.

The Defender and Seer reluctantly parted. In their last, passionate embrace both pledged life-long devotion to each other despite the different destinies that had been planned for them even before their births.

Aron took his time returning to his barracks. He expected to be playfully tortured by his circle brothers, but resolved not to give away his forbidden affair with a Seer. Much to his surprise and relief, Aron saw that his circle brothers also were straggling in after three days and nights of drinking and debauchery.

No one spoke as they shuffled in. A few collapsed on their cots, hoping to capture a few minutes of precious sleep. The peace of the barracks was abruptly shattered when the door flew open with a crash.

Witt Peyser stomped into the room and surveyed the scene with disgust. "What a sad sight this is!" he roared. "On your feet! Attention!"

Even the sleepers managed to jump from their cots. Most of the circle looked like they could hardly manage to draw a bowstring.

"The present fight might be over, but you are still Defenders. I expect you ten to remember that," Witt snarled. "Circle Sankarikiller has been ordered to investigate a disturbance in one of our mountain villages. Apparently no one has heard from this village for days and all roads to it have been blocked."

The steward paced up and down, shaking his head in disbelief at the sorry condition in which he found the circle brothers. "You have less than a day to prepare yourselves for this mission. Pack rations for about a week's outing. We leave at first sun."

Witt started to leave but turned back. "I expect you to act and look like Defenders when we leave the temple tomorrow." With a snort of disgust, the steward marched from the room.

Witt made sure he was well away from the barrack's door when he allowed himself to burst out laughing. The circle brothers were a sorry-looking sight, but he knew they would be ready the next day. The young always recovered quickly, especially when given the proper incentive.

While preparing to leave, Aron barely had time to scratch out a quick note to Verinya and leave it in their secret place in the garden. Even Tevan demanded attention, but the busy Defender barely acknowledged his kinsman.

"Time to go home. I want to see Mama and Papa," Tevan demanded, pulling insistently on Aron's shirtsleeve.

The Defender tried to be patient, but exasperation was evident in his voice. "Yes, yes, Tevan. As soon as I return l will take you home. I promise. Now go find Verinya. She will take you to market."

Tevan plopped down on the barracks floor with a heavy thud. "Now. I want to go now," he sobbed. "I miss Mama and Papa."

The other circle brothers stopped what they were doing and glared at Aron. Shaking his head in embarrassment, the Defender knelt down and gave his cousin a hug. "When I come back, we will ride home together, Tevan, but you need to be good until then," he said wiping away his kinsman's tears.

Tevan smiled as he rose and gave Aron a vigorous hug. "I wait for you, Aron. I will be good." With a hearty wave to all in the room he set out to find Verinya.

# # # # #

COMING THE FALL OF 2016

SEERS OF VERDE: BOOK TWO

Excerpt from Book Two

Aron Nels hid in the branches of the giant fruit tree fighting to quiet his heavy breathing after the frantic chase. The attack had come so quickly, he barely had time to flee. The orchard keeper stood straight up in the crook of two heavy limbs, he flattened his back snug to the tree trunk. The heavy canopy of leaves and flowers hid him — for now.

After finally regaining control of his breathing, Aron cleared his mind. As sweat slowly trickled down his face, he concentrated on all the sounds and sights in his area. A light breeze slightly swished the leaves around him. Bees and other insects flitted and buzzed among the flowers. A bird broke into a song in a nearby tree. All was as it should be.

What seemed forever but actually was only several minutes later, a twig snapped nearby. The bird cut short its song and flew away. Something moved through the underbrush near his tree. It stopped often, then continued slowly examining everything in its wake as if it was looking for something.

Aron knew what the hunter sought — him. This was the attacker who had ambushed him near the river. Somehow the assailant had tracked him to his hiding spot. The orchard keeper begrudgingly admired the hunter. Not many could have followed his frantic escape as he sprinted in a zigzagging pattern through the trees.

The orchard keeper had done his best to elude the pursuer. He leaped over fallen logs and scuttled through heavy brush until he found a familiar, ancient tree that's branches could support his weight. However, now he could hear the searcher pace from tree to tree, looking for his prey. At each tree, the hunter clumsily scaled the lower branches. Finding nothing, he would drop back to the ground with a thud.

Aron followed the other's progress. Finally, the assailant reached his tree. The branches shook as the other man scrambled up. Moving slowly and quietly, Aron positioned himself directly above the other. Assuming he would have only one chance to strike, the orchard keeper poised in a ready-to-attack position.

The other man stepped out on a lower branch in attempt to better scan the upper branches. This was his chance. Aron let his missile fly with tremendous force. Sensing movement from above, the pursuer moved with cat-like speed. But the large fruit still hit him, exploding after striking his shoulder, knocking him to the ground.

With a blood-curdling scream, Aron leaped from the tree to subdue his victim but found nothing when he landed on the ground. Out of the corner of his eye, a blurred shape shot toward his head, hitting him squarely in the face.

It was Aron's turn to be knocked down. Before he could sit up, a foot pressed down on his chest, pinning him. The two men stared at one another momentarily. Aron's captor removed his foot and sat beside him smiling broadly, proud of his achievement.

"You'll have to do better than a piece fruit to knock me down father," Flyn Nels chuckled as he watched Aron sit up and clean the pulp off his face.

The elder Nels finally managed a smile. "How did you find me so quickly? You don't know the woods that well."

Flyn said nothing but let out a loud sniff and pointed to his father. "You were working very hard to escape father. You left a heavy trail of scent. I recognized your odor," he said shrugging.

Aron raised his eyebrows questioningly. "Scent?" he asked incredulously.

Flyn nodded matter of factly. "On the ground, in the brush, even on some of trees where you must have stopped briefly. Why, are you looking at me so strangely? You have told me you can smell rain coming when its hours away. I have seen you find a herd of grazer by smelling them from downwind."

Aron shook his head in wonderment. "I've never trailed prey by following scent like one of the predators." Trying to look stern, he grumbled, "You still sound like an old woman when you climb, son. You will never ambush prey if they hear you."

Flyn grinned, "That's why I hunt the ravines and grasslands. I can see and smell the prey, plan my attack. Speed and a good aim with the bow will bring down most animals."

Tousling his son's thick dark brown curly hair, Aron laughed, "Perhaps you are right, most of the grazers don't run up trees when they're being chased."

Flyn laughed. "It would be quite a sight to see one of those fat grazers sitting in a tree, it would break all the branches." Both men grinned at the amusing thought. Rising together, they sauntered back to the stream where Flyn initially "ambushed" his father by hurling a rotten windfall that exploded all over his back.

"Just in time, son, you can help me carry some of these fruit baskets back to the cabin," Aron said.

Flyn grunted as he picked up one of the heavy baskets, "You will get your revenge on me yet."

"Can you stay for second meal?" Aron asked as they trekked toward the cabin with their loads of fruit. "Romal will be happy to see you."

An older man walked out the orchard, carrying more of the golden fruit. "Why should I be happy to see this cub?" Romal growled. "He never comes around to help anymore now that he finally learned how to use a bow."

Flyn sauntered up to Romal, "Good to see you, too, uncle," he said slapping the older man on the back.

"Well, as long as you're here, we might as well feed you," Romal said, his eyes twinkling, revealing his good humor.

Flyn licked his lips, "Sounds good after the trip here, but it will have to be quick." The two other men looked at him questioningly. Flyn looked away for a second then faced Aron.

"This is what I came to tell you father. The Tarylans have captured another Defender. A death duel will be held tomorrow, two hours after first light.

"I'm sorry father, I wanted you to hear it from me instead of some gossip who would have gotten the details wrong. Uh, there's one other thing," he paused, looking embarrassed. "My hunter circle wants me to go with them to watch the duel. I've never seen a Defender before."

Aron's face paled at the news. Saying nothing, he snatched up his basket of fruit and stomped angrily toward the cabin.

Romal glared at Flyn. "You know your father fought with the Defenders at Temple Darya, where he was wounded. He thinks one of them saved his life, dragged him to safety."

Flyn looked down at the ground, scratching a line with his boot toe. "I know how he feels uncle, but it's a chance to see a real Defender. Perhaps this duel will be different.

"Maybe the Defender will defeat more Sankari than the last one did. That would make father happy."

Romal shrugged as he picked up his basket. "Yes, but they always kill the Defenders don't they? How many of them have been killed so far?"

Flyn looked at his uncle, "This is the eighth one to have come forward."

Romal looked surprised, "Eight already. That probably means only two are left. Those damn Sankari won't be happy until all the Defenders are dead," he said sadly as he followed his brother to the cabin.

Nothing was said during the meal. Aron concentrated on his food, angrily stabbing the pieces of meat as he ate. Finishing, he pushed his plate away. Aron folded his hands together, his elbows were propped on the table. "Why do you want to go?" he said in a low voice, not doing a good job of masking his anger.

Flyn met his father's gaze. "I want to see one of the heroes of our people you have told me about since I was a crawler."

Aron's eyes narrowed, "Which side?" Romal stopped eating but said nothing. He looked at his nephew questioningly.

Flyn looked up and smiled. "Nuvan," he said proudly. "My circle brothers all have Nuvan blood. Don't worry father, I will cheer for the Defender."

Aron rose slowly from the table looking very tired. He said nothing, but the sorrow his eyes told his son exactly how he felt. Flyn rose to follow his father outside but stopped to squeeze his uncle's shoulder.

"Next time, stay longer pup," Romal growled good-naturedly. "We could use the help. Our backs aren't as young as they once were."

Flyn smiled, "I promise uncle." Aron did not look up when his son approached. He was busy rearranging fruit in small baskets, which would make for easier delivery to their customers. Without warning, Aron tossed two large golden apples to Flyn, who easily snatched them with both hands.

"Which one is the honey fruit?" Aron asked, testing his son. Flyn felt both apples then carefully sniffed each one. "This one," he said holding the apple in his left hand triumphantly aloft as if it were a prize. A deep bite of the fruit confirmed his declaration.

Rising, Aron reached out taking Flyn's face in his hands. Two sets of blue-green eyes stared into each other. "Your Nuvan blood is strong son, always remember that."

Father and son embraced, giving each other hearty pats on the back. "Don't worry father, I'm sure the Defender will give a good account of himself in the arena."

Aron allowed himself to smile, "May he send many Sankari to their ancestors." With a wave and a smile, Flyn turned and jogged steadily through the orchard.

Romal joined his brother on the porch to watch as Flyn disappeared into trees. "You don't have to worry about that one, he's grown into a fine man. Why, he's already a better hunter than you."

Aron snorted, giving Romal a strong brotherly shove. "There's more fruit to harvest or do you need a nap old man?" Aron said grinning.

"See if you can keep up for once," Romal answered as he grabbed two large empty baskets and headed for the orchard.